PRAISE FOR

THE FAMILY D

'*The Family Doctor* is a compelling thrill[illegible] frightening. But is more than that because it is a story that draws desperately needed attention to domestic abuse in this country, to institutional indifference, to the devaluing of women's lives. *The Family Doctor* is a cry for change.'

Sofie Laguna, Miles Franklin Award-winning author of *The Eye of the Sheep* and *Infinite Splendours*

'Brilliant. So compelling on so many levels.'

Chris Hammer, author of *Scrublands*, *Silver* and *Trust*

'Debra Oswald is always deft at capturing the nuances of female friendship and romantic attraction, but this time she brings them to a pitch of pulse-racing intensity. Delving into the dark world of domestic violence and society's abject failure to protect those most vulnerable, she has produced a gripping thriller, brimming with heart and intellect.'

Geraldine Brooks, author of *The Secret Chord*

'Mesmerising and heart-breaking. A perfect story for this moment in time.'

Sarah Bailey, author of *Where the Dead Go*

'*The Family Doctor* brings urgent news, taking the reader into suburban battlegrounds kept private by the threat and actuality of violence. In crystal-clear prose, Debra Oswald unveils an all-too-believable world of love and loyalty stretched to the limit, with agonising consequences when the best people are forced to do the worst things. When is it justified to fight fire with fire? The moment you finish this novel you will want to find someone else who has read it, and talk all night about the vital questions it raises.'

Malcolm Knox, author of *Bluebird*

Debra Oswald is a playwright, screenwriter and novelist. She is a two-time winner of the NSW Premier's Literary Award and author of the novels *Useful* (2015) and *The Whole Bright Year* (2018). She was creator/head writer of the first five seasons of successful TV series *Offspring*. Her stage plays have been performed around the world and published by Currency Press. *Gary's House, Sweet Road* and *The Peach Season* were all shortlisted for the NSW Premier's Literary Award. Debra has also written four plays for young audiences—*Dags, Skate, Stories in the Dark* and *House on Fire*. Her television credits include award-winning episodes of *Police Rescue, Palace of Dreams, The Secret Life of Us, Sweet and Sour* and *Bananas in Pyjamas*. Debra has written three Aussie Bites books for kids and six children's novels, including *The Redback Leftovers, Getting Air* and *Blue Noise*. Debra has been a storyteller on stage at Story Club and will perform her one-woman show, *Is There Something Wrong With That Lady?*, in 2021.

DEBRA OSWALD

THE FAMILY DOCTOR

This is a work of fiction. Names, characters, places and incidents are products of the author's imagination or are used fictitiously. Any resemblance to actual events, locales, or persons, living or dead, is entirely coincidental.

First published in 2021

Allen & Unwin
83 Alexander Street
Crows Nest NSW 2065
Australia
Phone: (61 2) 8425 0100
Email: info@allenandunwin.com
Web: www.allenandunwin.com

A catalogue record for this book is available from the National Library of Australia

ISBN 978 1 76087 778 1

Set in 13.3/18 pt Garamond Premier Pro by Bookhouse, Sydney
Printed and bound in Australia by McPherson's Printing Group

10 9 8 7 6 5 4 3

The paper in this book is FSC® certified. FSC® promotes environmentally responsible, socially beneficial and economically viable management of the world's forests.

FOR DALE DRUHAN AND SHELLEY EVES

ONE

BODIES ARE VULNERABLE PARCELS, SO MUCH SOFT TISSUE held in place by bone and skin. Walking around in them is a precarious business, considering their delicate physiological systems, prone to self-inflicted damage, susceptible to blows from the outside world and blows from other people. Not to mention the risk that the body could betray from within, suddenly, unpredictably.

Paula Kaczmarek had never been the kind of doctor who ruminated on such dangers excessively. She got on with doing the best that could be done for her patients—identify their problems, offer sensible remedies, chivvy them into treating themselves a little better. No nonsense, pragmatic. But underneath all of that, she felt an achy tenderness towards every one of those vulnerable bodies.

Just after five o'clock she smiled goodbye to Jemma on the front desk and headed out the door of Marrickville Family Practice. She fished out her phone and saw two missed calls from her friend Stacey, thirty and thirty-two minutes ago. During patient consultations, Paula always kept her phone on silent, zipped inside her handbag. It was disrespectful to be distracted by a caller ID flashing up on the screen at the same moment her hand might be probing some intimate cavity in a person.

In the car park, she tried to call Stacey back but it went to voicemail. On Tuesdays, Stacey took her kids to soccer training and Paula would usually be doing a few aged-care visits at this time. But she'd visited her current batch of old ladies yesterday, so this evening she was free to drive straight home.

Five months ago, Paula had offered Stacey a place to stay for as long as the family needed. Stacey had moved into the small room that used to be a study and the kids—Cameron was ten, Poppy just turned eight—shared the spare bedroom, next door to Paula's. It was the first time Paula had ever lived with children in her house. These days she found herself thinking a lot about what to cook, which dishes might appeal to kids. She had discovered that if she made any foodstuff sufficiently crunchy, Cameron and Poppy would happily eat it. Tonight, she bought the ingredients to make chicken schnitzel, sugar snaps and roast vegies with enough chopped pecans and parmesan sprinkled on top to make them crispy.

Paula and her husband Remy had bought the Californian bungalow in Earlwood years ago, and just as they'd finally finished renovating it, he got sick. Now, after Paula's long quiet stretch living there alone, she was enjoying having Stacey and Cameron and Poppy in the house, relishing the voices bouncing up the hallway. She'd developed a fondness for the earthy, tangy smell of grubby kids and their school clobber.

At the start, Paula had to forbid Stacey from saying 'Thank you' and 'Sorry for invading your house' ten or twenty times a day. They'd been friends since they were twelve, for God's sake. If Stacey was in trouble and Paula could help, then the solution was simple and there was no reason for I-don't-deserve-this gratitude. But Stacey's old buoyancy had been so eroded that the impulse to apologise for herself would overcome her. Paula would turn to find Stacey looking at her with tears oozing up, stammering out more embarrassed thanks. So they developed a jokey system whereby Stacey would add pen-strokes to a post-it on the fridge, like a prisoner marking off the days—a pen-stroke for every time she felt the urge to apologise or gush her appreciation. Paula agreed that, down the track, they could convert the tally into some appropriate Festival of Gratitude—a fancy weekend away or whatever.

Once she moved into Paula's house, Stacey pulled things together remarkably quickly—or at least, she threw herself into the practical processes with determination, even if she was still fractured below the busy surface. She made sure Cameron and Poppy were settled at their new school. She found Cameron a good counsellor. She took on a fill-in maternity leave contract as a teacher at a preschool and there was already talk of a permanent job. She was sorting out her finances and legal mess. She signed up for sessions with a psychologist herself.

To see Stacey now, to measure the change from the fragile woman her friends had found in the Ballina motel—well, Paula was relieved and surprised and bursting with admiration for her.

At night, after the kids were asleep, the two women would stretch out on the sofa and talk about what the future might look like. Paula was sometimes tempted to say, 'Stay living here for the next ten years,' but she resisted. That would be selfishness. She wanted to see her friend get on her feet, grasp her independence, maybe find a new partner eventually. So the fact that Paula loved having them here—the place humming with energy again—that shouldn't enter into Stacey's plans.

Anyway, for the time being, it was good. For the first time since Remy's death, Paula looked forward to coming home from work to this house.

As she swung her car into the driveway, she saw Stacey's old red Subaru parked outside. They were back from soccer training. So right now Stacey was probably in the process of hustling the kids through the shower and into pyjamas.

There was an unfamiliar white hatchback across the street, with a sticker from a car rental company on the back window. Most likely an interstate visitor at the Lees' house.

Both the kids' soccer boots were on the front porch, positioned precisely. Cameron would've done that. That boy had a commitment to tidiness his mother and sister lacked.

Paula unlocked the front door and drew in the breath to sing out hello, but with the intake of air her mouth was suddenly filled with a teeth-jangling sensation. She knew it very well—the brassy smell of blood.

'Stace? You okay?'

Two picture frames had been knocked off the hall table, scattering broken glass across the floor. That probably explained the blood smell—one of the kids had cut their feet.

But then in the living room, the coffee table was tipped on

its side and the carved granite bird from the mantelpiece was lying in the middle of the rug.

The skin prickled up Paula's arms, chest, neck, and she could hear her own rapid breaths, her throat stinging with the metallic blood smell. She spotted Stacey's mobile phone on the floor, its metal carcass bashed out of shape, the screen splintered into a white cobweb. Then she saw a woman's feet, and taking one more step around the sofa, she found her friend sprawled out.

Stacey's long hair was sodden, soaking up some of the pool of blood around her head and shoulders. The wound in her neck was meaty, with ragged edges, as if the skin had been torn apart by an animal. Paula had seen gunshot wounds like that—years ago, when she worked in emergency departments.

She knew Stacey was dead, but still her impulse was to lunge down and kneel by her friend, check for a pulse, find some way to staunch the bleeding. It was only once she was crouched low, facing the other corner of the room, that Paula had a sightline into the dining room.

She could see Poppy hunched in a tight ball where she'd squashed herself against the skirting board. Cameron had curled his body around hers, as if trying to shield his sister.

'Cameron,' Paula called out.

Both children were very still.

Paula stood up, but her knees crumpled and she steadied herself against the arm of the sofa for a second so she wouldn't fall. It was a wrench to leave Stacey's side. Paula felt she was abandoning her in this moment, even if that was illogical. But she needed to go to the kids.

She hurried across the room to reach them, grabbing on to the corner of the dining table as a pivot point to swing herself around and down onto the floor beside them.

That close, it was clear both children were dead, shot in the back of the head. Paula leaned over—she knew this was futile—to slip her hand inside the rucked-up collar of Cameron's soccer jersey and search for a pulse. With her other hand, she reached over him to hold on to Poppy's leg—the strip of bare skin between her red shorts and the top of the thick football socks. The impulse was to hold Poppy so she wouldn't look so defenceless. Her skin was still warm.

Paula heard the squeak of running shoes on the floorboards and Matt, Stacey's husband, lurched into view. He glanced down at Stacey on the floor, then turned to stare at the kids. His eyes appeared solid black—pupils dilated—and his skin was moist and pale, like uncooked dough. He stood very still, feet planted solidly, but then Paula saw his hands were shaking as he lifted the gun.

He raised his eyes to look Paula full in the face—he must've known she was there from the moment she came in the front door. He held her gaze for one second, then swung the muzzle of the rifle under his chin and fired.

TWO

ANITA WASN'T SURPRISED TO SEE THAT THE STREET OUTSIDE Paula's house was jammed with vehicles, cordoned off with police tape and unnaturally bright from the crime scene LEDs casting a harsh, astringent wash over everything.

She pulled her car to the kerb and texted Paula.

I'm here. They might not let me come inside. A xx

She'd been to ugly crime scenes—police rounds was her first job as a journalist—and covering the courts over the last six years, she'd seen plenty of photos of wounded bodies, blood-smeared kitchen knives, yellow markers numbering dismal objects strewn across a floor. She had a technique for looking at those images, blinking crisply so they couldn't burrow inside her eyeballs in a permanent way. But she wasn't sure she could manage this. She'd spent so many hours of her life in Paula's house, so many long dinners, TV binge festivals, boozy dancing nights, backyard afternoons yabbering over many pots of tea, weeping sessions after some misfortune for Paula or Anita or Stacey. And now she knew Stace was lying on the floor in that house. Beautiful Stacey and her beautiful kids.

Her phone dinged with a text: *Okay to come in.*

Anita tipped her head in greeting to the cops outside as she threaded her way around their gear and through the front door, her shoes crunching on the plastic runners temporarily laid over the rugs and floorboards. She was ushered away from the living room towards the kitchen, but on the way past she glanced into the room to see the crime scene officers working in their blue coveralls and white booties. Their faces were held almost rigid, as if they could only get through this with a tight professional mask. Anita had seen those solemn expressions before, whenever cops were required to deal with dead children.

As she moved one step further down the hallway, she caught a glimpse of Stacey's body and the bloody blur of Matt's scalp but she couldn't see Cameron or Poppy. Maybe that was just as well.

An officer carrying a tripod and an armload of camera equipment walked briskly towards Anita, so she ducked into a corner out of the way. From there, she could see through to the kitchen table where Paula was sitting, talking to a detective. Anita recognised him from a long murder trial she'd covered the year before. Detective Mehta. Rohan Mehta. She remembered thinking he was a good guy when they'd chatted in the courthouse corridors. And now she observed the gently respectful way he was treating Paula, leaning slightly across the table towards her, with a manner that managed to be tender without being intrusive.

'Paula. Hi,' said Anita softly, in keeping with the muted air in the room.

On her way to the house, Anita had told herself that Paula could handle this better than most people. She was a doctor, robust, not easily flustered, and a woman who'd already experienced the wallop of grief in her life, so she was someone who could be a strong centre for everyone else. But when Paula stood up, her movements were tentative, fragile. A papery version of herself.

She was only wearing a camisole tucked into her red-and-blue-patterned skirt. The shirt she had been wearing was now stuffed into a clear plastic evidence bag sitting on the bench. Through the plastic, Anita could see large bloodstains on the sleeves of the white shirt. The brightness of fresh blood had already dulled to a darker red.

Anita rushed forward to hug her, and it was reassuring to feel the warmth of Paula's skin, the underlying sturdiness of her body. The two women held the embrace for a long moment but they didn't look directly at each other. It might be too much. There was a risk this reality could hit with a force that would obliterate them.

Detective Mehta waited until they broke the embrace, then he stood up and offered Anita his hand to shake. 'Hello, Ms Delgado. We met on the—'

'Yeah, on the Richardson trial. Please call me Anita. Gotta say I'm glad you're the one here for—I mean, I'm relieved you're the detective handling . . .'

He nodded, so she didn't have to struggle to finish the sentence. He made eye contact with such direct, pure sympathy that Anita had to drop her head and fuss with her bag. One more second of that sympathetic gaze and she would lose it.

'I understand you were also a close friend of Stacey Durack,' he said.

'Yes, yes.' But Anita's throat clamped tight and no more words would come out.

'I'd like to get a statement from you, but it doesn't have to be right away,' Mehta explained. 'Might be best now if you concentrate on looking after your friend. Dr Kaczmarek thought she could probably stay tonight at your—'

'Oh yes, of course,' Anita jumped in, too abruptly and loudly. All her reflexes and gauges were off-kilter. 'Come to my place.'

The house was an active crime scene, so Paula wouldn't be allowed to stay there, even if she'd wanted to. Mehta suggested Paula fetch a few items of clothing from her bedroom before she left.

'Oh . . . No. I'll just take my handbag for now.'

Anita understood the impulse to walk out with nothing—every single thing in the house now felt contaminated with ugliness and sorrow.

Mehta nodded his understanding, but he asked Paula, 'Are you sure you don't need something warmer to wear now, though?' It was late April and the night was chilly.

Paula ran her hands over her bare arms, as if she'd forgotten she was only wearing a cami. 'Oh . . .'

'Don't worry,' said Anita. 'I've got a sweater in my car.'

As Anita drove away from the Earlwood house towards her own apartment, she glanced at Paula in the passenger seat. She looked even flimsier now, shrunken inside the folds of the loose green jumper Anita had found on the back seat.

'Did they say when you can go back to the house?'

Paula shook her head.

'Well, whatever. Stay with me as long as you want.'

'Thanks. I was an idiot. I should've brought some clothes with me.'

'Borrow mine,' Anita said.

When they were younger, Paula, Stacey and Anita had often shared clothes. Anita flashed on the image of the three of them, seventeen or eighteen years old, standing in front of her wardrobe, flicking through coat-hangers, chucking things on the bed to consider them in the light. Stacey was more voluptuous than the other two, even as a teenager, but she knew how to pick out the right borrowed garment that would still somehow fit her lavish breasts and hips. She was always coaxing the others to try different clothing combinations, whooping with laughter when a fashion ensemble proved to be tragic or gushing in her Barry White drawl about how sexy they looked.

Anita blockaded that memory of Stacey in all her fleshly life force. Instead, she fixed her eyes on the road and bunged on a hearty tone as she said to Paula: 'I've got plenty of I'm-a-doctor clothes you can borrow. We can make the sizes work, even if I've packed on a little bit of weight.'

'Thanks,' said Paula. 'Oh, but underwear . . .'

'Yeah, I guess you'll want your own undies. Broadway Kmart?'

The late-opening Kmart was so fluoro-bright it made Anita squint and the conditioned air was desiccated and chilly. A handful of people wandered the aisles, most of them on solo shopping missions. Who would choose to come here at ten o'clock on a Tuesday night? Maybe shiftworkers, restless individuals, shoppers who hated crowds, or people whose routine had been thrown off course by some sudden, unspeakable event.

Walking through the store, Anita felt disconnected from her body, apart from some faint nausea and a hollow sensation in the belly—the way she would feel at two a.m., prowling Dubai airport halfway through a long-haul flight.

Paula chose a three-pack of underpants and grabbed a couple of bras.

'Do you need to try the bras on?' Anita asked.

Paula shook her head. 'I'll take a chance.'

Anita realised that the process of going into a fitting room cubicle, undressing and dressing again was beyond Paula right now.

Paula sank even more deeply into a slumped silence as Anita drove to Newtown, parked in her underground spot and took them up in the lift.

Anita's apartment was on the fourth floor of a building with a real estate agent at street level, down the quieter end of King Street but within easy walking distance to live music or a tattoo parlour or the cinema, as required. Sometimes she wondered if it was time to move out of Newtown, away from the clog of cars and buses that left a grimy coating on every surface. Then again, the area was never boring, with plenty of weird shops and businesses giving it a spirited go, but without the hipster self-satisfaction of other inner-city suburbs. And there were always, reliably, fascinating humans wandering along the footpaths, laughing raucously and dodging their way between the cars to cross King Street.

Anita's apartment was tidy enough not to be embarrassing, with compact furniture that suited the small space and bursts of colour from textiles she'd bought on her South American travels. Even so, there was something provisional about it, as if Anita were camping here, making the best of it while she waited for her life to move into gear. The friends had always chosen Paula and Remy's house as the properly *homey* place to hang out, so it felt odd to invite Paula inside for more than a quick visit on their way somewhere else.

Anita made them toast and mint tea, while Paula stood over the rubbish bin in the kitchen, taking the tags and stickers off all the Kmart underwear as if that was an important and urgent task. On this night, any activity either of them did felt inappropriate, ridiculous, obscene. Ripping off tags was as good as anything to be doing.

Anita wondered when they would really talk. Probably not tonight. They—Paula, Anita, Stacey—had always been good at talking. But this was so overwhelming, it crushed any speakable words out of their throats.

The three of them had met as twelve-year-olds on their first day at Parramatta High School. Even though various clusters of school friends had crumbled and regrouped, the three had remained a strong unit. In the years since, circumstance had sometimes frayed the connections—Paula's impossibly long hours as a medical student, Anita's three-year stint in London, Stacey's move to a remote property off the communications grid—but the threads between them never snapped.

Paula was always the strongest, no question. Even when her husband Remy was terminally ill, it felt as though Paula was the one supporting Anita through the process, demonstrating how to manage it graciously, when to talk openly, when to joke and when to sit silently with the awfulness of it.

A year later, after Remy died, it became clear that Stacey was the one in desperate trouble, struggling to twist free of her abusive husband. Anita had dived in, been a devoted friend, showered her and the kids with love. But even then, Paula was really the anchor point, calm and generous, taking Stacey, Cameron and Poppy into her house.

'Should we try to sleep?' Anita asked when they had chewed their way through the toast.

Paula shrugged. 'Probably. There's going to be a huge amount to do tomorrow. A lot of phone calls.'

Anita's apartment had one decent-sized bedroom and a smaller room with a sofa bed. Together, wordlessly, she and Paula unfolded the mattress and put clean sheets on it.

'Good night, lovely,' said Anita, and they embraced briefly, lightly, careful not to tip each other over into emotional intensity they couldn't handle right at this minute.

Anita lay in bed, her mind still clenched against the initial shock of the killings. But then thoughts began to ooze up, unbidden. Picturing Stacey's face. How afraid she would've been. Imagining the moment she must've seen in Matt's eyes that he was going to do this thing. Hearing her voice—she would've pleaded with him, wept, whimpered with fear. Did Stacey suspect he would hurt the kids? Had she known that before she was killed? If she had realised, did her heart explode into ragged pieces? And the kids—those gorgeous fucking kids—did they register what was happening? Did they know their father was about to kill them in the moment before they died? Anita hoped they didn't. Jesus Christ, she hoped not. Those exquisite children. Their spectacular, clever, vibrant mother.

Rage towards Matt burned along Anita's arteries like a powerful fuel. But at the same time, she felt powerless, crumbling apart with self-pity at losing her friend, immobilised in the face of this ugliness.

Anita gave in to the weeping, sobs wrenching through her with such force she could barely breathe between them.

The bedroom door opened and Paula padded in, wearing borrowed pyjamas. She climbed into the bed and curled herself along Anita's back. Against her ribcage, Anita could feel Paula's jagged breathing—she had been crying too.

The two women didn't say anything, but they lay there together until the morning, either awake or slipping into shallow puddles of sleep, sometimes huddled together, sometimes keeping a hand on the other's waist or arm, hanging on to each other through the night, so neither of them could die.

THREE

CAMERON AND POPPY WERE FANTASTIC AT PARLOUR GAMES. Paula figured this was a happy by-product of having spent a sizeable chunk of their childhood living on a property off the grid, with no internet, no mobile reception. According to Stacey, the solar batteries often failed, and if the backup generator then conked out, which it frequently did, the house would be without power for an indefinite period. So Stacey had built up a repertoire of activities—puzzles, craft projects and board games—that could be done by the light from LP gas cylinders.

Charades was their favourite. When Cameron first moved into the Earlwood house with Paula, he was horrified that she didn't know how to play charades.

'I never learned,' Paula explained. 'We didn't play games in my family.'

Cameron frowned, finding this admission sad and barely credible.

She laughed. 'I guess I had a deprived childhood.'

Paula's disadvantaged childhood became a running gag between them. Cameron would tease her, adopting an exaggerated expression of pity. 'Did you get to eat chicken when you were a kid?' 'Did your parents ever read you books?' 'Were you allowed to drink water from the tap when you were little?' He loved that Paula would wail with mock angst, loved that this silliness was their special shared thing. And Stacey was relieved to see her anxious son daring to be cheeky with Paula. It was good to see delight on the face of a boy burdened by so many worries.

Cameron made a big deal out of teaching 'Poor Paula' how to play charades. The four of them would write movie, book or song titles on scraps of paper, four titles each, then put the folded scraps into Stacey's upturned straw hat. They never turned the game into a competition—there were no points or winners or time limits.

'We play for the glory of the doing and the guessing, don't we, guys?' said Stacey. 'And who needs time pressure? Too much pressure in the world already.'

They took turns—youngest to oldest—which meant Paula went last, being three months older than Stacey. It intrigued the kids that their mother had once been twelve and that she'd been friends with a twelve-year-old version of Paula back in those ancient times.

When it was Paula's go, Cameron patiently explained the rules, the signals to use, and if she looked stuck about how to act out a word, he would whisper advice to her. Paula made a big deal about relying on his help.

Poppy was barely eight, but she could confidently dissect words into their syllables and come up with rhymes in order to offer 'sounds like' clues. She threw the whole of her little body into the miming, especially if it required flamboyant emotion or imitating animals. But then some detail would crack her up and she'd dissolve into giggles. Cameron would pretend she was doing it on purpose as a clue and he'd call out guesses—'laugh', 'giggle', 'wee your pants'—which would send his sister into more flurries of laughter. If Stacey signalled to him to cool it, Cameron would nod earnestly and keep quiet until Poppy had controlled herself enough to complete the clue.

When it was Cameron's turn to perform, he would have his serious concentrating face on, sucking in his bottom lip a little, tiny creases in his forehead, determined to be precise and effective with his actions. He was especially satisfied if Poppy guessed his signals.

Now, Paula could still picture the exact spot in front of the fireplace where the kids used to stand when they played charades, and she could imagine the straw hat with the folded bits of paper sitting on the coffee table. That was why she wanted to move back into her house as soon as it was feasible. There were memories embedded in so many places in that house—images of her husband, and now Stacey, Cameron and Poppy too. She needed to be there.

For two weeks, Paula stayed at Anita's Newtown apartment, going in to work most days, taking off the occasional morning to do police interviews, meet funeral directors and handle the other administrative tasks that follow the killing of a close friend and her children. She preferred to keep occupied, seeing patients, driving to and from the practice, even if it meant she had to field the awkward, soggy but well-meaning questions from her fellow doctors. All the doctors except Li-Kim, who knew Paula too well to prod at her by constantly asking, 'How are you?'

Li-Kim was forty-two, smart, a diligent GP, dryly funny, discreet, loyal. She was forever trying a new weight-loss method. 'Paula, let's be realistic: I'm short and dumpy, with a sweet tooth. I'm born to be round. Why should patients pay attention to advice from a fat doctor?'

They'd joined the practice in the same month, immediately clocking each other as potential friends. Then Remy met Li-Kim at a medical conference dinner and the two of them hit it off straight away. Two years later, when Li-Kim and her wife Connie had their first daughter, they asked Remy to be the godfather.

Since the murders, Li-Kim had been shepherding Paula's work schedule with gentle care and unobtrusively covering any necessary absences.

When Paula decided it was time to move back into her own house, Anita tried to talk her out of it.

'Oh, Paula, are you sure?' she asked. 'It's only been two and a bit weeks. Is it too soon? If ever a location was primed for PTSD . . . shit, your place . . .'

'You can't let bad memories trump the good ones,' Paula argued.

'Okay. I get you want to go home,' said Anita. 'But should I—I mean, do you want me to come and stay there with you for a few nights or something?'

But Paula could see Anita was nervous about the idea of sleeping in the Earlwood house, as if malevolence was now soaked into the walls in transmittable form. Anita had always had an anxiety problem, sometimes being gripped by quite irrational fears, so Paula understood this offer would truly cost her. It wouldn't be right to burden her friend with more than she could handle.

'Don't worry,' said Paula. 'I'll be fine. I'll call you if I'm not.'

On her way to the house, Paula stopped by the supermarket and bought vegies, milk, bread, fish, fruit, cheese. By stocking the fridge with fresh food, she would reclaim her home, inserting wholesome ordinary things into it.

Turning into the street, she saw the bank of flowers stacked along her front fence. Seventy, eighty, maybe a hundred bunches, forming a burial mound of vegetation and cellophane wrapping, piled against the low brick wall of Paula's front yard. Some of the flowers were decaying, clearly put there very soon after the deaths, but others looked fresh, with intensely blue delphiniums, pink stocks and the crisp whiteness of chrysanthemums sitting on top of the half-rotten mass.

Tucked between the bouquets were envelopes, addressed to Cameron or Poppy or Stacey, many written in children's chunky lettering. There were also two sheets of cardboard, the kind kids use for school projects, covered in messages and little drawings. One was from the primary school Cameron and Poppy had attended, the other from the preschool where Stacey had been teaching. Paula tried to imagine how the other kindy teachers would explain what had happened to Ms Durack.

She left the flower pile where it was for now and approached the front door. She had readied herself for this—walking in there again—and she tensed her abdominal muscles, like someone guarding against a gut punch. In the preceding days, she'd arranged for crime scene cleaners to go over the place and she'd bought new rugs to replace the bloodied ones the police had taken as evidence.

She walked into the living room. The cleaners had put some items back in the wrong places—the granite bird was on a side table instead of the mantelpiece—but, really, the place looked bizarrely normal.

The doors to the kids' bedroom and Stacey's room were shut. Paula left them shut for now. Anita and she had agreed they would sort through the stuff together at some point. No rush.

She turned the TV on, volume high, to fill the house with the burble of voices while she cooked herself some dinner. Afterwards, she sat gingerly on the sofa, as if any sudden physical move might trigger a disintegration. She clicked on an old series of *Frasier* and found she could pretty much enjoy it, letting the episodes roll on, one after the other, lulled into a welcome stupor by the sitcom's humour and goodwill.

A storm had gathered itself up since she'd been in the house and, over the sound of the TV, Paula heard the rain start to sluice down. She ran out into the front yard to rescue the paper tributes, tucking them under her shirt to bring inside. After wiping off the water droplets with a tea towel, she laid the letters and cardboard sheets on the kitchen table. Once they dried, she would slip them into plastic sleeves. It would be a sorrowful but satisfying task. It would be something, anyway.

Her hair and clothes were now quite wet—it was the kind of rain shower that soaked you through within minutes. In wet socks, she padded into the bathroom to towel her hair dry and it was then, in that undefended moment, thrown off her careful course by the sudden storm, that she was pierced by a memory.

'Paula, can you come?' The sound of Poppy's voice calling out from the room she shared with Cameron. The little girl had just had a shower, her pyjamas slightly damp from the steamy bathroom, and she was rubbing her long hair dry with a towel.

'Can you please get the knots out of my hair?' Poppy asked, holding out a brush and a bottle of leave-in conditioner. 'Mum's gone to the shops and I can't do the knots by myself.'

'Oh sure,' said Paula, but not feeling sure—she'd never de-knotted a child's hair before.

Poppy plonked herself on the edge of the bed and flicked her hair back, trusting Paula could do this. Paula worked gently through each section of hair, trying not to tug too hard, while Poppy chattered on about a school excursion to the Maritime Museum. Once Paula was confident she wasn't yanking Poppy's scalp in a painful way, she enjoyed the ritual of it, the satisfaction of turning the tousled clumps of hair into a smooth, straight curtain down the girl's back. She was moved that Poppy trusted her so simply, and she was struck by the intense sweetness of having a connection with a child who wasn't her own, but a child she'd been given the chance to love.

Now, Paula shook off that remembered scene, gulped a breath, and walked out of the bathroom. But she couldn't stop the memories coming. Next she saw Cameron, the day the family moved in with her. This beautiful, earnest boy, his face pinched with anxiety. Paula saw him prowling the whole house, checking the window latches, making a mental inventory of external doors, escape routes, potential dangers. According to Stacey, Cam felt it was his job to ensure the safety of his mother and sister.

Paula squeezed her eyes shut to rid her mind of that memory, then opened them to find herself in the spot Matt had been standing when he shot himself. And in that moment, she was hit by an image that forced its way into her brain like something whooshing up under pressure from deep under water: she saw herself with a scalpel in her hand, slicing into Matt's neck until she severed his carotid artery. In this urgent fantasy, she saw him fall to the floor, bleeding out rapidly, as still and harmless as a cadaver in an anatomy class.

~

When Anita went back to Paula's place after the funeral, she guzzled two big goblets of shiraz very quickly. She figured she should get well pissed to reduce the risk that her first time being in this house again would freak her out. Paula had moved home more than a week ago and seemed to be handling it.

Mind you, Anita noticed Paula was also knocking back the wine, as the two of them picked at a platter of food left over from the post-funeral afternoon tea. The congealed fattiness of the cold mini quiches needed to be washed down with even more gulps of shiraz.

Paula yanked the clip out of her hair and shook her head to loosen the spongy curls. She had kept her hair exactly the same ever since Anita had known her—long brown hair, naturally wavy, worn tied back when she was working or attending formal events like funerals, left loose around her face when she was off-duty. When Paula was nine, her mother had taken her daughter to a salon and requested the child's hair be cut short and square—a style known thereafter as 'the Doctor Spock

Hairdo'. Anita had seen a photo and it really was as alarming as described. Typically, Paula herself made a compassionate diagnosis: her mother had been overwhelmed at the time and wanted to reduce maintenance of her daughter's long knotty hair. But in her quiet way, Paula asserted herself—never again allowing her hair to be cut, not ever, apart from minor trimming.

Over the same period of years, Anita had lurched between different hairstyles in desperate attempts to find herself or solve whatever personal mess she was in at the time by means of personal grooming. She'd worn her hair long, short with shaved sides, feathered, bobbed, layered, even permed during one especially misguided phase. She'd dyed it blonde, goth black, cartoonish blue, russet, peroxide-tipped and so on. Presently, she had reddish foils through her dark brown hair, but she was contemplating cutting it pixie short again. She envied Paula's certitude about matters like hair.

As Paula kicked off her shoes, Anita followed her lead, both women undoing zips and buttons on the formal outfits they'd worn to the crematorium.

Once the police released the bodies, it had fallen to Anita and Paula to organise the funeral. By the time Stacey was four, her father had disappeared to New Zealand to construct a new life for himself with a second family. And by the time Stacey finished her teacher training, her mother had died. There was no other surviving family to speak of. The father did manage to fly in to Sydney to attend the funeral, but Matt's parents chose to stay away, instead sending flowers with a loving message for their dead grandchildren.

Anita had delivered the eulogy, at Paula's insistence. ('You're much better than me at words and speaking and all that.') Paula organised the slideshow of photos and there was a video of kids from the school singing a song in honour of Cameron and Poppy. A celebrant conducted the whole thing with what felt like the right pitch of warmth and solemnity. (But what about this thing could ever be considered 'right'?) They ensured there was no religious blah blah in the service because Stacey wouldn't have been able to stomach any talk about God.

The crematorium chapel was full and many mourners had stayed for the afternoon tea in the function area—old friends as well as Stacey's recent work colleagues and parents from the school.

After hours of well-meaning talk and the emotional workload of dealing with people at the funeral, Anita thought it would be a relief to retreat here, just the two of them. But in fact, without all those distractions, the more painful stuff, the impossible stuff, seeped into the room where the two of them were sitting.

Anita gave up on the claggy mini quiche she was trying to digest and filled her wineglass again.

'Should we have known it might happen? Should we have done more to protect her?' she asked.

Paula shrugged limply. 'Everyone did all the right things. And there was no reason to think she wasn't safe here.'

When Stacey moved into Paula's house, Matt was securely in jail in Queensland (refused bail, charged with assaulting Stacey, driving a car through a shopfront window and assaulting a police officer). But four months later, he was released and no one informed Stacey. That piece of information had accidentally fallen into the crack along the Queensland–New South Wales border.

'Of course,' Paula added, 'if we'd known he was out of jail, we could've helped her find somewhere to hide for as long as she needed to.'

Anita felt a flush of rage burn up her neck. 'Why should Stacey have to live like a fugitive because of him? Why should she have to drag her kids around and hide out like—fuck . . . it's just . . .'

Paula responded in her measured doctorly tone. 'Because you have to be realistic and do what works in practice. Whatever can keep people safe.'

Anita pulled herself more upright on the sofa and suddenly realised how woozy drunk she was. 'I understand that. I'm just saying—'

'And the thing is,' said Paula, 'Matt must've been mentally ill.'

'Was he? Was he*?*' Anita could hear her own voice coming out sharp and hectoring. 'I guess he was. But what the fuck does that mean? He planned this. It wasn't some temporary brain snap. He planned this for fucking weeks.'

Anita had, properly, avoided covering the case for the newspaper because of her personal connection, but she'd been talking unofficially to the cops and the other journos, gathering every detail about the days leading up to the killing.

'Matt kept watch on this house, knew everybody's schedule, knew you were usually late on Tuesdays so he'd have time alone with them. He rented three different cars to avoid making Stacey suspicious. Before he headed to Sydney, he drove back to the Maryvale property to pick up the gun he'd hidden. This wasn't impulsive. It wasn't some kind of blind uncontrolled explosion.'

'No, clearly not. But for someone to do what he did—'

'No. Fuck him. I don't want to understand Matt. Or wonder about Matt. I don't want to psychologise this. I don't want anyone to explain this away or analyse it in a way that drains the blood out of the primal bare fact of it: a man murdered his own children and their mother. All I want to do is shoot that monster dead.'

Paula exhaled heavily. 'Come on, revenge doesn't do anyone any good—well, it might give you a burst of immediate satisfaction. But it doesn't fix anything.'

'Okay. Yes. True. Revenge isn't the answer. Okay. I want to go back in time and shoot him *before* he had a chance to do it. That would've done some fucking good, wouldn't it? We just need to kill all the dangerous men.'

Anita realised that she'd been barking at Paula, aggressively stabbing her head at her friend as if she were the enemy. And Paula looked so profoundly tired that Anita felt terrible for adding to the pain of the day.

'Sorry, Paula,' Anita muttered and hoisted herself unsteadily to a standing position. 'I'm pissed and I'm—look, I should go home. I'll call an Uber.'

In the back of the Uber, Anita made brief eye contact with the driver in the rear-view mirror.

'Sorry if I'm not chatty,' she said. 'Had a friend's funeral today.'

The guy made a sympathetic noise and left her alone. Maybe it was a cheap move, playing the dead friend card to be excused from the obligation to chat. But there was a strong risk she would dissolve into a weeping jag or a shouty rant, so really she was doing the driver a favour by shutting up entirely.

She felt queasy with booze and the familiar niggle of regret in her belly. Anita often came away from encounters with Paula feeling like a fool, replaying certain things she'd said, ashamed that she'd spilled her guts so messily—blurting out every wild thought, every gust of emotion—while Paula was always so controlled and mature and patient with her. Even now, in the shadow of this catastrophe, the old insecurities still buzzed between them.

Anita was disgusted with herself for indulging in this sulky self-absorbed shit. And the thing, the overriding thing, was that they'd always backed each other, relied on each other, whatever annoyances simmered and spiked.

Anita pulled out her phone to type a text, poking clumsily at the screen because she was drunk and because the car was bumping through the suburban streets. She eventually managed to hit send.

Dear P, Sorry for hectoring you. A xx

She saw the three little dots moving to indicate Paula was typing a response straight back. Which was a relief.

You didn't. I get it. I'm angry too. P xx

And then, thirty seconds later, there was another text from Paula: *Maybe you're right and we should kill all the fuckhead men.*

Let's do it. Goodnight, my lovely. A xx

Later, Anita came to wonder if the things she'd said that night had set Paula's mind spinning along a certain path. Once an idea had been said aloud, even in a flippant way, it could establish its own blood supply in a person's imagination.

FOUR

WALKING INTO THE DOWNING STREET COURT BUILDING, Anita was generally sure-footed. She knew how to do her job and she mostly did it well, unlike her performance in the messier areas of life. She'd started covering court stories when she was working for a newspaper in London. Then she came home, four years ago, just as the Sydney paper's long-time court reporter was transferring to the Washington bureau, leaving a gap Anita could slide into. At a time when any print media job was rare and precious, it had been a piece of luck.

On her way through the foyer, she said hello to the security screening staff, waved to a cop she knew, nodded to a barrister she'd observed shredding a witness on the stand yesterday. She liked that this was her patch. She was familiar with the players and used to the rhythms of the place. This building was really her workplace, much more than the newspaper office.

Lately, she'd been covering a defamation case as well as assembling whatever background stuff she could on the upcoming Santino trial. Today, she was determined to wrap her head around a labyrinthine fraud case that was testing her grasp of fiduciary terminology.

She sat through the fraud hearing into the afternoon session, the lists of financial statistics unspooling for hours. After a while, the voices in the courtroom blurred into a meaningless drone in Anita's ears.

Lapses of concentration had been happening in the weeks since Stacey was killed. Arguably, Anita should've taken leave from her job until her head was clearer, but time away from the noise and activity and deadlines, time alone with her thoughts—no, that held little appeal. Mind you, even at work she would still find herself revisiting moments with Stacey, replaying them again and again.

Twelve years ago. Dinner for Paula's twenty-fifth birthday. Stacey had introduced them to her new boyfriend Matt. He was good-looking in a boyish way, hair flopping over his face, labrador puppy eyes. Stacey was fizzy, so infatuated was she with this guy, and that seemed to make her even more vivacious as she greeted the dozen people around the restaurant table.

Stacey was smitten with Matt, but it was obvious he was even more besotted with her. Anita recalled the way he'd gazed at her with those sooky eyes. As if he couldn't believe he'd nabbed himself a woman this vibrant and clever. As if, by winning Stacey's love, he'd won a prize he didn't deserve. Which he fucking well didn't.

Ten years ago. The day after Cameron was born. Anita went to the hospital to find Stacey propped up in the bed, puffy in the face and wincing with pain from the caesarean, but so beautiful.

When Stacey looked at her newborn in the transparent plastic crib, anyone could see there was light shining out of her.

That day in the hospital, Stacey cradled tiny Cameron and said to Anita, 'If a huge monster lumbered in here right now and tried to hurt this baby, I reckon—even with my belly freshly cut open and stitched up—I reckon I could tear that monster apart with my bare hands.' Then she laughed, surprised to hear herself express such a ferocious thought out loud.

A bit over two years ago. Between Christmas and New Year. Shortly before Remy's sarcoma was diagnosed. Anita twisted around in the passenger seat of Paula's car, watching Stacey through the back windscreen. As they drove away, Stace was standing in long grass, waving goodbye. Cameron, an eight-year-old by then, had planted himself beside his mother and six-year-old Poppy clung on to the seam of Stacey's shorts.

Paula and Anita had driven up to Queensland together to stay a couple of nights on the remote property outside Maryvale where Matt was trying to make a go of cattle farming, despite having no agricultural experience. On the eleven-hour drive back to Sydney, the two women spent much of the time talking about Stacey, the troubling details they'd noticed, the way Matt's black mood could suddenly change the air pressure in the room. They knew Stacey had put on a show of cheerfulness for her friends, and they still worried about how tired she looked, how weighed down. Then again, neither Anita nor Paula had kids. What did they know about the strains of motherhood, and life on a farm without mains power or town water? Maybe it was natural and understandable to look as exhausted as Stacey.

Still, after that visit, Paula and Anita were both on alert, trying to speak to Stacey once a week at least. But it was difficult, given she had no landline, internet or mobile reception on the property, and the stretches of time with no communication grew longer.

Anita often thought about one particular phone call: Stacey had used the landline at the preschool in Warwick. She'd started teaching there two days a week to bring in some off-farm income. It was a quick call—Stacey chatted about the kids, but she sounded preoccupied and then ended the call abruptly.

Two minutes later, Anita's mobile rang again. It was Matt. He'd followed Stacey into town and appeared at the preschool to check on her. Now he wanted to know who Stacey had just been speaking to.

'Oh—hi, Matt. This is Anita. Me and Stacey were just catching up—'

He cut in. 'I love her more than she loves me. There's an imbalance. She says that's not true. But you know and I know it's true.'

Before she could respond, he had slammed down the phone.

Anita was sunk so deep in those memories that she only realised the court had adjourned for the day when people around her were standing up and shuffling out. Shit. How long had she been lost in her head? She'd have to beg favours from colleagues to fill in whatever chunks she'd missed.

There was a move on by a few journos and lawyers to hang around for Friday afternoon drinks. Anita had been avoiding social gatherings. She didn't want to keep talking about Stacey but she couldn't bear to talk about anything other than Stacey. Any kind of regular chat felt scratchy or awkward or phoney, so she'd kept to herself. The only exception was time spent with Paula. The two of them could rave on about the killings without polite limits or apology. And when it was the two of them, they also felt free to say nothing or talk trivia or laugh about silly stuff, whatever—but all the while, the fact of what had happened would be suspended in the air they breathed together, in a way that felt essential, compulsory.

Of course, it was self-indulgent and unhealthy to continue avoiding social events. Anita ought to ease back into human interaction. So that Friday, she let herself be swept along in the chattering group heading to the pub.

By the time Anita arrived in the back bar, the courthouse mob had colonised one of the long tables and people scooched over on the bench seat to make a spot for her in the middle of a noisy group of lawyers. That suited her—being immersed in loud opinionated voices and raucous laughter, she was free to listen and smile and not really engage with people. It still felt a bit phoney, but it was a start.

A few minutes later, three cops joined the group, and Anita realised Rohan Mehta was one of them. He must have been around the Downing Street courts today because he was a detective on the Santino case, which was coming to trial soon.

As they dragged extra chairs up to the far end of the table, Mehta nodded hello to her. Two days after the killings, Anita had gone in to his office to give a statement. He'd called her a few times since then to check details about Stacey—part of the job of preparing material for the coroner. It could be eighteen months or two years before a coronial inquest would be scheduled, but the bulk of the police work on it needed to be done now.

Over the next half-hour, there was a flurry of comings and goings from the pub. Anita declined an invitation to make it 'a big night' at some bar down at the Quay with the bunch of noisy lawyers. She wriggled out of having dinner at a Thai place with one of the journos (a lovely woman) who was making sympathetic 'I know you're struggling' faces at her.

As people left, others swapped seats and slid along benches, so that when Rohan Mehta came back from a run to the bar, there was an obvious empty spot next to Anita.

'Okay if I sit here?'

Mehta stood, waiting for her to respond, and Anita realised she was gawping at him without answering.

'Oh. Yes. Yes!' she said quickly. 'Please.'

He sat next to her on the bench seat.

'Sorry if I'm a bit . . .' Anita mimed being spaced out and, by way of explanation, she added, 'I was on that fraud trial today.'

'Phoo . . . those endless pages of figures.' He shook his head. 'That stuff fries my brain.'

'Me too. I was never good at sums. Had a maths teacher who made me chant "Numbers are my friends" over and over.'

'Did it help?'

'Apparently not. I'm still barely numerate,' she said.

Rohan smiled.

Anita closed her eyes and puffed out a breath, defeated.

'You okay?' he asked.

'Please excuse me. I don't think I'm capable of chatting like a regular human being. Not to you, especially.'

She felt him looking at her, concerned more than offended, but she still worried she might have been rude, so she added, 'Sorry if that sounds—I just meant that because you're connected to Stacey's case, engaging in small talk is hard to—y'know . . . Sorry.'

Rohan nodded. No explanation was required. Then he said, 'I'm happy to engage in big talk, if you want.'

He said the words lightly. No pressure. She felt her stomach muscles—permanently knotted tight these days—relax a little, with that sense of being at ease with the other person. She turned the beer glass on the table in front of her and let a silence sit there. It struck her that even the silence was comfortable with this guy.

Eventually, she said, 'I wish you could've met Stacey. Oh shit—is it okay for me to talk to you about a victim in a coronial case that you're working on?'

'It's okay.'

'If Stacey was here right now, she'd be like an energy source in the room. But she wouldn't try to be the centre of attention or anything. She'd *galvanise* the place, connect people, get them talking to each other. Contagious enthusiasm. People used to wait for her to arrive at a party, you know? And she wasn't only like that in a crowd. I mean, even when it was just the two of us, I was always the best version of myself with Stacey. I was funnier and smarter and nicer—if that makes any sense.'

'It does. I've got a cousin who's that person for me.'

He smiled broadly just thinking about this cousin. Anita realised she'd only ever seen him in the context of crime scenes and court appearances and sombre moments, when a bold smile would not have been appropriate. This was the first time she'd seen Rohan Mehta smile with full wattage. It was a good smile.

Then he asked, 'Do you reckon you *were* smarter and funnier with Stacey, or did it just feel that way?'

'Legitimate question. I don't know. I'm such a suggestible person, I can't judge. With my friend Paula, I often feel like I'm too impulsive, neurotic, a "silly duffer", but that's not Paula's fault. It's not because of something she's *doing* to me. Well, Paula can radiate a bit of that patronising doctor thing—but it's totally benign and it comes from good intentions. Shit . . . sorry, I feel disloyal saying that.'

'No, don't worry, I get it,' he assured her. 'It's a manner a lot of doctors take on, don't you reckon?'

'I do. And look, the main thing to say is that Paula's a wonderful doctor. I've snooped online—those review sites where people rate their doctors. Patients all love her, really rely on her, trust her advice.'

'And you do too.'

'God, yeah. Sometimes I vow to hide my fuck-ups from Paula, but I never can. I have to tell her every important thing in my life, even if I know she's going to tell me I'm a silly duffer. In the end, I always *want* that bracing advice from her.' Anita barked a laugh and Rohan smiled.

'Mind you,' Anita added, 'I'm a woman with a long CV of defunct relationships, dealing with the internet dating circus, so how can I realistically discuss my experiences with a woman who met Mr Perfect on her first day at medical school?'

'This is Paula's husband who died?'

'Yeah. Remy. He was a neurologist. Described himself as an ABC—Australian-born Chinese. Very kind guy and so handsome—I'm talking joke-handsome. We were expecting them to have absurdly beautiful children soon. Until Remy was diagnosed with sarcoma. He was gone within nine months.'

'That's brutal. Poor Paula.'

'Yes. Impossibly sad. But, y'know, she was incredible all through it. Handled it like a fucking goddess.'

As more people left the table—heading home or to dinner or to another drinking establishment—Anita stayed talking to Rohan. It struck her that he was a guy who actually listened to the person he was with and—a miracle—asked follow-up questions. Anita knew how rare that was. So often, when she was supposedly having a conversation with a man, she would find herself *interviewing* the guy, asking questions, then follow-up questions, as the gentleman yabbered happily on. Sure, as a journalist, it was easy for her to fall into interviewer mode, but it wasn't only her. She'd heard many other women complain about the same experience. When stuck at dreary functions, Anita had a game she played in her own head. *How many questions can I ask this guy in a row before he asks me one single question?* The record stood at forty-eight.

On this evening, she found herself in the unfamiliar and embarrassing position of being the one doing all the yabbering without asking questions of the other person. She quickly changed gear to balance things up.

'So tell me,' she asked Rohan, 'why did you decide to become a cop?'

'Oh . . . Do you want a short answer or the quaint childhood idealism version?'

'As quaint and idealistic and childhood-y as possible, please.'

'Okay, well, when I was a kid, my parents had a restaurant—they still do. Indian restaurant.'

'Delicious food?'

'Yes, very delicious. We lived in the flat above, and when Mum and Dad were working downstairs, my sisters and I would be minded by our grandparents. My grandparents were addicted to old British TV detective shows, so I was too.'

'Your dream was to be a gruff, tweedy detective inspector?'

'Pretty much, yeah. What got me hooked—I liked the way an episode would start with all this confusion and mess after a murder, people upset, and then the detective would march in, put the pieces together, and create—you know . . .'

'Harmony.'

'Exactly,' he said. 'I decided I wanted to do that: calmly show up after a bad thing has happened, find the solution and make everything better for people.'

'So it was a noble career choice.'

'The trouble was, my parents—' Rohan stopped mid-sentence and groaned.

'Oh wait,' Anita gasped with mock horror, 'don't tell me you got good marks in high school? Oh no, hang on, you didn't have good enough results to get into a law degree, did you?'

Rohan went with the joke, nodding with exaggerated sombreness.

'I'm so sorry,' said Anita.

'Thank you. Clearly you can understand how devastated my parents were when I studied criminology and joined the police force.'

'But they're proud of you now?'

Rohan laughed. 'Oh no, still wretchedly and loudly disappointed.'

Anita winced with serious sympathy this time.

Rohan shrugged. 'I'm a thirty-six-year-old man. I can deal with it.'

'And being a real-life detective, how close is it to what Little Rohan imagined?'

'Ha. Well, different in a multitude of ways, as you might guess,' he said. 'For one thing, in a TV detective show, if someone looks guilty but it's only thirty-five minutes into the episode, you think, "Oh, that obviously guilty guy can't be the murderer," because you know there's another twist coming. In TV, the audiences are trained to expect twists, to assume that "nothing is what it seems".'

'But in reality . . .'

'In reality, we get a call and walk into a house—'

'Walk in to see a woman and two kids dead on the floor, and the estranged husband with a self-inflicted gunshot wound,' Anita said.

'Yes. And that scene—it *is* what it looks like. The thing about real police work, there are virtually never any twists. Might be a more constructive process if there *were* twists we could undo. But I mean, we walk into that house—we know what's happened, we know what it *is*—but . . . oh fuck . . . then what?'

Anita realised that she'd steered the conversation into a dark place, but Rohan seemed okay with that. That was an advantage of hanging out with cops and the journos who routinely covered ugly stories. They were used to ugly. Dark things were understood, with no need to discuss them overtly. But then, if you did end up going there, you knew the other person could handle it more easily than a civilian could.

'You mean because the tragic scene in that house isn't a mystery with an answer?' said Anita.

'In a TV drama or a mystery novel, the puzzle gets solved by the end of the story and that neutralises the danger from the psychopath or the "unlikely killer" or whatever kind of monster it is. But in the real job, we can't kid ourselves. Things are usually pretty much what they seem. We can't hope for twists. And monsters are still out there.'

Mehta sounded resigned to that, and Anita felt a spike of annoyance. 'But even if there's no puzzle to solve, there's *urgency*—I mean, to stop it from happening to the next woman, that's an urgent fucking matter, isn't it?'

Anita realised she'd snapped at him, firing an unfair amount of anger in his direction. But he seemed to understand and not take it the wrong way.

'It is,' he said. 'It's urgent.'

'But I guess at the point you homicide guys are involved in a case, the terrible thing has already happened,' Anita said.

Mehta nodded bleakly.

'Same for me. I sit in court covering one murder trial after another. Another dead woman and then another woman, and I don't . . . The system is fucked.'

'I don't disagree,' Rohan said. 'How could I disagree? We're failing every day.'

'Sorry, I don't mean to suggest what you do isn't . . . Getting justice for people *after* the terrible thing has happened—that's still something.'

'Yes, it's something.'

They both stared at the tabletop for a few moments, letting the weight of that settle around them—settle enough that they could give themselves permission to talk about something else. Eventually, they got talking about a recent trial, about food, about their families.

Anita realised quite a few people had left by this time. It occurred to her that she could stay longer, and if he stayed longer (he was making no sign of leaving), it would just be the two of them.

She felt comfortable with Rohan. Really, she had to admit, she was attracted to him. He was a thoughtful man and certainly a very beautiful man. But the attraction felt incongruous, improper. This was the detective working on her friend's murder. Even Anita—not renowned for the wisdom of her choices with romantic partners—could see that might not be a wise move at this point.

'I should go,' she announced abruptly and stood up.

'Oh,' Rohan said. 'Sorry. Was it a mistake to talk about—'

'No. You haven't made any mistakes. I was up for talking about it. And thank you. It was good. Good to chat.'

She gave an awkward farewell wave and slipped out towards the street. Good to chat? Chat? What sort of ludicrous way was that to describe the exchange they'd just had? Sometimes Anita reckoned she had the social skills of gormless fourteen-year-old.

On the bus home, she texted Paula.

Went to the pub tonight and talked like a regular human being. A xx

I'm proud of you. P xx

Anita decided not to mention her conversation with Rohan. Instead, she texted: *It's good to get out of the house. Shall we find some live music to go to this weekend?*

I'd love that. Call you tomorrow morning. Sleep well. P

~

By the time Paula received Anita's text, she'd already accepted *she* wasn't going to sleep well that night.

She was sitting in the kitchen, drinking ginger tea, scrolling around on her laptop. Since the funeral, she'd been methodically sifting through old photos of Stacey and Matt, hunting for the first hints of what was going to happen. This was her version of a hospital morbidity and mortality meeting, reviewing available evidence to understand what symptoms she'd missed, how she should have handled it better.

There was a shot taken in Stacey and Matt's first year, in the garden of the house Anita, Paula and Stacey were renting together. Stacey and Matt were both so inconceivably young, with luminous skin and shining hair. Paula examined the curl of Matt's mouth—the way the smile was always on the verge of turning into a self-pitying pout.

He used to tell anyone who would listen that Stacey had 'rescued' him. She would always add that the rescue was mutual. Since she was a teenager, Stacey had talked about her 'family deficit', the feeling that she'd been rejected by her father and by extended family on both sides. Right from the start, Matt offered to fix the deficit she felt. 'We will make our own family,' he would say and Stacey would nod, eyes full of tears. He got a hook into the most vulnerable part of her.

By the end of their first year together, he had ditched all his other social connections and invested his emotional life entirely in her. He rang Stacey countless times a day, left romantic notes for her to find and would pop up unexpectedly at events to bring her some cute gift or food treat. Matt's obsessiveness had always made Paula and Anita uneasy and the two of them analysed it endlessly.

One Easter weekend, still in the early years, the three women had rented a holiday cottage at Bundeena. This was not long before Stacey fell pregnant with Cameron, so it should have been the opportunity for Paula to say something, to intervene and prevent the catastrophe.

Bundeena was meant to be a girls-only weekend—no boyfriends invited. Remy had been happy to stay home (he was on call at the hospital anyway) and Anita's then beau, Secretly Married Martin, was also content not to come. (It would later become clear that he had family duties, including an Easter egg hunt with his small children, whose existence he had not yet revealed to Anita.) Matt was a different story. He hated Stacey being away. He phoned her several times and finally manipulated her into agreeing to return a day early.

On Sunday morning, Paula and Stacey headed off on a bushwalk, leaving Anita to sleep off a hangover in the cottage. Paula figured this might be a good chance to broach her worries. More low-key, just Stacey and Paula, so there'd be no sense of two ganging up against one.

Paula aimed to keep her tone chatty as she asked, 'Do you ever worry that Matt is a bit . . . I don't know . . . a bit too dependent on you?'

Stacey barked a laugh and prodded her finger into Paula's ribs. 'I love the way you phrase that as a question when clearly what you're thinking is "Stacey should definitely worry that Matt is too dependent on her".'

'Oh. Well—sorry. I was only—'

Stacey clutched Paula's arm with mock panic. 'Ooh, do you think I should be worried, doctor?'

'Okay. Piss off. I'll shut up.'

But a few steps further along the path, Stacey said, 'The thing is, Paula, I'm not an idiot. I hear the way Matt talks—as if I'm a hundred per cent responsible for his happiness. Which I realise is unhealthy. And the kind of sludgy underside of that is he thinks I'm responsible for his unhappiness too. If anything goes wrong—like when he failed his course last semester—he can only *process* it by blaming me, by finding some reason that what's happened is my fault. He thinks I'm the only person who can make him happy, but flip that and it means if he ever feels bad about himself, I must be the one making him feel bad. Do you understand what I'm saying?'

'Yes. Yes, I do. And look, you can obviously see—'

'That's it—I *do* see what's going on. Me and Matt are working on it. Because I love him and we'll find our way through this.'

Even way back then, Stacey had insight into what was happening. But the insight didn't save her. She was an intelligent, capable woman with friends who cared about her, and that didn't save her either.

By the time Cameron was five and Poppy was three, Matt had been sacked from many jobs, dropped out of courses, regarding himself as a victim of rip-offs by bad people. Stacey stuck by him, joked him out of sulky moods, boosted his confidence, financed his schemes. Really, Matt had exploited the very best impulses in Stacey—her stoicism, her generous heart, her ability to forgive. He took those strengths and twisted them back on her, made them into shackles. Paula despised him for that.

Next, she clicked on a photo from two years ago—Remy in hospital, having chemo in that ghastly floral armchair she spent a lot of energy hating, as if tasteless upholstery was the main problem they were facing. Stacey was perched on the side of the chair, one arm around Remy and the other pointing to the chemo drugs with a flourish, like a TV presenter. As soon as Stacey heard about Remy's diagnosis, she had arranged to come down from Maryvale to visit.

In the next photo, Cameron was in the armchair, folding himself around Remy as if he could cure him through the power of his fervent wishing. Poppy sat cross-legged on the floor between Remy's legs, her little hands planted on his bony knees. Remy loved those kids and he was so grateful Stacey had brought them down. Paula should have persuaded her to stay in Sydney then and not go back to Matt. That was what she should have done.

There was a photo taken the last time Paula and Anita visited the Maryvale property: Stacey posed in front of the new tractor, draping her hair forward to cover the bruises on her jawline.

Anita had asked straight out, 'How did you get those bruises?'

'Oh lordy.' Stacey laughed. 'Clumsy me tripped over in the machine shed, landed on top of this very tractor, sprawled out like a cartoon character.'

Paula and Anita had known the explanation was a rehearsed lie. But they'd both also sensed the shame Stacey was feeling and they didn't want to embarrass her. So they let all the lies she told that weekend go unchallenged.

The most recent photo was taken on a day trip to Whale Beach. By then Remy was dead, Matt was in jail, and Stacey and the kids had been living with Paula in the Earlwood house for four months.

In the shot, Poppy was posed on the sand with her legs far apart and arms in the air, as if about to do a cartwheel. She couldn't, in fact, do cartwheels but she requested that Paula take this optical illusion photo now, on the understanding that Poppy promised to learn to actually do cartwheels very soon. Cameron stood closer to the waves, looking back at the camera anxiously. He had heard Stacey's voice calling out encouragement to Poppy and he was compelled to check it was happy yelling, not frightened yelling.

They should have been safe in Paula's house. Stacey and Cameron and Poppy should have been safe in her house.

FIVE

PAULA HAD PLANNED TO FLY TO MELBOURNE IN LATE MAY and join two medical school friends for a walking holiday along the Great Ocean Road, figuring it'd be considerate to give Stacey and the kids a break from her, a chance for them to swan about the house on their own.

Now she didn't feel up to the social duties of being a travelling companion. In the two months since the murders, Paula had excused herself from her book club and sidestepped all other invitations, including dinners at Li-Kim's place and events with Remy's extended family—lovely people of whom she was genuinely fond. She had been using cheerful texts and the occasional short phone chat to hold friends at bay. Every friend apart from Anita. For both women, all personal connection had telescoped down to their friendship.

So Paula cancelled the holiday leave and worked on into June, doing fill-in sessions at the practice on top of her regular load. She found that with a busy run of patients through a day, she might not think about Stacey and the children for an hour at a time.

She arrived at the surgery on a Tuesday morning to fill in for Mark Lang. Mark was the youngest doctor at Marrickville Family Practice—an eager, big-hearted guy, a good GP, even if he still needed a bit of guidance when it came to the more delicate judgements the job required. He was a fervent mountain biker, rock climber and scuba diver. Just hearing Mark cheerfully recount his strenuous weekend activities made Paula feel limp with tiredness. This week, he'd flown to the Solomon Islands for a diving medicine conference and Paula was covering his open appointment morning.

The first patient was already waiting on the blue chairs—six-year-old Brody with his mother Rochelle. Paula smiled hello to Rochelle and gave Brody a little wave.

'Hi, guys,' she said. 'I'll be with you in one sec.'

Paula stopped by the front desk to check on a few bits of admin with Jemma. Meanwhile, she could see Brody pressed up close to his mum, holding her hand. He was a sweet kid, shy, always keeping his mother in his sight and usually clinging on to her. The family had moved into the area a year ago and, even though Brody was on Mark Lang's patient list, Paula had treated him three or four times. His mother often brought him in with stomach pains and the doctor's role was to check it wasn't anything alarming and then to offer reassurance. Paula figured that Brody missed a lot of school because of anxiety-related ailments.

The mother, Rochelle, was a reserved person, on the anxious scale herself. Clearly devoted to her son. On a previous visit, she'd explained to Paula that she worked as a beautician but only in the middle chunk of the day, so she was available to take Brody to and from school.

She was a woman who made an effort to keep up a look—face always made up, spray tan even in winter, long foiled auburn hair, acrylic nails in a muted pink colour at a tasteful length, not talons. Today Rochelle was wearing high-heeled boots with jeans and a close-fitting zip-up blue jacket. She'd draped a burnt orange pashmina around her neck with one of those chic knots that Paula could never manage.

'Come with me, guys,' said Paula, ushering mother and son into her consulting room.

'What can I do for you today, Mr Ferguson?' Paula asked Brody, as he slid onto a chair next to Rochelle.

Brody didn't answer; he just looked to his mum, who smiled apologetically at Paula and mimed that there was a problem with her son's throat.

'Can I have a bit of a look at your throat?' Paula asked.

Brody dutifully opened his mouth and Paula peered in with the otoscope, being as gentle as she could with the tongue depressor. It wasn't difficult to see that his tonsils were swollen and dotted with pus. She checked his ears, took his temperature, examined the slightly enlarged glands in his neck.

As she felt the delicate pulse under the skin, she was struck by the softness and vulnerability of his small body. Whenever she was treating children now, Paula could so easily find herself flooded with memories of Cameron and Poppy. She consciously fought off those images. She couldn't do her job properly if she gave in to intrusive thoughts.

'Well, Brody's tonsils are infected,' said Paula, 'so I think some antibiotics would be a good idea. Is he allergic to anything?'

Rochelle shook her head and Paula turned to the computer to type up the prescription. The infection probably explained why the boy was so subdued and clingy.

Paula ran through the standard advice for looking after a kid with a bout of tonsillitis and Rochelle listened, attentive.

'I reckon three days off school,' said Paula. 'Is that okay with you, Brody?'

He nodded earnestly, but then he quickly glanced at his mother to check.

'Can you get the time off work, Rochelle?' Paula asked. 'Or is there someone else who can stay with Brody?'

Rochelle squeezed her son's hand. 'I'll take time off.'

Paula heard it—the cracked sound in her voice—and realised that those were the first words Rochelle had uttered since she'd walked into the surgery.

'Ooh, sounds like Mum might have a sore throat too.'

Paula turned to smile at Brody, but in her peripheral vision she saw Rochelle's hand go to the scarf that was swaddling her throat. A centimetre above the edge of the bright fabric, the purple bruising on her neck was unmistakable. She tugged the scarf back up to cover the marks, but it was too late—Paula had seen.

'You know what, Brody? I need to look after your mum for a little minute. Would it be okay if you hang out in our playroom for a while?'

Brody grabbed on to the sleeve of his mother's jacket.

'I'm okay, sweetheart,' Rochelle assured him. There was that fractured rasp of a voice. 'I'll have a chat to the doctor and then I'll come right out.'

Paula showed Brody down the hall to the corner of the waiting room. It had been Jemma's idea to make a little corral out of play furniture to define a kids' zone, with plastic bins full of toys and a bright 'roadmap' rug inside.

'Jemma, can you keep an eye on Brody for a few minutes?'

Jemma grinned and waved extravagantly at Brody.

By the time Paula walked back into her consulting room, Rochelle was sitting on the edge of the examination bed, shaking.

'Look, if you could just check my throat is—y'know—check it's basically okay and then I'll go.'

'Let's have look,' said Paula softly.

This woman was clearly ready to bolt out the door at any moment, so Paula knew better than to bombard her with questions.

The moment Rochelle removed her scarf, Paula took a sharp intake of breath. Doctors weren't supposed to react audibly like that, but the lurid strangulation bruises, the handprints around her throat, were so vicious that Paula's immediate response was the instinctive human one.

Many abuse victims who showed up in a GP's surgery had been cowed into secrecy and were reluctant to reveal anything. The doctor would need to coax them gently in order to elicit information.

'Can you tell me what happened?' Paula asked. 'Who did this?'

Rochelle answered with surprising bluntness. 'My husband. But it's the first time in a while.' This woman was a veteran.

Taking her cue from Rochelle, Paula jumped straight to the direct questions. 'Did you black out when he strangled you? Did you lose consciousness?'

'Not this time. He said he didn't want to actually kill me this time.'

'But he wanted to demonstrate that he could kill you if he chose to?'

'Bingo,' Rochelle answered, with a small mordant smile. 'You've met my husband, have you?'

Paula examined the woman's injured neck as tenderly as she could, not wanting to add to her physical pain. She could feel the tension in Rochelle's entire body, every muscle and sinew braced tightly.

'Do you have any difficulty swallowing?'

'No. Well, it hurts when I swallow, but no trouble getting food down.'

Paula examined Rochelle's eyes and saw some petechiae—tiny red haemorrhage marks. The throttling attack had been brutal. It was amazing she hadn't lost consciousness, hadn't died.

Paula recalled seeing Rochelle with her husband outside the practice once. Ian Ferguson was much older—she in her early thirties, he in his early sixties—and he was physically much bigger than her too. Paula had observed them for a few moments as Ferguson steered Rochelle into the car, his fingers digging into the flesh of her upper arm.

'Can you take off your jacket?' Paula asked.

'Look, if you reckon my throat's okay, I'd rather just go home and get my sick little boy into bed.'

'Be good if I could take a proper look at your neck.'

Rochelle hesitated, then unzipped the blue jacket and slid it off. Paula noticed a small bony lump along her clavicle, where a previous fracture had healed.

'How did you break your collarbone? Was it your husband?'

'That was ages ago.'

Rochelle's hand went up to touch the slender line of her collarbone. That's when Paula saw the puckered red skin on the pale underside of her forearm—the healed scar from a large rectangular burn.

Rochelle met Paula's gaze. 'He pushed my arm onto the barbecue.'

'Did our Dr Lang treat this burn?'

Rochelle shook her head. 'I never come to the doctors at this place. My husband does. And I bring Brody here when he's sick. But I go to other medical centres if I really need to.'

She made sure she moved between doctors, never seeing the same person twice, to avoid anyone noticing the string of suspicious injuries.

'This . . .' Rochelle looked down at the scar on her arm. 'This was because I told him I didn't want to have another baby.'

'Is Brody his son?'

Rochelle nodded and then scrunched up her eyes, squeezing tears away. 'Look, he never hurts Brody. Never lays a hand on him. Please believe that. Please believe I would never let him hurt Brody.'

Paula reached out to put her hand on Rochelle's arm. 'I believe you.'

'But no way I want any more kids with him. That's why I have injections every three months.'

'Depo-Provera?'

'Yep. Those. He searches through my stuff, so if I tried taking the pill, he'd find them.'

'But with the injections he doesn't have to find out you're using contraception.'

She nodded, then pulled her jacket back on, started wrapping the scarf around her neck again. This woman was used to finding work-arounds and survival tactics.

'No, no, please don't go yet,' Paula said. 'For one thing, I want to send you for some tests to make sure you don't have other damage from—'

'Better not,' Rochelle interrupted. 'Then he'd know you'd seen my neck. I'd pay for it.'

'Rochelle, please wait.'

'Dr Kaczmarek, I know what you're going to say. I should leave. He's dangerous.'

'He is. Clearly. I'm worried you could be—'

'Look, I'm handling this the only way I can. Main thing is he doesn't hurt Brody. Trust me about that.'

'You don't have to put up with it.' Paula reached for the pamphlets on domestic abuse, women's refuges, support services.

'Forget that stuff. It's no good to me.'

'I can't let you leave here without—'

'No. You don't get it.' Rochelle's voice, fractured and hoarse though it was, came out with a steely edge Paula had not heard before. 'I tried leaving him—couple of times. I did all that stuff they reckon you should do.' She waved her hand at the pamphlets Paula was holding. 'He tracked me down every time. The last time, this happened.' She indicated her healed collarbone. 'And the thing is, I'd never leave without Brody.'

'Of course not. No one would suggest—'

'No. I really don't think you get it.' Rochelle was shaking, but there was a firmness in her gaze as she tried to make Paula understand. 'He said if I leave again, he'll find me. And he can find people—that's what he does for a living, okay? He said he'd find me, then kill Brody in front of me. And I believe he'd do it.'

To punish her. He'd kill his child to punish her.

'Thank you. I know you want to help me and everything, but the best way you can help me is if you don't say anything to anyone.'

'Come on, Rochelle, if you go to the police, they can—'

She shook her head emphatically. 'He's got lots of old mates in the cops. Even if they did arrest him, he'd be released on bail, then he'd find me and . . . Look, it's better if—I'm asking—I'm really begging you: do not say anything to Ian or the police or anyone. That'd come back on me, okay? Make things worse for me. It'd be much safer for me if you don't even—if you just leave it.'

Paula felt paralysed, useless, as she watched Rochelle pick up her handbag and open the door.

'I'm going to take my sick boy home and look after him.'

'Rochelle, please . . .'

'I've been handling this a long time, okay? You don't need to worry about Brody. You don't need to worry about me.'

When Rochelle headed out into the corridor, Paula scrambled to follow. She watched Rochelle open her arms as Brody bolted out of the play area to reach her. She saw the relief on the boy's face as he wound his fingers around his mother's wrist.

Paula realised she'd been seeing Brody's clinginess from the wrong angle. Really, this little boy had assigned himself the task of protecting his mother, so when he complained of illness, it was so he could stay home and keep watch over her—a child's logical response to the danger she was in. Paula recalled Cameron's vigilance around Stacey, constantly checking she was safe. Maybe the tonsillitis was a piece of luck, if it brought Rochelle here, if it meant there was a way to help her.

Rochelle was steadfastly avoiding eye contact but Paula demanded her attention with her authoritative doctor voice. 'Rochelle, can you make an appointment to bring Brody back on Monday, so I can check his tonsils have cleared up?'

'Oh. Okay. If you think . . .'

'In the meantime, ring me if you're worried at all,' Paula added. 'Ring anytime. Please.'

Paula wasn't naive. However strong the urge to swoop in and wrap that woman in a protective force field, this had to be handled cautiously. The risk was clear, and instruments like apprehended violence orders had their limits. An AVO wasn't a magic spell that kept all danger away. But still, but still, she would find a workable solution for Rochelle Ferguson.

For the rest of the day, whenever there was a gap between patients, and then at home in the evening, Paula conducted her research, tackling the problem methodically, compiling a list of refuges, welfare agencies, private companies that advertised their ability to help someone disappear. She discussed the situation with a smart woman at a refuge interstate (possibly a safer option) and put in a call to a police sergeant who'd offered helpful advice a couple of years ago. In all her enquiries, she took care not to let slip any identifying details, just in case.

The emotional burn about Stacey was fuelling this—in part, at least. Paula was conscious of that, which was why she made an extra effort to check herself against the steps any responsible GP would take. Rochelle was like a prisoner wearing an electronic ankle bracelet, her range of movement restricted by the realistic fear her husband would kill her or her child. Any doctor would work hard to find an escape route for that woman.

Paula had looked after people for whom there'd been no true solution. On that list was Andy—one of her favourite patients, even if it was inappropriate to have favourites—who'd been diagnosed with motor neurone disease three years ago. There was the super-chatty woman who'd wanted a baby so fervently but, after throwing IVF, multiple surgical procedures, hypnotherapy and money at the problem, had been forced to give up.

And Paula had been sitting next to Remy when the specialist told him they'd exhausted every treatment. She'd peppered the oncologist with questions, mentioned a new drug trial cited in an online journal, asked for tests to be run again. But Remy had put his hand on her arm, without needing to say anything aloud. *Stop now. There's no way to fix this.*

After that day, Paula had shifted tactics, throwing her energy into researching the most effective drug combinations for end-stage pain and the best ways to manage the dying process. She was pretty sure this had made things easier for Remy towards the end. He had said so, anyway. But it never felt like a solution to the problem they faced.

That was a lesson she'd had to learn as a young doctor—learning to sit with your inability to *fix* some patients. But Rochelle Ferguson didn't belong on the unfixable list. The follow-up appointment on Monday would be another chance to talk to her without arousing her husband's suspicion. This time, Paula would be equipped with information and viable options, even if she had no protective magic spells to offer.

SIX

ANITA REALISED SHE HAD UNCONSCIOUSLY STARTED TO car-dance, bum bouncing on the driver's seat, shoulders twitching and hands drumming the steering wheel to the rhythm of the dance music on Fernanda's playlist—a string of cumbia numbers, mostly Colombian, pulsing with percussive energy.

Anita loved all her Chilean cousins but Fernanda had always been her favourite. After the news about Anita's dead friend spread to the relatives back in Chile, there were many loving messages and boxes of sweet treats posted to her. Fernanda sent a short, beautiful text and a link to a Spotify playlist she'd put together for Anita.

Meanwhile, in Sydney, Anita's mother was cooking on an industrial scale. In emergency mode. The woman already had a full schedule, ferrying Anita's dad to his many medical appointments, as well as wrangling her own health issues, but she was staying up past midnight preparing batches of *pastel de choclo* and *cazuela* to deliver to her daughter in this time of sadness.

Anita's freezer was now jammed with containers of Chilean comfort food. She must take some around to Paula's next time.

Anita glanced out the side window of the car to see a truckie looking down at her as she danced in the driver's seat. Anyone cruising past would assume this was a happy woman in high spirits. But it was only the music, the irresistible beat and effervescence of it, making her move like this, in defiance of her true mood. Maybe it was inappropriate, fake, wrong. Still, it felt beneficial, as if she was keeping circulation going to dead limbs and maintaining muscle tone ready for a future when genuine good feelings might return. That was why she'd been playing that cumbia playlist on a constant loop in the car, on walks, in her apartment.

She didn't tell Paula about the dancing around the house or the moments when she forgot about Stacey and the kids for stretches of time. Not that Paula would judge harshly. It would be Anita judging herself and putting that on her friend (which was something she must stop doing). In fact, Paula was a generous-spirited person who would appreciate the value in finding joy again. In fact, fuck it—Anita should suggest they go on a trip to Chile together soon. Then again, Paula might be better off travelling with someone else if she wanted to have a fun, joyful time. Maybe their friendship would forever be in a special category, a precious but painful category, draped in black fabric.

She turned off the music as she neared Lidcombe.

Anita pulled into the car park of the coroner's court complex, but she wasn't there to cover a current inquest. In recent weeks, she'd made several visits, gathering material on past cases for an article she'd pitched to Caroline, the editor of the paper's weekend magazine: a long feature about how the system failed to protect women and children killed by men.

Caroline was pushing her to go with the personal angle—'my friend was murdered'—but Anita baulked at that approach. For one thing, that would feel self-absorbed and tasteless. But more importantly, she wanted to write a ferocious but surgical piece, bristling with statistics and meticulous research. She didn't want anyone to diminish the power of the story by sympathising with her as a bereaved friend nor to explain it away as personal angst.

Paula kept expressing doubts about the project, not sure it was wise to wade into this stuff. Anita knew how Paula regarded her: as a person too unstable, too 'emotionally labile', to handle such material right now. And sure, Anita could be impulsive and reactive sometimes, but Paula didn't understand the solid base of her journalistic skills. No point trying to explain or defend herself. And anyway, Paula was only worrying out of love for her.

'I'll manage,' Anita reassured her. 'It's a way to funnel my rage. It's therapeutic.'

'Is it, though?' Paula asked.

'Look, doing this project helps me control the urge to punch random men in the face. So it's therapeutic for those guys, isn't it?'

Of course, scrolling through the newspaper files and coroner's office archives made for hard reading. So many dead woman, so many dead children. So fucking many.

The reports often showed a common pattern. First, the man would charm the woman, seducing her in the fullest sense of the word. One detail that jumped out at Anita was the number of men who made a point of characterising the woman as the stronger, more dominant person in the relationship. She'd seen Matt do that with his forlorn puppy adoration of Stacey. 'I love her more than she loves me. There's an imbalance.'

Next, the man would isolate the woman from other people in her life. And it would be hard to be more isolated than Stacey had been living on the Maryvale property: off the grid, eleven hours' drive from friends, with no way to communicate with the outside world.

Usually, there were threats of violence before the physical abuse began. The safety of the children would be used as a control mechanism. Then threats to kill would be woven into the abuse. Finally, the man would murder her.

Stacey's case slid into sharp alignment with the pattern. Recognising the common pattern didn't suck any of the poison out of her death, but it formed a structure in which Anita could *place* Stacey's story when it was too hard to hold it in her head.

Anita walked into the coroner's records office and exchanged smiles with the two staff members. Bronwyn and Yianni had become used to her showing up, requesting their help to find documents for the feature article.

Bronwyn was a short, blocky woman in her late fifties who maintained a short, blocky haircut. Yianni was slightly younger, with silver-haired, dark-eyebrowed Greek good looks.

Anita's default setting was to be outgoing. (Sometimes she worried she was excessively gregarious, in a way that made certain people back off.) Both Bronwyn and Yianni could be a little wary and officious, holding tight to their authority in this place, nursing the solemn duty of their jobs. But in the face of Anita's relentless friendliness, they'd loosened up and turned out to be very helpful. She expressed her gratitude profusely. (Maybe a bit too much so.)

Before Anita had a chance to mention the case files she was hoping to see this afternoon, her phone vibrated with a message from the newspaper office. The subeditor was querying a few chunks of wording in the court story she'd filed an hour ago. Anita ought to sort out any problems before the piece was lawyered too savagely.

She held up a finger to indicate to Bronwyn and Yianni that she'd be back in a second, then sat down in the waiting area to respond to the sub's questions.

While Anita hunched over her phone, typing, she was aware that Bronwyn had called Yianni over to her desk to look at something on the computer screen. They were conversing in low voices, but certain words spiked in Anita's hearing and caught her attention.

'Her and the two kids were living at a friend's place,' said Bronwyn.

'The friend was a doctor? Is it that one?' Yianni asked.

'Yep. The GP. That's who found the bodies.'

They were talking about Stacey and Paula.

Anita kept her head down. Presumably they didn't know about her connection to the case. Just as well—she'd prefer not to get into a discussion about it with them.

'Apparently, no one even told her the husband had been let out of jail,' said Bronwyn.

Yianni responded with a groan of disapproval.

'I know—terrible,' Bronwyn agreed. 'Have you seen the photos yet? The two kids were shot in the back of the head. Execution-style almost.'

'By their own dad.'

'Yeah, it's a nasty one. In the end, he shot himself in front of the wife's friend,' she added.

This wasn't a moment of necessary professional discussion of the case. This was straight-out gossip. It hit Anita how ugly gossip could sound. She'd often heard the horror-movie thrill in people's voices, the titillation they felt, when picking over the details of shocking cases. Anita had been guilty of indulging in such talk plenty of times and she must've sounded as unattractive and sticky-beaky as these two. She felt a pang of retrospective shame.

When Yianni started speculating about the order in which the family members were killed, Anita struggled to tune out their voices and focus on her email.

But then she heard a different voice.

'*Please. Please.*' It was Stacey's voice.

Anita jerked her head up and Bronwyn must have mistaken the shock on her face for curiosity.

'Yeah. Come and look at this, Anita.' Bronwyn beckoned her closer to the computer monitor. 'You know that guy who killed his family? The police got this off his phone.'

Anita moved close enough to see the footage playing on Bronwyn's screen. She recognised the interior of Paula's house and the sound of Matt's voice, his breathing. He walked past the hallway mirror and there was his reflection, holding the phone out in front of him. As he moved into the living room, the picture lurched around, so you could see his runners clomping across the floor. Then, for a brief flash, the rifle was visible in his free hand.

The image tilted up again and Anita saw Stacey scrambling to her feet near the living room fireplace. Her neck wasn't bloody—this had been filmed in the moments before he shot her—but she was groggy, as if she'd been knocked down.

'*Matt, what are you doing?*' Stacey was saying. '*Cameron! Cameron, sweetheart—I'm here. I'm here. Please, Matt. Let's talk. Can we talk? Please.*'

Next the camera angle jerked around to show Matt's shirt up close and the picture went dark. He must have put the phone in his pocket. But it was still recording audio.

Matt's hoarse breathing dominated the sound, but Anita could hear him saying, '*This is your fault.*'

Stacey's voice pleaded with him, then two rifle shots tore through the recording, followed by the animal sound of Stacey howling.

Matt took the phone out of his pocket again and focused the camera on Stacey, her face contorted with shock. A primitive mask of pain.

'*This is your fault, Stacey,*' he repeated.

Stacey lurched towards the dining room where the children had been lying curled together against the skirting board, trying to hide from their father. Then the footage cut out.

Yianni stared at the monitor, exhaled heavily, then murmured, 'Far out . . .'

'Yeah, right?' said Bronwyn. 'The guy knocks her unconscious so he can chase the children through the house. But then he waits till she comes to before he shoots them. That psycho wanted to film her reaction as he killed her kids.'

'And—what—was he gonna watch it back later? Like a trophy?'

'Guess so. Except he shot himself. Hang on, maybe we can see . . .'

As Bronwyn clicked on the file to watch the footage again, Yianni gave her a warning nudge on the shoulder. She swivelled around on her office chair and saw Anita's face.

Anita didn't speak a word—she would not have been capable—but the other two immediately checked themselves. Possibly they remembered she was connected to this case, or maybe they understood at some gut level.

Bronwyn paused, cautious, but then inhaled, clearly about to launch into some explanation or apology. Anita didn't want to listen to any of the possible things that might be said in this moment. She didn't blame Bronwyn or Yianni, but she didn't want to engage with them right now.

She grabbed her stuff, pushed through the door towards the exit, and ran across the car park, hands splayed to hold her bag and notebook and phone and keys against her chest so she didn't drop anything. She opened the passenger door and let everything tumble onto the seat. She needed to speed away from what she'd seen as quickly as possible.

But once in the driver's seat, her hands trembled on the steering wheel and her field of vision was bleached out, as if she'd just stared directly at a bright light. The reality of that video was pressing in on her skull—too potent, too enormous, for the small, sealed space of the car. But she couldn't move. And she wasn't fit to drive.

Anita had been sitting there, stranded in the car, for fifteen minutes when the phone rang—*Paula* on the caller ID. She should've let it go through to voicemail, but she was caught off guard.

'Paula. Hi.'

'Oh, you are there. Where are you?'

'Uh—in the car. Parked.'

'What's wrong? You sound—'

'Nothing. I'm okay.'

'I can hear you're not okay,' said Paula.

'I'm just—I've just . . . The police found a video on Matt's phone.'

'From that day?'

'Yeah. He filmed Stacey.'

'You've seen it?' Paula asked.

'Just now. By accident.'

'Tell me.'

'I dunno. It's . . .'

'What about the kids? Does it show the kids?'

'You hear the gun but you can't see the—y'know—the moment, thank Christ.'

'But on the video, can you tell if—I mean, does Stacey see what happened?'

'Yes. He wanted her to watch him do it. Before he shoots, he says, "This is your fault." Says it again afterwards. Then the film cuts out.'

There was a silence on the phone line.

Eventually Paula spoke, stepping carefully from one word

to another, as if trying to maintain control of her own thought process. 'Well, so, it's what we thought probably happened.'

'I guess it is. But knowing for sure is—fuck . . . We can't hope it was different. We can't kid ourselves.'

'No,' Paula said, but then she went very quiet on the other end of the phone.

'You still there?' Anita asked. 'I'm sorry . . . I shouldn't've told you.' Blurting it out in the moment—Anita immediately saw that had been a mistake. 'Do you want to grab dinner tonight or . . . ?'

'Can't. I'm working until nine. And I've got a patient waiting right now. Talk tomorrow?'

'Yes. Yes. For sure. Bye, lovely.'

The instant the call ended, Anita regretted even mentioning the video existed. The details would have come out at the inquest in any case, but that would be many months down the track, when they'd all be better fortified to handle it. Not that Anita ever described the footage in graphic detail. But Paula would be imagining every beat of it anyway.

A car pulled into the car park, and Anita saw Rohan Mehta hop out of the driver's seat while an older detective, Gary Walsh, emerged from the passenger side.

As the two cops headed towards the entrance together, Rohan spotted Anita sitting in her car. He waved hello, squinting against the afternoon light that bounced off the windscreen. As he walked further on, he must have caught a clearer view of her face through the glass, because he stopped and exchanged a few words with Walsh. Then the older cop continued into the building on his own while Rohan approached Anita's car.

Through the side window, he said, 'Are you okay?'

Anita shook her head.

Rohan indicated the front passenger seat, miming *Should I get in?*

Anita nodded, then swept the notebook and bag and other stuff onto the floor so he could sit.

'I saw the phone video.'

'Oh.' Rohan sighed. 'I'm sorry. How?'

When she explained, he wanted to march straight inside and tear strips off Bronwyn, but Anita urged him to leave it be.

'This isn't anyone's fault,' she argued. 'Well, it's Matt's fault. Let's save our anger for fucking Matt.'

Rohan nodded, though he still didn't look happy about it.

'And the video only confirms what we already thought happened,' Anita said. 'As you said: no twists.' She attempted a dry smile but her mouth was quivering.

'Are you okay to drive?' he asked.

'I'll be fine.' Anita saw him looking at her hands, which were jiggling on the steering wheel. 'Do you believe I'm a danger on the roads in my current state?'

'I do. Why don't I drive you home?' he offered. 'I can ask Walsh to handle things here and bring my car back later.'

On the half-hour drive from Lidcombe to Newtown, Rohan driving Anita's little hatchback, they agreed not to talk about the video or about any of their mutual work stuff, given that it all revolved around people being murdered. They tried listening to news radio, but that threatened to add another grim layer to the mood. Then they tried an easy listening music station, but the wailing ballads with their cloying string arrangements made them both sick. Finally, Anita played the cumbia music playlist and chatted about her many cousins.

In the car park under Anita's building, Rohan handed back her car keys with a small courtly bow.

'Thank you,' she said. 'Very much.'

He smiled and shrugged. No problem.

'Look, um, if you fancy some early dinner,' said Anita, 'I happen to have a freezer full of Chilean comfort food.'

'Oh.'

'Was that "Oh" as in "How do I politely sidle away from this shaky woman and her offer of a stodgy corn-based meal" or "Oh" as in "I would love to eat a stodgy but tasty corn-based meal but I'm not sure if it's a genuine invitation or she's just being polite"?'

'The latter,' he said.

'Goodo. And it's a genuine invitation.'

They headed upstairs, and Anita watched Rohan Mehta pace around the small living room of her flat making work calls. She liked the way he was in his police detective mode—steady, well-mannered, firm. She liked the way he scrunched up his face slightly to concentrate as he listened, and how every now and then he would nod or laugh softly at something the person on the other end of the phone was saying.

Meanwhile, Anita extracted a terracotta dish of *pastel de choclo* from the freezer to defrost in the microwave and then heat up in the oven. She assembled the most interesting salad she could out of the vegetable matter in her fridge.

By the time Rohan finished his string of calls, she'd opened some wine. By the time the food was ready to eat, they'd finished most of the bottle.

The top part of the *choclo*—the slightly sweet, pudding-y corn layer—had caramelised around the edges the way Anita hoped it would and the bottom layer of beef, onions, olives and spices was as juicy with flavour as it should be.

'This dish is kind of a Chilean cottage pie. I realise it isn't exactly sophisticated,' Anita said.

'Yummy is what it is,' Rohan mumbled around a mouthful of food. 'Thank you for introducing me to *choclo*—never heard of it before.'

'I always think there's something sort of infantile about this dish—the spongy top, the combo of salty and sweet, the whole lot soft enough to be shovelled into your mouth with a spoon.'

Rohan nodded. 'That's why it works as comfort food.'

All evening, she could feel thoughts about Stacey sitting on the edge of her mind, even while she was enjoying the food, the wine, the talking with this man, the laughing. Those good things felt real—they *were* real—but strangely disconnected from the other reality which was always there, like an indigestible lump in her belly.

Anita and Rohan kept excavating their way to the bottom of the terracotta dish and talked about their mothers force-feeding them in times of stress. Rohan described his experience as a fat teenager, the weight piling on from his mother's feeding plus his own secret eating to console himself about being a pudgy, unconfident loser. In the end, it was his desire to join the police force that gave him the drive to lose weight and cultivate some muscles.

Anita had developed a theory about men like Rohan. If you encountered an attractive grown-up man who was *not* an up-himself dickhead, it often emerged that the guy had been considered deeply unattractive as a seventeen-year-old. Those adolescent males who were chubby, the late developers, those blighted by acne or whatever—they were the best value as adults. They didn't carry the unconscious arrogance of the good-looking man and they maintained a sympathetic understanding of insecurity in other people. Now it turned out Rohan Mehta was one of those cases. That explained his slight diffidence about himself, despite his undeniably handsome looks. Maybe it also helped to explain his kindness and the cautious, humble manner. Anita decided not to share her theory with Rohan right now. She didn't want to embarrass him or give the impression she was sucking up, coming on to him in a desperate way.

They opened a second bottle of wine, with a verbal contract to drink only half of it, and Anita filled a platter with sweet biscuits that had been posted from Chile.

Taking dishes to the sink, she was aware of their bodies close together in the small kitchen space. When Rohan reached behind her to put something down, she leaned against his arm, leaning firmly enough that it would be clear it was a purposeful lean rather than an accidental brushing past.

He took the cue and pulled her close against him, but gently, waiting for her to confirm that this was what she meant. He was restrained, not wanting to presume or push her or take advantage, so she would have to make it even clearer. She lunged forward to kiss him.

For a moment, she worried she might have been the one to misread the clues—maybe he was merely offering kindly physical affection to a sad woman. But no, when he kissed her, it wasn't in a kindly way. He kissed her in an unrestrained and lustful way. Even then, he didn't want to take anything for granted beyond the kissing, so Anita knew she would again have to offer a clear invitation. She led him by the hand into the bedroom.

The next morning, because there was only insipid light leaking in around the window blind, Anita realised that it was early, not long after dawn. Rohan must have assumed she was still asleep because he was very quiet as he fished around to find his clothes on the bedroom floor.

Anita should sit up, switch on the light, offer to make him breakfast or at least a beverage. But instead she lay there pretending to sleep while she rehearsed what she should say.

Possibly she should say, 'Good morning, Rohan Mehta. Thank you for noticing I was a mess in that car park yesterday and driving me home without being pushy or patronising or fussy about it. Thank you for staying and thank you for a really good night, including the—look, I have to say, the *great* sex. Also, I slept surprisingly well—so it seems you're an ideal person to share a bed with as well as an excellent sexual partner. I'm pretty sure you're a truly good man. But the problem is, this whole thing feels strange—kind of *off*—because of the way we know each other, so this can never be a relationship.'

But she didn't say that. She stayed curled under the doona, eyes closed, as she listened to Rohan pick up his shoes and slip quietly out of the apartment.

Only when she was sure he was gone did she emerge from the bedroom. After a shower and coffee, she tried to ring Paula, but her friend's phone was switched off. She must be seeing patients. Hopefully she'd had a decent restful night.

SEVEN

THE FLOOR WAS ROLLING SLIGHTLY UNDER PAULA'S FEET. The woozy seasick sensation of jetlag. Elevated levels of cortisol and insufficient sleep the night before. The accumulated minutes of flimsy dozing might have added up to two hours, but the whole night had been infested with visions of Stacey and the kids—the ones Paula already carried in her head, now spliced together with imagined moments from the video on Matt's phone.

Briefly, at three a.m., she'd considered driving to the surgery and rummaging in cabinets for some heavy-duty medication to knock herself out, but she couldn't risk feeling dopey, not now when she must stay clear-headed to find a helpful strategy for Rochelle Ferguson.

At four a.m., she'd made the decision—she had to be resolute with herself about this—to temporarily *stop* thinking about Rochelle. In Paula's current state, her thought process kept sliding into pessimistic spirals which wouldn't do that poor woman any good. So she must put the problem aside for now. Come back to it when she was in a more fit state.

In the morning, she contemplated ringing Anita but then let the idea go. She didn't have the capacity to deal with her friend's distress on top of her own right now.

Paula managed the morning's appointments—luckily nothing cropped up that required too much fine judgement or dexterity. At lunchtime, she stepped out into the street and deliberately soaked up some sunlight, feeling it reinvigorate her a little, like a solar battery being charged. Then she bought a banh mi to take back to the surgery, in the hope food might help her to feel more normal.

Sitting at the desk, she ate quickly, worried that the smell of the pork roll would permeate the room. If the food didn't help—if she didn't feel she could function at a proper level through the afternoon—Paula resolved to finish work early, reschedule a few people, ask Li-Kim to cover anything urgent.

Even with her consulting room door shut, she could hear an altercation building at the practice's front desk. There were the loud bass notes of an angry male voice, punctuated by Jemma's placating responses. Paula shoved the rest of her lunch in the bin and went out to the hallway.

A large man stood at the reception desk, his forearms planted on the upper counter as if he was about to rip it up off the floor. Every time Jemma stammered out a reply to his badgering questions, he huffed his contempt and waggled his massive skull, as if nothing she could say was worth taking into his head.

Paula recognised the man. Ian Ferguson, Rochelle's husband.

There was a flush of panic through her ribcage. Maybe Rochelle had confronted him, with Paula's encouragement, and that was why he'd shown up here, angry.

'Is there a problem?' she asked. 'Can I help?'

Jemma swivelled around in her chair and Paula saw how much she was floundering in the face of his bullying. 'Mr Ferguson was hoping to see Dr Lang but I explained that, um . . .'

'Yes, that's right. I'm sorry. Mark Lang is overseas at a conference,' said Paula, moving closer to the desk in order to draw Ferguson's attention onto herself and away from Jemma. 'If it's something urgent—'

'It's this fucking hand.' He waved his right hand, which was wrapped in a tea towel, with a small patch of blood soaking through. 'I've been trying to make missy here understand that I need to see a doctor and I always see a *male* doctor.'

Jemma threw Paula a tiny smile—*This guy is such a fuckwit*—but Paula could also see that the poor young woman's eyes were swimming with tears.

'Ah. Right.' Paula nodded, surprised by how calm she was managing to sound. 'Well, both our male doctors are unavailable this afternoon, but I have some time right now if that would suit you.'

Part of her wanted Ferguson to stomp away, but another part of her was curious.

'You could go down to the hospital emergency department,' Paula added, 'but there's no guarantee you'll score a male doctor there either.'

The man gave a little snort.

'Look, Mr—is it Ferguson? Hang on . . . are you Brody's dad?'

'Uh, yes,' he replied, a bit confused.

'I'm Dr Kaczmarek. I've seen your son a few times.'

Paula was careful not to mention seeing Brody two days ago, in case Rochelle hadn't told her husband. In case that caused him to wonder if his wife had revealed anything.

In fact, Ian Ferguson looked blankly at her—he didn't know or care much about his son's doctor. His being here right now was simply a coincidence. It could be a useful coincidence, though: an opportunity for Paula to check out this man and assess the danger.

Ferguson hesitated for a moment but eventually he muttered, 'Well, might as well get this hand sorted out.'

Paula indicated that he should follow her to the consulting room. She heard his heavy footsteps up the corridor behind her and suddenly her chest tightened. She was back in her living room, half crouched, breathless, hearing Matt's shoes on the floorboards. Then a lurch in her belly, and she was in the moment when Matt paused by the bodies of his children and looked her in the eye.

Inside the consulting room, with Ian Ferguson sitting at the treatment table, up close, Paula was conscious of the bulk of the man. He was a head taller than her, hefty, with a wide barrel of a torso, his fair skin ruddy and sun-damaged, eyes so pale they were almost colourless in that massive head, like an enormous, sallow, weatherworn bull. He was carrying too much weight and there were hints of old injuries in the way he moved, but the power was still there in him, in those colossal shoulders and huge mottled hands.

Ferguson unwrapped the tea towel and placed his right hand on the surgical sheet to show Paula his injury. The gash down the outside of his thumb wasn't deep and had already stopped bleeding.

'How did you do this?' Paula asked.

'Oh, I tripped on the stairs at work and turned out there was a jagged bit on the railing. Badly made piece-of-shit railing.'

'Well, the good news is that it's not too deep.'

'Won't need stitches?' he asked and Paula could detect the nervous little boy inside the weathered middle-aged bully.

'No. A clean-up and some steri-strips will do.'

Paula turned away to fetch the items she needed to dress the wound.

Ferguson cleared his throat awkwardly and offered, 'I'm sure you know your stuff. Medical stuff. But I'm more comfortable with a man. Someone who's going to do what needs to be done without a lot of chat. That's why I steer clear of female doctors, wittering on with a load of babble.'

Paula was astonished at how blatant he was. Most men would hedge and dissemble to cover their misogyny, but not this guy. She consciously fought the disgust off her face and focused on his hand as she sluiced the wound with saline.

These were the powerful hands that had left a string of purple bruises around his wife's throat, her voice cracked and hoarse, her eyes flecked with red.

Ferguson made teeth-sucking noises at the sting of the antiseptic Paula was applying. She relished the little stabs of discomfort she was causing him and she felt the sinews in her arm tighten, repressing the urge to jab her fingers into the raw flesh to make this bastard wail with agony.

She took a breath, gathered herself, then concentrated on the task of peeling the backing off steri-strips to hold the edges of the wound together. She didn't speak because she didn't trust herself not to spew out invective at this man. Her silence made Ferguson uncomfortable. Her lack of female doctor 'wittering' threw him off balance, and in fact he was the one who started wittering.

'Don't think I'm a wimp,' he said. 'The reason I'm checking if I need stitches is because I have to take care of my hands. For my business. Can't afford to have my hands out of action.'

'Oh yes,' murmured Paula, then let him fill the silence with more babble. Clearly Ferguson found the sound of his own voice soothing when he was stressed.

'I've got a security and investigations business. Bit of keyboard work with that, but the major issue is I also do some shooting instruction. I like my security guys to be up to speed with handling nine-millimetre pistols and I don't trust the clowns you usually get teaching that stuff. So I got myself qualified as an instructor. Need my hands in top working order.'

Paula saw the gun in Matt's hand. The ragged wound in Stacey's neck.

She swung around to the computer and scanned Ferguson's medical file. Most of the clinical notes had been entered by Mark Lang. She must talk to Mark when he came back to work—ask for his take on this guy, see if they could come up with a solution between them to ensure Rochelle's safety.

'I see that Dr Lang referred you for a cardiac stress test and other tests but there's no record here of—'

'Oh no,' he interrupted, 'I haven't got time for that carry-on.'

'Well, you might want to take more care with your health. You're a sixty-two-year-old man with a young child.'

'Yeah, yeah. My boy's only six. Brody.'

The sound of the child's name coming out of this man's mouth made Paula shiver. He pronounced 'Brody' and 'my boy' with serrated edges, possessive, controlling. Was she imagining it? She might be. She might be. Even so, right now, she would do anything—she would rip his tongue out of his revolting wet mouth—anything to stop him saying the boy's name again.

Paula pushed herself to regulate her breathing and fixed her eyes on the computer screen, but she kept seeing Brody's anxious little face, checking his mother was okay. Then she saw Cameron, fretting, scanning the house for danger signs, keeping close to Stacey.

Paula heard her own voice coming out on autopilot. Her benignly firm doctor voice. 'The thing is, Mr Ferguson, cardiac health is not something to ignore.'

'I'm not gonna have a heart attack this week, though, am I?'

What a blessing it would be for Rochelle, for Brody, for anyone else in this man's orbit, if a sudden heart attack took him out.

'Since you're here,' said Paula, 'we should take your blood pressure and talk about a few other tests.'

'Rightio, you don't have to earbash me about it.'

Paula put on the blood pressure cuff, pumped it up, read the gauge—using the familiar steps of the task as a way to settle herself.

'One eighty-six over one twenty . . . that's worryingly high,' she said.

'If it's high, that's because you got me riled up about all this,' snorted Ferguson. 'That's from you putting stress on me.'

For this man, every setback, every irritation, would always be someone else's fault.

Paula turned back to the computer monitor. 'I see that Dr Lang prescribed some medication for hypertension a while ago.'

'Yeah, I stopped taking it. Gave me headaches.'

Paula should allow this man to walk out of the consulting room and pray he had an almighty heart attack or stroke, thereby releasing his wife and child from fear and violence.

'Look, Mr Ferguson, you can ignore my advice—it's up to you—but I think you should follow up on some of these appointments. Is there a reason you never got the blood tests Dr Lang ordered?'

'Aww . . . he gave me one of those—y'know . . .' He flapped his hand at the sheaf of test forms on the desk. 'I hate those pathology joints. Too much waiting. I'm busy.'

'Well, why don't I just take some blood right now?'

Paula usually sent patients off to one of the private pathology places to have blood drawn, but sometimes she did the simple stuff herself in the consulting room, on the spot. With certain patients, reluctant or unreliable ones, it was the safest way to ensure proper follow-up. As she suggested this solution to Ferguson, Paula was observing herself, hearing herself be the responsible doctor again. Her habits of mind were so strong, feeling the obligation to offer good care even to this vile man.

'It would only take a few minutes and then it's done,' she added.

She saw him wince.

'I'm not big on needles.'

A needle phobia. Paula felt a surge of vengeful anticipation—it would be satisfying to see this man squirm for a moment. 'Ah, right. Well, I find that when a patient is scared of needles, it helps if—'

'I'm not scared,' he shot back. 'Just not a fan. I mean, who in their right mind likes getting stuck with needles?'

Paula pressed her lips together in a forgery of a sympathetic smile.

Ferguson scrambled to regain some dignified ground. 'It's a physiology thing. I come over faint. My blood pressure or some issue.'

'That can happen,' Paula said. 'But if you lie down flat, you'll be fine.'

She indicated the examination bed he could lie on. Ferguson waggled his head to register his doubt, but he climbed onto the bed.

Paula immediately regretted that she'd persuaded him to accept follow-up tests. Why had she pushed it? She should've let him walk his loathsome carcass out of the consulting room with his hypertension buzzing and his dodgy heart ticking inside him like a fucking time bomb. Without proper treatment, there was some hope this guy might keel over and die. Of course, with or without treatment, there was a strong chance he would survive long enough to keep tormenting Rochelle for years. And a chance he would kill her one day very soon.

While Paula printed off ID labels and stuck them on the blood sample vials, Ferguson stretched out on the bed, his needle phobia making him run off at the mouth even more.

'I hope Brody isn't a brat when he comes in here,' he said.

'No, always beautifully behaved,' Paula responded.

'At least there's a chance Brody won't turn out as useless as my three oldest kids. All of them in their thirties but they still blame me for their pathetic lives. Want nothing to do with me now, which suits me fine. Basket cases, the lot of them. Mind you, if my mentally challenged wife—my current wife, I mean—if that woman keeps treating Brody like a little wuss, then that kid's just as likely to—'

Paula jumped in to shut him up. 'Because I need to take several samples, I'm going to use a butterfly catheter to make things easier.'

'Oh right. Whatever.'

Ferguson tucked his right arm, the one with the injured hand, against the wall and stuck out his left arm, stiff with apprehension.

'Try to relax,' suggested Paula.

As she slipped the tourniquet around his upper arm, the touch of his skin under her fingers was disgusting to her. She tightened the tourniquet with slightly too sharp a tug and enjoyed hearing his nervous intake of breath. But apart from these petty satisfactions, she was amazed to find herself operating on autopilot again, searching for a good spongy vein to tap, calculating how to insert the needle without hurting the patient unnecessarily. Even if the patient in front of her was a violent, controlling, dangerous piece of shit.

As Paula reached for the butterfly catheter, she couldn't prise Rochelle out of her head. Ferguson might be here in the consulting room right now, but his wife was more truly her patient. And it was Paula's responsibility to protect a vulnerable patient from likely harm. It was her responsibility to help Rochelle, to get her safely away from this man without increasing the risk to her or the little boy. By leaving Rochelle in danger, she was failing a patient. She just needed to think, talk to some cops, talk to social services. Even if she couldn't see a safe escape route for that woman quite yet, there must be a way.

'Your hands are shaking,' Ferguson scoffed.

His voice halted the tangle of thoughts in Paula's head. She looked down and realised her hands were trembling as she held the catheter.

'Not gonna stick that thing right through me, are ya?' he asked, jokey but nervous too. 'Do you even know what you're doing, apart from all the bossy crap you bang on with?'

The urge to punch him in the mouth was so overwhelming, she felt the electricity buzz down her arm.

'I know what I'm doing,' she said firmly. 'Many people find if they face away from the needle site, it's more comfortable.'

Ferguson twisted his torso round slightly and turned his head to face the wall beside the bed. Paula steadied herself, then inserted the needle in the plump vein in his forearm.

'That part's done,' she said.

'Hardly felt it,' he said. 'Maybe you're not so bad at this.'

Paula had always allowed herself a bit of vanity about her needle technique—she could give injections with minimal pain and take blood skilfully from even the most decrepit elderly patient with crumbly veins.

While Paula drew up blood into the vials, Ferguson kept rabbiting on. 'Yeah, I'll award you points for being good at that bit,' he said. 'I'm the kind of guy who respects someone who can do their job properly. I'm always having to remind clients how good I am at my job. You get some people—they go, "There's no way you can pull off X result or fix Y problem or find Z person." And I say, "Mate, watch and learn." Fact is, I can track down any-fucking-body any-fucking-where they're hiding. That's why my business is successful.'

He was boasting now, keen for Paula to be impressed by him.

'People don't realise how doable it is to track people. With the right know-how, that is,' he crowed. 'I employ a couple of scrawny kids who are across the digital stuff, backed up by the old-fashioned legwork involved in tracing an individual. I will find that individual eventually, even if they try very hard not to be found.'

He grunted a laugh and Paula heard Rochelle's voice in her head. *He can find people—that's what he does for a living, okay? He said he'd find me, then kill Brody in front of me.*

Paula gave in to the urge to dig a little. 'Rochelle mentioned you have your own business, but I don't think I really understood—'

'Pfft, don't waste brain cells listening to her blab on too much. She's a fucking whiner, my wife. You've probably seen her fussing over that boy like—oh . . . And then, Jesus H. Christ, she whines at me!'

'Oh well, I'm sure Rochelle has her own point of view about—'

Even that tiny amount of pushback from Paula ignited Ferguson into more open belligerence.

He shook his head. 'She talks a lot of bullshit. Mind you, she understands she's on a good wicket. She tried leaving me once, but I found her. We laid down a few ground rules after that.'

'Ground rules? What sort of ground rules?'

'Point is, I'm very clear with her. And if Rochelle ever tries to take my kid, I'll find her, sort her out.'

Paula knew she should leave him to keep talking, keep revealing himself, but she couldn't bear to let that go unchallenged. 'Sort her out? What do you mean?'

Ferguson responded with a few breathy laughs, realising he'd revealed more aggression than he'd intended. 'I'm joking.'

His left hand, palm upwards on the exam bed, twitched a bit as he tried to control his temper. Paula pictured his hands encircling Rochelle's slender neck, mashing her larynx, crushing the blood vessels to frayed threads, squeezing the oxygen out of her.

Should Paula confront him? Call the police right now? They wouldn't arrest the guy just for making menacing boasts about tracking down his wife. Paula had no proof. Rochelle would be too afraid to speak openly. And if Paula called in the authorities, Rochelle would be the one to cop it later. But to allow this man to speak like this and then walk out of the consulting room . . . The prospect was unbearable.

'What's the hold-up?' asked Ferguson. 'We all done?'

'Give me a second. Lie still for me while I, uh . . .'

Her body followed her usual practice, on automatic, reaching for a cotton ball and bandaid to cover the needle's puncture site. On the shelf, she noticed two glass ampoules of adrenaline lying in one of the plastic storage tubs. They kept some in each consulting room for use in an emergency anaphylaxis situation.

Paula pictured herself—as clear and precise as a training video—picking up the yellow ampoules one at a time. They would feel like glass bullets, cool and smooth in her palm. She would wrench the top off each one with a sharp yank of her wrist and draw the liquid up into a syringe. She would then turn around and inject the adrenaline into the catheter in Ferguson's arm. Two one-millilitre doses would send him into extreme cardiac dysrhythmia and probably into full cardiac arrest, given his existing medical problems. The injection site would be explained by the catheter she was using to collect blood, and an autopsy would be unlikely to be incriminating. It could be done.

Paula stood very still to listen to her own sensible voice in her head. The voice spoke slowly and calmly, leaning into the rhythm of the phrases to gain some control over her ragged breathing.

Injecting the adrenaline into this man would be murder. A doctor couldn't deliberately kill a patient like that. She was not that person. This was not her. This was grief. This was crazy thinking. If Rochelle was in danger, Paula could not hold herself responsible. Not to this degree. She was not a person who would murder a human being, however foul a human being, however dangerous he was.

She took a deep breath, squared her shoulders, stern with herself, then picked up the cotton ball and bandaid.

Right at that moment, Ferguson started going off at the mouth again.

'Will this take much longer? This is what I was meaning before—the way females make a fuss, trick you into talk-talk-talking about whatever shit they manufacture in their heads. Look, the point I was making, I've got certain skills and I'm . . . The point is, I'm not a gullible idiot. I'm never gonna let a woman make a fucking fool of me again.'

He made a hissing noise—a kind of sour laugh. Paula turned around in time to see him lift his bandaged right hand off the bed so he could inspect it.

'You done a decent job? I need this hand. Does it still work?'

He made a strangling gesture with his large meaty hand, bending his fingers to throttle an invisible creature.

Before Paula had a chance to block them, she was slammed by rapid-cut images, like a movie trailer on fast-forward. The crackle of fear in Rochelle's eyes. The gun in Matt's hand. Stacey's hair soaked in blood. Brody's gaze darting back to his mother again and again, checking. Cameron's anxious, burdened little face. Poppy curled up against the skirting board. Ferguson's huge paw around Rochelle's arm, fingers digging into her flesh like the teeth of an animal trap. The meat of Stacey's neck where it was torn open. This man's hand squeezing Rochelle's throat, squeezing the life out of her.

Then Paula was aware of her body operating on a different kind of automatic pilot. She'd rehearsed it in her mind already, so there seemed to be no decision-making at all as she followed each step of the process.

She picked up the two ampoules, the glass bullets smooth in her hand, twisted off the tops and drew up the liquid into a syringe. As she moved closer to Ferguson, she didn't dare speak, in case her voice betrayed her.

'You going to get this finished now? Is this it?' he asked, so all Paula had to do was make a small murmur of assent for him to stay lying there, still and vulnerable.

She carefully inserted the needle of the syringe and pushed all the adrenaline through the catheter and into the man's vein. She immediately took a step back, as if to step away from what she'd just done.

Within seconds, Ferguson's heart rate surged, accelerating, tachycardic. He gulped a breath sharply and wrenched his head around. He swung his torso upright and made eye contact with Paula—his expression surprised, panicky, pleading rather than accusing. But a moment later, he sank flat again, clutching at his chest as his heart was failing him.

Paula slipped the empty glass ampoules and the syringe into the yellow plastic sharps bin. By now, Ferguson was in deep trouble, writhing, breathless, groaning on the examination bed.

Paula forced herself to spin away, turn her back to him. She crossed her arms across her chest, holding one wrist down with the other in order to fight the deep-seated impulse to save a patient. Over and over, she reminded herself this action was being done to save Rochelle and her little boy. This was saving innocent lives from almost certain danger. To hold steady to this course, she conjured up the image of Rochelle and Brody huddled in the corner of the consulting room, while Ferguson thrashed on the bed.

After a minute, maybe more, he flung his arm out, knocking a metal basin onto the floor with a loud clanging noise. Anyone in the practice might have heard that.

Paula swung open the door of her consulting room.

'Need some help here! Patient in cardiac arrest. Li-Kim, can you get the—'

'I'll grab the defib,' said Li-Kim.

'Jemma, ring the ambos.'

By the time Li-Kim wheeled the practice defibrillator into the consulting room, Paula was making a show of doing CPR.

The two doctors worked on Ferguson for five minutes, until the paramedics hurried into the surgery. Paula rattled off a quick handover: 'Sixty-two-year-old man, had a fall during a dizzy spell, history of hypertension and cardiac disease, untreated.'

Then Ferguson was rushed out the door on a gurney.

Paula and Li-Kim flopped back against the doorframe, out of breath.

'Do you reckon he'll make it?' asked Li-Kim. 'Didn't look good.'

Paula only managed a vague noise in her throat.

'You right, hon?' asked Li-Kim, squeezing Paula's shoulder.

'Uh, yeah. Well . . . you know . . .'

'Yeah, stuff like that always throws you off. Want me to ask Jemma to move the rest of your appointments?'

'No, no. I'll be fine.'

Paula sat back at her desk and saw that Ferguson's medical file was still open on the screen. She added a few notes.

Came in with a minor hand injury after a dizzy spell led to a fall. Discussed the need to take prescribed hypertension medication and to follow up on cardiac tests previously ordered. Patient is reluctant to do so.

She looked down at the keyboard to see her hands were still trembling. She had no idea if Ian Ferguson would survive.

The smell of the half-eaten banh mi in the bin drifted up, suddenly overwhelming her. She lunged for the metal bowl that had fallen onto the floor and vomited into it, bringing up her stomach contents, then retching up bile, then dry-retching with painful spasms.

Eventually her guts settled and she mopped at her mouth with tissues, shivering a little from the chill of the sweat on her face.

EIGHT

ANITA WAS UNCERTAIN OF THE ETIQUETTE SURROUNDING an encounter like the one she'd had with Rohan Mehta. It hadn't been a date and didn't fall comfortably into the one-night-stand category. It was sex between sort-of colleagues, but last night wasn't the equivalent of fucking a fellow journalist. She'd never slept with a policeman before. And the backdrop, the context, or whatever you wanted to call it—the killing of three loved ones—threw standard guidelines out the window. There was no accepted practice here.

She definitely should've handled things differently this morning: sat up in bed, said a decent goodbye to him, like civilised adults acknowledging a mutually satisfying but once-only event. By pretending to sleep and letting him leave, she'd allowed a murky gap to open up.

Around midday, he texted her.

Hi Anita. Thanks for last night. Rohan.

She responded immediately.

Well, thank you. Thanks for the lift home.

Ridiculous—as if the transport had been the notable part of the evening. She wondered if her tone was too prim, given the fact that the two of them had 'rubbed their pink bits together' as Stacey had always liked to call it.

A moment later, he sent another message.

No worries. And thank you for the comfort food.

She texted straight back.

Thank you for the comfort.

The second she hit send, she regretted it. Had she jumped awkwardly from polite to playfully suggestive? She didn't want to give this very decent man the wrong impression, so she added a follow-up text: *I'll see you round the courts. Anita.*

She waited for a reply but the phone was silent in her hand. Which was to be expected. Her last text didn't require any response from him and, arguably, her message had a closing-things-off crispness, punctuating the exchange with a clear implication that their interactions would be purely professional from now on.

Then, after twenty minutes—had Rohan been considering how to respond or was he just busy with a work matter during those twenty minutes?—he replied: *You will. All best, Rohan.*

Anita glanced at that text several times over the course of the afternoon. Did the wording suggest disappointment that she was shutting down intimacy? Or was the 'You will' a clue that he was hopeful things would spark up again when they saw each other? Then again, 'All best' was quite formal, like the sign-off to a business email. Or did his 'All best' indicate he was being self-protective, having realised she was parking him back into the 'colleague' slot? Or were all the words in his text soaked with relief, glad that Anita had re-established a cordial, professional distance and he was therefore free of obligation to her?

'For fuck's sake, stop now.'

Anita uttered those words out loud as she walked across the newspaper office. She often berated herself aloud in order to wrangle useless ruminations into mature thoughts. Hearing her own voice come out strict and sensible was sometimes enough to shut down foolish thinking. And this adolescent fussing about Rohan Mehta was certainly foolish, as well as being horribly inappropriate, given the far more important matters of the last twenty-four hours.

She was hanging out to talk to Paula. They still hadn't talked properly about the video on Matt's phone. Anita needed to know how her friend was handling the news. They needed to share this moment in some way, carry the dark weight of it together.

~

Once Paula recovered from the bout of vomiting, she cleaned her teeth at the sink in the consulting room then took a few minutes to steady herself before packing away the defibrillator and tidying up the paraphernalia that had been knocked onto the floor when Ian Ferguson thrashed and when Paula, Li-Kim and the paramedics worked on him. She kept the small window open and turned on the ceiling fan so the vomit smell could disperse a bit, before spraying a eucalyptus-scented disinfectant around the room.

There was a temptation to ring the hospital and ask about Ferguson. Would she be glad to confirm he'd died? Or would it be a relief to discover he'd survived, so she wouldn't have to confront the consequences of what she'd done? She didn't know what to feel. This seemed so unreal, there was no way to align it with the regular structures of her mind.

Eight more patients were on her appointment list and Paula made it clear to Jemma that she would see everyone, with apologies for running late.

Through the afternoon, Paula listened, smiled, nodded, pulled perky faces at a baby, examined a skin lesion, offered advice about hormone replacement therapy, did a pap smear, vaccinated a toddler, filled out a workers compensation form, prescribed hypertension medication and referred patients to various specialists.

During the months Remy was sick and then during the bleak stretch of time after he died, she had been determined not to impose her grief on patients or on people she encountered in a casual way. In the process, she had developed strong muscles for faking regular behaviour, functioning as a doctor, functioning as a human being, in a way that would appear entirely normal from the outside. It was the same in the weeks after Stacey and the children were killed. By now, Paula was match-fit for faking normal.

Even when her last patient had gone, she remained in that 'I'm a normal doctor' mode, sitting at the computer in the consulting room to catch up with test results and emails.

When Jemma buzzed from the front desk, Paula stepped out of her room into the corridor. From there, she could see a police officer standing at the counter.

Her heart rate shot up, blood whooshing in her ears, belly lurching as if she might start retching again. Ferguson had died and she was about to be arrested for his murder. Or Ferguson had recovered and reported what she'd done. Attempted murder.

'Good afternoon,' said the cop. 'Are you Dr Kaczmarek?'

Paula just nodded, not sure she could trust her voice to come out plausibly.

'You treated Mr—uh . . .' He consulted his notebook. 'Mr Ferguson?'

'Yes. Yes, I did. Yes.' Too many yeses. 'Did Mr Ferguson . . . ?'

'He died.' Then the cop winced, realising there were two little kids behind him in the waiting area, and he lowered his voice. 'The gentleman passed away en route to the hospital.'

Not a gentleman. And now dead. Because she'd killed him.

'That's why I'm here,' added the cop.

Paula was suddenly light-headed, grabbing onto the upper counter so she wouldn't fall.

The policeman reached out to steady her. 'You right there, doctor? Must've been full-on today. Oh, but I guess you handle stuff like that all the time. Part of the job.'

'Oh well, yes, but no, it's . . .' Paula mumbled.

The police officer indicated that he'd like to move away from the desk, out of Jemma's earshot, for a private exchange. This was it. They wanted to take Paula in for questioning, conduct a full investigation.

'The thing is, Dr Kaczmarek,' explained the cop, 'the docs at the hospital thought we could avoid having to do an autopsy on this gentleman, if you'd feel happy to do the death certificate.'

'Oh.'

'I mean, based on your medical records and what you saw when he had his—you know . . .'

'His cardiac episode.'

'Right. Exactly. If you reckon that's appropriate, it'd save everyone a lot of unnecessary trouble.'

This officer was not here to arrest her or even to question her. She was being asked to sign the death certificate for the man she'd just murdered.

As her breathing and heart rate steadied, Paula was able to take a clear-eyed look at the person inside the police uniform. The guy was young, maybe not long out of the academy, self-conscious, awkward. He was trying to hide his nerves about handling this duty on his own, but at the same time she could see he was relishing the authority and importance of the job, occupying the uniform with a slightly pompous stiffness, like a boy playing police dress-ups.

Based on Mark Lang's files, Ferguson's health status and the episode in her surgery, Paula could justifiably write the man's death certificate and it wasn't uncommon for police to make this request of a doctor. In the past, Paula had signed death certificates in similar situations, even if this situation was—well, not entirely similar.

The young cop handed her paperwork from the hospital emergency department and she found the other necessary information from the practice records. As she completed the form, she took a deep breath, wanting to monitor her own reaction to this: the certainty that she had killed a man. Her hand trembled as she held the pen, but she controlled it enough to sign her name with her usual sweep and definition.

*

When Paula switched her phone back on to active mode, there were several missed calls from Anita. Then her phone dinged with a message.

How are you? Can we have dinner or something? I could come to your place. A x

Paula's instinct was to retreat, go directly home, engage with no one. How should she act now? How did someone who'd killed a human being behave? Would she feel compelled to blurt it out to Anita the minute she saw her? That would be foolish. It would be unfair to do that to her friend before she'd thought this through properly herself. She typed, *Not tonight . . . too tired*, but then deleted it. Anita would be anxious about how Paula was handling the phone video news and she would not be fobbed off without explanation for the second evening in a row.

Instead, Paula texted back: *Movie maybe? Too tired to be good company for anything else. P x*

She wasn't sure Anita would be satisfied with that—she might insist on an all-emotions-hanging-out debrief about Stacey—but five minutes later there was a reply.

Good thinking. I'm shredded too but need to see you. Only found one movie that isn't a) violent, b) grim or c) superheroes. So it's Japanese Quirky Family Drama. OK? Can you make 6.45 session in Newtown?

Anita booked tickets online and Paula drove straight there from the surgery. There was only time for a quick greeting hug before the two women found their seats in the darkened cinema, the ads already playing.

Paula was relieved she'd suggested a movie. It gave her time to settle a bit before any conversation would be required of her.

Sitting together would hopefully neutralise Anita's worry, but because they were sitting in the dark Anita couldn't scrutinise her too closely.

Paula felt excoriated by the last week—Rochelle, the video of Stacey, Ian Ferguson—as if all her protective coating had been scraped off, so now her emotional responses were overwrought, overly reactive. During the three-minute trailer for a mawkish English rom-com, she found herself actually crying over the sixty-something couple finding love in the autumn of their lives in Umbria.

Anita must have heard the tearful sniffing, because she glanced sideways to check on her. Then she leaned against Paula, arm pressed against arm, and rolled her shoulder with wordless affection. Paula leaned back into Anita and rolled her shoulder in reply. It was comforting. It was good.

The next trailer was for a squawky French farce and Paula wound up laughing way more than the galumphing comedy warranted. Again, she saw Anita sneak looks at her, smiling this time, relieved to see her cheerful.

The Japanese movie started and the subtitles proved handy, something to hook her focus on. The film was eccentric and straining to be so. ('Kwerky with a capital K' was Anita's term for such films.) But the lead actor was charismatic and the family reconciliation story drew Paula in. It was pleasing to see the Tokyo locations and recall the week she'd spent there with Remy not long before he was diagnosed.

When the lights came up at the end, Anita was in one of her bouncy, slightly manic moods.

'In a fitting thematic link to the movie, I reckon we need to go to a Japanese restaurant,' she said.

'Oh honey, I'm so whacked, I won't last long,' Paula moaned. 'I mean, food's a good idea but it has to be something quick.'

'Which makes Japanese the ideal choice!' Anita grinned. 'It's quick. They don't waste time cooking the fish!'

Anita knew a Japanese place not far down King Street; as promised, the service was swift. Paula didn't eat much—her guts were still knotted, touchy—but she speared a gyoza with chopsticks and levered in enough rice that Anita didn't question her lack of appetite.

Anita was still fizzing, words tumbling out of her mouth, with or without sashimi in there at the same time. She was chattering about the 'theme nights' Stacey used to arrange when they were in their early twenties. She would choose a foreign movie for the three of them to watch on half-price Tuesdays, followed by a cheap restaurant with cuisine that matched. During the themed meal, Stacey, Paula and Anita would plan an itinerary for the perfect holiday in that country, even though they couldn't possibly afford it.

As Anita yabbered, Paula's head swam with the unreality of this moment—to be here eating Japanese food given what she'd done that day. Could she ever share this thing with her friend? Should she offer Anita a redacted version? An account of Ian Ferguson's death which omitted the adrenaline ampoules but included the part about Paula deliberately delaying the attempt to resuscitate him? Then again, maybe she could never tell any of it.

Anita suddenly stopped mid-sentence, inhaled sharply and said, 'Okay, Paula. What is going through your mind right now?'

'Sorry?' Paula felt caught out, as if what she'd done to Ferguson was oozing out of her pores, and Anita had detected it.

'I can see you're thinking about—I mean, are you thinking it's wrong we haven't talked more about the video of Stacey?' asked Anita. Her buoyant mood had suddenly deflated.

'Oh. Well . . .'

'But look, maybe we don't have to go through it all right now.'

'I don't think we have to,' Paula said quietly.

'No. But of course, I mean, yeah, we can, anytime, if you need to or—well, if either of us needs to—down the track. But tonight I reckon we should have a break.'

Paula nodded and Anita reached across the table to squeeze her hand.

'You look so exhausted, P. Your eyeballs are lolling out of their sockets.'

'In an attractive way, I hope.'

'Gorgeous. Hey, I'm sorry for dragging you out for quirky Japanese cinema when you're so tired. You should've told me to fuck off.'

'No, no, I'm glad you dragged me out,' said Paula. 'But I now need to fuck off to bed.'

'Yep. I'll sort the bill.' Anita jumped to her feet, switching back into her hyper mood. 'I'm prescribing you a big dose of sleep. You need to be ready to heal the sick and save lives tomorrow.'

Anita waved away Paula's proffered cash and darted over to the cash register. Paula watched her chat to the Japanese waitress, doing a little floorshow to describe the movie they'd just seen. The waitress was baffled at first, but eventually she was smiling and laughing.

Paula found herself consciously drinking in the sight of Anita being her awkwardly delightful self with the waitress. Paula did that a lot now; she was determined to store moments, images, scraps of the people she loved in some part of her brain that might not be infected with bad things.

NINE

ANITA SOMETIMES IMAGINED A WILDLIFE DOCUMENTARY AS she observed the journalists and TV crews outside the court buildings. One moment, the media would be hanging around as solitary birds or in groups of two or three, pecking at their phones, swivelling their heads to survey the area, waiting for something to happen. Suddenly, someone from a high-profile trial would appear on the footpath, and the journalists and crews would swoop in, flapping around the person like a flock of pigeons encircling the remains of a discarded hamburger.

For a regular individual caught up in a juicy trial, the walk to the entrance of a court building must be unnerving, the media pack shuffling with them every step of the way. The legal bods were fine, of course. They strode through, safely zipped inside their lawyer costumes, holding big white folders like shields. But the people fronting the court system for the first time were clearly overwhelmed, faces pinched against the questions being squawked at them, clinging to the advice they'd been given about not responding and not hitting out at the cameras in their path.

As a print journalist, Anita wasn't right in there shoving a microphone in anyone's face. Unlike the TV journos, she wasn't required to provoke distressed people into blurting out a sound bite in the street. But she was still obliged to hover close enough to hear if anything was said that should be part of the coverage. In a way, she got the benefit of the TV journos badgering these poor people, so she couldn't pretend she wasn't morally complicit. What did that make her? A scavenger bird? Maybe best not to run the birdlife analogy too far.

This morning, waiting to cross the street, she saw the media flock around a figure emerging from a black hire car. Then she recognised Gilbert Woodburn's luxurious curve of silver hair, always easy to spot because he was several centimetres taller than anyone around him. Woodburn, one of the most expensive criminal barristers in Sydney, still handled a hefty case load at the age of seventy-two. He'd made a career of renting his authoritative presence (the hair, the height, rich baritone voice, patrician demeanour) to clients of questionable reputation.

Woodburn moved calmly towards the main doors of the building as if the flapping media pack were not even there. He was followed by his courtiers (junior members of the legal team), who kept their arms tucked in to their bodies, making themselves physically small so as not to draw attention away from the magnificence of their boss.

When a second vehicle pulled up, Woodburn turned and walked at a stately pace towards it. His courtiers clustered around him to form a human shield so the passengers emerging from the car wouldn't stumble directly into the media scrum.

First out onto the footpath was Woodburn's client, John Santino, charged with the murder of Kendra Bartlett almost two years ago. He was pleading not guilty, claiming his girlfriend had committed suicide by jumping off a motorway overpass into oncoming traffic.

Santino was thirty-six, with Italian-pretty-boy looks and a gym-muscled body visible inside the sober suit he'd obviously been advised to wear to court. Whenever Anita saw pictures of Santino, she was puzzled that his face was so shiny, you could even say glossy. In person, his face looked as if it had been lacquered. It must be the skincare regime he followed.

Stepping from the far side of the car was Santino's younger sister Marina, who had been by her brother's side at his committal hearing and every other public appearance. Marina was there to demonstrate the adamantine support being offered to John by his wealthy and tightly interlocked family. His father, the patriarch of the Santino family, had started out as a labourer and ended up making serious money in the concreting business which the elder sons now ran. John had never worked in the family trade and instead had been indulged, bailed out of several failed ventures, installed in a huge apartment in Darlinghurst and, in recent years, had been subsidised by family money to run a couple of bars in the eastern suburbs.

Marina walked around the vehicle to join her brother. She was made up for the cameras, her dark hair freshly blow-waved and clothing carefully chosen—today's corporate suit with a high-throated silk shirt was considerably toned down from the sexy clubbing outfits Anita had seen in Marina's posts on Instagram.

Santino lunged over to help another woman out of the back seat of the car. Brooke Lester had been photographed on Santino's arm several times over the last year, but it wasn't until she stepped out onto the footpath that everyone could see she was pregnant.

Anita noticed Brooke tug on the waistband of her skirt where it was cutting across the tightness of her belly. The pencil skirt was too restrictive, even with one of those expandable maternity panels at the front. Along with her stiffly fitted jacket, low-cut clingy jersey top and high heels, it was an uncomfortable outfit for a pregnant woman.

The TV journos peppered Brooke with questions about her pregnancy, and after a huddled conversation with John Santino and Gilbert Woodburn, Marina was the one delegated to speak to the media.

'Yes, as you can see, my brother's beautiful partner Brooke is thirty weeks pregnant. Our whole family is thrilled. We pray that the truth will come out and my brother will be acquitted, so he can be the wonderful father I know he will be. Thank you.'

With his usual smooth choreography, Gilbert Woodburn swept the three of them away from the media pack. Just outside the entrance, there was one last moment of pageantry.

Marina took Brooke's hands and held them in her own for a moment. 'I'm not allowed to be in there with you today,' she said. She was on the defence witness list, so could not attend court as an observer until after her testimony.

Before she left, Marina Santino made a show of hugging her brother, then clasped his and Brooke's hands together, urging him, 'Take care of her.'

This was all a show for the cameras. How could Santino be guilty of a horrible misogynist crime when two women who knew him well—his girlfriend and his sister—would kiss him on his glossy cheekbones because they loved him, felt safe with him, believed in him?

As John Santino headed inside the court building, he slipped his arm around Brooke, hooking her in close to his side. The gesture, his hands on that woman's body, hit Anita like a thump in the solar plexus.

The trial was being held in the courts just off Phillip Street in the CBD—an elegant stone colonial building with all the period trimmings: red wine carpet, toffee-coloured timber seating like church pews and arched windows high in the walls. For a trial like this one, with intense public interest, it was an awkward choice. The narrow corridors barely allowed for the security screening set-up and the extra bodies milling around.

In Court 3, seats were limited, so Anita was quick to grab a good spot in the public gallery to set up her laptop. There was a bit of *sotto voce* chat with the other journos, helpful swapping of seats to gain access to power points and a palpable buzz of anticipation.

Following the official thumps at the chamber door, everyone rose for the judge's entrance. It was only then that Anita saw where Brooke Lester was perched, surrounded by a contingent of Santino family members.

Justice Roland Burke swept through the door to take his position at the bench.

In her years covering trials in Australia and the UK, Anita had generally been impressed by the judges. Sure, there were exceptions—arrogant dickheads, dozy muttering guys who didn't comprehend much, or other varieties of woeful—but mostly she found judges to be thoughtful people, wearing their huge responsibility with great care and with sympathy for the bewildered civilians in their courtroom. Justice Burke, though, was a hard one to classify. Anita had seen him snort contemptuously at something he considered to be 'whining, self-indulgent codswallop'. 'Codswallop' could be respect for a transgender person or making allowances for disadvantaged people. But he'd also made unexpectedly compassionate judgements. Other judges had told Anita off the record that Burke was regarded as a worry, too unpredictable, but here he was, in his scarlet robes and wig, presiding over a high-octane murder trial.

The first decision Burke made was an absolute fucking cracker.

Before the jury was brought in for the start of the trial proper, a ruling on evidence needed to be made. The Crown wanted the jury to be made aware of Santino's prior assault conviction and to hear testimony from two previous girlfriends who had gone to police, claiming he'd physically abused and threatened them. One of those young women had taken out an apprehended violence order, but neither woman had wanted to proceed with assault charges at the time. The Crown argued this showed Santino's tendency to become explosively angry and violent when his wishes were thwarted. For the defence, Woodburn argued the incidents bore no relation to the Kendra Bartlett case. The assault conviction was for bashing a male business associate with a pool cue. The allegations by the two previous girlfriends involved slapping, punching, objects being thrown and threats of stabbing. In none of the previous scenarios had Santino threatened to throw a woman off an overpass. According to Woodburn, threatening to kill women by other methods—for example, stabbing—was not sufficiently alike to count as 'similar fact' evidence.

Woodburn had barely laid out this dubious argument when Burke made his ruling: the assault charge, the history of violence, none of it would be admissible in this trial. Journalists could not report any of it. The jury would hear none of it.

'I don't want a string of disgruntled ex-girlfriends parading through my courtroom,' the judge said. 'Let's just look at the facts of the case in front of us.'

Anita saw the Crown's barrister, Irene Pileris, slump slightly with the unwelcome surprise of the ruling. Even Woodburn looked startled for a moment, then quickly converted that expression into a knowing smile.

Pileris regrouped quickly, locking her spine back into its usual upright posture and calmly rearranging her notes.

Anita liked Irene Pileris. She was in her early fifties, smart, tiny, birdy, sinewy from cycling astonishing distances across the city. Her red bicycle helmet was tucked under the bar table, ready to be swapped with her barrister's wig for the cycle home. Irene was methodical and unflustered rather than a showy court performer, but there was something deeply plausible about her that tended to convince jurors.

The jury filed in—six men and six women, ages ranging from mid-twenties to late sixties. All twelve looked slightly nervous, as if determined to do this properly but not sure what that involved. As the judge described their role in the weeks ahead, the jurors shifted position in their chairs. Should they cross their legs? Sit up to attention? Slouch in a more casual fashion? They moved their facial muscles awkwardly too, like people uncomfortable about being photographed. They were all self-conscious, trying to adopt the look serious jurors were supposed to have—the way Anita had seen fresh batches of jurors do in pretty much every criminal trial.

The opening statements for prosecution and defence laid out two possible narratives, like trailers for the movie the jury would be watching over the next six weeks. The Crown would tell the story of John Santino—a controlling bully and possessive partner who could not endure the idea that Kendra Bartlett would leave him. He had followed her as she attempted to escape and, in a fit of anger, threw her off the overpass with the intention of killing her. The defence narrative rested on a portrait of Kendra as a mentally unstable young woman, further unhinged by the failure of her acting dreams, who took her own life.

Every day of the trial, the new girlfriend, Brooke Lester, arrived on Santino's arm. He made a big fuss of protecting her from jostling media, leaning his head right into the crook of her neck to murmur reassurances into her ear. She wasn't as demonstrative with Santino as he was with her but, even so, she clung to his arm and played the loyal partner.

Anita noticed the way Brooke kept her face tilted down, so she was always looking up at people from a low angle, big green eyes peering through her blonde fringe like a nervous forest animal hiding in foliage. It was reminiscent of Princess Diana's defenceless baby fawn pose, which had always struck Anita as disingenuous and irritating. It was easy for women to slip into such self-deprecating postures. Some years ago, Anita had noticed her own body language in photos: her head tipped slightly to one side in the pose many women adopted. The head tip said, *It's only little me.* It was a woman reducing her own power in a group shot, next to suited men who would be staring directly at the camera, heads square on their thick necks. Anita had consciously trained herself not to do that head tip.

During the trial, Santino periodically turned to seek out where Brooke was sitting in the courtroom and mouthed 'I love you' to her. She would look up at him through her pale fringe and smile back. Anita scrutinised the faces of the jurors. Were they convinced by this or sickened by it?

The morning the forensic pathologist was on the witness stand, Anita craned her neck to catch a glimpse of Brooke's face. What was going through that young woman's head as she heard the pathologist describe Kendra Bartlett's catastrophic injuries, caused by the fall from the overpass onto the road surface ten metres below and the impact of the truck that then hit her? Her skull shattered, her face pulpy and unrecognisable, her pelvis and so many other bones splintered into pieces it took the pathologist a long time to list them all.

When it was Woodburn's chance to cross-examine the pathologist, he didn't ask any further questions about the injuries. It wouldn't help Santino's case to conjure up more appalling visions in the jury's mind. Instead, Woodburn shrank all the information about Kendra Bartlett's battered body down to one detail: the toxicology showed she had escitalopram (sold as the antidepressant drug Lexapro) in her system. The drug was present at the level you would expect for someone taking a therapeutic dose, but that was enough for Woodburn to polish up his picture of Kendra as mentally unwell.

'So, this poor young woman was depressed enough to be taking serious antidepressant medication,' he intoned, offering his big sad eyes to the jury.

Anita felt the burn of rage and the urge to yell out to the jurors. Could they see what Woodburn was doing? He was co-opting the pity they felt for Kendra and dragging it sideways to support Santino's version of the story. It was an act of embezzlement, stealing the goodwill of these twelve people, misappropriating their decent human feeling.

When the pathologist was finally excused from the stand, there was a shift in air density in the courtroom, pressure dropping a little now that the gruesome stuff was done with.

Anita had become accustomed to hearing gory forensic pathology reports in court. She'd peered at blown-up photos of victims, the kind where you needed help to discern which part of a person's body was on display in the mangled red tissue. Since the murder of Stacey and the kids, she found she was still able to listen to such evidence. She was still able to write up the grisly information into newspaper language. But now, as her fingers were typing the words, it felt peculiar, as if they were not her hands, the mechanical process disconnected from the churning mess in her head.

Anita glanced at the journalists around her in the gallery. One guy was doing a crossword on his phone during a boring bit of the proceedings. She could see another journo's laptop screen—the woman was toggling between the story she was writing about Kendra Bartlett's horrendous death and the eBay page on which she was bidding for a set of garden furniture.

Anita didn't judge their behaviour. She'd been like that herself. When you were covering long distressing trials, you had to find ways to flush the toxicity out of your system. But it couldn't be like that for her anymore. Now there was a level of separation between Anita and the people who used to be her gang around the courtrooms. She hoped the separateness wasn't visible to anyone.

When Justice Burke called the lunchtime adjournment on the Friday, Anita stayed in her seat, fiddling on her laptop longer than necessary, to allow time for the other journos to wander outside. The last thing she wanted to do was engage in any gossipy chat about what happened to Kendra Bartlett. She needed a little airlock of time between the courtroom and the world, time alone before she could engage with people.

She eventually headed out of Court 3, thinking she'd find a cafe a few blocks away from the court precinct. Through the doorway to the street, she could see out to the verandah, where Rohan Mehta was in close conversation with the earnest young lawyer from the prosecution team. As one of the detectives involved in the Santino case, Rohan was slated to give evidence for the Crown and so wouldn't be allowed in court until then.

Anita noticed that Rohan kept glancing at the doorway. Was he hoping to see her among the stream of people coming out? Was he keeping an eye out for her? She checked her own reaction—yes, she would like it if he was looking for her.

When they made eye contact, she raised her hand in a little wave. She aimed to make it the same kind of wave she would give any detective she'd met a few times and got on with, as opposed to the wave she would give a detective she'd had sex with.

Rohan smiled and took a step towards her, but then his phone rang. He looked at the caller ID, winced to Anita—*Sorry, I have to answer this*—and strode around the corner to take the call.

Half an hour later, when Anita walked back with a sandwich, Rohan was still on the courthouse verandah, swivelling back and forth as he talked on his phone. When he saw Anita perch on the stone wall to eat her lunch, he wound up the call and came over to sit beside her.

'How's it going?' he asked.

She assumed he meant the trial.

She made a growling noise in her throat. 'I have to sit on my hands sometimes, so I don't launch myself across the room and smash the sharp corner of my laptop into John Santino's evil fucking skull. Is it okay for me to say that to you?'

'I think it's okay,' said Rohan.

'Hey, I heard talk Santino was being looked at for drug charges before he decided to kill his girlfriend. Is that true?' she asked.

'Well, there were possible connections to serious quantities of cocaine. Lots of stuff goes through the bars he runs, for sure. And Santino himself—always known to be a big white-powder boy.'

'He had a possession conviction way back,' Anita said.

'He did. And by all accounts, in the last few years he's developed a taste for oxy and heroin too.'

'Right. Wow. Perfect fatherhood material. Because he got bail—'

Rohan jumped in, defensive. 'We tried to have his bail revoked. Several times.'

'I know. I'm not blaming you guys. But because Santino's been out on bail, he was free to spray it around and get that poor bloody woman pregnant.'

Rohan nodded, grim. 'Lot of chat in the DPP about the pregnancy being a clever tactic.'

'Reckon. Brooke Lester sitting in court with that huge belly is the best defence he's got going for him. But Jesus, that poor woman. She's so young.'

'Twenty-three,' Rohan confirmed.

'So now she's having a baby with an abusive, weapons-grade arsehole.'

'Well, that arsehole is going to jail.'

'Is he?' Anita asked. 'I mean, Burke ruled out the priors and the previous girlfriend stuff.'

Rohan puffed out a breath slowly. 'That was annoying. Really fucking annoying. But don't worry. We've still got a strong case against this guy.'

'Good. And the prosecutor, Irene Pileris—she's excellent value. Not a show pony, but effective.'

'Yeah, glad we got Irene.'

There was a brief pause, enough of a pause to allow the other stuff in Anita's mind to whoosh forward and tumble out of her mouth.

'Listen, Rohan, I'm sorry about my cryptic texts. Awkward and confusing and—I mean, I'm supposed to be a skilled communicator but—oh . . .'

'Well, yeah, you are a professional wordsmith,' he said, deadpan.

'Supposedly. But a wordsmith who doesn't know how to use words clearly to another human being. Sorry.'

'No need to apologise. My texts were clunky too.'

Anita took a breath, keen to blurt this all out in one go. 'It's just—look, Rohan, I like you very much and I think you're almost certainly a really good man and I very much enjoyed the other night, but it doesn't feel right, under the circumstances, because of the way we properly got to know each other and I think—Look, maybe when this is all over . . .'

'You mean, when the coronial inquest into your friend is over?' he asked.

They both knew that was so long off—many months, possibly years—she was effectively saying there was no chance of them pursuing anything.

Anita shrugged. She wasn't sure about any of it.

'Okay. I understand,' Rohan said quietly. 'I respect that.'

She was disappointed he didn't argue back. But then if he had argued back, had not respected her position, she would've thought less of him. It was impossible.

But even as they seemed to talk themselves into a dead-end, the words didn't entirely match the body language. Their hands had edged closer on the stone wall, close enough for the side of her finger to be leaning against his hand, and neither of them had shifted away.

'Time for you to go,' said Rohan.

'Sorry?' Anita wondered if he was sending her away.

'Don't you need to go back in there? Starting again at two, I believe,' he said.

'Oh yes. Shit. Two.'

Anita scrambled to shove the sandwich wrapper into her jacket pocket and scoop up her laptop bag to hurry inside.

'See you,' she said.

'Yeah, see you.'

When the court rose at four p.m., Anita perched on a bench in the corridor to finish the day's story for the paper and send it off. It only took her ten minutes but that was long enough for the rest of the media pack to have left the building.

When she came out onto Phillip Street, Rohan was waiting there. He was waiting for her. It seemed like the most natural thing in the world.

They walked through Hyde Park and then up to where Rohan's car was parked at the Surry Hills police station, stopping by a supermarket to buy food to cook dinner at the Alexandria apartment Rohan shared with a flatmate.

His place was in a group of neat, uniform residential towers built on old industrial land, resembling a plantation forest that had sprouted in a flat paddock. Those apartment block clusters always made Anita think of an architectural sketch and she pictured herself as a line drawing of a human figure included to indicate scale and the potential of life existing in the development. Well, there were now two human figures walking through the building foyer—her and Rohan Mehta, carrying groceries and intending to have a lot of sex.

The flat was tidy and perfectly comfortable, if a little impersonal. The flatmate travelled so much for his marketing job, he was rarely there, and it was clear Rohan was really only using the facilities of the place rather than occupying it as a home.

That Friday night spilled over to the entire weekend. They stayed in bed for much of the time but did venture out for food. They also went walking, including a hike to Anita's flat to fetch more clothes.

They fell easily into the rituals of a fresh relationship, including the traditional telling-of-the-romantic-history. Anita did her routine about the string of unfortunate men she'd chosen in her twenties, including Secretly Married Martin and The Masturbator. In her early thirties, in London, she lived for two years with an Australian guy, an intellectual property lawyer, and there'd been talk of babies and real estate back in Australia. But when she returned to Sydney, he never got around to booking a flight. Underneath all their plans, the flesh of the relationship had atrophied without them realising. They agreed to let it go.

Up until a year ago, Rohan was living with the girlfriend he met at uni and, like Anita and London-based Lawyer, they too had talked of babies and real estate. He had no clue she'd been sleeping with her old high school boyfriend for six months.

'Does that make me a shit detective?' he asked Anita.

'No, no. Well, in matters of the heart maybe,' she said. 'And you've got no worries about me being a secret cheater. I'm such a useless and unconvincing liar. I mean, if I try to lie, I sweat, my neck goes red and my eyeballs flick from side to side—so, you know, with me no detective work is required.'

Over the next week, Anita and Rohan spent every night together, sometimes at her place, sometimes at his. If they ran into each other around the courts during the day, they didn't let on they were together. It was simpler that way.

Anita enjoyed drifting in the permanent state of dreamy sexual anticipation that came with a new relationship, her whole body slightly achy with lust. The speed of this thing with Rohan Mehta was giddying, but at the same time it felt surprisingly calm and harmonious. She wasn't an infatuated girl with him, as she usually was in the early days with a new man. With Rohan, she felt like her most grown-up self. That was a new experience for Anita. A very good experience.

TEN

PAULA WAS SPENDING MORE AND MORE OF EACH DAY IN THE food court at Marrickville Metro shopping centre.

In a food court, a person could go unnoticed. A woman could sit alone at a table and no one would think anything of it. Paula kept phone earbuds in her ears so that if one of her patients recognised her, she could smile hello and pretend to be on a call.

Sometimes the smell of cooking at one of the vendors would make her bilious. The meaty odours seemed to slide into her mouth, down her throat and into her belly like a solid greasy influx her gall bladder couldn't handle. When that happened, she would move to another section, away from whichever food smell was upsetting her.

On the other hand, hanging in the food court was also a tactic to coax herself to eat. Since Ian Ferguson, the prospect of most food made her nauseous. She couldn't face cooking at home. She tried having food delivered, but the smell would linger in the house for hours and she'd be retching over the sink. She couldn't order a meal in a cafe in case she couldn't eat it and might draw attention to herself. But she discovered that in the food court she could wander between the eating options without commitment. If and when something looked appetising—a fresh juice, a tub of salad, a sandwich—she would buy it. That way she could put enough nutrition into her body to sustain herself.

She understood that her low appetite and digestive problems were a symptom of stress. She understood that perfectly well.

On the day she killed Ian Ferguson, there was the initial rush of the act. It wasn't a euphoric rush, but there was still a strong energising process in her body. Next, there was the thrill of getting away with it as she wrote the death certificate. That was followed by the relief of going to the movies with Anita, as if everything was the same, as if the universe was not forever altered by what she'd done.

Since that night, she and Anita had been to the cinema, to a Latin music gig at the Camelot Lounge, jogged the Bay Run. Paula kept suggesting outings that involved more activity than talk, activities in which they could be together but side by side, so she wouldn't have to face her friend too directly. In recent weeks, Anita had been busy with a big trial and they were getting together less.

Just behind the spot she was sitting in the food court, the guy at the noodle bar chucked a handful of pork into a wok, which made a loud hiss. The pungent smell enveloped Paula, flipping her stomach over. When she got up and moved away, closer to the juice kiosk, her guts settled again.

After Ian Ferguson's death, Rochelle cancelled the follow-up appointment to check Brody's tonsils. Not surprising. The woman was dealing with the sudden death of her husband.

Paula considered sending a condolence message, but it felt obscene to send a sympathy card about a man she'd killed. In the end, Mark Lang sent an email to Rochelle on behalf of the practice. It made sense—the dead man had been Mark's patient.

When Mark Lang first returned from his diving medicine conference, Paula waited for him to quiz her about what had happened with Ian Ferguson, but questions never came. The one time they discussed it, Mark said, 'Nah, not surprised. I tried to talk him into taking medication and getting some tests but—well, Ian Ferguson wasn't a bloke you could argue with. Never let you win a point.'

As more days unspooled after the murder, it was incomprehensible to Paula that nothing had changed. She kept expecting a squad of police to pound on her front door or march into the practice or show up at the food court right now to arrest her, but the police never came.

This was one of those times when she felt the ache of Remy's absence strongly. Since his death, she'd sometimes thought her way out of problems by imagining what Remy would advise. And she often consoled herself by imagining the delight Remy would've taken in some funny or lovely moment. By conjuring him up, she could squeeze a bit more out of life.

Now, it was agonising he wasn't around to talk to about the situation she was in. But, really, what wisdom could Remy have offered? There were doctors who had upped a dying patient's morphine dosage, knowing it would suppress their respiratory system and hasten death. You could consider that to be a doctor killing a patient. But that was nothing like this.

She felt spikes of childish temper. If Remy hadn't been snatched away from her, she never would have done this. If Matt hadn't murdered Stacey and the children, she never would have done this. If Ian Ferguson had not happened to come into the surgery so soon after Rochelle's visit, during a week Dr Lang was away at a conference, on the day after Paula learned about Matt's phone video, she never would have done this. But Paula had never been a person who indulged in *if only things were different* thinking and she didn't approve of shifting blame to other people or circumstances to wriggle free of responsibility for her own actions. She'd done what she'd done.

After that initial rush and then dizzy panic, Paula hoped she might settle down, regain her equilibrium. But she was surprised to find she was growing worse, unravelling inside, however normal she appeared outside. Why should it surprise her? Surprise was ridiculous. She had zero experience of the progression of a person's mental state after they'd committed murder, had no knowledge or case histories to draw on. Now she was increasingly anxious, gullet scalded with reflux and abdomen burning, as if the remorse was her own bile eating away her stomach lining.

At the juice bar, the blender started whirring and Paula was hit by the smell of creamy yoghurt and strawberries mulching up for a smoothie. She feared she might vomit up the toast she'd eaten earlier.

By the time she made it into the ladies the nausea had passed. She stood at the basins to splash her face with water and regarded herself in the mirror, droplets of water hanging off her nose and jawline.

She had killed a man. She had murdered someone. She was not this person. The universe was out of kilter because she had done this thing. It wasn't superstition. It was a simple matter of right and wrong.

She must face up to what she'd done, go to the police and confess.

She shivered, dry-mouthed with fear, cortisol flooding through her system. She didn't want to face the police all on her own. So, she would admit everything to Anita first and ask her friend to accompany her to the police station. Anita knew how such things worked and would guide her, as well as being the emotional support she needed.

She texted Anita.

Hi. I know you're busy but can we meet up this evening? V. important thing to tell you. P xx

Finishing the afternoon's session at the practice, Paula made some effort to tidy her consulting room and leave things in a decent state. She made sure important emails were sent and patient files were up to date.

Once she'd reported herself to the police this evening, she might not ever come back here. Probably they wouldn't hold her in custody but she presumed she would no longer be permitted to practise as a doctor. Better not to stew about any of that now. No point speculating about lawyers and trials and the future.

For the two hours since she'd resolved to confess, she had been mentally rehearsing the wording she would use. There was a good chance the police would find her story unlikely. She would have to give them medical details, but she would also have to offer plausible motivation, talk about Stacey, all of it. She wanted to explain her exact thought process before she killed Ian Ferguson. Not to excuse anything, but to clarify.

She was terrified, no question, but still, this was necessary. She didn't allow herself to think beyond the moment of confession. She needed to focus on the moment itself, the correcting of the universe, so she would be able to breathe properly again.

~

Anita plonked herself and her laptop bag on the bench seat in the Enmore restaurant where they'd chosen to meet. Paula insisted on buying the first round of drinks and bringing them to the table.

'I ordered us some share plates too,' she said.

'Thanks,' said Anita. 'It is fucking good to see you, lady. Sorry I've been so busy.'

It was true she'd been preoccupied with the Santino trial, but it was also true that she'd been preoccupied with Rohan Mehta.

Traditionally, she would have shared every detail of the new romance with Paula and Stacey by this point. Stacey would've insisted on a blow-by-blow account, mock-swooning at the excitement of it all, enthusiastically analysing the subtext of key moments. Paula would be excited for Anita too, but in a more measured way, running through a checklist of questions to ensure this new guy was good enough for her friend. Nothing important in Anita's life felt real until she'd shared it with those two.

The way things were now, she didn't know how to tell Paula about Rohan Mehta. The story of how they got together might be painful. And parading her happiness might be painful too. She should wait for the right time to say something.

The two friends clinked glasses.

'I'm glad this place isn't too noisy,' Anita said. 'Don't you reckon restaurant reviews should have an acoustic rating alongside the price guide and however many stars? Do I sound like a curmudgeonly old deaf man?'

Paula smiled. 'No, no, I agree.'

'Anyway, sorry, I'm prattling.' Anita made a little show of gulping her wine and wriggling her bum firmly into the seat to indicate Paula had her full attention. 'Please tell me your "*v. important thing*".'

Paula stared at the tabletop for a second. 'You know how we agreed we wouldn't constantly talk about what happened to Stacey . . .'

'But we can, Paula,' Anita jumped in. 'Anytime either of us needs to, I reckon we should.'

'No, of course. And in fact, something happened at work and I wanted to tell you about it.'

Anita nodded, ready to listen.

'It's about a patient of mine. A woman. And her husband.'

Paula described Rochelle's visit to the surgery, the marks of strangulation and other injuries her husband had inflicted on her. She described Brody's anxiety, maintaining a watchful cordon around his mother.

'Like Cam,' Anita murmured.

'Yes. Made me think about him so much.'

'So I'm sure you're trying to persuade this woman to—'

'Yes, I offered all the usual advice and referrals.'

Paula explained Rochelle's fears, the husband's threats to kill her or their child if she ever tried to leave him again.

'The stats on that are terrible,' said Anita. 'The period of time when a woman tries to leave an abusive partner, the risk of him killing her goes way up.'

'And Rochelle's husband had the skills and the means to track her.'

'Yes, yes,' Anita agreed fervently. 'That's a very real danger. A scary percentage of the women in refuges are being tracked electronically in some way by their ex-partners.'

Anita heard herself adopt a slightly lecturing tone with Paula. Since she'd started writing the feature on men murdering their partners, she'd been quoting the statistics to her brothers, her parents, her friends, her colleagues. It wasn't as if she and her female friends didn't know this stuff already, but wading into it waist deep, then dunking down and soaking her brain in the horrendous data, had turned Anita into a zealot.

'What can you do to help that poor woman?' Anita asked. 'Oh, don't tell me she's—'

'No, she's okay now. That's why I wanted to tell you what happened.'

Paula described Ian Ferguson coming into her consulting room, the threatening way he spoke about his wife, his untreated heart problems, then his fatal heart attack.

'So he can't hurt her now,' said Anita.

'No. She's not in danger anymore.'

Anita was relieved—not only to hear that the woman was safe but also to see there was a calmness about Paula: the way she used to be.

~

Paula took a breath to steady herself and gauge how she was feeling as she described Ian Ferguson's death to Anita, but excluding the part about injecting a lethal quantity of adrenaline. Only hours before, she had been determined to reveal every detail, but between sending Anita the text and arriving at the restaurant, Paula's thinking had shifted. There was no confession of guilt. Instead, she went on to tell Anita about something that had happened forty minutes ago.

Paula had been about to leave the surgery when Jemma stopped her as she passed the front desk.

'Oh, you're off,' Jemma said, then dropped her voice to a whisper. 'I was hoping you could fit in one more patient before you go.' The receptionist flicked her head in the direction of the play area.

Rochelle Ferguson was crouched down by the toy table, helping Brody pack away pieces of a plastic construction set. Paula couldn't breathe. She had killed this woman's husband, this child's father.

Then Paula saw Rochelle stand upright, facing Brody. She was smiling—lightly, playfully. The two of them, mother and son, were laughing about who could throw the bright plastic pieces into the box with the most accuracy. Every time Brody successfully landed a piece in the box with a satisfying plonking sound, he did a gleeful wriggle. Rochelle would make a huge fuss, as if he were a sporting star who'd scored a goal.

Observing Brody in the play area now, Paula hardly recognised the anxious, clingy little boy he'd been. This child was sparky, happy, enchanting.

And when Rochelle turned towards her son, Paula saw the delight on her face and the ease in her body, as if the armour she'd kept strapped around herself for years had melted off.

Paula felt a wave of—maybe it wasn't like the euphoric rush from an opioid drug, but a lovely warmth spread through her limbs and she was able to breathe deeply again.

'Hi, Rochelle,' she said.

'Oh hi, Dr Kaczmarek.'

'Am I seeing you or Brody this afternoon?'

Rochelle glanced at the bags in Paula's hands. 'Were you about to go home?'

'Well, going out to meet a friend,' said Paula. 'But I can definitely fit you in.'

Rochelle squatted down next to Brody. 'Okay if I see the doc and you hang out here for a minute?'

Brody nodded. He was happy to keep practising his throwing skills. He was happy to let his mum out of his sight for a little while.

Paula ushered Rochelle into the consulting room.

'I'm so sorry about your husband,' Paula said.

Rochelle looked at the floor, pressing her lips together. 'Well, I don't reckon I have to pretend to be super upset with you, doctor.'

'No, you don't.'

'Please don't get me wrong. I feel guilty that I don't feel sad—but y'know, it's like someone let me out of prison. Which is a terrible thing to say about someone dying.'

'I don't think it's terrible. It's understandable,' said Paula. 'How are you going in practical terms? I mean, are you okay financially?'

Rochelle grimaced. 'Money's tricky.'

'Did your husband have life insurance?'

'No. Ian thought all insurance was a waste of money. His money was tied up in the business and there's actually heaps of debt. That's one of the things that used to make him riled up.'

'Ah,' said Paula. 'If things were going badly in his business, he used to take it out on you.'

Rochelle nodded. 'But it's alright. My mum's helping now. Ian couldn't hack having my mum around. She hated his guts and he knew it. But now Nana picks up Brody from school two afternoons a week. Means I can work longer shifts. We'll get there.'

'I'm really glad to hear that, Rochelle. And how is Brody going? He looks pretty happy.'

'He is. He is.' Rochelle choked up and Paula handed her the box of tissues. 'I used to kid myself Brody was okay. But when I look at him now, it's like, "Oh, that's who you are, Brody. That's the happy little kid you were supposed to be." Because he doesn't have to worry about me all the time.'

'Well, that's great.'

'Yeah, yeah, it is great. But makes me feel guilty. For letting it happen.'

'Don't waste emotional energy feeling guilty, Rochelle,' said Paula. 'You're a brave person and a loving mother who did the best she could in an impossible situation.'

Rochelle looked up at Paula, desperate to believe what was being said to her.

'Yes,' said Paula firmly. 'I'm a doctor so you have to believe me.'

Paula smiled and Rochelle laughed. They filled out the paperwork for a mental health plan so Rochelle could see a psychologist over the next few months.

'Thanks for this. And thank you for being so kind to me and trying to help when everything was, y'know . . .'

Paula reached forward and hugged Rochelle. She felt the strength of this woman's body.

'The thing is,' Rochelle said, 'when you've been in a situation for so long, it feels like that's normal life—well, even if you know it's not normal, it's how things are. But then something changes and it's like, "I remember this! This is what safe feels like."'

By the time Paula finished telling the story, Anita was sniffling and rummaging in her handbag for tissues.

'Jesus, Paula,' said Anita. 'That's spectacular. That's . . . fuck . . .'

'Sorry. Didn't mean to make you cry.'

'Don't apologise. I love that story.'

'Yeah. It made me feel a little bit better about everything,' said Paula. 'I mean, it doesn't change anything about Stacey and the kids but it's . . . I dunno . . . I think there's some consolation in it.'

'Yes. *Yes*. Thank you for telling me.'

Paula shrugged. 'I guess I wanted us to share the good things as well as all the painful stuff.'

Anita nodded and reached across the table to squeeze Paula's hand.

Paula twisted around in her seat, trying to catch the eye of the bar staff. 'I wonder where our food is? We ordered it ages ago. I'm starving all of a sudden.'

'Hey, can we go back a step?' Anita asked. 'The guy died in your surgery?'

'Well, he had a heart attack in the surgery but he actually died in the ambulance shortly after.'

'So when this homicidal piece of shit started, you know'—Anita mimed a man clutching his chest in agony—'you *helped* him?'

Paula nodded.

'Jesus, Paula. You must've been tempted to stand back, not lift one of your highly qualified fingers to revive him and let that man die on the floor in front of you.'

'Well, you tend to go onto automatic pilot and do the standard emergency stuff.'

'Sure,' said Anita, but she flipped her head, dubious. 'Not sure I'd be so fucking nice.'

Paula gave in to an urge to push it—not to confess, but she wanted to poke a little, tease out what Anita would think. 'Well . . . the thought did run through my mind.'

'I bet. I mean, you could've found some ingenious way to kill the fucker outright, couldn't you?'

Paula shrugged, playing it nonchalant, even though her heart was beating fast now. 'I could.'

Anita leaned forward and gripped Paula's hands, this time with jokey concern. 'Are you telling me you murdered that guy?'

Paula nodded with exaggerated gravitas. 'Yes, that's what I really came here to tell you.'

'Then, hurrah! Good on you!' Anita laughed and then swerved into a jokingly worried tone. 'Ooh, but hold on a minute . . . Is murdering patients—even the truly nasty ones—is that considered ideal practice under the Hippocratic oath, Dr Kaczmarek?'

'No. I believe it's generally frowned upon.'

'I mean, it's probably okay just this once. But don't you go murdering any more patients.'

'I won't. Ian Ferguson's my one and only. The process is too stressful.'

'I can imagine. Although, now I think about it, let's not be too hasty. There are a lot of deadshits cluttering up the world. You could go through your patient files, make a list of all the violent, dangerous men and then . . .'

Paula shook her head, mock earnest. 'The connection to me would be too obvious. One murder per practice is all you can reasonably get away with.'

'Point taken,' said Anita.

The share platters they'd ordered finally arrived. Paula used the opportunity to look away and focus on spooning food onto their plates.

It was a relief to hear her friend approved, in theory, of what she'd done. Of course, if Anita knew the truth—that this murder was real, not a joke, not a hypothetical act—she would feel differently. And it wasn't fair to burden Anita with that knowledge.

Another thought crystallised in Paula's mind: it wouldn't be beneficial to do anything that might overturn the new peace Rochelle and her son had found. A confession, a murder investigation and the resulting publicity would bring more distress to that fragile little family.

Paula certainly felt the weight of what she'd done. She felt the wrongness of it inside like a large tumour pressing on vital organs. She would never do something like this again, but at least some good had come from her criminal act. And no good could come from admitting it. If that meant she had to carry the weight of it inside her alone, then that was how it had to be.

She realised that Anita was gazing at her, watching her eat. Paula was suddenly aware that she'd been shovelling food in ravenously.

'Oh honey,' said Anita, smiling with deep affection, 'it's good to see you looking happier. And eating. I've been worried about you.'

'Don't worry. I'm okay.'

'Yeah, well, seeing the way you're ploughing through this meal, my theory is that for the last few weeks you were just really fucking *hungry*.'

Paula laughed and made a show of wolfing down the food like a person who hadn't eaten for weeks.

Anita cleared her throat pointedly. 'There's something I need to tell you.'

'Sure—as long as I can keep gorging myself as I listen,' Paula joked.

Anita made a 'please continue' gesture and said, 'I've got involved with a man. It's become serious pretty quickly.'

'Oh! Oh, Anita, that's brilliant! I'm so, so glad.'

'It's Rohan Mehta.' Anita looked hesitant, clearly anxious about how Paula would react.

Paula took a moment to absorb this. 'Oh.'

'Rohan's the detective who—'

'Yes. I know who he—he seems like a really lovely—'

'He is. He's lovely,' said Anita. 'But I know it's weird, because of the connection to Stacey. So I understand if you feel . . . I don't know . . . weird about it.'

'No. No,' Paula said firmly, then smiled. She did feel a little weird about it, but mostly she felt delighted. 'I'm really happy. And to the extent there's a connection to Stace, it's kind of wonderful to think that something good has come out of something horrible.'

Anita grinned, obviously relieved.

'Do you understand what I mean?' Paula asked. 'This is a good outcome—like organ donation after someone's died in a car accident.'

'Ha. I'll tell Rohan you likened him to a deceased donor liver.'

Paula laughed. 'Don't tell him that!'

'No, I will. He'll like it.'

For the rest of the meal, the two friends talked about Anita's new relationship, gushing like teenagers, giggling until they were snort-laughing like old times, as if Stacey hadn't been killed and Paula hadn't murdered a man.

ELEVEN

IRENE PILERIS HAD CHOSEN TO OPEN THE CROWN CASE IN the Santino trial with the forensic pathology evidence about Kendra Bartlett's injuries. In screen drama terms, it was like a flash-forward scene to the grisly denouement—designed to shock the jurors into confronting the crime they were here to consider. Then Pileris took the jury back, to lead them chronologically through the narrative of how Kendra found herself on that overpass.

First, Kendra's mother was on the stand. She was forty-four but looked older, with dog-tired eyes and brittle hair dyed too luridly red for her sallow complexion. At the same time, she came across as much younger than a woman in her forties, shifting nervously on the witness stand like a teenager hauled up to face the school principal.

Through a series of gentle questions, Pileris elicited the story of Kendra growing up in various places around Tasmania. The mother was candid about her own struggles with alcohol and described her daughter as well-behaved—'a goody-goody really'—and by necessity a self-reliant girl. Even as a schoolkid, Kendra looked after the house and held down a part-time job.

When Kendra was nineteen, there was a falling-out over her mother's latest boyfriend. ('He was not a good man,' the mother conceded.)

Kendra left Hobart and travelled to Sydney to pursue her ambition to be an actor. For the next three years, there was little contact between mother and daughter, but Kendra would send a message once a month, reliably, to say she was okay.

'She was still annoyed with me, but she didn't want me to worry. She was a very thoughtful person.'

Finally, Pileris prompted the mother to describe the day the police called to say Kendra had died. The woman's face crumpled like a scrap of paper and there was a doleful silence in the court for the moments it took her to collect herself. She refused the offer of a break from testifying, and after a few more simple questions, Irene Pileris expressed her personal sympathy and then handed the witness over to the defence.

Anita was surprised at the toughness of Woodburn's cross-examination of Kendra's mother. It obviously suited his defence narrative to characterise this woman as a bad mother who'd driven her daughter to depression and suicide. In particular, he badgered her to admit that Kendra had been obsessed with losing weight.

The mother was rattled by his relentless questions about the dieting, until she finally cried out, 'Kendra was never anorexic when she lived with me! Is that what you're trying to make me say? She wasn't!'

Woodburn turned to the jury then and raised his eyebrows. Gilbert Woodburn was seventy-two but in his facial expressions, in the way he held himself, it was possible to visualise the sixteen-year-old he had once been: the smarty-pants third speaker on the debating team at a posh school. Back then, and still, he believed he was the cleverest person in any gathering.

As he continued to bully Kendra's mother on the stand, reducing her to tearful, stammering replies, Anita checked the reaction of the jurors. For many of the twelve, at least half of them, their faces were twisted into looks of disapproval, uncomfortable about watching the defence barrister humiliate and demolish a bereaved woman. Woodburn had misread his audience. He'd fucked up. Which was hugely satisfying.

As the trial days rolled on, Anita's loathing of Gilbert Woodburn, Justice Burke and John Santino held her in a state of constant simmering anger. That anger was strangely welcome. It was bracing, invigorating enough to keep despair at bay.

Pileris continued Kendra's story through testimony from friends she'd made in her early days in Sydney: a flatmate, the photographer who took her acting headshots, colleagues from various jobs. Each witness added scraps that formed a coherent portrait of Kendra as an energetic, kind-hearted, naive, determinedly optimistic young woman.

A former assistant manager from John Santino's Darlinghurst bar described Kendra's first shift working there. Santino had spotted the new, pretty twenty-one-year-old serving behind the bar and he'd 'swooped' on her, 'serving up all his charm'.

The next witness, Kendra's friend Damien Ross, was expected to be on the stand for at least two days, possibly more, so Anita was especially curious to watch him sworn in.

Damien Ross was twenty-four, tall, slender, with a stylish haircut and clothes. His strawberry blond hair and overall creamy paleness—eyes, skin, even his eyelashes—gave him an unusual kind of beauty.

Irene Pileris guided him through the standard who-are-you bit. Damien explained he'd grown up in Perth, completing an arts degree there before moving to Sydney. He began attending part-time acting classes the same day Kendra Bartlett enrolled at the drama school. These days, he was having some success as an actor, with several television roles so far, as well as performing in fringe theatre. To supplement his acting income, he worked occasional shifts in a call centre for a wine merchant.

Damien Ross looked nervous on the stand—you rarely saw a first-time court witness who wasn't—but it became clear to Anita that this guy wasn't lacking confidence. It was more that he was keyed up, determined to do right by his dead friend. From time to time, during his long hours in the witness box, he stretched his long, pale neck and shook the tension out of his limbs, like an athlete keeping calm and focused at the start of a major race. He was there to honour Kendra Bartlett.

Damien and Kendra had become enthusiastic friends, devoted to each other from that first day in class. Both were new to the city, with no support system, broke, lonely. Both were juggling casual jobs to pay for acting classes and planning to audition for the big 'proper' drama schools later in the year.

'Was this a romantic or sexual relationship?' asked Irene Pileris.

'No. I'm gay. We were good friends,' Damien Ross answered.

'And you would describe your friendship as close?'

'Yes, very close,' he confirmed. 'We texted or called each other several times a day. Saw each other pretty much every day. Because we were both blond and pale, we had a running joke that we were secretly Norwegian brother and sister. We shared everything—money, secrets. We even shared energy, if that makes sense. I mean, if I was having a shaky time, Kendra would love me up, boost my confidence, you know? And then I'd do the same for her other times. We looked after each other. But it was fun—we were always teasing each other, being silly, creating wild fantasies about what we'd do in the future.'

'So, would you have described Kendra as a happy person when you first met her?'

'Yes, yes. I mean, she was sad sometimes. Things were difficult with her mum and she worried about making it as an actor. She fretted about her weight sometimes—I mean, actors have to, that's the reality—but the main thing was, Kendra always lived healthy. It was one of the things we had in common. Both of us had alcoholic parents, so we didn't drink or do drugs. But, look, yes, Kendra was happy. If you met her, you would say, "Oh, that girl is so vibrant!"'

Damien described the day Kendra pirouetted into class having met John Santino the night before. She was dizzy from the intense and flattering courtship by her new boss. She didn't care that the guy was fifteen years older. The relationship progressed very fast, with Kendra moving in to Santino's apartment three weeks after their first meeting.

Pileris asked Damien Ross, 'When did you first meet John Santino?'

'One night, I went to a bar he owned, the one where Kendra worked. I was sitting on a bar stool, chatting to Kendra. She was due to finish her shift in half an hour and we were going out to catch up. We must've been laughing about something because behind me I hear, "What's so fucking funny, mate?" Really aggro voice.'

'And this was the accused, John Santino?'

'Yes. He grabbed me by the shoulder and said, "Getting a good fucking eyeful of my girlfriend's tits, are you?" He was making a fist with his other hand and the veins on his temples were bulging. The guy was ropable. I thought for sure he was going to hit me. Kendra quickly explained who I was and he calmed down. He told me he hated men staring at her in the bar. He was okay with me because I was gay.'

Soon after that night in the bar, Santino persuaded Kendra to give up work entirely.

'He boasted to me about how he was going to support Kendra,' explained Ross. 'He said—and trust me, this is word for word, because he sounded so up himself, doing his charming routine, it's burned into my memory—he said, "I'm gonna support Kendra to be an actress. My princess won't need to do any more shit jobs. I'll pay for the acting classes, clothes, photos, cosmetic surgery, whatever she needs. I'll be like a patron of the arts. I'm Italian. There's a long, long history of rich Italian families being patrons of the arts. Heard of Lorenzo de Medici, mate?"' His impersonation of Santino was so plausible and sharply funny, some of the jurors had to suppress a smile.

At the beginning, Anita had feared this trial would be too distressing, too close to Stacey, too much. She'd gone into it with muscles clenched tight, guarded against letting any excess emotion leak into the process. She'd avoided discussing it with Paula, mentioning it briefly, but nothing compared to the detailed accounts of fascinating court scenes she used to offer as entertainment over dinner in the past. She figured it was best not to add to the store of horrible images in her friend's head.

But seeing Damien Ross on the stand, bearing witness to Kendra Bartlett with such precision and strength, changed Anita's mind. There could be consolation in seeing the dead woman and her story acknowledged through this formal process, seeing her killer held to account by Irene Pileris's methodical work, by the evidence the police had piled up and by the testimony of Kendra's friend.

That afternoon, she sent Paula a text—*I'm bringing dinner to you*—and arrived at the Earlwood house with wine, cheese, bread, prawns and salad stuff.

The two women spread the food out on the dining table and picked at it as Anita bounced around the room, fired up to convey the satisfaction she was extracting from the trial.

'I reckon it could give us some cathartic goodness. Seeing Kendra get some justice, publicly, it's . . . I mean, we won't ever get that for Stacey and the kids—'

'There'll be an inquest,' Paula pointed out.

'Yes. Which will be something. But Matt will never stand in a courtroom and have the truth of what he did wrap around him the way I'm seeing it wrap around John Santino.'

Paula shrugged and then nodded.

'What I'm trying to explain—explaining this badly, sorry . . .' Anita went on. 'The point is, I could let myself be upset by this trial, I could be totally undone by it, or I can try to draw moral satisfaction from it.'

'Hey, I'll take whatever moral satisfaction is available on the market.'

From then on, Anita started giving Paula her own daily bonus-material reports on the Santino trial.

In his second day on the stand, Damien Ross spoke about the way Kendra had altered her appearance to please John Santino. Under pressure from her new boyfriend, she became more anxious than ever about her weight. Santino had joked to Damien about setting Kendra weight 'goals'. If she lost three kilos by August, she would be rewarded with a trip to Hamilton Island. Before Santino, Kendra had never used much make-up and she usually wore second-hand boho dresses and Doc Martens, but her new boyfriend insisted she wear full make-up every day, high heels and sexy-corporate clothes—low-cut silk shirts and tightly tailored suits.

'I was standing with them in the street once,' said Damien Ross, 'and Kendra went back to fetch something from the car. He pointed at her as she walked away from us, and he said, "Look at that, mate. Is there any better sight on the planet than a woman's arse in a tight skirt when she's walking in stilettos?" And then he laughed and said, "Oh no. That's right. You don't care because you're a fucking fag."'

After Anita related this bit of testimony to Paula, she spun her laptop around on the table.

'Check out these photos of Kendra—pencil skirt, stilettos, long blonde hair blow-dried straight, heavy eyeliner. Now here are shots of the new girlfriend who comes to court with him.'

The resemblance was unmistakable, apart from Brooke Lester's pregnant belly. Both women were in their early twenties, slim, with similar facial features and made to appear more similar thanks to their identical long straight blonde hair, heavy eyeliner, high heels and pencil skirts.

'How creepy is that!' Anita exclaimed. 'It's like he wheeled Brooke into a hairdresser, taped a photo of Kendra to the mirror and said, "Make my new one look like my old dead one." And Rohan reckons the previous girlfriends—including the one who took out an AVO—they look like this too.'

'And the pregnant woman, Brooke—how is she going?' asked Paula. 'She comes to court with him every day?'

'Every day. Arm in arm. Makes my flesh crawl to see him paw at her and parade her in front of the cameras.'

'Jesus . . . the poor woman. Who's going to look after her once she has the baby?'

'Don't know,' Anita said. 'Santino's sister Marina hovers around outside court, fussing over Brooke. So I guess we have to hope his family will take care of her once he's in jail.'

On the afternoon of his second day on the stand, Damien Ross spoke about the many occasions he had witnessed Santino's flares of temper and the times Kendra had showed up at class with injuries. As her confidence eroded, she dropped out of acting school and gradually withdrew from her friends. Because Santino was enraged by men staring at her, Kendra was allowed out of the apartment less and less frequently. When Damien did manage to see her, he saw the bruises and burn marks.

The day after Damien Ross confronted Santino about the abuse, he was cut off from all contact with Kendra. John Santino phoned to say, 'She doesn't want you in her life anymore.'

Within a twenty-four-hour period, Damien discovered Kendra's phone number had been changed, all her social media accounts deactivated and the couple had suddenly moved to a new apartment at an unknown address. In desperation, Damien went to the police and expressed his fears for her safety. Officers spoke to Kendra but she declined to make a complaint.

~

Paula sat in her consulting room after her last appointment of the day, closed her eyes and imagined the next patient to walk in the door was Kendra Bartlett, presenting with three broken fingers or hot liquid burns to her thighs or a deep knife laceration to the cushion of flesh below her thumb.

Paula knew from court reports that Kendra had gone to medical centres with each of those injuries. She had always offered an explanation, joking about her own clumsiness.

'Oh, my hand slipped when I was lifting a kettle of boiling water.'

'I tripped and I guess I landed with my fingers scrunched up in a stupid way.'

'I was cutting up sweet potato and the knife slipped.'

The GPs who'd treated Kendra's injuries were all questioned in court. Each of the three doctors worked in a different practice. None of the doctors had seen this woman before and none of them would see her again. All three suspected abuse, questioned her, tried to arrange a follow-up consultation, and each felt they could do little in that moment to stop her from disappearing out the door and sinking back into whatever dark world she was living in.

Paula was struck by how convinced Anita sounded, almost evangelical, about the idea that following the Santino trial would be a healing thing, offering the chance for some sense of justice, even if it was only vicarious justice, given the man who killed Stacey would never stand trial. If it helped Anita to talk obsessively about Kendra's case, then Paula was prepared to listen.

Paula's thinking about Kendra kept spilling over into thinking about Stacey. Stacey with her face bashed into a swollen, pulpy mess, scrambling to the car to flee the Maryvale property. Stacey kneeling on the floor of Paula's lounge room as she watched her children being shot in the head.

The rage towards Matt would build up like a painful pressure under Paula's skin. Sometimes she would deliberately, methodically, summon up the memory of him blowing his head off in her house. She hoped that image would offer swift release of the pressure inside her, like cutting into a cyst to expel the pus. But by the time Matt shot himself, Stacey and the kids were already dead. There was no release in picturing him dead after he'd killed them. That was too late.

Only one fantasy was worth anything: if she rewrote the narrative of that evening so she arrived home earlier. Poppy would be in the shower, Cameron playing *Minecraft* on his iPad, Stacey unpacking their schoolbags, rinsing out lunchboxes. Paula would see Matt with the rifle before he had a chance to hurt anyone. She would come up behind him silently, with the granite bird in her hand. She would smash the sharpest edge of the bird into the softest part of his temple. She might manage to do crucial damage to his temporal artery but it didn't really matter. There would be no need to kill him. She didn't care if he lived or died. She would only need to hit his skull hard enough so he dropped the rifle and went down. The police could have him after that.

Paula realised her hand was in spasm, her body unconsciously rehearsing the action of picking up the chunk of granite. This was disordered thinking, a post-trauma reaction. She had adequate insight into what was happening to her, but insight didn't necessarily solve the problem.

She needed to get out of this room, away from the online news reports, and find some way to decompress. Better to avoid going back to her own house in this agitated state. Better to avoid contact with Anita right now, with the risk more talk about Kendra could increase the pressure. She must find some other way to anchor herself.

One thought came to mind. She decided to follow it and not let herself interrogate the thought too much.

Paula swivelled her office chair back around to the computer, clicked on the patient records and found a street address for Rochelle Ferguson. She waved goodbye to Jemma on her way past the front desk and headed out to her car.

Turning into Rochelle's street, Paula slowed down, checking the house numbers. She wasn't sure how to go about this without behaving like a stalker. Well, in truth, she was a kind of stalker.

Maybe she should pretend she was lost or interested in buying real estate in the area. She berated herself for not having prepared a cover story.

She pulled her car over to the gutter, across the road and one house down from the Ferguson place. The house had been subjected to an ugly renovation in the seventies, with an outer skin of red brick, aluminium windows and garish blue roof tiles, but the hard edges were softened by foliage from lovely big trees and banks of overgrown shrubs. Paula had no idea if Rochelle would be home or even if she still lived at this address.

By now it was almost five o'clock, late June, with the sun already sinking, which meant Paula's silver-grey car might hopefully fade into the dusk light. When a man walking his dog down the footpath glanced at her sitting there, she snatched up her phone and feigned sending a text. She didn't want to arouse suspicion.

She should leave right now. Giving in to this impulse was ludicrous. If Rochelle walked down the footpath and saw her doctor sitting in a parked car outside her house, the poor woman would freak out. Paula should definitely go.

As she put on her indicator to do a U-turn, a Mazda approached from the other direction and pulled into the Fergusons' driveway. Rochelle emerged from the driver's seat, wearing a pale blue pantsuit with the logo of the beautician business embroidered on the chest pocket. She went around to open the boot of the car and started to unload bags of shopping.

The front door of the house swung open and Brody galloped out onto the porch and down the steps. An older woman—presumably Rochelle's mother—stayed back, leaning against the doorframe, waving hello.

Paula sat very still in the car. She held her phone in front of her so if anyone happened to glance over, they would think she was checking something on the screen rather than gazing at the woman and child. Spying on them, even if it was, arguably, a benign form of spying.

Brody, wearing a red puffer jacket over his school uniform, bounded down the driveway and threw his arms around his mother's hips. Rochelle bent over to land a volley of staccato kisses all over his head. Brody laughed, shook his head as if he were ticklish, but then submitted his face for more kisses.

From across the street, Paula couldn't hear what they were saying, but it was clear Brody was chattering to his mother, telling her some tale of his school day that required melodramatic hand gestures. Rochelle listened, gasping with appropriate amazement at his story.

The grandmother stepped out onto the porch, offering to help bring in the groceries. Rochelle waved her off, smiling—Brody would help with the shopping.

Mother and son joked around about what goodies might be inside the bags. Then Rochelle did a little pantomime about one of the bags being too heavy to lift, so they would have to carry it together, one handle apiece. Brody nodded, very earnest about the task, and helped her hoist the bag up onto the porch. And meanwhile, Paula sat in her car like a crazy person, watching a woman and a child carry in groceries.

When they eventually went inside the house, front curtains were drawn and interior lights switched on, Paula drove away.

She felt anchored again, as she'd hoped she might. But it struck her that she didn't only feel soothed, she was also revived, as if she had drawn power from the sight of Rochelle and Brody alive, safe, not afraid.

TWELVE

ON HIS THIRD AND FINAL DAY IN THE WITNESS BOX, DAMIEN Ross looked exhausted, too drained to continue. The pale skin around his eyes was raw and puffy from crying or sleeplessness, probably both.

Anita had the urge to run over and shake his hand—no, fuck it, she wanted to fold that young man in her arms, do whatever she could to transfer the energy he would need to hold strong. She wanted to hand him caffeinated beverages and muesli bars and herbal remedies, shower him with praise and reassurance and gratitude for the way he was standing up for Kendra.

When Irene Pileris stood up at the bar table to ask Damien Ross the first question of the day, she paused for a moment and smiled at him. She was silently letting him know that he was doing a good job, this was nearly over, and there was just one more part of Kendra's story he was required to tell. Damien took a breath and Anita saw him soak in Pileris's smile as the fuel he needed to keep going.

First, Irene Pileris questioned him about his efforts to find Kendra, his appeals to anyone who might've known where she was, even following John Santino as he left the bar one night, hoping Santino might lead him to wherever the couple was living. All these attempts failed.

'So you had no contact with Kendra for three months, is that correct?' asked Pileris.

'That's correct.'

'Then on the thirtieth of September that year, there was a missed call on your phone.'

'Yes, from a number I didn't recognise. That's why I didn't call back,' he explained. 'After that, I had to go into a rehearsal session so I put my phone on silent. Four hours later, I turned my phone back on. There was a text from that same number.'

'Can you read that text for us, Mr Ross?' asked Pileris. 'Do you need a copy?' She reached for a piece of paper to hand to him.

'Thank you, no. I remember it word for word.'

Pileris gestured to indicate he should go ahead.

'The text said, *Hallo, my Norwegian bror. Miss you. Sorry for disappearing. Got kinda crazy here with J. But I'll be free soon and we'll see each other again. I love you, my beautiful friend. KB.*'

'Did you respond to the text?'

'I tried ringing the number but it was switched off. So I messaged back saying I loved her and I'd see her soon.'

'And did you?'

'No. By the time I saw her text, Kendra was already dead.'

As Irene Pileris concluded her questioning and sat down, Damien Ross took a wad of tissues out of his pocket and pressed them against his eyes. Anita noticed two female jurors were reaching into their handbags for tissues to mop at tears.

At first, in his cross-examination of Damien Ross, Woodburn came on smarmy.

'I'm impressed by the way you've made the witness stand your stage, Mr Ross! I love all the voices you do. You strike me as a good actor. Would you say you're a good actor?'

Damien frowned, cautious, not falling for the smarm, and answered in a flat tone. 'Not for me to say. I hope I'm a good actor.'

'And good actors are skilled at playing a character, are they not? Skilled at making a fictional story sound convincing?'

'I suppose so.'

'So in a way, Mr Ross, your acting training has made you a trained liar. How can the jury be sure this isn't a convincing performance of a sequence of lies?'

Damien inhaled sharply, furious, and Anita silently urged him to keep his cool. He did keep his cool. 'I'm not telling lies. Why would I do that?'

'Well, is it possible you're lying to the court because you loved your friend Kendra and you don't want the world to think she was mentally ill enough to kill herself? Are you lying to us to protect her reputation?'

'No.'

'Or perhaps you're lying to yourself because you can't bear to believe Kendra rejected you as a friend? You'd rather believe some fictional version in which my client forced her to end the friendship, is that so?'

'No,' Damien responded.

He was distressed, no question. But then Anita watched this remarkable young man transform his distress into power, right in front of her in that courtroom. The more Woodburn pushed him, the more firmly Damien planted himself on his feet.

'I was upset when Kendra cut contact. I missed her very much. But my main emotion was fear that she was in trouble.'

'I see.' Woodburn nodded with fake thoughtfulness. 'You were afraid because you knew Kendra was struggling with anorexia, had a dysfunctional relationship with her mother, and worried she would never achieve success in her acting career? Afraid because you knew Kendra Bartlett had fragile mental health?'

Damien Ross was shaking visibly, squeezing away tears with brisk eye scrunches. His whole body was blazing with rage but his voice came out steady and strong.

'I'm not pretending my friend didn't have a few problems—like most people do. But Kendra's biggest problem was John Santino. Her problem was being trapped in a relationship with a controlling, violent monster. Do you reckon any woman with a few problems deserves to be chucked off an overpass? Kendra was a beautiful person. She didn't deserve any of the shit he put her through. Not the thousand sneaky humiliations. Not the constant surveillance. Not the bashing. Not killing her. None of it.'

Anita's heart was thumping in a glorious rhythm. As soon as there was a break, she found a quiet corner of the corridor to leave Paula a voice message.

'Hi. It's me. Just now, in court, Kendra's friend Damien—fucking hell, Paula, he was fierce for her. He was magnificent. I wish you could've seen it. Anyway, talk soon.'

Once Damien Ross stepped down as a witness, Irene Pileris brought the Crown narrative around to Kendra's final day.

There was testimony from a tradesman who'd gone to the Santino apartment that last morning. A carpenter who did small home repair jobs, he was hired to replace the splintered wooden jamb of the bathroom door. It was the kind of damage you would expect from a locked door having been kicked open. (The defence's version was that Santino had broken into the bathroom to stop Kendra from slashing her wrists.)

While the tradesman was working in the apartment, he heard Santino yelling at Kendra in the bedroom. When she came out of the room, she was wearing heavy make-up but the swelling and rawness on the side of her face were still visible through the thick layer of foundation. She was shaking and unsteady on her feet.

The tradesman turned to address the jury directly. 'That woman was scared.'

He then described going to the kitchen, on the pretext of fetching a glass of water, so he could ask Kendra if she was okay. She whispered to him, 'I'm leaving. Don't worry. I'm outta here.'

Very soon after that, Santino hustled the tradesman out the door.

In cross-examination, Woodburn made a performance of being confused by the tradie's testimony.

'So—excuse me if I've misunderstood—if you thought Kendra Bartlett was in danger, why didn't you do anything to help her?'

'I should've punched him in the face,' the witness snapped back, flicking his head to where John Santino was sitting. 'Should've punched his lights out and got her out of there.'

'Oh dear,' Woodburn responded with fake dismay. 'There's no need to punch anyone. We have systems in place in this country to protect people. If you were so worried, why didn't you ring the police?'

'I should've,' answered the tradie, his voice low, dragged down by lead weights. 'I think about it every day. I should've.'

Again, Anita saw that Woodburn had miscalculated. By pushing this witness, all he'd succeeded in doing was provoking a decent man to express what many people in that courtroom were feeling.

After the lunch adjournment, it was Rohan's turn on the stand. As one of the detectives on the case, his task was to present the evidence that had been gathered about Kendra's last hours.

Bank records showed she had withdrawn all the remaining cash in her account at an ATM near Santino's apartment. She put the cash and her passport in a travel pouch concealed under her clothing, suggesting she was escaping Santino rather than leaving the apartment with a plan to kill herself.

Her Opal card records indicated she caught a train from Edgecliff station and then changed trains at Central to travel to Kingsgrove.

In CCTV footage from Kingsgrove station, Kendra could be seen alighting from the train at speed, running along the platform, looking behind her with a fearful expression. The accused, John Santino, could be clearly seen running after her. He later explained to police that he used an app installed on Kendra's phone to locate and follow her.

Kendra ran from the station in the direction of the M5 Motorway. She was next seen running towards a pedestrian overpass that was closed for maintenance, creating an effective dead end for a person fleeing on foot. Because the overpass was under repair, the usual high protective mesh was not in place.

A passer-by told police she saw a woman frantically climbing around temporary barricades to go onto the overpass, with a man running after her. The two people had a loud argument on the bridge. The passer-by was concerned enough to ring 000, then hurried towards the overpass. The pair was seen to struggle, then the woman was hoisted up by the man and thrown over the low railing onto the roadway. A truck hit her within one or two seconds of her landing on the road surface.

In cross, Woodburn queried Rohan on a few matters.

'If Kendra Bartlett was planning to leave my client, why didn't she take any luggage, any clothing with her?'

'I don't know. But I could guess, based on common sense, Mr Woodburn. If she was afraid John Santino would prevent her from leaving or she was afraid he would hurt her, she could have tried to hide her intentions from the accused.'

'The CCTV footage, Detective Mehta—you assume this shows a woman running in fear from a man chasing her to do her harm. Is it possible that it shows a distressed woman intending to harm herself, being pursued by a man who loves her and wants to protect her from committing suicide?'

'I suppose it's possible,' conceded Rohan. 'But I think that's very unlikely given other evidence and the expressions on the faces, which you can see quite clearly in the footage.'

Rohan was thrillingly good on the stand: well prepared, polite but resolute in the face of Woodburn's battery of questions. In his quiet way, Rohan was going in to battle for Kendra Bartlett.

This was what he'd spoken about to Anita that evening in the pub, the first time they'd had a proper conversation. He'd talked about the drive to obtain justice for people after a terrible thing has happened. It couldn't change the terrible thing but it was still of value. It was important. Watching him on the witness stand, Anita realised she was almost certainly in love with this man.

Finally, Woodburn questioned Rohan about John Santino's demeanour in the hours immediately after Kendra's death. The defence barrister was keen to characterise Santino as a bereaved man, distraught at the loss of his partner. Woodburn suggested that the police officers had prejudged his guilt, so had misread his behaviour. Santino's refusal to cooperate, his bravado and apparent lack of sadness were, in fact, manifestations of genuine grief.

Again, Rohan held steady in his answers and he took the opportunity to sneak in an extra detail.

'Well, Mr Woodburn, I can't know what was in the accused's mind,' Rohan acknowledged. 'But I do know John Santino put up a new dating profile on Tinder two days after Kendra Bartlett was killed.'

There was an audible intake of breath and a wave of appalled muttering through the courtroom.

Anita noticed Santino turn, searching for Brooke, but she kept her head tilted down, staring at her huge taut belly. It was hard to tell if she was hiding from the curious stares of others in the courtroom or if this was a meaningful vote of no-confidence in her boyfriend.

Even Woodburn didn't look quite as relaxed and smug as he usually did. Several members of the jury were looking at Santino with open disgust now.

From her seat in the courtroom, Anita texted Paula.

They've got him. This monster is going to jail. A xx

That evening, Rohan and Anita conducted a ceremonial opening of the remaining containers of Chilean comfort food to mark one full month of their relationship. Anita resolved to ring Paula in the morning and arrange for the three of them to have dinner together—an official 'boyfriend introduction' dinner.

THIRTEEN

WHEN PAULA ARRIVED AT THE RESTAURANT IN CHIPPENDALE, she could see the new couple already sitting at a table and she waved. Anita jumped up, slightly clumsy, as if nervous about how the evening would go.

The two women hugged and kissed hello, and then there was an awkward little moment as Paula turned to greet Rohan. Should they shake hands solemnly like two people who had met over the murdered bodies of her dear friend and two children? Or should they exchange pecks on the cheek as a best friend meeting the new boyfriend?

Paula could see Rohan Mehta hesitate—calm, but clearly waiting for Paula to make the call. In the end, she decided to split the difference.

'It's really good to see you again, Rohan,' said Paula, and she reached out to put her hand on his forearm.

'You too,' he said, squeezing her arm affectionately.

Through dinner, Anita was flustered, laughing a bit too loudly, fiddling with the buttons on her shirt. At one point, when Anita was gabbling about the food, Paula met Rohan's gaze. They shared a faint smile, silently acknowledging that they should both calmly ride out Anita's nervous energy until she felt sure enough the evening would go well.

And the evening did go well.

Rohan and Anita were so *together*, so clearly enjoying each other, that it gave Paula a pang of missing Remy. But seeing Anita happy was worth it. And anyway, sometimes the ache of missing her man, remembering him with ramped-up intensity, had its own consolation. She didn't say any of this out loud, of course.

When Anita was in the middle of an anecdote, hands flying and voice swooping to give the story its best telling, Paula noticed the way Rohan looked at her. Attentive, delighting in her energy, enjoying Anita being the centre of attention, besotted by her. That was how Paula and Remy used to look at each other.

She recalled how Matt hated Stacey being the centre of attention. That had always been incomprehensible to Paula—why would you fall for a woman as vivacious and magnetic as Stacey if you didn't appreciate her being that person? In Matt's mind, when Stacey was shining bright at some social occasion, she was 'winning' the moment in a way that was a defeat for him, as if there was a scorecard in the sky and every social point Stacey earned cost *him* a point. He would chip at her, ridicule her, petulant. Sometimes Stacey could handle him, cajoling him back into a sociable mood, and other times she would make an excuse for them to leave.

At one point during that first dinner with Rohan and Anita, Paula was aware of Rohan Mehta looking at her intently. She felt a sting of fear—maybe, as a police detective, he could somehow intuit that she was guilty of murder—but with a moment of calm breathing, she assured herself that was irrational. Ian Ferguson's death was not considered a murder. It wasn't even a subject of investigation or any scrutiny. If Rohan was trying to read anything in her, he was probably looking for clues to whether he'd passed the test as Anita's new boyfriend. Paula decided to cover her moment of unease by mentioning the subject that was there at the table with the three of them, unspoken.

'Rohan, can I ask where are things at with the inquest about Stacey and the children?' she asked.

Anita froze, her gaze darting between the two of them. But she need not have worried. Rohan handled the question with grace, explaining the process, the timeline, what would be required of Paula. He didn't only answer her procedural questions. He also spoke about how distressing he'd found Stacey's case at a personal level and how keenly he appreciated the loss her friends must be feeling. He spoke with delicacy and without pulling focus onto himself in an egotistical or condescending way.

Paula decided Rohan Mehta was a properly grown-up man with a good heart. She was glad Anita had found him, whatever the context.

The next morning, Dr Kaczmarek's first appointment was booked in as a 'long consultation' and she smiled when she saw the name of the patient.

Paula had seen Judy and her family through the normal run of illnesses and some personal tangles in recent years. There'd been Judy's own gynaecological woes and the bout of depression after her marriage broke down. There'd been the teenage daughter's bad scoliosis, but spinal surgery had gone well and the girl was now studying physiotherapy and playing high-level basketball. There'd been the substance-abusing son who veered close to self-destruction. Paula had helped Judy coax him into detox, residential programs and whatever threads might hold him in life during the most precarious phases. That son was now in his mid-twenties, sober for over a year and doing a TAFE course. Then Judy's mother had suddenly showed up, dying from lung cancer secondaries. Paula had helped organise home nursing until the mother went to hospital for her final days.

Judy flashed her fabulous earthy smile as she walked into the consulting room and plonked herself on the chair. 'Hi, Paula.'

'Good to see you, Judy.'

Judy always made Paula feel like a person in her own right and not just a doctor fixing problems. She'd sent Paula a thoughtful, tender note when Remy died and another one when Stacey and the children were killed. She was a good woman, stoic, a warrior for her kids.

'Work's slowed down a bit,' Judy said, 'and no one in my family is currently in crisis, so I've got a window of time to do some body maintenance. I'm thinking mammogram, check cholesterol, get skin cancers burned off, grease and oil change, all that palaver.'

'Good idea.'

Paula took her blood pressure, organised the referrals Judy wanted, wrote repeat prescriptions for her regular meds. Judy chattered on, updating Paula on how the kids were doing—both pretty well, even the errant son.

When they were finished and Judy was clutching her fistful of paperwork, she hesitated a second too long in the chair.

'Ah,' said Paula. 'Looks like there's something else, Judy.' She could always tell when a patient presented with a few straightforward problems but was really there to talk about some more delicate or embarrassing matter.

Judy laughed. 'Oh, Paula, you do know me!'

She reached into her large handbag and pulled out an object wrapped in a couple of tea towels.

'Remember when I was looking after Mum at home and the palliative people prescribed her this liquid painkiller stuff?' Judy unwrapped the tea towels carefully to reveal a brown glass bottle of Dilaudid. 'I remember thinking at the time—that's a bloody big flagon of a powerful narcotic they handed to me.'

'Looks like it's almost full.'

'Yeah, because Mum ended up in the hospital two days after I got it. Anyway, it's been in my wardrobe for months. And now that I've got my son back living with me, I don't want to leave temptation lying around the house.'

'Of course. Wise move. Do you want me to dispose of it for you?'

'Could you? That'd be great,' said Judy. 'I didn't want to pour it down the sink in case it got into the water supply and sent all the fish off their faces. That's if fish even have faces.'

After Judy left, Paula picked up the bottle, which still contained at least two hundred millilitres of hydromorphone, a synthetic opiate. It had always struck her as an anomaly that prescribing Schedule 8 drugs was so regulated, with a strict paper trail, but then situations like this would often arise—a patient died or was admitted to hospital, leaving their unused medications sitting in bathroom cabinets, no longer controlled or traceable. For now, Paula stowed the bottle in a lockable cupboard in her consulting room.

The plan to nurse Judy's dying mother at home had collapsed after a hip fracture landed her in an emergency department. That was how it played out for so many people. Paula's father had died in a hospital ICU because her mother had insisted on all possible measures being taken to extend his life. By the end, his crumbly body had been barricaded behind so much equipment, it was difficult to embrace him. Two years later, her mother fell onto her kitchen floor, toppled by a stroke that most likely took a further few hours to kill her, with no one around to offer any human touch in those final moments. Neither parent had experienced the kind of death Paula would recommend to a patient.

She was grateful that during Remy's last week of life she was able to stay close, lying in the bed with him for pretty much twenty-four hours a day. Visitors would come and go, perching on the edge of the mattress to chat or play music or just sit quietly.

From time to time, she would jump up to make food or to help the palliative nurse, but otherwise, she lay beside Remy, feeling the warmth of his body next to her, wanting to bank up the feeling, lock it in.

Afterwards, she had found it hard to sleep alone in their bed and the insomnia persisted, like a stubborn injury, for months after he died. She tried temazepam, which helped her drift off for a few hours, but she would usually wake up at three or four a.m. and that would be the end of sleep for the night. In desperation, she had experimented with opioids. Not every night. Only occasionally, only when her eyeballs were scraping inside their sockets and her bones felt abrasive under her skin. Only when she needed seven or eight hours of unconsciousness so she could be rested and functional for her patients. An occasional short-term fix.

Eventually, she admitted to herself that she relished the initial rush from the medication—a euphoria that filled the window of time before the drug made her drowsy enough to fall asleep. Paula hadn't felt any kind of intense happiness for so long. It was astonishing to be reminded what that felt like, even if it was a brief, synthetic version of happiness.

She wasn't a fool. She understood how addictive these drugs were. She made sure to leave gaps of several days between using them. And when she found she was really craving that brief moment of opioid bliss, yearning for it, she would back off for a good long while. Then there would be a night when she felt the need again.

She had convinced herself this was a phase, temporary and under control, but looking back on that period of her life with an honest gaze, she knew she had been in dangerous territory. And in truth, she had only been saved from sliding into opioid abuse by Stacey.

One evening, Stacey had phoned Paula from a motel in Ballina. In an explosion of anger, Matt had slashed the throats of the three alpacas they kept in the home paddock. Stacey—her face swollen and pulpy, body bruised, ribs broken, all at the hands of her husband—had hustled the kids into the car before they saw the corpses of the animals and driven to the nearest police station. The instant Paula heard Stacey's voice in that call, a sobering charge of energy went through her body. She never touched opioids again.

Now, in her bedroom at home, sleepless at two a.m., Paula could picture the bottle of Dilaudid Judy had handed over that morning. A small amount of the liquid hydromorphone would mean blessed sleep. Paula felt the vibration along a thread that connected her body lying here in bed with the brown bottle sitting in the locked cupboard at the practice.

She should've disposed of it straight away but she hadn't. She could drive there now and use some but she wouldn't. She trusted she could fight the temptation because she'd managed it before.

~

One Wednesday towards the end of the Santino trial, Anita and Rohan travelled into the city together by train. As they walked from the station towards Phillip Street, Rohan made a call, trying to arrange his schedule so he'd have time to duck into Court 3 at some point in the day.

While he was speaking on the phone, there was a bombardment of missed calls from the same number. He frowned and answered the next call.

'Hi, do you need me?' he asked. 'I thought we were all set for today.' But then he stopped and stepped out of the stream of pedestrians into a shop doorway, so he could listen with closer attention. Anita could faintly hear the voice on the other end talking rapidly, with the high pitch of someone in a panic.

'What? Oh no . . . How is she? Can you find out more?' Rohan asked. Pausing to press the phone against his chest, he said to Anita, 'Irene Pileris was in an accident last night. Her bike skidded—road was wet or something—and she slammed into a bus shelter.' Then he went back to his call. 'Yes, please, mate—whatever you can tell me would be helpful.'

Anita waited in the shop doorway with Rohan, watching his anxious face as he called more people.

Finally, he slapped his phone against his forehead in frustration and turned to her. 'Irene's basically okay but she's having surgery now and in hospital for—well, I don't know, a while.'

'Can't the DPP get an adjournment?'

'Argued for it, but no go,' he said. 'So the junior guy has to finish the trial.'

'That's Hugh Warby. I don't really know him. What's he like?'

Rohan grimaced. 'Look, he's not a total idiot.'

'Oh fuck . . . okay. Still, still, let's not be silly about this. The prosecution's been strong up to now and you told me there's some dynamite stuff to come.'

'There is,' Rohan confirmed. 'Great eyewitness. Even better piece of audio.'

'Good. Good. It'll be okay.'

Walking into Court 3, Anita saw Hugh Warby, the junior barrister now running the Crown case, at the bar table, rearranging his white folders, looking sweaty and flustered before the day had even started. The poor guy was anxious that he was out of his depth and that anxiety was dragging him further out to sea.

His first task was to question Maram Hafda, the nineteen-year-old woman who had been walking near the overpass when Kendra was killed. According to Rohan, Maram was the kind of eyewitness you want—a bit too young, perhaps, but smart, sober and unconnected to the people involved.

On the stand, Maram started off well, even while Warby stammered out awkwardly worded questions as if he'd lost his grasp of syntax.

'Can you, Ms Hafda—you can describe—well, can you, for us, relate the . . . You were that day walking close to the overpass at the—hold on, let me be absolutely accurate re the street . . .'

Despite him, Maram was lucid and composed as she described the two people arguing on the overpass. She observed the man aggressively grab the woman and yank her around, as he yelled abusive things, including, 'Is this what you want, you stupid bitch?' She heard the woman repeatedly plead, 'Let me go.'

Maram rang 000 to report what was happening, then moved closer, considering how to intervene. A moment later, she saw Santino lift Kendra up, shove her over the low railing and let her fall onto the roadway. He leaned over the edge to look down and made a 'ha' noise of triumph.

Hugh Warby finished his questions, then plonked his weight heavily into the chair. He let out an embarrassingly obvious sigh of relief which he then converted into an unconvincing fake cough. However clumsily, Warby had extracted what he needed from the young woman's testimony, which was unequivocal and so damning that Gilbert Woodburn would have to work hard to subvert it.

'Miss Hafda,' said Woodburn in his most unctuous voice, 'what a horrible scene you witnessed by chance, when you were simply going about your day. My sympathy. That must've been a very upsetting sight to see. Was it?'

'Oh,' Maram responded, not expecting this. 'Yes, it was.'

'My goodness, I'm sure it was. Your head must've been spun around by such an upsetting scenario. Do you think there's a chance you, in your distress, got little bits and bobs of detail wrong?'

'If you mean—no, I remember pretty clearly.'

'*Pretty* clearly?'

'Very clearly. Because it was so horrible, the memory is clear.'

Woodburn nodded but then did a stagey little frown. 'But from that distance, could you be sure what you were seeing?'

'I was only a hundred metres away. And after I rang triple zero, I moved closer. Maybe only fifty metres away.'

'Did you know Kendra Bartlett was on antidepressant medication?'

'Uh, no,' Maram answered, puzzled to be asked this. 'I just saw a woman on the overpass. I didn't know anything about her.'

'Indeed,' said Woodburn with an arch tip of his head. 'You didn't know anything about her. When you claim you saw my client holding Kendra's arm and heard him say, "Is this what you want, you stupid bitch?", did you—'

'I definitely heard that.'

'I don't doubt for a moment, Miss Hafda, that you think that's what you heard. But is there a chance that the scene you were observing from a distance was my client arguing with Kendra Bartlett to dissuade her from committing suicide by jumping?'

'Oh well, I don't . . . It didn't look like that.'

'Mm. And when you heard Kendra Bartlett say, "Let me go," you jumped to the conclusion that she meant "Let me leave". But couldn't she have meant "Let me go" in the sense of "Let me jump", "Let me die"?'

The cross-examination went on and on, with Woodburn circling back to ask questions again, laying traps to catch Maram Hafda out, implying she was incompetent, flipping through his repertoire of smarmy noises and snorts of contempt.

'I'm simply quoting something you said a few moments ago, Miss Hafda. Remind me—how close were you to the two people at this point?'

'A hundred and twenty metres. He was shouting loudly, so I was close enough to—'

'Ah . . . one of us must be confused—earlier you said a hundred metres. We can play back the tape, if you need to remember the version you told the jury a moment ago.'

'Oh. No. I guess I said that.' Maram was becoming rattled after almost an hour of this.

'So which is it—a hundred metres or a hundred and twenty?'

'A hundred, I guess.'

'You guess.' Woodburn snorted. 'Mm, we've had a lot of guessing from you. So the moment when Kendra fell, are you sticking with your guess of fifty metres?'

'Um, I don't . . . um, yes.'

Ambushed and confused, Maram threw a look of appeal to the Crown team, but she couldn't seem to catch Hugh Warby's eye. He was fussing with his papers, not even looking at the young woman on the stand. Anita wanted to shake him. *Why aren't you raising objections?*

Many times in situations like this, Anita had seen judges step in to protect the witness from being bullied, but Justice Burke said nothing. In fact, Roland Burke had a half-smile on his face, relishing Woodburn's floorshow too much to curtail it.

By the end, Anita could hear the confidence, the triumph, oozing out of every word Gilbert Woodburn spoke to Maram Hafda.

'When my client saw his girlfriend fall to her death, is there a chance the sound you heard him emit was a guttural cry of anguish from the man who loved her?'

'Oh. I don't—I don't know.'

'You don't know. Is it possible, Ms Hafda, that what you saw on the overpass, in the distressed state you must've been in—so much so that you're now struggling to keep the details clear—I completely understand it's difficult to be accurate—is it possible, Miss Hafda, that what you saw was a man grabbing his girlfriend because he was desperate to stop her from jumping?'

'Oh, I . . . I guess so,' she murmured.

'Thank you. No further questions.'

Straight after the break, there was to be a voir dire, so the jurors were held back in the jury room. Woodburn was challenging the admissibility of a piece of evidence—far too late in the proceedings for a challenge like this, but Justice Burke had agreed to it anyway.

There'd been some back and forth about who would be allowed in the courtroom, given the sensitivity of the evidence to be discussed, and Anita was expecting the judge to close the court entirely. He finally decided that family, friends and the general public would be excluded, but the 'ladies and gentlemen of the press' could remain while the legal teams presented their arguments. Burke loved an audience.

The evidence was thirty minutes of audio on a USB police had found among Kendra Bartlett's possessions—recordings the young woman had made on her phone during the week before her death and transferred to a USB to avoid detection by Santino. The defence maintained that the recordings were inadmissible because they were made without Santino's knowledge or consent and potentially had been faked by Kendra.

Hugh Warby stumbled through arguments in favour of the evidence being presented to the jury. 'The probative . . . ah, the probative value of . . . If Your Honour could excuse me a second while I find the notes on—um . . .'

'Let's just have a listen to some of this audio, shall we?' suggested Burke, making no effort to conceal his contempt for Warby's inept performance.

When the recording began, Kendra Bartlett's voice sliced through the air in the courtroom and hit Anita with a force she wasn't ready for. She'd been looking at pictures of this woman, she'd been imagining her life and her death for weeks now, but hearing her voice was electrically charged at another level altogether.

'Johnny, I just need some time away; I need some time to think,' Kendra could be heard saying at the start of the section played in court.

After that, the audio was dominated by John Santino's voice, either sneering in a nasty little singsong tune or spitting words at her with raw aggression.

'*What's that you've got, Kendra? Is that a backpack? Is that your little bug-out bag? Your little escape kit? You brainless fucking slut. Did you honestly fucking think you could sneak off and I wouldn't know?*'

As Santino continued hectoring her, you could still hear Kendra's voice, but faintly, as she tried to appeal to him.

'*What? What? I can't hear you!*' he bellowed at her. '*You don't get to decide to walk out on me. I've put money into you. I've spent my money on all your shit. That makes you my investment property. My investment property can't decide to walk out my door and go off to play with her little fag friend. Fuck me, sometimes you shit me so much, I can't stand to look at you one second longer—but I'm the one who decides if and when you go, okay?* Okay?'

By this point Kendra was barely audible. Anita could just make out the sound of her crying and her voice, thin and friable, pleading, '*Please, Johnny. Please, baby, let me go.*'

She was mostly drowned out by Santino ranting. '*Kendra, if you ever try to sneak off, you won't be hard to find—on account of you're as dumb as a box of hammers. I will find you and I will throw you off the tallest building in this city or—hey, I know, maybe I should cut your stupid fucking throat so I don't have to listen to your whiny fucking voice one second longer.*'

As the audio played, Santino kept his head down, eyes fixed on his shoes, but his voice filled the courtroom, making every particle of the air vibrate with dark energy.

Anita was breathing too rapidly, tipping close to a panic attack. At the same time as she sat listening to Kendra's tape, her mind was replaying the phone video of Stacey pleading with Matt. And as two women pleaded for their lives, here was Anita paralysed in her seat, useless. She couldn't do anything for Stacey or Kendra. She couldn't do anything for either of them.

Anita was still so light-headed from hyperventilating that when the recording ended and the barristers put forward their arguments, the words were indecipherable to her.

When Justice Burke announced his decision, his voice seemed muffled, as if the sound had to push through viscous air in the courtroom to reach her.

Burke ruled for the defence. The recording had been made without consent and could have been doctored. It would not be admissible.

Anita forced herself to sit very still, head in her hands, hoping her dizziness would settle. The three journalists near her in the gallery were whispering to each other, but Anita kept her head down.

None of the journalists would be permitted to report on anything they'd heard during the voir dire, but not one of them could unhear that audio. If they'd held any scrap of doubt about Santino's guilt—if only to maintain the storytelling interest in the trial, holding out for a narrative twist or whatever—that was gone now.

The young female journo sitting next to Anita nudged her and pointed out Brooke Lester, who was walking back into the courtroom along with other spectators.

The jurors were then escorted back into court through a side door. Anita watched as each juror resumed their seat. They would make their decision about John Santino without ever hearing that audio.

FOURTEEN

PAULA COULD SEE ANITA WAS WINDING HERSELF UP INTO one of her agitated states. Ever since they were teenagers, she had been the one to coax Anita to dial back her escalating anxiety about whatever she was fixating on and steer her away from doing something foolish. It was a pattern they were both familiar with. A running joke even. Sometimes Anita would be resentful, feel patronised by Paula, but mostly she said she was grateful.

The two friends had agreed to go for a Sunday walk along the coastal path from Coogee. Anita had suggested this activity, explaining, 'I've been sitting on my arse in that courtroom for so many weeks, my leg muscles will waste away if I don't stomp in weight-bearing mode for at least ten kilometres.'

Sometimes Paula found the Bondi and Coogee area unappealing, almost harsh—mostly treeless hillsides covered in squat, unlovely apartment blocks, swathes of concrete, with a few patches of stunted salty vegetation. But then she would turn her head and the ravishing beauty of the ocean would gazump all of that.

Paula and Anita walked for an hour, then stopped for a sandwich in a cafe along the route. But as Anita talked nonstop about the Santino case, her fervour was ratcheting up, too loud and too intense for the crowded communal space of a coastal cafe on a bright Sunday afternoon.

'Just take a breath,' Paula advised her.

'You're right. Yes. Sorry. I'm talking too loudly. Are people looking at me—"Why is that woman so fucking loud?" Am I being too loud?'

'Maybe a bit.'

'Let's scurry out of here. You've finished eating, haven't you?'

They resumed their walk, following the curve of the beach, with Anita striding along, burning up some of her excess voltage. But she continued talking, barely pausing to breathe between words.

She ranted to Paula about the sixty-something male GP who had testified as part of the defence case. This doctor had prescribed antidepressants to Kendra Bartlett when she was brought to see him by Santino's sister Marina. He had asked Kendra only a handful of questions—most of which Marina answered on her behalf—and then he wrote her a prescription for Lexapro.

'Is he allowed to do that?' Anita asked. 'I mean, he sees Kendra one time and he can pump her full of happy pills?'

The doctor's negligence frustrated Paula as much as it did Anita, but she wasn't entirely surprised—guys like that were out there. 'Look, I can't explain exactly what that doctor was thinking.'

'No, I know. Sorry. You're not responsible for every GP in the country. Although—sidebar—things would work much better in our nation if you *were* running everything. And really, it's Marina: she's the dodgy character in that scene.'

Anita gave Paula a run-down on Marina's performance on the witness stand during the week, acting out the testimony in character, conveying Marina's motherly protectiveness towards Santino, even though she was several years his junior.

'My brother is a very loving person,' Marina had declared. 'Johnny can lose his temper sometimes but it's only ever verbal, never physical. My brother is a gentleman with women. He's always fallen for his girlfriends with—I guess you'd say with blind devotion. Oh, but it's not like I'm saying Kendra wasn't a lovely girl. She was really sweet. I adored her.'

Marina presented herself as the person Kendra confided in about her anxieties and, eventually, her suicidal thoughts. Marina spoke, with a lyrical sadness, about how fragile Kendra had become.

'If my brother is guilty of anything, he's guilty of believing his love could save Kendra. He loved her too much to face how mentally unwell she was, until it was too late,' Marina said directly to the jury, dabbing a few tears from the edges of her eye make-up.

'Do you reckon Marina knows he killed her?' Paula asked.

'I think about that all the time when I watch her up there on the stand,' Anita replied. 'She must realise. But she loves her brother. And there's a great big concrete slab of loyalty there.'

'People can refuse to face a thing. They can choose not to face it as an act of will.'

Anita wasn't really listening to Paula; she was winding herself up into a state again.

'Fuck their family solidarity bullshit. They're all lying to paint Kendra as a suicidal nutcase. Santino killed her and now . . . oh . . . I mean, it's stupefying to sit in that court and watch how quickly the prosecution is crumbling to pieces.'

'The defence barrister—he's obviously clever,' said Paula.

'Oh yes, the man is an evil wizard. Woodburn gathers up all the evidence that shows Santino is guilty and then uses his sorcerer alchemy to transmute it into evidence she killed herself.'

'What does Rohan say about the way the case is going?'

Anita shrugged. 'When I ask, he goes quiet and weird with me. So then I worry he thinks it's inappropriate for me to talk to him about it. Professionally inappropriate, I mean. Or maybe he thinks it's unhealthy for our relationship to bring this toxic stuff into it. Do you reckon that's what he thinks?'

'I don't know. Ask him.'

'If I push—"Come on, what do you think is going to happen?"—he says, "The jurors aren't crazy." Which is probably right, don't you reckon?'

'I guess so. I don't know enough about how it works.'

'Then again—fuck . . . the jury don't know any of Santino's prior history, they didn't hear the audio. Marina's a good performer on the stand, plus Hugh Warby's making a hash of everything.' Anita abruptly stopped on the walking path and pressed her hand against her lips as if to prevent the words coming out of her mouth. 'I can't believe I'm saying this, but there's a chance Santino might get off.'

Paula felt a flush of panic wash through her chest as she recalled the news footage she'd seen of Brooke Lester outside the court building. Brooke arriving on John Santino's arm, one hand on her eight-months-pregnant belly, as if her small hand could shield her baby from the TV crews and the noise and the hazardous energy that bristled around the courthouse.

It was clear that Anita's thoughts had also gone straight to Brooke. 'Did I tell you I've seen Brooke Lester's parents?'

'Oh. Do they come to the trial with her?'

'No. They stay outside. I didn't know who they were to start with. Last week, this couple started appearing across the road from the court building. One of the camera guys told me who they were. Trish and Rob Lester.'

'Does Brooke talk to them?'

'No, that's the thing. She won't even look at them. One day I saw the mother call out something, but Brooke turned away. Pointedly turned away.'

'Shunned them?'

'That's what it looked like, yeah,' said Anita. 'And Marina glared at them as if they're the enemy.'

'What did the parents do?'

Anita shook her head. 'Just stood there looking shattered. They've turned up every day since then but Brooke never acknowledges them.'

At home on her own, Paula had been playing and replaying news footage of Brooke Lester outside the court, pausing on any shot that offered a glimpse of her face. The young woman was so guarded, it was hard to read much into her expression. She was clearly nervous, but then again, anyone would be tense in the face of all the media commotion. And a pregnant woman who thought her partner might go to jail would be in an edgy state. All of that might explain her frightened manner. She might not be afraid of her boyfriend. But she might be. If Brooke was estranged from her parents, she would be bound more tightly into the Santino family, however the trial turned out.

Paula and Anita resumed walking. By now they were almost at the end of the beach section. Paula was so absorbed, trailing after thoughts about Brooke that it took her a moment to register that Anita was sniffing back tears.

Paula clasped her friend's hand. 'Are you okay? What are you thinking?'

Anita gulped, then brushed away tears with her free hand. 'She nearly got away—Kendra. He'd trapped her, worn her down, but she dredged up enough confidence to make the decision to get out. She had cash, she escaped his apartment, made contact with her friend. She nearly made it. She was almost safe.'

The two friends walked back up the steps towards the car park, each with an arm around the other's waist.

~

Anita had to slide further along the bench seat to make room for the extra spectators showing up in Court 3 during the last days of the trial.

Because her testimony was completed, Marina Santino was permitted inside the courtroom now. She stuck close to Brooke like a combination of attentive carer and prison guard. Even from two rows behind, Anita could hear the hissing sound as Marina whispered a stream of commentary into Brooke's ear.

Up the back of the public area—in the I'm-not-sure-I'm-allowed-to-be-here seats—Anita recognised a few individuals who had testified for the Crown earlier in the trial. The tradesman who'd fixed the bathroom door on the morning Kendra died was there. On the witness stand, he'd been upset and regretful; perhaps that was why he felt an obligation to be here now. Anita also spotted two young women from Kendra's first Sydney share house and the former manager who had employed her at Santino's bar. Anita was heartened to see them there—at least there were people in that courtroom who cared about Kendra, who carried memories of her as a lively young woman.

Right up the back, she saw the milky-pale figure of Damien Ross. He sat very still, listening as if his unwavering focus was crucial to the outcome, as if he could save Kendra by paying vigilant attention. Anita swivelled her upper body around and tried to catch his eye, but Damien didn't notice. Why should he? She was just one of the pack of journalists assembled there, tapping out his dead friend's story on their laptops.

The final defence witness was John Santino. It wasn't common for the accused person to risk being cross-examined, but the narrative Woodburn was weaving required the jury to see this man play the role of the bereaved partner.

Santino began by relating how he'd met Kendra, the whirlwind romance, his commitment to support her acting dreams, how he'd adored her 'bubbliness' and her 'beautiful soul'. Anita made an effort to identify this man's possible charm. He radiated a boyish fervour that could conceivably come across as attractive, and if a young woman was swept up by him, becoming the focus of his emotional intensity, it might feel compelling.

Woodburn was careful to stare down the problem areas that had come up earlier in the trial and he adopted an austerely authoritarian tone for the next run of questions.

'Mr Santino, would you describe your relationship as volatile?' he asked.

'Yes. I would have to say yes to that.' Santino straightened his shoulders, like a schoolboy bravely owning up to some minor transgression. 'Because of the passion of the connection me and Kendra had, we had arguments sometimes. I'm not proud about that. But Kendra, she would get mad and shout at me just as loud.'

'Did you ever hit Kendra?'

'Oh no. Never.' Santino made a show of being sickened by the suggestion. 'I would never hurt her in any way.'

'But you could feel quite jealous over your girlfriend—is that so?'

'Yes, that's true. I mean, if other men thought she was hot, it made me feel good—she was hot and she was mine. But I didn't like it if guys came on to her too obviously, panting over her. But then Kendra could be possessive too—she hated other women coming on to me. The jealousy was only because we loved each other so strongly.'

Woodburn sighed sternly, playing it with an edge of disapproval. He eyeballed the jury, so they could take a good look at how rigorous he was being with his client. But eventually he nodded slowly, letting the jury know that he, Gilbert Woodburn, was finally satisfied with Santino's answers to these tough questions.

Surely no one would be taken in by this farce. But when Anita scanned the jurors, some of them seemed to be going with it.

Next, Woodburn took John Santino through the last months of Kendra's life. The answers were prepared, well calibrated to present Santino as the imperfect but devoted boyfriend, answers that folded the foul-tasting evidence into a more palatable mixture.

'It was her idea to drop out of acting classes. I kept telling her she was talented but she had too much self-doubt.'

'I loved the way Kendra looked. But she begged me to help her lose weight. "Be my body coach, Johnny," she said. So we came up with the plan, together, to have rewards like the Hamilton Island trip as incentives. I regret that now. I blame myself for maybe making her anorexia worse.'

'Kendra started withdrawing from her friends when she got depressed. I kept saying 'Ring your friend Damien." I liked the guy. But Kendra said Damien always pressured her about going back to acting and he made her feel bad about herself.'

Anita turned her head enough that she could see Damien Ross in her peripheral vision. She felt agonised for him. He must have wanted to pound down the aisle and smash Santino's shiny fucking forehead against the wooden edge of the witness box. But Damien stayed very still, just staring at the man who had killed his friend and was now telling lies about her.

'It was Kendra's idea to change her phone number and cut contact with Damien and her other friends. Now, I realise that was part of her mental illness and I should've argued back more.'

The voice coming out of John Santino's face was sweet, hesitant, loving, but it was the same voice Anita had heard on the recording threatening and ridiculing Kendra. Anita looked at the jury. They hadn't heard that recording and they didn't know his history, so they could only judge this man on what they were seeing now. And now, many of the jurors were softening with sympathy.

Woodburn shifted into a new gear, adopting a gentle, you-poor-thing tone as he asked about Kendra's final days.

Santino let his voice break a little bit as he answered. 'I blame myself. Kendra told me she wanted to kill herself but I didn't want to believe she would really do it.'

'Did you wrest a knife off Kendra on one occasion?' asked Woodburn.

Santino dropped his head, as if too overcome to answer, but then went bravely on. 'Yes, she was holding the knife up to her own throat. I kind of dived over, got the knife off her, but she accidentally cut her hand—here.' On his own hand, he indicated the location of the laceration Kendra had had stitched up in the medical centre.

'On another occasion, did you find a packet of oxycodone tablets in Kendra's handbag?' Woodburn asked.

'Yes, I did. She told me she had enough there to kill herself with.'

'Do you know where she obtained those serious opioid drugs?'

'No clue. I guess there are places in the Cross you can buy stuff like that illegally.'

'Did you go to the police?'

'No. I flushed them down the toilet as soon as I found them. But I regret that now. I should've gone to the police. Kendra might still be alive if I'd . . . I thought we could get help for her and it'd all be okay. But I was wrong.'

Santino then let rip with his full grief performance, complete with snotty crying, and Woodburn requested an early lunch adjournment so his client could gather himself.

As spectators filed out of Court 3, Damien Ross zigzagged quickly between the ambling people and out the door, so Anita lost her chance to throw him a fortifying smile or whatever feeble attempt at supportiveness she would've tried.

She stayed in her seat to finish typing the morning's notes, then made her way through the dog-legs of the courthouse corridors to reach the ladies. Anita sat on the loo for a few extra moments, trying to breathe away some of the distress from the morning.

Eventually, she hauled herself up and went out to the basins to wash her hands and wet down stray bits of hair. She was about to leave when she heard a toilet flush and one of the cubicle doors swung open. Brooke Lester had obviously been sitting silently in that cubicle for some time, taking the chance for a moment of privacy and solitude.

Anita flashed her an automatic friendly smile and Brooke smiled back, not unfriendly but not quite meeting Anita's gaze.

Brooke did a little embarrassed grimace at herself in the mirror. 'I have to wee all the time now.'

'Oh right, of course,' said Anita, scrambling to think of a way to continue chatting without being intrusive.

But the young woman herself seemed to want to hang on to the conversational thread and keep talking to this stranger in the ladies. She said, 'The baby kind of jumps around, dances on my bladder.'

'Ha. Right.' Anita nodded. 'I've never been pregnant, but I've always imagined it must be a crazy feeling—having a separate human moving independently inside your body. It's a wild idea, really.'

Shut up, Anita. Why was she prattling on with this nonsense?

But Brooke puffed out a little laugh. 'Ooh, yeah! Never thought about it like that.' Then she leaned down to address the baby. 'Who are you in there? And what music are you dancing to?'

The two of them exchanged goofy smiles and Anita was struck by how lovely this woman was and how very young.

Then Brooke sighed, the delight evaporating from her face as if she'd suddenly remembered something grim. She arched her back and wriggled her shoulders to relieve aching muscles.

Anita offered, 'Those wooden seats in the court—they can't be super comfortable for hours on end when you're pregnant.'

Brooke stood there rearranging her overly tight clothes—a peach-coloured narrow skirt with an elastic maternity panel and cream wraparound top made from clingy jersey—yanking at the fabric to give her belly more room.

She was apparently in no hurry to leave the ladies. 'You're a journalist, aren't you?' she asked.

'I am. How are you going with it all? This must be hard,' Anita ventured.

Brooke looked at Anita via the mirror and murmured, 'Yeah, I mean . . . yeah, it's hard.'

Her tone was tentative but there was definitely an invitation to talk seriously. This was Anita's opportunity. Fuck protocols.

She should warn her about the man she was tied to. But it wouldn't work to grab this woman by the shoulders and simply screech at her, 'Run away! You're not safe! Escape now!' Anita should rattle off a full list of John Santino's previous assault charges and accusations. And she should not let Brooke Lester leave that bathroom until she'd described every menacing word Santino had uttered on that recording.

But before Anita had a chance to say any of the words, the door behind her squeaked open and, in the mirror, she saw Brooke's face harden with fear.

'There you are, Brooke, my darling! Are you okay?'

Marina Santino's tone was syrupy—sweet enough to bring on a diabetic coma—but there was no denying the anxiety on Brooke's face when she saw her boyfriend's sister walk into the ladies.

Marina slid her manicured hands across the young woman's shoulders and steered her away from the basins, away from Anita. 'We've got to get you to a doctor's appointment, honey!'

Then Marina flipped her attention to Anita, explaining, 'Obstetrician appointment. Very exciting. But we're late!'

She whisked Brooke out into the corridor.

After the encounter in the ladies, there was no sign of Brooke Lester for the remainder of the trial, but Marina was in Court 3 for the final two days, a conspicuous and potent presence. She announced—loudly enough to be overheard—that Brooke was 'shaken up to see Johnny getting upset on the stand', so she was staying home to rest.

The closing addresses by the two barristers were as Anita would have predicted. Hugh Warby's summary of the case against Santino was pedestrian, with a vocal intonation that dribbled downwards towards the end of each statement, as if Warby himself was unconvinced by his own arguments.

Gilbert Woodburn was at his magnetic, cunning best, sweeping the jury through the evidence as if he was retelling the plot of a mesmerising true-crime podcast about a man falsely accused. He appealed to the jurors' vanity: surely they were smart enough to see through the apparently suspicious material they'd heard; surely they were wise enough to appreciate that a man could be foolish, but that didn't mean he was homicidal. Woodburn left space for the jury to feel huge sympathy for poor anguished Kendra Bartlett, so there was no need for them to swing that sympathy into the guilty column of the ledger. He concluded by using his deep, authoritative voice at its most compelling—this was a sad story but not a story of murder. Acquittal was the only sensible verdict.

Anita surveyed the faces of the jury as they listened to Woodburn. She'd developed theories about each juror, assumptions based on gender and other markers, plus her observation of their reactions during the trial. But there was really no way to know.

When the twelve people retired to deliberate, Anita kept replaying Rohan's reminder: 'The jury aren't crazy.' Despite the omissions in the evidence and the clunkiness of the prosecution, there had to be a filament of hope the jurors would make the right decision.

When the jury deliberations spilled over to a second day, Anita took her laptop to work in a cafe close to the courthouse. The moment word came through that a verdict was imminent, she would be ready to dash over there.

To justify the time she was occupying the cafe table, she ordered beverages every hour, and at lunchtime she paid for a big healthy salad. Probably just as well from a nutritional point of view too. Given the volume of caffeinated liquids sloshing around her body, it felt good to chomp through a bowl of greens and feta and grainy bits.

She forked in salad with one hand, scrolling through notes on her laptop with the other, so focused on the computer screen that at first she didn't register the woman standing right by her table. When she finally glanced up and realised it was Trish Lester, Brooke's mother, Anita smiled—an invitation to talk.

'Hello,' Trish said. 'I've seen you going into the court.'

'Yes. I'm a journalist. Anita Delgado.'

'So you'd know how the system works for this next part?'

'Basically, yes. You're Brooke's mum?'

'That's right.'

The father, Rob, came over to join his wife, holding a metal stand with the number nine for the food he'd ordered.

'Don't bother her, Trish,' he said. 'The woman's having her lunch. And working.'

'It's okay,' Anita assured him and quickly scooped her belongings into a corner of the table to make space. 'Would you like to join me? There's plenty of room.'

Trish threw a look to her husband. 'She might be able to help us understand what's going to happen.'

Rob pressed his lips together. He was reluctant, but at the same time keen for any help they could find.

The two of them sat down at Anita's table.

'If the jury say he's guilty, will he be sentenced straight off?' Brooke's father asked.

'No. There'll be sentencing submissions and other procedures,' Anita said. 'But almost certainly, he would be taken into custody straight away.'

Rob Lester nodded soberly.

'You know you can come into the courtroom,' Anita explained. 'Any member of the public can watch the trial.'

'Well, we didn't know that to start with,' said Rob. 'Doesn't matter, though. The trial isn't really why we're here. Really, it's, uh . . .'

Anita nodded and waited for him to fill in the rest of the thought. That was a habit she had learned as a journalist—don't swoop in and finish people's sentences with what you assume they were going to say. Don't be afraid to let a silence run. People usually felt obliged to fill the silence and more of the truth would tumble out of their mouths.

'We don't care about the trial,' he said. 'We just want to talk to our daughter.'

Hearing the distress in her husband's voice, Trish jumped in. 'We saw it on the news—Brooke going into the courthouse. We didn't even know she was pregnant until we saw it on TV. Then one day I turned to Rob and I said, "Let's drive up there, try and talk to her."'

The Lesters had been driving up from Wollongong every day during the last weeks of the trial. They'd taken leave from their jobs—Rob was an electrician and Trish worked in the kitchen of an aged-care home.

'How long since you've spoken to Brooke?' Anita asked.

Trish looked at Rob, as if making the calculation in his face. 'It'll be a year next month,' she said. 'We got into a big argument with her—about him.'

'Santino.' Rob Lester pronounced the name with a shiver of distaste.

Trish described Brooke meeting Santino on an online dating site and being spun around by the seductive bombardment from her new boyfriend—flowers delivered every day to the homeware shop in Sydney where she had been working, romantic texts filling her message bank, limousines arriving to take her to expensive restaurants, weekends in posh hotels, and promises of overseas holidays they would go on once he wasn't restricted by his bail conditions.

'So did Brooke talk about the murder investigation her new boyfriend was facing?' Anita asked.

Rob Lester nodded. 'She always defended him: "Poor Johnny".'

'In a weird way, I think it tied her to the guy more strongly,' Trish added. 'Like, here's this man suffering over his girlfriend's death, who gets unfairly charged with murder. It made Brooke feel an urge to support him even more.'

'She quit her job so she'd be available whenever he needed her.' Rob sighed heavily. 'She stopped seeing her friends because Johnny needed her.'

'We tried to get on with the bloke,' Trish insisted. 'I mean, that's what you do. You can't question your daughter's choice of boyfriend . . .'

'But what if her choice is a grub like John Santino? What do you do then?' Rob asked.

Anita made a murmur of helpless sympathy.

'A year ago, she tried to break up with him,' Trish said. 'She came home to Wollongong, crying and crying, wouldn't say why. Rob thought—'

'He hit her. I saw the bruises. That mongrel hit her,' the father growled.

'But then John kept ringing, sending flowers and whatnot to the house, and she said she was moving in with him. That's why we had the big row.'

'And when she went back to him, she cut off contact with you?' asked Anita.

Rob nodded and flopped his head back. 'Look, I lost my temper on the phone a couple of times—said some things I wish I hadn't said.'

Trish rubbed the back of her husband's hand, reassuring. 'Santino made it like Brooke had to choose—him or us.'

These were loving, honourable people who'd never encountered the domineering force of someone like John Santino until the day he swooped in to snatch their daughter. They'd been taken by surprise, not equipped for this fight.

'And since you've been coming to the court, has she talked to you?' Anita asked.

Rob shook his head, too upset to speak.

'He's always right there next to her,' explained Trish. 'Or the sister. Rob reckons Brooke's too scared of them to talk to us.' And now Trish was the one fighting tears. 'Is it better to think your daughter hates you or better to think your daughter is scared to death?'

Rob leaned across the table, eager to convey something to Anita. 'Look, I feel bad about what I said to you a minute ago, when I said we didn't care about the trial. We do care.'

'We think about that poor girl he killed,' said Trish. 'We think about her all the time.'

'Of course,' said Anita.

'And now our daughter is pregnant to that bastard.' The rage was seeping up into Rob Lester's throat, tightening his vocal cords. 'What are we supposed to do?'

'Mr Lester, I would hate it. I'd want to kidnap her and try to talk sense into her.'

Anita was tempted to blurt out everything she knew about John Santino, but she couldn't. Not because of the journalistic ethics, breaking court rules and all that, but because it would only cause these parents more pain, futile pain, given there was no clear way for them to rescue their daughter from danger.

But she did say, 'Mr and Mrs Lester, I don't know what's going to happen. Hopefully this man will go to jail and you'll have a chance to reconnect with Brooke. And even if he's acquitted, the baby might be—well, let's hope the baby helps you all to reconcile. What I would suggest you do, as soon as the trial is over—talk to the police about John Santino. Talk to this man . . .' Anita tore out a page from her notebook and wrote down *Detective Rohan Mehta*, then his mobile number.

Rob Lester took the scrap of paper and nodded his thanks.

Trish squeezed her husband's hand. 'We'll be at the court when the verdict comes in—whatever happens. Even if Brooke won't talk to us, she'll see us. She'll know we love her. She'll know we're there if she needs us.'

Anita rang Paula that night and described her meeting with the Lesters. It felt important for Paula to know that if Santino was sent to jail, Brooke wouldn't have to rely on the Santino family. She had her own doggedly loving family to support her and the baby. Paula agreed it was a reason to be hopeful.

Twenty-four hours later, Anita got the heads-up that a verdict was imminent. Walking into Court 3, she saw Trish and Rob Lester sitting in the corner and she nodded to them in greeting. Damien Ross was there, in his usual spot near the door, and Brooke was back in the courtroom, wedged between Marina and one of the Santino cousins.

The jury filed back in. The instant Anita saw two of the female jurors crying and several of the others looking at their shoes, sheepish and awkward, she guessed the result.

The foreman was a man in his fifties, square-bodied and square-headed. The muscles under the skin of his jawline were tensing in a combative rhythm, ready for an argument.

When the foreman pronounced the words, 'Not guilty', Anita heard an agonised wheezing sound behind her. Without needing to turn and look, she knew it was Damien Ross.

Murmured conversation bubbled through the courtroom, but cutting loudly across all of it was Marina's braying voice repeating, 'Yes. Yes. Yes.'

John Santino was crying, blowing kisses to his jubilant family. His emotional display was punctuated a couple of times by a strange vocalisation—a grunting 'ha' of satisfaction. Exactly like the sound the eyewitness had recalled when Kendra Bartlett fell from the overpass.

Hugh Warby appeared to be disappointed, ashamed, but unsurprised. Gilbert Woodburn looked smug, but rather tired. Even though he shook hands with John Santino, he broke contact with his client as soon as he politely could and busied himself with collecting up his folders. Anita liked to imagine Woodburn felt a tiny bit regretful, maybe a tiny bit grubby, for using his powers to release this dangerous creature back into the world. But probably not. And anyway, that was the system they worked in and the barrister had just been doing his job.

Anita stayed in her seat to watch Santino stride out of Court 3, with Marina on one arm and Brooke hooked in close on the other side. Brooke maintained a fixed smile, almost robotic, as if she was somehow mentally distant from this moment. It was impossible to read her expression with any certainty.

As the trio walked close to where Brooke's parents were sitting, Anita couldn't quite hear but she could see Trish Lester bleating, 'Brooke. Sweetheart, talk to us. Please. Brooke.'

Santino swept the pregnant young woman away like a prize he'd won, and that was when Brooke's mother dissolved into shuddering tears, slumping forward as if all her vertebrae had come apart. Rob Lester had to hold her upright on the bench.

Damien Ross sat near the exit and kept his eyes pinned on Santino, holding the man to account with the fierceness of his gaze. Santino turned his head and, for a brief moment, he smirked at Damien. He smirked.

Outside, with all the commotion of courthouse steps interviews and jostling camera crews, Anita was busy doing her job, covering this as the big story it surely was, and she lost sight of the Lesters and Damien. But once John Santino and his entourage had driven off in hire cars, the crowd dispersed quickly, leaving only the usual population of the street—a few legal bods and office workers going about their business.

Anita hung around Phillip Street, trying to get hold of Rohan. He would've heard the result but she wanted to talk to him anyway. As she walked around the side of the courthouse building, leaving another voice message, she noticed Damien Ross slouched against the sandstone wall, weeping helplessly, not caring that passers-by were gawping at him.

Anita decided not to waste time with introductions—he would've recognised her as part of the journalistic pack.

'I'm so sorry about Kendra.'

He nodded, polite, but not interested in hearing platitudes.

Anita launched straight in. 'Three months ago, my friend Stacey was killed by her estranged husband, straight after he'd shot her kids.'

'Fucking hell.'

'Yeah.'

'I'm very sorry,' Damien said. 'Did he go to jail?'

'No. He shot himself.'

'Ah.'

'Shame John Santino didn't do the world the same favour.'

Damien scrunched up his mouth, relishing that image.

'Then again,' said Anita, 'it would've been satisfying to see him go to jail.'

Damien nodded and Anita leaned against the wall next to him, sliding her laptop bag down between her feet.

'I'm Anita, by the way.'

'Hi, Anita.'

She let a silence go by and then said, 'I've spent a lot of time going over and over what I could've done to keep my friend safe.'

'Ooh yeah,' Damien sighed.

'Me and another good friend—we didn't know how to help Stacey. Whenever we asked questions, she just retreated further away from us. I'm not sure if we helped or made it worse.'

'Right. That's the trouble.'

'The thing is, Kendra was so fucking brave. She left the coercive dickhead who'd taken her prisoner. She was coming to find you.'

Damien shrugged, eyes swimming with tears. 'I should've answered the phone.'

'He was already tracking her by then. And anyway, anyway, please don't blame yourself. John Santino is the fiend in Kendra's story. Don't you siphon one drop of blame off that guy and soak it into yourself. Save all your rage for him.'

Damien pulled a face. *Maybe you're right.*

'Look, Damien, I don't know you, but I know a lot about the background of this case, and I watched you in that court. You were a wonderful friend to Kendra.'

Damien swayed his head from side to side, not accepting that.

'Yes. Yes, you were.'

Damien started sobbing again, but more in grief than rage now.

'Would it be really weird and inappropriate if I hugged you at this point?' Anita asked.

Damien spluttered a laugh. 'I work in the theatre. We're forever hugging each other.'

So on the Elizabeth Street footpath, Anita wrapped her arms around Kendra's friend.

FIFTEEN

WHEN THE SANTINO VERDICT CAME UP ONLINE, PAULA thought she would be ready for it. Anita had prepared her for the possibility that the case had careered out of control, but still, the news hit her like an unexpected shove and she had to hang on to the edge of her desk to keep her balance.

And then there was the voicemail from Anita, describing the way Santino had smirked as he strolled out of the courtroom with his arm hooked around his pregnant girlfriend.

Driving home from the surgery that day, Paula reminded herself not to give in to catastrophic thinking and jump to the worst prognosis for Brooke Lester.

John Santino had killed his previous girlfriend and then lied about it, but he might now regret what he'd done. The shock of Kendra's death, followed by the scrutiny of the trial, could render him less of a danger to his current girlfriend. And maybe his sister—manipulative as she was—now had the measure of her brother and would hold him in check in the future.

There must also be hope the new baby could ease things. Paula had seen that happen in the past when patients were entangled in family conflict. The arrival of a baby sometimes softened hard edges and led to a negotiated peace.

When Stacey was heavily pregnant with Cameron, she and Paula used to meet up at Enmore pool.

'I love floating this giant belly in here,' Stacey said. 'The water holds up the weight and gives my tragic swollen ankles a break.'

Gliding along, swishing from side to side like a happy dugong, Stacey chattered about how excited Matt was about the baby.

For a long time before this, Paula had been worried about Matt—his childish jealousy, the moodiness that could contaminate the air around him. On a couple of occasions, Stacey had confided in Paula about some cruel thing her husband had said to her. But he was always torn up with remorse afterwards and Stacey understood that the eruptions of meanness sprang from Matt's insecurity, so she was confident she could help her husband find his way. Paula heard stories from mutual friends who'd witnessed him verbally abusing Stacey, but Matt was always careful not to do it in front of Paula or Anita. He was too canny for that.

In the pool, Stacey let herself hang, suspended in the deep water, eyes scrunched against the sting of the chlorine, and smiled. 'Matt's going to be a great dad,' she said.

And it was true that Matt took to fatherhood surprisingly well for a man who had always seemed so infantile himself. From the start, he was devoted to the kids—energetic, playful, more upbeat than Paula had ever seen him.

There were photos Paula still had in a folder on her phone: Matt with Poppy on his shoulders and Cameron swinging like a monkey off his outstretched arm; another shot of Matt and both kids asleep in a happy tangle on the sofa. No one who looked at those photos could imagine that man would pursue his two children through a house and shoot them in the back of the head.

Halfway between the medical practice and home, Paula pulled over to the side of the road, not sure she was safe to drive.

Twice during the last week, Paula had driven past Brody Ferguson's school at three-thirty in the afternoon. There were so many vehicles and people around at pick-up time, no one would notice one more car proceeding slowly past the school gates. The first time, she spotted Brody among the pack of kids before he trotted out to meet his grandmother. Paula smiled and absorbed the immediate calming effect, like an infusion of a wonderful drug that someone should've invented. The second time, Rochelle was the one waiting at the gate to meet her boy and that was even better—to see the mother and child together and safe.

This afternoon, it was too late for school pick-up time and, anyway, it felt creepy to drive past the school or the Ferguson house again. She considered parking near the day spa where Rochelle worked. Paula had done that one morning—hopped out of her car, wandered by the shopfront and glanced in to see Rochelle at the front counter chatting to a client. Luckily Rochelle hadn't noticed her, but even if she had, Paula could easily have made a fancy-seeing-you-here face without making the woman uncomfortable. Through the swirly mauve signage on the plate glass window, Rochelle had appeared cheerful, strong, calm, and that was consoling to Paula.

Even so, she knew she had to stop this behaviour. Instead, she drove straight home and made do with visualising Rochelle and her son, alive and safe.

~

For a couple of days, Anita was flat out writing newspaper stories and doing radio and TV interviews about the trial, and Rohan would've been busy too. He kept missing her calls, then sending apologetic texts in reply. She would suggest a time and place to meet but he would apologise—he hadn't seen her text until it was too late. When she tried to get their usual text banter happening, Rohan would always answer but in brief, flat messages that tied off the thread. This wasn't ghosting—he answered every message, always in a friendly or at least polite tone—but he definitely wasn't communicating in a way that assumed any intimate connection between them. Finally, she had to face the fact he was avoiding her.

Had he suddenly realised he wasn't interested anymore? Had he grown annoyed by her constant questions about the Santino case? Had he decided that a police detective and a journalist who covered criminal trials was a bad mix? Had he secretly been in a relationship all along? Married even? Had he simply gone off her and so he was dousing her in politeness until she floated off? Was he trying to give her the message as painlessly as possible? Rohan was a considerate guy, so that was the kind of thing he would do. Had he fallen for someone else recently?

Were he and his new girlfriend lying in bed right now, snorting with laughter about what a hopeless joke Anita was?

Anita knew she could spiral into paranoid, self-lacerating thoughts for an impressively long stretch, but the last few months had made her impatient about indulging in shit like that, anything that wasted time or love or energy. She had become more likely than she'd ever been to say, 'Fuck this,' and cut through to the centre of things.

She drove to Rohan's apartment in Alexandria and hit the buzzer outside the building entrance.

'It's me,' she said to the intercom panel.

'Oh. Oh hi.' His voice was tinny through the speaker. 'Come up.'

Anita climbed the flights of stairs in big strides, three at a time, like a little kid trying to feel powerful, and quickly reached Rohan's floor, where she found him standing in the open doorway.

'Come in,' he said.

But she stayed outside on the landing, still puffed from climbing stairs with giant steps. 'Have you been avoiding me? Am I going crazy?'

'You're not crazy. I have been sort of avoiding you. Come inside.'

Anita stayed where she was. 'Is it because you've gone off me?'

'Not at all. No. God, no. I've just been . . . Look, the way that trial went—I shouldn't've let it get to me, but it did. I wanted us to put him away and we didn't and now—shit. Look, when I feel like I've failed at something, I just—aagghh . . .'

'You shut down and go to ground instead of sharing it with your girlfriend?'

'Yes. I know it's not ideal. Please come inside, Anita.'

She shook her head. 'You seemed perfect. But of course—I mean, of course everyone has flaws.'

'Yeah. I'm definitely not perfect.'

'And this—what I'm seeing now—is this your main flaw? You clam up and won't engage if you feel bad about something?'

He nodded.

'I guess that's not so bad,' Anita said. 'Plus you admit this flaw and you'll talk about it, so it's not even that bad.'

Rohan shrugged. 'That's not for me to say.'

'I'm saying that if this is the worst thing I can expect from you, it's pretty tolerable as flaws go.'

'Well, okay. Good. Great.'

'But as long as you know that I can spin myself up into an anxious hissy-fit if I imagine someone—for example, you—is thinking something bad about me and they won't say it.'

'I get that,' he said. 'And I'm sorry for contributing to any anxiety.'

'So your clamming-up thing with my paranoid thing—that's not a good mix.'

'No. But I think we can handle it. Would you like to come inside?'

'Yes, I would like to come inside.'

When they walked down the little hallway into the living room, Rohan reached to put his arms around Anita but she took a step back.

'Sorry,' he said. 'You don't want me to touch you?'

'Not quite yet. Not while I'm still upset about the things I imagined you were doing—for example, laughing about me with your new girlfriend.'

'Which I wasn't doing. And there is no new girlfriend.'

'Right. But it's like when someone is horrible to you in a dream and you still feel cranky about it when you wake up. The imaginary feelings need time to settle. Like a cooling pond in a nuclear reactor.'

'A cooling pond in a nuclear reactor.' Rohan pulled his mouth down to fight off a smile.

'Yes,' said Anita, but she couldn't stop herself grinning. 'There's a requisite period of decontamination.'

'Oh, is there?'

And then they both spluttered into laughter, much more laughter than the moment warranted, releasing a little of the tension that had built up in the last weeks and the weeks before that.

The sex that night was good. They were slightly more self-conscious and courteous with each other than usual, but it was still better than the sex Anita had ever had with anyone else.

Afterwards, lying there together, Rohan rested his hand gently on the spot where her ribcage stopped and the soft part of her belly started. She put her hand on top of Rohan's, holding it against her skin. She wanted to remind herself that a man could hold a woman's body with tenderness. She didn't explain what she was doing, but she figured there was a good chance he understood anyway and was considerate enough not to diminish it by saying anything.

*

The next Sunday, Anita and Rohan decided to catch the ferry to Manly—aiming for a restorative day of inhaling the ocean, walking along the wintery beach, stuffing their faces with burgers—and they invited Paula to join them but she said no.

Anita was still worried her friend might be shaken by the Santino verdict, especially after Anita had persuaded her to invest emotional currency in the trial, building up expectations of a satisfying result.

Paula had sounded okay when they talked on the phone, but Dr Kaczmarek could always bung on that calm doctor voice, so Anita remained uneasy.

Change your mind and come to Manly with us today. A xx

Don't be silly. I'm fine. Go and have a delightful day with your lovely man. P xx

And they did have a delightful day. And he was a lovely man.

Walking back towards the ferry wharf at the end of the afternoon, Anita said, 'I think our restorative outing was exactly what we needed.'

'I agree,' said Rohan.

'But look, I gotta tell you I feel a bit guilty about having a lovely time when—y'know . . .'

'When so much horrible shit has happened?'

'Yes. And you need to know that whatever is going to happen with us, Paula is a huge priority for me—I mean, I can't just . . .'

'No, no, I understand,' he assured her. 'You've got to take care of your friend.'

She halted abruptly on the crowded footpath in order to kiss him, causing a minor pedestrian pile-up. He kissed her ardently, but at the same time steered her out of the path of an oncoming power-walker with the assured grace of a ballroom dancer.

When they stopped kissing long enough to come up for air, Anita urged him, 'Let's always be open, please—let the air get to things so they don't go all festy and putrid.'

'Mmm, festy and putrid,' Rohan said with jokey growl of lust.

There were delays with the ferries, so they had to sit on the slippery gloss-painted benches and wait ages for the next one. But in their contented mood, that felt fine, as if it was happily prolonging their excursion rather than causing irritation.

Sitting there, the two of them agreed that they should, sometime soon, introduce each other to their respective families. There was much discussion over how to go about this. The Delgado and Mehta families presented different issues, requiring different manoeuvres. Rohan's strategy would be to introduce Anita to his sisters first, then allow them to talk her up to his parents, before the eventual parents/new girlfriend presentation. With the Delgados, Anita's favoured tactic was the surprise meeting—bring Rohan to a large family gathering unannounced. All her relatives would be smitten by him and fall over themselves to be the one Rohan liked best. Thereafter, Anita's mother would take credit for having identified him as a much better man than the usual losers her daughter chose.

On the ferry back across the harbour, Anita stuck her head over the side and let the chilly salty air cuff her around the face in a way that felt wonderful. She was slightly windburned, full of food, pleasantly weary from walking on sand and talking earnestly and having a lot of sex in the last few days.

Anita headed back to her own apartment, alone, in order to get a decent night's sleep. As she flopped on the bed, she made a mental list of bushwalks she and Paula should do together, music gigs they must book, restaurants they could try. She wouldn't allow her relationship with Rohan to create any separation from her friend, not ever and especially not now.

SIXTEEN

PAULA HAD A MONDAY MORNING OF TREATING THE VERY old and the very young.

She placed the stethoscope on the ribcage of a three-year-old girl with bronchitis, apologised to her for the coldness, then listened to the air sighing in and out of the tiny lungs.

She examined the raw, vulnerable toes of an eighty-year-old man with peripheral vascular disease, then talked through the management options with him as gently and candidly as she could.

She swabbed the perfect, almost translucent skin on the arm of fifteen-month-old baby having his MMR booster. Paula let the baby wail and glare at her, so the infant's sense of betrayal about the needle was directed at the doctor rather than his own mother. He quickly settled and glued his little body to his mother for protection. By the time they left the surgery, Paula did manage to elicit a wary smile and a finger-scrunching wave from the baby.

When Paula slipped out to the kitchenette to make tea, she noticed two missed calls from Anita. As she waited for the kettle to boil, the phone vibrated again, with *Anita* on the caller ID, and this time Paula answered it.

'Hi, lovely,' said Paula. 'You okay?'

'What's a placental abruption?' Anita asked urgently, garbled. 'If a pregnant woman has an abruption, what does that mean? That's bad, isn't it? Does it mean—fuck . . .'

'Take a breath, Anita. It's when the placenta comes away from the wall of the uterus.'

'It's caused by trauma, yeah?'

'Can be. Not always. But yes, sometimes it's from abdominal trauma, like a car accident. Why are you asking? Has someone—'

'Brooke Lester. She showed up at Royal Women's last night bleeding. She rang her mum and dad, or the hospital did—I'm not sure. Anyway, the parents called Rohan from the hospital and they told him she'd had an abruption.'

'How serious? Did she lose the baby? Did they have to—'

'Hang on a sec. Rohan's talking to someone right now about that. Hang on.'

Paula stood in the kitchenette, listening to the burble of voices in the background of the call. She could vaguely make out the sound of Rohan talking to someone on another line and Anita interjecting with questions.

It was a long time since Paula had done obstetrics, but she'd never forgotten a case she'd observed during her residency—a baby stillborn after the mother had been injured in a car smash. She reminded herself that most babies survived an abruption and mothers almost always did, unless the injury was severe, unless a lot of blood had been lost. Paula ran her hand rhythmically back and forth along the curved laminate edge of the benchtop to calm herself.

Eventually Anita came back on the line.

'Sorry about that. Good news: Brooke's okay. She needed a blood transfusion and they had to do an emergency caesarean. Shit—sorry, I need to go. Have to take this call.'

'Wait. The baby? Have they said if the baby is okay?'

'I'm not sure.'

Paula heard more indecipherable talk with Rohan, then Anita came back to say, 'Yes, both okay, apparently. Let me find out more and I'll ring you later.'

During her afternoon appointments, Paula kept her phone on silent but face up on the desk. That way, if a call came in from Anita, she could excuse herself and take it.

This urgency, the electric current running through her, the need to stay on alert for any news about Brooke Lester—well, it was ridiculous. There was no practical need for Paula to be kept informed and she was of no use to the woman. But for her own sake, Paula needed reassurance. And that was understandable. If a patient were to come in to the surgery right now with anything like Paula's recent history of trauma, she would respond to that person with compassion.

'Of course you feel distressed,' she would say. 'Of course you're excessively focused on this young woman with an abusive partner. Of course you're seeking peace of mind by assuring yourself this woman is safe.'

Paula would never scold or shame such a patient and she

understood she should offer herself the same kindness. But it wasn't easy to do that.

When Anita finally called back, Paula hurried out into the street with her phone, needing more clear air around her than she could find inside the practice building.

'Hi,' said Paula. 'Have you found out any more?'

Anita was steadier now, no longer in that wound-up state she could pitch herself into sometimes. In fact, she was in journalistic mode, laying out information in short sentences, careful to clarify when details were verified and when not. Paula appreciated that—it was like a page of medical notes, composed and precise.

Anita had learned that Brooke had collapsed in the foyer of the Royal Women's Hospital at about eleven p.m. the night before, bleeding heavily. Her parents arrived some time later. It was still unclear if Brooke or the hospital had contacted Trish and Rob Lester. The Lesters then rang Rohan. Anita had previously given them his direct number.

Brooke told hospital staff and her parents that she'd been assaulted by John Santino. She said he had shoved her repeatedly against a table. Her abdomen had been slammed onto the hard edge several times. After the assault, Santino went out, leaving Brooke alone. She experienced severe pain and bleeding, so she caught a taxi to the hospital. Shortly after that, she underwent an emergency caesarean section. The baby was in a stable condition and although Brooke needed a blood transfusion, she was recovering well under the circumstances.

Paula exhaled heavily, prowling up and down the footpath outside the medical practice.

'Has Santino shown up at the hospital?' Paula asked.

'No. But Marina's been in there to see her. By the time the police had a chance to interview Brooke, she denied he ever assaulted her. "I tripped and fell against the table", she's now saying. Rohan reckons she looked really petrified.'

'Can the police do anything?'

'They've got a provisional order to restrict Santino from going near her. Cops don't need Brooke's consent to do that,' Anita explained.

'Well, that's something.'

'Yeah, for sure. But don't know how much use that'll be in the long run—I mean, if she's too scared to make a formal complaint and he fights the order in court and whatever . . . who the fuck knows? How long will the docs keep her in hospital now?'

'Hard to say,' said Paula. 'After a caesarean, if there were no other problems, she'd only be in there about five days. But in this case, probably longer.'

'Okay. So Brooke should be safe in there for a week or so. Get this—the cops reckon Santino's been out boozing every night since his acquittal. Boozing and/or doing drugs. Apparently he can't go near the bar he owns because people hassle him there. Rohan reckons he's been hanging out at some other bar called Protozoa. What kind of name is that for a drinking establishment? Anyway, he's in Protozoa, getting out of it, talking shit to strangers. Maybe he'll do everyone a favour and stumble drunkenly in front of a bus.'

A week after John Santino was acquitted and three days after Brooke Lester's baby was delivered by emergency caesarean, Paula drove straight from work to the Royal Women's Hospital.

Walking through the foyer towards the bank of lifts, she recalled the times she'd been here to visit friends who'd had babies. Cameron and Poppy were both born here.

It was half past seven, towards the end of visiting hours, so the lifts were busy with people heading back down to ground level to leave the building. Paula pressed the button for the floor she figured she would be most likely to find Brooke Lester. She was carrying her medical bag with the stethoscope poking out through the opening. People were more inclined to trust a doctor, more inclined to confide in you.

She told herself she was only there to assure herself Brooke was safe and well, without disturbing the woman.

The lift dinged and a family group stepped out, loaded up with stuffed toys and helium balloons proclaiming *It's a boy!* Paula exchanged a cheerful smile with them. The maternity hospital was such a happy place. Of course, on any given day, there would be a few unfortunate people dealing with a loss or anxiety about a sick newborn or some other painful complication, but for almost everyone, it was a happy place.

When she emerged from the lift on the postnatal floor, there was a flurry of activity in the corridor. Nurses were rushing about, a couple of them running, stopping for quick consultations with each other before dashing off.

One of the nurses turned to Paula with a harried smile. 'Every baby in Sydney decided to be born in the last three hours!' She didn't look unhappy about it, just busy and distracted.

Paula smiled back and called, 'Good luck!' before the nurse hurried away.

Paula wasn't sure Brooke was on this floor and she had no idea which room she might be in. Better not to ask at the nurses' station—they might wonder who she was and it would arouse suspicion. And anyway, the one staff member behind the desk was preoccupied, juggling several phone calls.

The corridors were relatively quiet. Most visitors had left, the dinner service was long finished and the nursing staff were occupied elsewhere for the moment. Paula did her best to look like a regular visitor, a slightly lost one peering at the room numbers.

She walked around for ten minutes but saw no sign of Brooke. If she stayed any longer, it would start to look peculiar. She reached the far corner of the floor and was about to turn and leave when she caught a glimpse of a young woman with blonde hair—blonde hair Paula recognised from the TV coverage outside the courtroom. Brooke Lester moved slowly past the open doorway of the room with the typical stooped posture of a woman recovering from a recent caesarean.

Paula froze, not wanting to be caught gawping. Coming to the hospital was a mistake. An invasion of this woman's privacy. She should leave immediately.

'Excuse me. Are you a doctor?' asked Brooke, standing in the doorway of her room. She pointed at Paula's medical bag, the stethoscope clearly visible.

'Yes. I'm a GP. But not a doctor here,' Paula responded. 'I'm just visiting.'

'Oh right. Sorry.'

'Are you okay? Do you want me to find someone for you?'

'No, no, I'm okay. Well, except for—you know . . .'

Brooke indicated her hand cupping her sore belly and mimed the line of her caesarean incision through her nightgown. But she was grinning too, sending herself up. She was so open, eager to connect, in a way that was hugely winning.

'I don't want to bother them when they're busy.' Brooke waggled her hand in the direction of the nurses' station. 'I've got a question about my baby. You'd know about babies, yeah?'

'Oh—a bit. But if you need a paediatrician to—'

'Can you just check if something looks normal? Do you mind?' asked Brooke.

'Sure,' said Paula. Nerves were fluttering in her chest but she reminded herself: she was simply responding to a request for help.

Brooke beckoned Paula into her room then shuffled across the floor in her sheepskin slippers. It was a private room, fresh and cheerful, with a large window, a rocking chair in one corner and an armchair next to the bed. Pink paraphernalia filled every available surface and a blanket printed with pink and red koalas was wrapped around the newborn lying in the transparent plastic crib.

'Oh my God, she's so beautiful,' Paula whispered. Her instinct was to whisper—reverence for this tiny exquisite creature. 'How old is she?'

'Three days.'

The baby was half awake, squirming in the crib, stretching one body segment at a time, trying out her new limbs now that she was out of the uterus and had more room to manoeuvre. Whatever the trauma of her arrival in the world, this infant looked full-term and healthy enough to thrive.

'See this whitish bit?' Brooke pointed out a pale spot at the centre of the pink curl of the baby's top lip. 'Is that bad?'

'Ah. That's a milk blister from sucking. It's normal, nothing to worry about.'

'But it can't be from sucking. I only just started doing proper breastfeeding and that blister thing was there as soon as she was born.'

Paula had heard that same breathy edge of anxiety in many new mothers she'd cared for over the years. She smiled at Brooke in the warmly reassuring way she had smiled at other mothers. 'It's really nothing to worry about. It'll go away naturally. Some babies are born with that little blister because they've been sucking their thumbs inside the womb.'

'Really? Ha! That's what you were up to in there, little baby.'

Brooke and Paula looked down at the newborn then looked up to grin at each other with the gormless delight of people disarmed by the impossible loveliness of an infant.

By now the baby was fully awake, twisting her head, mouth open, searching for a breast, making surprisingly loud yowling sounds. Brooke jerked with fright.

'Ooh, she wants milk,' she said, lunging towards the baby, flustered. 'This is all so hard. Don't even know how to—oh, shit . . .'

'You can take your time,' Paula suggested. 'Would you rather sit in the chair to feed her?'

'Yeah, might be easier on my tummy.'

'Okay. You make yourself comfortable and I'll bring her to you.'

Brooke sat on the upholstered chair and took a pillow off the bed to cushion her caesarean incision. Once Brooke had undone the top buttons on her nightgown and unclipped her maternity bra, Paula calmly handed her the wailing baby.

She was ready to help the young woman get the baby properly attached to the breast. It had always intrigued Paula that something as essential to human survival as breastfeeding was often so difficult. The difficulty seemed like a biological design flaw.

In fact, it turned out Brooke was managing fine on her own.

'Wow, you're good at that,' said Paula. 'A lot of people have trouble but you're doing so well.'

Brooke looked up, her eyes welling with tears. 'Really? I've been worried this poor kid got a shit deal having me for a mum.'

'What? No way. She's lucky to have you as her mum. You're going to be great.'

'Thank you for saying that.' Brooke sniffed back tears and tucked her head down.

Paula listened to the little sucking noises the baby was making. She recalled visiting Stacey when Cameron was born, watching her feed him, and being astounded by the happily animal nature of the process. Then Paula checked herself—she mustn't let memories of Stacey leak across and distort her perception of the person in front of her now.

The peaceful moment was broken by a groan of pain from Brooke. 'Aww . . . my belly hurts,' she said.

'Ooh, I bet. Breastfeeding helps the uterus to contract back. After you've had a caesarean those contractions can be extra painful. You okay? Want me to find someone to bring you something for the pain?'

'No, no, I'll cope. Thank you, though. The baby likes your voice—it's making her calm. Would you mind passing me some water?'

'No worries.' Paula poured a glass of water from the jug on the bedside table.

'Thanks,' said Brooke, taking the glass with her free hand. 'Shit . . . sorry—am I holding you up? You're here visiting someone?'

'Oh yeah.' Paula was uneasy, not wishing to tell any more lies than she had to. 'I'm here to see a woman I've been worried about. I don't need to rush off this second, though. Have you chosen a name yet?'

'We talked about names ages ago, but now I'm thinking I like Ava. It means breath of life.'

'That's beautiful.'

Brooke pulled a goofy face. 'Sorry, I'm blabbing on and you're being so nice to me and I don't even know your name. I'm Brooke.'

'Paula.'

'Well, thank you for being so nice.'

Then Brooke cooed to the baby, 'Hello, baby Ava, I was spinning myself into a tizz until this lady turned up, wasn't I?'

'Will you have help when you go home?' Paula heard her own voice coming out sounding normal, using the tone and wording she would use with any young new mother. There was nothing in Paula's manner to indicate she had any particular agenda. 'Have you got grandparents on hand?'

'My parents've been amazing since everything went—' Brooke stopped herself from finishing the sentence. 'Mum and Dad want me to live with them.'

'Oh terrific.'

Brooke's breathing shivered with anxiety. 'Nah, well, the baby's dad wouldn't like that.' Then she pulled a grim face. 'Not that he really wants the baby.'

'Ah. Are you sure he doesn't want her?'

'Pretty sure.' Brooke did a sharp impersonation of John Santino. '*I don't want that baby.*'

'I see. So does that mean he'll—'

'But he wouldn't want to let us go either. I don't know. Anyway . . .' Brooke broke eye contact, sinking away from any connection with Paula.

Paula was tempted to fire out dozens of questions but she couldn't risk pushing in a way that might make Brooke shut down.

The baby may have picked up the surge of stress through her mother's body because she fell back from the nipple and started fussing and writhing. Brooke's fragile confidence crumbled and she was on the edge of panic about how to help her whining baby.

'I don't know how to . . .' she mumbled. 'Could you, for a sec, could you . . . ?'

Paula picked up Ava from Brooke's lap and held her high on her shoulder, letting the baby grumble and snuffle into her neck. Paula inhaled the smell—breastmilk sweetness mixed with the scent of the child's delicate skin. Ava did a small burp and quickly settled.

Brooke hauled herself slowly to her feet and shuffled towards the bedside table. Meanwhile, Paula placed Ava on the koala blanket and swaddled her into a tight little parcel, the baby relaxing the way newborns often did when they were enveloped.

'You're good at that,' Brooke observed. 'Bet you're good at gift wrapping.'

Paula smiled. 'I always like it when my patients bring tiny babies into the surgery. It's one of my favourite parts of the job.'

Paula wondered if she'd been too reticent a moment ago, if she'd missed her chance to coax the young woman into talking about her situation. Now Brooke seemed keen to change the subject, trying to sound light-hearted.

'I feel a bit embarrassed about scoring this fancy private room,' she said, as she poured herself another glass of water. 'It's only because I had a blood transfusion. Because I had a—um . . .' She swirled her hand over her belly, searching for the word.

'An abruption?' Paula offered.

'That's the one. Turns out the trick is: bleed enough and you score a private room.'

'Do they know what caused the abruption?'

'Oh . . . I got—I landed against a table pretty hard. A couple of times—well, three times. Anyway, the doctor reckons I've recovered really well. And my baby wasn't affected in the end and that's all I really care about.'

Paula kept her mouth shut. She couldn't appear too nosey. And she shouldn't launch into a lecture on coercion and abuse.

As Paula gently lay baby Ava in the crib, Brooke eased herself back into bed, worn out by pain. But she smiled as she gazed at her daughter's face through the side of the clear plastic crib.

'I'm really glad I had a girl,' she said. 'Even if she's got Johnny's genes in her, there's less chance she'll turn out like him—because she's a girl. If that makes sense.'

Paula decided to pick up on this chance. 'Brooke, I don't want to pry, but are you afraid of this man, the baby's father? Did he hurt you?'

Brooke shrugged and her face crumpled into tears.

Paula plucked a couple of tissues from the box and handed them to her. 'You shouldn't have to be hurt or afraid. No one should. There are people who can help you. The police can help you take out an AVO, for one thing.'

Brooke shook her head. 'Johnny would hate that. It'd rile him up even more. He's got money and lawyers and he'd fight it. The thing is, sometimes Johnny says he doesn't want the baby, but other times he makes a lot of fuss about how we all have to be together and he won't—I mean, I think he'll settle down in the end and I'm hoping it'll be okay. Hopefully he'll love her when he sees her. I hope so.'

So much hoping. Paula wasn't convinced hoping was going to be enough to keep this young woman safe. But there was no point pushing her or bombarding her with information about John Santino. Brooke was essentially open-eyed about the man with whom she was entangled. Her survival tactic, for now, was to yield power, to endure and to hope. She couldn't envisage any other safe path.

'Hey, look,' said Paula. 'Ava is fast asleep, sucking her thumb. Very happy.'

'Oh yeah,' said Brooke, managing a wan smile. 'That's how she got her little milk blister.'

'You need a nap too. First bit of advice I give all my patients when they're new mothers: you sleep when the baby sleeps.

Forget all the jobs around the house, forget all your worries and have a snooze.'

Brooke laughed and did a little mock salute. 'Whatever you say, doctor.' Then she flopped back against the pillows, looking so vulnerable and too young to have this many burdens.

'Second bit of advice: call your mum and dad,' Paula added softly. 'Ask them to help you. Anyway, I'll disappear now and let you sleep.'

'Thank you, um . . . I've forgotten your name, sorry. Thank you.'

Brooke's eyelids were already fluttering closed, so Paula was able to slip out of the room without any fuss.

SEVENTEEN

THE FOLLOWING DAY, PAULA RETRIEVED JUDY'S BOTTLE OF unused Dilaudid from the locked cupboard in the consulting room, cocooned it in bubble wrap, wedged it in her handbag and took it home. She wasn't sure she would use it. She wasn't sure she would do anything at all.

Her thinking was vacillating constantly. After Ian Ferguson, she had vowed she would never do anything like that again. But she couldn't ignore the fact that Brooke Lester was in real danger from a man who had assaulted women and murdered his previous girlfriend when she tried to leave him. That man had almost killed Brooke and their unborn child, and he would almost certainly not allow the young mother and baby to slide out of his control. There was no guarantee the authorities could protect her, especially if fear kept her silent.

Two ideas were suspended in Paula's head simultaneously:

It would be wrong to use her knowledge of the situation and her skills to intervene.

It would be wrong, given her knowledge of the danger this woman faced, not to use her skills to intervene.

Near the medical practice, there was a hair salon Paula went to occasionally to have her split ends trimmed. She avoided that place and walked into a salon where no one knew her. On this Friday afternoon, there were several women having foils done or big-night-out hairdos. Was there any chance they could dye her hair blonde right now, even though she didn't have an appointment?

The hairdresser was intrigued by the impulsiveness of Paula's request and, as he smeared her long wavy brown hair with the eye-watering chemicals, he asked a few tentative questions. Paula just smiled enigmatically.

She felt the peroxide tingle and sting as it cooked on her scalp. She had considered using a blonde wig instead, but whenever she'd seen her patients wearing wigs while undergoing chemotherapy it always looked so fake. Any hint of fakery would arouse suspicion. She couldn't risk it. Still, going blonde was a big call. She mentally drafted an explanation she could offer Li-Kim when she arrived at work on Monday morning, leaning on the notion of seeking the boost from a radical change in look.

Paula went home from the hair salon with the stink of the dye chemicals wafting around her head like her own personal toxic cloud. She ate dinner and watched some TV, as if this were any normal Friday night. At nine p.m., she held her head under the shower, then draped a towel across her shoulders and dug out Stacey's old hairdryer from the bathroom cabinet.

Paula had never been much good at doing anything with her hair beyond pinning it up or back, so she watched a YouTube tutorial on how to blow-dry wavy hair straight. Copying the video, she aimed the blast of hot air from the dryer as she rolled the brush through each section until she ended up with more or less straight hair. She was surprised how much further her hair fell down her back once the kinks and waves had been smoothed out.

She gazed at her reflection in the mirror. The straight blonde hair was an alien sight, like a ridiculous wig for a fancy-dress costume. Which in a way it was. She reasoned that John Santino would be more likely to chat to her if she turned up looking a certain way, and straight blonde hair was one component of the look. She was a good ten or fifteen years older than the women he was usually attracted to but hopefully that wouldn't matter—she wasn't trying to seduce the guy, just hook his attention long enough to start a conversation.

She dug out a pair of stiletto shoes she hadn't worn for years and found a tight, low-cut top that fitted the look. She didn't own anything like the pencil skirts Santino favoured, so she had gone out and purchased one in her lunchbreak.

With the outfit on and the long straight blonde hair loose around her shoulders, Paula resembled one of those lookalike mannequins police set up on street corners to jog the memories of passers-by, to help an investigation. Dr Kaczmarek was now a mannequin of Kendra Bartlett and Brooke Lester. But she wasn't trying to solve a crime. She was contemplating committing a crime in order to prevent one.

She took an Uber to a busy corner in Surry Hills, and from there she walked the four blocks to Protozoa. It was too chilly a night for a short skirt and pantyhose, and she'd forgotten how uncomfortable very high heels could be, pitching her pelvis forward, pushing too much weight onto the balls of her feet and chafing the skin into blisters within minutes. There was an additional degree of difficulty walking in the pencil skirt, which only allowed for small, restricted steps.

According to the information Rohan had given Anita, Protozoa was where John Santino had been hanging out since his acquittal. Because it was unconnected to his own businesses, the place afforded him some anonymity.

As Paula walked down the stairs from the street and into the basement bar, she reminded herself that this was only a reccy, or possibly a practice run for something she might eventually decide not to do at all. She could pull out of this trajectory at any moment.

Protozoa was a dark rabbit warren, with a few tables near the bar and booths tucked along the walls. Business appeared slow at ten-thirty on a Friday night. It was one of those places that had so little trade, you could only assume it was a front for illegal transactions. The dim lighting went some way to concealing the disgusting interior, but the fuggy smell—a soup of beer, cheap cola syrup in the mixed drinks and body odour—was hard to disguise. Every surface was slightly sticky and Paula's shoes made a wet *thock* sound with every step she took on the tacky floor.

The music coming through the sound system was an incongruous playlist of old rock anthems, poppy dance tracks and sentimental ballads. It covered over the fact that there wasn't much in the way of sparkling conversation happening in the place. Once Paula's eyes adjusted to the gloom, she noticed there were several patrons drinking alone, scrolling through their phones. Even the half-dozen people sitting in pairs were sucking on their drinks in morose silence or engaged in sporadic, awkward dialogue.

Protozoa was a gobsmackingly sad establishment. Presumably the owners had fancied the sound of the word when they chose it as the name without investigating the meaning. In fact, 'a single cell parasitic microbe' accurately captured the microscopic life breeding on the fixtures and furniture inside.

Paula felt self-conscious as she walked between the tables. Luckily, the new hair, shoes and clothes helped—a costume to play the role of someone who would feel confident about strolling into a bar like this alone.

She made a show of scanning the place, as if looking for someone she knew, before she fronted up to the bar. She ordered a bottled beer, on the basis that a sealed commercial product was the thing least likely to be contaminated by the E. coli which clung to every surface.

Taking the beer to one of the small round tables, she took off her warm jacket and sat down, crossing her legs in the braided, vampy way which was the only possible position in such a tight skirt. She tugged her top a bit higher on her shoulders, self-conscious about the two centimetres of cleavage.

Her phone was a handy prop—checking messages was a way to keep up the performance that she was waiting for someone who was late. Even so, she was conspicuous. Within ten minutes a guy sidled over and stood a metre away until she eventually looked up. He was only in his late forties, but already alcoholism had mottled his face with enlarged blood vessels and his abdomen, tight with ascites fluid, was stretching the front of his T-shirt.

He stood there smiling at Paula. Was it a come-on smile? Too hard to decipher in the low lighting.

Finally, he said, 'Hi there. Are you, uh . . .' The guy didn't even have enough confidence to finish whatever pick-up line he'd planned to use.

Paula jumped in quickly. 'I'm waiting for my boyfriend.'

He showed her the palm of his hand to indicate he would leave her alone, then he sauntered over to the bar, as if that had been his destination all along.

Paula felt a swell of pity for the man. What a miserable, exposing business mating rituals could be. She glanced around the room and wondered if the solitary individuals were waiting here for their dating app prospects and if the awkward couples had arranged to meet via a dating site but things weren't going well. Paula knew the basics of the current dating world, thanks to her patients' stories and the media, plus Anita's vivid tales of misadventure, but it was all so far from Paula's own experience, she felt like a naive observer from another era. Early on, she'd had two proper boyfriends—one at school and one in her first year at university—but soon after that, she and Remy became a couple, when they were both only twenty. Which meant Paula had never had to deal with the shuddering vulnerability of the whole dating palaver.

She made the beer last for twenty minutes, then headed to the ladies so she could survey other corners of the bar on the way there and back. She couldn't see Santino anywhere.

She bought a second beer, read a few articles on her phone, scanning the tables and booths every now and then, as if looking for someone she knew. After another fifteen minutes with no sign of Santino, she gave up and walked out into the street.

Maybe he'd stopped coming to this bar. Maybe this whole idea was a stupid mistake.

The following night, she went back to Protozoa. She wore the same outfit but with a different top so her return appearance might be less obvious. This time she chose a corner booth which offered a good view of most areas of the bar. She held her phone to her ear, nodding and murmuring as if in the middle of a call, while she discreetly scanned the faces of the patrons.

When her gaze swept past the fire exit, she spotted him. John Santino. Sitting on his own in one of the booths. Wearing jeans and a polo shirt rather than the suits he'd worn in the TV footage, but it was definitely him.

Paula felt the whoosh of adrenaline through her chest, making her skin prickle, but it was hard to interpret her fight-or-flight response. Was it an aggressive urge to attack this predator? Was it a fear response—the instinct to flee a dangerous man? Or was it panic about her own potential actions? The function of her sympathetic nervous system was too primitive to offer much high-level interpretation. Whatever was going on, she wanted to override instinct and take control of the process.

Santino was drinking a neat brown spirit, maybe bourbon, as he flicked at the screen of his phone. After a few minutes, she observed him conducting a phone conversation with someone who was clearly annoying him. After the call, he was huffing, petulant, and he threw his energy into irritable texting, stabbing at his phone with his index finger.

Paula slid along the booth seat, planning to walk to the bar so she would be in Santino's field of vision, but as she got to her feet, Santino received another text, shoved the phone in his pocket and stalked out of Protozoa at speed.

All through that weekend, Paula kept herself in home detention and barely went outside in the daylight. That way she could avoid questions about her newly blonde hair and steer clear of any regular chat that would throw her off course. She watched a lot of television and ate a lot of toast.

On her third night at Protozoa, Paula was worried the barman might recognise her as the woman who'd been there alone the previous two nights. Maybe he'd assume she was a sex worker touting for business. Then again, that might not be considered a problem at a joint like this. In any case, when she walked down the stairs she clocked a different guy behind the bar, so there was no problem anyway.

She ordered a bourbon and ice. It was Sunday, so the place was almost empty, and she had her choice of spots to sit. She followed her usual routine, feigning busyness with texts and murmured phone calls. There was no sign of Santino and she figured coming here on a quiet night was probably a waste of time.

She did notice one guy—a man with a receding hairline that slid into a pepper-and-salt ponytail tied with a strip of leather. He kept strolling past Paula's booth, trying to catch her eye. She steadfastly avoided meeting his gaze, but that didn't discourage him.

On his fourth stroll past, ponytail guy said, 'You look lonely.'

'I'm waiting here for my boyfriend,' she replied.

'Yeah? That boyfriend's been keeping you waiting a while, yeah? I could keep you company until he shows up, yeah?'

'No, thanks. I'd rather wait on my own.'

She flashed him a steely enough look that he tilted back on his heels then retreated to one of the round tables. But he sat facing her and she could feel his eyes still on her.

Paula was thinking she should go home and never come back to this dismal place. She turned to rummage in her handbag on the seat beside her—partly to avoid the staring of ponytail guy and partly to find a roll of mints to counteract the cloying taste of the bourbon.

'Is that clown bothering you?'

It was John Santino, standing right next to her booth seat. The first thing Paula noticed was that his face was as shiny as Anita had described. Glossy enough that even the dim overhead lamps bounced brightly off his forehead and cheekbones. The man must exfoliate with sulphuric acid and coarse sandpaper to have a complexion like that. Paula couldn't believe she was distracted in a moment like this, thinking about Santino's skin care choices.

'If that guy's creeping you out . . .'

'No, no, I'm fine,' Paula replied. 'I told him I'm waiting for my boyfriend.'

Santino nodded and twisted slightly away from her. Paula worried that she'd discouraged him too much and squandered her chance. But a moment later, he swung back with a charming smile.

'So are you really waiting for your boyfriend or are you waiting for a guy who isn't a loser to say hello?'

Santino turned the smile up full bore, like a naughty but adorable kid. This must be his standard manoeuvre and Paula could see how it might work on some people. She responded with a slight smile, wanting to keep him talking. But then she found that meeting this man's gaze made her nauseous, so she quickly looked down at the tabletop.

He interpreted that as a coy, flirtatious move by Paula—an invitation of sorts. So now he sounded even more confident. 'I mean, I'll cruise out of your way if you like . . . or I could buy you another drink.'

Paula froze. This was exactly what she had hoped might happen, but now that she found herself here she felt too panicky to follow through.

'Oh, I get it,' muttered Santino, suddenly sulky, offended. 'You saw me on TV. That's why you won't have a drink with me.'

'Sorry? I don't know what . . . Are you on TV? Sorry. I don't really watch TV so I never recognise famous people.'

Santino's mood bounced back again, like a kid who flipped between petulance and exuberance in a flash. 'Cool. You don't watch TV, but I see you do drink—what is that? Bourbon?'

Paula nodded.

'I'll get us a couple more.'

She watched him walk over to the bar. Compared to other men in the place, Santino was attractive in a certain way, with a handsome enough face, meticulous haircut, good jeans, expensive leather jacket hanging off one shoulder, tailored shirt chosen to indicate the well-muscled physique underneath.

He returned to the table with a bourbon for her, a double bourbon for himself. They clinked glasses and Paula sipped at it cautiously.

'Can I just explain,' Santino said, 'that this low-grade place is not my usual style. But I've attracted a bit of media attention lately, so if I want a quiet drink, if I don't want to be harassed, I have to come somewhere like this.' He hooted a little laugh. 'No one I know is going to show up here.'

'Makes sense,' said Paula.

'Gotta say, I'm surprised to see a classy woman like you in Protozoa.'

'Well, my reasons are similar to yours. Don't want to run into anyone I know.'

'I'll pay that.' Santino smiled. 'I'm John, by the way.'

'Hello, John.'

'This is where you say your name.'

'Oh. Well, uh, call me Doc.'

'Short for . . . ?' he asked. 'Or because you're a doctor?'

Paula shrugged.

'Mm. Intriguing,' he said.

Santino wasn't intrigued for long. Being an A-grade narcissist, he preferred to talk about himself and Paula let him rattle on with a self-pitying rave for thirty minutes. The guy was puffed up with outrage at the way he'd been persecuted. Without mentioning the actual crime, he gave Paula his version of the last few months—the way he'd been falsely accused, put through a trial, forced to spend buckets of money, upset to see his family traumatised. Even now he'd been acquitted, people were still giving him shit. And it wasn't just cops and journalists. His own girlfriend was shooting him filthy looks, as if he was some terrible monster, even though he'd been acquitted.

Paula made sympathetic noises. She sipped on her one drink and declined a refill, claiming she'd already had several. But Santino went to the bar and brought back two double bourbons for himself. On top of whatever he'd drunk earlier, the guy was clearly well pissed by now.

As he complained about the way he'd been wronged, Santino drifted away from slick charmer and closer to angry guy.

'There are women out there,' he said, skewering Paula with his hard brown eyes, 'I mean, present company excluded—but there are bitches out there who want to tear your balls off.' He smirked. 'Well, those bitches can try but they don't always get away with it.'

Then he frowned at Paula, registering the look on her face. She realised she must have let some disgust creep into her expression.

'Bad unfair shit can happen,' he insisted. 'Don't believe me? It can happen.'

'I know unfair shit can happen.'

'Too fucking right it can. You were looking at me just now like . . .'

'No, no, sorry if I seemed—it's not . . .' Paula sighed. 'Listening to you got me thinking about some of the stuff I've been going through.'

'Oh yeah?'

Paula had rehearsed the next part in her mind and now seemed the right moment to drop it in.

'My husband died of cancer eighteen months ago,' she said.

'Sorry to hear that. My condolences.'

'Thanks. It was hard. Afterwards, I had killer insomnia.'

'Yeah, tell me about it,' moaned Santino.

'I thought if I didn't get some sleep, I'd go crazy.'

'I know that feeling,' he said. 'All the shit in your head whirling round and fucking round. What's your fix for that? Valium?'

'Wasn't strong enough for me.'

'So what else?'

'Well, because I'm a doctor, I have access to serious drugs. Oxycontin, Vicodin.'

'Handy.'

'Hmm, yes but no. I got addicted—well, dangerously close. In the end, I hauled myself off the opioids entirely. All good.'

Santino nodded, but then he squinted at Paula. He obviously fancied himself as an astute reader of people. 'But what's going on now?'

'Oh . . .' Paula sighed, reluctant, as if he was drawing this out of her. 'A few months ago, my best friend died and I kind of lost the plot. In my bag, right now, I've got a syringe loaded up with Dilaudid.'

'Which is?'

'It's hydromorphone.'

'Sounds intense.'

'Yeah, it's a Schedule 8 painkiller. The thing is, I know if I use it, I'll feel mighty good for a while . . .'

'Like, you're saying it's an excellent high?'

'Ooh yeah,' Paula said with a sly smile. 'Especially if you inject it. You feel so fucking wonderful and then you have the best sleep.'

'Ah.'

'But I don't want to slide back into that. If I go home now, I can't trust myself not to use it. That's why I'm staying out, so I'm not tempted. Hoping I can talk some sense into myself.'

'Right. Right. I get you.' Santino's gaze flicked to Paula's handbag, like a hungry child envisaging a cupcake.

'Excuse me a sec,' said Paula, dabbing at her eyes as if she were on the verge of tears. 'I need to go to the ladies.'

'Sure. I'll be right here,' he said. 'Let's keep talking.'

Paula took her handbag with her as she hurried to the toilets. She hoped her clumsy rushed manner would be explained by the sad tale of loss and addiction she'd just told Santino. It brought her a perverse kind of satisfaction that she was using the truth of her life to draw this man in.

The ladies room of Protozoa was as putrid as you would expect—cramped, with grimy broken tiling, a pervasive smell made up of mildew, urine and acrid cleaning products, rust-coloured leaks down the walls and mysterious puddles on the floor.

Paula stood at the basins and dabbed cold water on her temples and neck to calm down. Faced with herself in the mirror, seeing the blonde hair, she was jolted by images of Brooke and Kendra and then of Rochelle. As she stared at her reflection, her own long hair became Stacey's beautiful hair splayed out on Paula's living room floor soaked in blood. Her heart rate shot up and her breathing accelerated. This was PTSD. This was a kind of insanity. She was in no fit state to make extreme choices. She needed to find some professional psych help. And right now, she needed to go straight home and avoid doing anything crazy.

By the time she'd settled herself enough to head back out into the bar, John Santino was standing up beside the booth where they'd been sitting.

'Hey, listen, while you were gone, I did some thinking,' he said with a seductive smile. 'Staying in this dump is making both of us depressed. Let's go to my place.'

Paula was on the edge of saying no, making an excuse to slide out of there quickly and never come back. Then she saw Santino lift his glass to drain the last of the bourbon, and she noticed the ropy tendons in his wrist. His shirtsleeves were folded back to the elbow to reveal his powerful forearms. Paula imagined those arms heaving Kendra Bartlett over the guardrail and slamming Brooke Lester against a table. She imagined him picking up baby Ava with his strong hands and shaking that tiny body until her head flailed back and forth on her fragile neck.

'Sounds good,' Paula said.

Santino slid his arms into his leather jacket and handed Paula her coat, smiling as if he'd always known she would accept his invitation.

'Is it far?' asked Paula. 'Can we walk? Be good to sober up a bit.'

As they walked the half kilometre to his apartment, Paula found she could manage surprisingly well on the high heels, having grown accustomed to them over the last three nights.

Santino was clearly drunk and at one point he had to grip the edge of a bus shelter to steady himself. He talked nonstop. It was destiny that the two of them had met tonight because they had so much in common. He understood her grief because his girlfriend died around the same time as Paula's husband. Like her, he was nowhere near over it. And then, with all the pressure from the police and the court case and some other shit that was going on in his life right now, he was feeling the pain of it hard.

'You know what I believe, Doc?' He lowered the pitch of his voice, going for a combination of intimacy and profundity. 'I believe there are times when people like you and me—people who've been through a lot—we should go easy on ourselves. You know what I'm saying?'

His gaze kept shooting towards her handbag, as if he could X-ray through the leather to see the Dilaudid inside. Presumably he wasn't aware of how obvious he was being about his fixation on the contents of the bag.

'You do whatever you need to do to get through the dark times, you know?' he continued. 'And if that means sometimes you rely on alcohol or a drug to make you feel good, give you a little bit of peace—well, hey, that's okay.'

He smiled at Paula and she returned the smile. His mind was moving exactly where she had envisaged it would.

It was almost midnight on a Sunday, so there weren't many people around when they turned into the Darlinghurst side street. As Santino punched in the code at the entrance to his apartment building, Paula was relieved to see there was no one around to notice him go inside with a blonde woman.

They travelled up in the lift to the fifteenth floor and Santino unlocked the front door of his apartment, ushering Paula inside with a welcoming flourish.

There was an entrance hall with a chrome and glass side table and a mirror with a chrome frame. The hallway was otherwise a dark tunnel, swathed in charcoal carpet and black-on-black wallpaper—matte black background with shiny black embossed circles on top.

Turning the corner out of the hall, the apartment opened up into a huge space, with the kitchen and living room looking out over the night cityscape through floor-to-ceiling windows. The place must be worth a packet—paid for by his family, according to Anita.

The interior was a symphony in black, white and chrome. Two white leather sofas, black high-gloss kitchen, glass-and-chrome dining table with white leather chairs. There was another large mirror—how clichéd a narcissist could this guy be?—and the only artworks were a couple of enormous chiaroscuro photos of naked women.

Santino's face, its surface as glossy as his apartment, had settled into an expression of expectant smugness about his home. Paula made the impressed 'mm' noise she knew he was expecting.

'Cleaners haven't been this week,' he said as he darted about, kicking a few items of clothing into a corner and sweeping takeaway containers into a cupboard. Otherwise the place was pretty neat, or at least uncluttered, with lots of hard, bare surfaces. The opposite of homey. Paula tried to imagine bringing a baby into this apartment.

'Another bourbon?' he asked.

'Yes, please,' she replied.

Santino dumped his leather jacket onto a bench and said, 'Want to take your coat off?'

'Might keep it on for now, thanks. Feeling a bit frozen through from the walk.'

He shrugged. He didn't care about taking another look at her body under her coat. In fact, there was no sexual tension in the room, thankfully—that was pretty clear. His only interest was the Dilaudid. Paula held on tight to her handbag, the shoulder strap slung across her torso.

'I see you hanging on to your bag there, Doc,' he said with a little hoot of laughter.

'Ha. Yeah. Do you live here alone?'

'Well, my current girlfriend's been living here. She's away right now.'

Away in hospital having been assaulted, suffering an abruption, requiring a blood transfusion, now nursing a newborn and too afraid to tell the truth about her predicament.

Santino handed Paula a glass with a generous splosh of bourbon.

'To be totally honest with you, I'm not sure how much longer I can put up with her bullshit,' he said. 'She was sweet when we first got together but, fuck me, she's turning out to be a crazy fucking bitch. Do you mind me saying that?'

She shrugged and Santino chose to interpret that as her being fine with it. He was very drunk now, running off at the mouth.

'Now she's sicking the cops onto me all over again. I mean, *fuck* . . . I don't wanna go into the whole thing with you, but my girlfriend, she's meant to be on my side, right? But now she keeps looking at me like I'm going to kill her or something. And that's because of the bullshit the cops and those other losers put in her stupid head. She's driving me crazy, just when everything should be good, you know? Like, last week, we got into a bit of an argument. Because she was giving me the, y'know, the "You're a bad guy" look—and she got me so riled up . . .'

He flicked his gaze in the direction of the glass-and-chrome dining table. He didn't say anything, but Paula understood why: he had slammed his pregnant girlfriend against the hard edge of that table repeatedly.

Again, there were two compelling thoughts suspended in Paula's head:

This was crazy, and she should make some excuse to leave this place before she did something she would almost certainly regret for the rest of her life.

If she was going to do something, it would have to be now. The time pressure was clear. Because Brooke was still in hospital, no suspicion would fall on her if Santino were to die tonight. If Paula did nothing, it was probable that Brooke would move back in here with him. There was a high likelihood that he would hurt her, maybe kill her. He might also hurt the baby. And then it would be too late for Paula to do anything to keep them safe. She would have missed her chance.

Santino shook his head. 'No way I'm letting that brainless slut tell me what I can and can't do with my own kid. I never know what she's gonna do to me next. The point is, accidents can happen. Accidents fucking happen.' He bunged on a smile, to mark the end of that rant.

'Anyway, let's sit down,' he said. 'Good to chill out, have a drink, not be around losers. Yeah?'

'Uh, yeah.'

Paula sat on one of the white leather sofas and Santino sat on the other, facing her. He tipped his head towards the handbag Paula was holding by her side. 'Because you're a doctor, you can procure the really good stuff, am I right? You can do it nice and safe, pure, proper dose, the whole bit.'

'Well, that's true. But . . .'

'Look, I'm in a place right now where I really need a little bit of the good stuff. But because I've had the cops breathing down my neck, it's been tricky to get my hands on anything. Anything high quality, I mean. And fuck it, I deserve something good after what I've been through.'

Paula nodded and let him keep talking.

'This is what I'm thinking, Doc: you want to resist temptation, you don't want to use that—what's the name again?'

'Dilaudid.'

'Here's an idea: we could share what you've got in there. Half each.'

'Oh, I don't think . . . I mean, the dose I've got is—'

'Okay. Okay. Not worth splitting. Here's another idea: I buy it from you, take the temptation away. I get some of the good stuff, prescribed by a doctor—ha!—and you keep yourself lovely and clean? Everyone's happy.'

'Umm—I don't know if that's . . .'

Santino stood up, prowling the space between the sofas, wanting to position himself closer to Paula's bag. He was jittery, the pitch of his voice rising, like a kid building to a tantrum.

'Come on,' he urged, managing a smile but barely. 'If you don't want it, no point wasting high-quality medical-grade stuff. And I'm doing you a favour if I stop you using it, yeah?'

'No, look, I should probably go home.'

And that was when Santino flared into sudden, intense anger—exactly the way several witnesses had described during the trial. As Paula went to stand up, he lunged down to bellow in her face. 'Do you think I'm an idiot? You came back here with me because you wanted me to give you an excuse to use that stuff. Right? *Right?* I'm right and you know it, you stuck-up bitch.'

Paula had put herself into this situation on purpose and now it was clear she couldn't handle it. She'd been a fool ever to think she was a person who could do something like this. She needed to abandon any plan and get out of there rapidly.

She shrank away from him. 'Please, I'd just like to leave.'

'Do you think I'm a fucking idiot?'

'I don't think you're an idiot. But I want to go now.'

Paula slid her bum along the slippery leather upholstery to shift closer to the door.

'You prick-teasing bitch! Did you honestly think you could go on and on all fucking night about that pure stuff in your bag and then just walk out? Are you trying to make me look like an idiot? Fuck me dead . . .'

'I'm not trying to—look, I'm sorry. I should go.'

Paula clutched her handbag under her arm and stood up, but then lost her balance on the ridiculous high shoes. That gave Santino a chance to grab for the bag. As he went to yank it out from under her arm, she was still holding tight to the shoulder strap. He got hold of the handbag itself and slammed it hard into Paula's face to make her let go. One of the metal corners on the bag whacked into her cheekbone and the force of the blow sent her staggering across the room, but still holding the shoulder strap. Santino was so clumsy-drunk, he must've lost his grip on the smooth leather surface. That seemed to make him even angrier and he let out a growl of frustration.

'Please don't hurt me,' Paula stammered. 'I'll give you the syringe, okay? Please don't hurt me.'

Santino was panting, ready to hit her again, but controlling the urge if that meant he'd get the Dilaudid.

'It's here. You can have it,' Paula said, in the most calming voice she could manage. 'You can have it. You can have all of it.'

She opened her handbag and took out a travel-sized toiletry bag, just long enough to fit the syringe snugly. On the kitchen table at home, she had taken the bubble wrap off the bottle of Dilaudid Judy had asked her to dispose of safely. She had then put on latex gloves to remove a syringe from its packaging and draw up a large quantity of hydromorphone—more than twice the dose considered lethal. Still wearing gloves, she had dropped the loaded syringe into the toiletry bag and zipped it up.

Now she unzipped the bag and held it out to Santino. He reached in and took out the capped syringe. His fingerprints would be on it, but not Paula's.

'You can have it,' she repeated, 'if you let me leave.'

'Yeah, whatever. Piss off.'

'Do you know how to use the syringe?'

'Yeah, yeah. I've done this heaps of times. I might not be a doctor but I'm not a fucking moron. I know what I'm doing.'

'I'm going to go.'

'Good, because you are shitting me to tears, woman. Fuck off.'

Paula slung her bag over her shoulder and hurried down the black-wallpapered hall. She took a silk scarf from her bag and wrapped it around her hand before touching the doorhandle. Once she opened the front door, the fresher, cleaner air of the landing filled her lungs. She wanted to go straight home now and have a shower. But then she hesitated. She needed to know the hydromorphone was going to kill him. It was a huge dose, but what if he didn't inject all of it? What if he'd been using opioids so much, he'd built up a tolerance? She needed to be sure.

Paula shut the door of the apartment loudly, so he would assume she'd left. She was trembling so much, she pressed her shoulders blades against the black embossed wall and slid down to sit on the carpet, staying as quiet as possible. She didn't dare step back round the corner in case he spotted her, but from the hallway, she could hear Santino in the living room.

She listened to him prowl around, muttering, barely audible, but a few words were decipherable—'bitch', 'cops', 'baby', 'fuck-wits'. The next thing she heard was the squeak of leather and the whoosh of air being pushed out of the cushions as he flopped down on the sofa.

There was silence for a few moments and then the sound of him sighing, making little satisfied vocalisations, punctuated by a couple of triumphant 'ha' sounds. This was him experiencing the initial euphoric rush of the drug he'd injected.

Paula leaned against the black wallpaper and listened to John Santino breathe. His respiratory rate dropped quickly but after ten minutes it seemed to sustain at a certain level. The dose in that syringe, assuming he had injected all of it, plus the alcohol in his system, should definitely be enough to suppress his breathing so severely he would die.

Her cheekbone was throbbing with pain where he'd walloped her. Putting her fingers to her cheek, she saw a small amount of blood, where the metal corner had broken the skin. She was careful to wipe her own blood onto herself rather than smear it anywhere in this apartment.

After another ten minutes, Paula heard Santino's breathing grow rougher, rasping slowly in and out of his lungs. A few more minutes on, and she was listening to his Cheyne-Stokes breathing—that laboured breathing pattern, crunchy on the inhalation, with a wet mucosal sound on the exhalation. She'd heard such breathing many times, when elderly patients were in their final days. Many of those deaths had been peaceful in their way, family gathered around, and the final breaths could have a solemn, dignified quality. This wasn't like that.

For a moment, Paula indulged the idea that she wasn't murdering this man. He had willingly taken the drug from her—in fact, he'd assaulted her to get his hands on it—and he had injected it voluntarily. But she couldn't delude herself. She had deliberately tricked him into taking a fatal dose. This was a murder.

John Santino inhaled, weakly, hoarsely, and there was a long silence. Was that the last breath? But a moment later, there was a snuffling sound and another breath. Then finally, the silence extended and he stopped breathing forever.

Paula hoisted herself to her feet, about to turn the doorhandle using the silk scarf. But then she remembered the bourbon glass she'd drunk from. There was very little—nothing, really—to connect her to this crime, to this man. But still, she didn't want to leave any of her DNA lying about.

She found herself creeping back into the main living area—creeping as if the dead man might suddenly wake up and catch her. There he was, sprawled on one of the white sofas, a bright red latex exercise band tied around his upper arm as a tourniquet and the empty syringe fallen from his hand, lying next to his thigh. He was cyanotic, eyes closed, lips blue, with a purple tinge across his clammy face. Even though Paula knew he was dead, she still stopped to watch his chest for a few moments to assure herself there was no movement, no air going into those lungs.

She gulped the last of the bourbon he'd poured for her, shoved the glass in her bag and walked out of that place.

At home, she wiped off the handbag to remove any traces of her blood and his fingerprints. At work the next day, she whacked the bourbon glass against the edge of the sink and dropped the shards of broken glass into the medical sharps bin.

EIGHTEEN

THE MINUTE ANITA WALKED INTO THE DOWNING STREET court building on Tuesday morning, she heard the buzz of talk through the foyer. There was a particular timbre to the gossiping voices—a sign something juicy had happened.

She raised her eyebrows to one of the TV guys, Brad, as he was gunning it back outside.

'John Santino found dead. Yesterday arvo. In his apartment,' said Brad, then he dashed through the doors to join his camera crew.

Anita tucked herself into one of her little secret alcoves on the ground floor where she could have some privacy to phone Rohan.

'What can you tell me? Off the record?' she asked.

Rohan puffed out a breath. 'This really does have to be off the record,' he warned.

'Sure, sure.'

'Looks like an accidental overdose of hydromorphone. We found traces of it in the syringe.'

'Hydro-what?'

'Hydromorphone.' Rohan pronounced each syllable distinctly, as if he was reading off his notepad. 'Heavy-duty painkiller—used for cancer patients mostly, I think, but there are people who use it recreationally. Can be lethal, especially mixed with alcohol.'

'Right, so you think Santino was drunk?'

'Pretty sure the tox report's going to show he was full of booze as well. He'd been drinking at Protozoa for hours the night before.'

'So then he goes back to his place, pissed, and injects too much of the party painkiller?'

'A not-so-tragic accident,' said Rohan. 'Remember, me saying that is so off the record it's in outer space.'

'Of course. Are you considering—I mean, he would've had a lot of enemies . . .'

'No forced entry, no sign of a struggle. And look, I've seen the photos—the guy injected himself.'

'Suicide possibly?' Anita asked.

'Possibly. But did he seem the type to you?'

'No.' Anita felt sure of that, but then again, she was also sure that you could never be sure what was going on in people's heads.

'Nah, look, this was an accidental overdose on top of booze,' Rohan said.

'Yeah, yeah, makes sense. Are you sorry?'

Rohan paused for a moment. 'I'm sorry we didn't get the conviction. I'm sorry he's not sitting in jail. But no, I can't be sorry about this.'

Anita spent the afternoon in the newspaper office, writing up background material on John Santino that could be published now he was dead, plus as much about the conduct of the trial as she thought she could get past the lawyers and into the paper. She kept an eye on the bank of TV screens in the corner of the room. Whenever anything popped up connected to the case, she darted around the desks so she was close enough to hear the soundtrack.

Early afternoon, camera crews had footage of Marina Santino emerging from the Lidcombe mortuary and being bundled into a black car by a clutch of family members.

Marina stopped behind the open car door to address the cameras. She looked wretched, no make-up, face puffy from crying.

'My beautiful brother had finally cleared his name, which makes this terrible accident even more heartbreaking. Please respect our family's need to grieve in privacy.'

Then Marina ducked her head and disappeared into the back seat of the vehicle, hidden behind tinted windows.

Late afternoon, the crews were waiting outside Royal Women's Hospital as Brooke Lester was discharged. She came out the main glass doors in a wheelchair with the baby cradled in her lap, swaddled in a blanket covered in pink elephants. A nurse was pushing the wheelchair while Brooke's mother, Trish, walked alongside, her arms loaded with bunches of flowers and a bundle of pastel gifts.

Brooke kept her head tilted down, cooing at the baby and avoiding the glassy gaze of the camera lenses. But then she lifted her head to say something to her mother and she beamed a smile. Seeing that young woman smile, Anita made a small involuntary sound in her throat—relief, gladness, whatever.

A white Corolla pulled up in the hospital pick-up zone and Rob Lester hopped out of the driver's seat. Trish put the flowers and other items in the boot, then carefully lifted the baby from Brooke's arms and into the newborn car capsule. Meanwhile, Rob ran around the vehicle to help his daughter hoist herself out of the wheelchair. He held Brooke's arm steady as she took cautious post-caesarean steps to the car and lowered herself gingerly onto the back seat next to the baby.

Rob Lester raised his hand, palm open and flat, in acknowledgement of the camera crews. He didn't appear annoyed—in fact, the man was grinning—but he was tacitly requesting privacy.

Anita sent Paula a text.

Hello, lady. Did you see the news? A xx

Yes. I saw. P xx

Good to know Brooke and baby are with her parents. Safe.

Definitely.

Anita was aware that she hadn't seen her friend for almost a week—too long—so a few minutes later, she texted again.

I could make a late movie session tonight?? A x

Yes please.

Anita pushed on with work until late, leaving her with no time to eat dinner before the eight forty-five p.m. movie session. As she hurried up the stairs into the Norton Street cinemas, there was no sign of Paula, so she jumped in the queue at the bar to buy the biggest glass of wine they sold plus a bag of cashews that would have to do as an evening meal.

Anita scanned the crowded foyer looking for her friend.

A woman she didn't know was raising her hand—*I'm over here*—but must've been signalling someone else.

It took Anita's brain a couple of seconds to process what she'd seen, then she whipped her head back to see the waving woman was in fact Paula. With blonde hair.

Paula was grinning, pointing at her newly bleached curls, loose around her shoulders. As they walked towards each other, zigzagging through the crowd, Anita did a pantomime of being surprised and dazzled by Paula's glamour.

Paula laughed. 'Your mouth's hanging open.'

'It looks great,' said Anita.

'Don't feel obliged to say that.' Paula ran her fingers through her new fair hair. 'I still haven't decided if I like it yet.'

'Well, okay, so the reason my mouth was hanging open is just surprise. On account of the fact you've had exactly the same hair since the age of twelve. Until now.'

'I guess I had a rush of blood to the head. You've always done a radical hair change when you need to reboot yourself after heartbreak or whatever.'

'True. I have to come clean with you: it doesn't actually work as a life-rebooting method,' said Anita. 'But meanwhile, I think it looks fantastic.'

Paula shrugged. 'I can always cut it off if I hate it. Ooh, quick, we need to get in there.'

'You can share my bucket of wine,' said Anita, as they headed into Cinema 2.

Once they were settled side by side in their seats, Paula tucked her hair behind her ear and Anita noticed her friend's cheekbone was slightly swollen. There was a large bruise almost concealed under foundation, with a small scabbed area where the skin had broken and healed.

'What happened there?' Anita asked.

Paula's hand shot up to her face. 'Oh, a patient was in a bit of a state, arm kind of flew out and knocked me against a cupboard.' She then bunged on a Liam Neeson tough guy voice. 'Doctoring is a dangerous game.'

'It looks hurty.'

'My professional medical opinion is that it is indeed hurty. But won't scar, luckily. I mean, I need perfect skin to go with my new glamour-puss hair.'

If it were anyone else, Anita would have pushed a bit, challenged them. Is that the truth? Were you stumbling about drunk? Did someone hit you? But there was something about Paula's certitude, her deeply adult assurance, that made Anita feel as if she couldn't question her.

The movie was the species of British bonnet drama usually seen on TV. There seemed to be a lot of lavish period gowns swishing through opulent rooms, sumptuously filmed. Famous actors seemed to be doing a lot of award-worthy acting. But Anita barely engaged with the film. She couldn't stop sneaking looks at Paula's blonded hair and bashed cheekbone. She couldn't stop her thoughts pinging off at wild angles.

After the movie, Paula drove them both to Newtown to find somewhere still serving food so that Anita could obtain more sustenance than cinema wine and nuts. While she wolfed down a kebab and Paula took tiny nibbles on baklava, Anita talked on and on about Brooke Lester.

'I mean, how horrifying is it that she almost died from being shoved against a table.'

'Well, a thick glass tabletop—that makes for a hard edge. It's effectively the same as a blow with a blunt instrument to her pregnant abdomen,' replied Paula.

Anita held her hands to her belly in sympathy. 'But she'll be okay now, won't she?'

Paula reached across to squeeze Anita's arm reassuringly. 'She will. Don't worry. And baby Ava is fine and healthy.'

'Oh, Ava's a lovely name. I didn't know Brooke had gone public on the name.'

Paula smiled. 'I must've heard it somewhere.'

Anita was distracted for a moment, wrestling with the last messy handful of her kebab and wiping the sauce off her chin. 'Tell me this, doctor, would you say there's any chance Santino actually intended to kill himself?'

'Well, I've known of people using hydromorphone recreationally, but I've never come across anyone using it to kill themselves. And anyway, did John Santino seem suicidal?'

'He didn't, no. That's what Rohan reckons too.'

'Ooh, the lovely Detective Mehta.' Paula grinned. 'Let's talk about more cheerful stuff. I need to hear the latest romantic developments with your new man.'

The two women launched into the kind of relationship dissection they'd always enjoyed, flipping comfortably between candour, teasing and earnestness. The conversation felt entirely normal. Bizarrely normal, except that Paula had dyed blonde hair and an injured face and Anita had suspicions running through her head that she couldn't fathom.

The following evening, Rohan went over to Anita's place for a night of easy dinner and telly. They talked, only for a moment, about John Santino's death.

'Hey,' asked Anita, 'in the official statements, did you guys ever name the drug that killed him?'

'Uh, no. We said "an opiate drug", that's all. But I think I told you it was hydromorphone.'

'Yep, you did. I was just wondering where he would've got hold of hydromorphone.'

'Guy like Santino would've had resourceful dealers.'

Anita shrugged and nodded. She figured she must have mentioned the name of the drug to Paula earlier. That would explain how Paula knew.

'And Brooke—she was injured when he pushed her against a table? Like a wooden table or—?'

'No. Glass top on an ugly chrome base,' said Rohan. 'I've only seen photos, but it was definitely glass.'

'But the glass didn't break when he pushed her?'

'Nah, those tables are more sturdy than they look.'

Later, when Anita was curled up on the sofa next to Rohan, her eyes were aimed at the TV screen but her mind was far away, churning through other possible narratives. Then she realised he was looking at her, aware that she was absent somehow.

'What are you thinking about?' he asked.

'You don't want to know.'

'I do. I mean, if you want to tell me.'

'Silly thoughts. Nothing to do with you,' she assured him. 'Labyrinthine female friendship stuff with Paula.'

Rohan did a jokey wince. 'But you know, I can handle it if you want to tell me. In my career, I've seen human beings at their worst. I can take it.'

She shoved him in the ribs with her socked feet. 'I know you can, detective. But I'm fine. If I talk about it, I'll inflate small stuff into a bigger deal than it should be. Have I warned you I have a tendency to do that?'

'You have. And I've accepted that challenge.'

The evening after that, Anita's plan was to keep to herself. Walking up King Street from the bus stop, she passed a bar with half-price happy hour cocktails. She went inside and ordered a margarita. The rush of the tequila coupled with the astringency of the lime and the mouth-puckering hit of the salt seemed to strip away the fuzz in her head so she could think more clearly—well, at least she told herself that was so. She drank a second margarita and then a third.

Anita knew she had a propensity to lodge a thought in her skull and whip it up into something way bigger than the thought deserved to be. It annoyed her that for years she'd wasted so much energy on paranoid fantasies and dangers that didn't really exist. Meanwhile, she'd failed to appreciate the very real peril Stacey had been in. Sure, Anita had been worried about the situation with Matt, but she never ever imagined the catastrophe that had been brewing all along.

The jolt of the murders in the Earlwood house had knocked some clarity into her stupid head, but Anita could still be troubled by irrational thoughts that adhered to her brain cells like burrs. Sometimes she would give in to the anxiety and scurry around to investigate if her fears were founded in any reality, checking and double-checking until she calmed down.

A therapist had once advised her that she should not indulge in such frantic checking, but instead she should just sit with any paranoid notion until it subsided. Anita generally tried to follow that method. But sometimes, like tonight, she couldn't manage it. She needed to march right up to her anxious thought and scotch it once and for all.

She flagged down a cab outside the margarita bar and, en route to Earlwood, she sent Paula a text.

Are you home? A x

Yes. Just watching TV. P x

I'll be there in five mins. A x

When Paula opened the front door, she was wearing track pants, a comfortably sagging old T-shirt and ugg boots. The blonde hair was pulled back in a scrunchie.

'Sorry,' mumbled Anita. 'You're in comfy-at-home-alone mode.'

'Don't be silly. It's great to see you. Come in.'

The two women wandered into the kitchen to open a bottle of wine.

'I've already had dinner,' said Paula. 'But I could make you something to munch on if you like?'

'No. Thanks. No. I'm a bit too churned up in the guts for food.'

'Un-huh,' said Paula and looked at Anita with her worried, caring face.

Anita wasn't in the mood for that benign condescending shit tonight.

By the time they settled on the sofa in the living room, Anita was already pouring a second big glass of wine.

'Go easy,' Paula warned. 'You were already a bit pissed when you got here.'

It was true that the three margaritas had surged through Anita's bloodstream quite forcefully between leaving the bar and arriving here, but she didn't feel like admitting that to Paula.

'I know you think I'm a neurotic,' Anita said.

'What? I don't.'

'You do, and don't insult my intelligence by bullshitting me about it,' Anita snapped back.

'Hey, Anita, you're a bit pissed and it's been an intense couple of weeks. Let's not—'

'I know you think I get a silly idea in my head and escalate it into a huge dramatic thing.'

'Well, you say that about yourself. I mean, I think—'

Anita flapped her hands, wanting Paula to shut up and listen.

'What I'm going to say is absurd,' Anita said, then she stood up so she could pace around the room. 'But I need to blurt out this insane theory in one go, scoop it out of my head and let the oxygen in this room kill it once and for all. Okay?'

'Okay,' said Paula in that patronising, calm-down-you-crazy-person voice of hers.

'First, you told me about your patient—the one who was strangling his wife and she was too scared to leave because he tracked her. Next thing you know, nasty strangling husband dies of a heart attack in your surgery.'

Paula opened her mouth to respond but Anita put up her hand—*let me finish.*

'Not so suspicious, sure, if sixty-something guy has a heart attack. But mighty convenient. Good news for his wife and kid, good news for the world. Anyway, I didn't think any more about that at the time except, y'know, goodo. Couple of months later, I tell you bucketloads of stuff about John Santino—behind-the-scenes intel most people don't know. About his prior assault charges, what he said on the audiotape, the drug abuse, the name of the bar he was hanging out in after the trial, the fact that he assaulted Brooke Lester so she almost lost the baby, almost bled to death. I tell you all of that and then a few days later the guy ends up dead from an overdose of a drug a doctor would have access to. And then, somehow, you seem to know other details I never told you—like the hydromorphone—and stuff *I* didn't even know, like the glass table and the baby's name . . . and fuck, how would you know any of that? So then I find myself thinking: maybe the first guy, the patient, maybe he just carked it in your surgery—natural causes, whatever—but then once you saw how his wife and kid were safe and happy with him dead, that put an idea in your head. It inspired you to—and then, fuck, then I started thinking about that patient from a different angle. In theory, a doctor could have done something, induced a heart attack or . . . I don't know enough about the medical side. Anyway, a doctor could kill a person and make it look like—fucking hell, how wild is that thought, right? I mean, after what happened to Stacey, after some of the conversations you and me have had about killing dangerous men—those were hypothetical conversations. We were being hyperbolic, letting off steam, but now I can't help wondering . . .'

Anita could hear she was blathering, speaking too fast, sounding like a demented person. But she could also hear that Paula wasn't interjecting, wasn't laughing at the ridiculous suggestions.

'You'll say I'm a nutcase,' Anita went on. 'I'm sure you think this is just Anita going off on one of her—Are you going to say anything?'

Paula sounded quite composed in the face of Anita's ranting. 'What do you want me to say?'

'Say it's a crazy idea. Say you didn't kill anyone—or, fuck, say you didn't kill two people.'

Paula stared at the table and exhaled slowly.

'Jesus, Paula, you're scaring me now.'

'Do you want me to tell you what happened?' Paula asked.

'Do I?'

'I don't know. I wasn't going to say anything to you. Not to anyone. Maybe it's better if I don't.'

'Fuck, you can't say something like that and then not finish the sentence.'

'Maybe I do need to tell you.'

Over the next hour, Paula described, step by step, how she killed Ian Ferguson and then John Santino. Along the way, Anita managed to chuck in a few clarifying questions.

'You decided then—on the spot?'

'You signed the death certificate?'

'Did anyone see you go into the building?'

'Am I having a stupid and horrible dream right now?'

But mostly Anita listened, her brain scrabbling to process what she was hearing, her chest too tight to suck in enough air to speak many words at all.

Paula looked like a different person as she told the story. The weird blonde hair was part of it. But her friend was different in a more fundamental way, at a cellular level. Or maybe she wasn't. Maybe she'd always been a woman capable of murdering people in certain circumstances and Anita had been too self-absorbed or too innocent to notice.

In the course of telling the story, Paula outlined her moments of doubt, the moments she had come close to abandoning her plans. She described the day she had resolved to admit everything to Anita and hand herself in to the police. She closed her eyes for a moment as she recalled seeing Rochelle and Brody so happy, explaining how that had changed her mind about confessing.

Paula moved on from the narrative straight into the justifications for what she'd done before Anita had a chance to catch her breath and respond.

'I did what I thought was necessary. I couldn't see any other realistic way to protect those women from serious harm,' said Paula.

'What? Sorry? What? Murder was the only answer?'

'No, no, no. But I looked at other options, other solutions. I checked the facts—that's why I went to see Brooke in the hospital, so I could be sure that—'

'For fuck's sake, you stalked that woman!'

Paula tipped her head, acknowledging that, but then kept going. 'I needed to establish, as surely as possible, if she was or wasn't in danger from John Santino. I mean, look at all the trials you've covered, all the case histories you've been reading. You know the system doesn't always protect women, not a hundred per cent.'

'Well, okay, everyone knows things are . . . So we should—what? We should all think, "Fuck it, let's murder the bastards"? You were so sure killing people was the only way.'

'I wasn't sure,' said Paula firmly. 'No one can ever be sure. I mean, in my job, I've always had to deal with the randomness of what happens to human bodies, the uncertainty, the unknowable stuff. In the face of that—the chaos of it—you try to be logical. I mean, if a patient comes to a doctor with a problem, the treatment can't ever be a hundred per cent the right choice. All you can do is weigh the risks and choose the most effective course of action, accepting it's not ever going to be perfect. I think an imperfect fix is better than doing nothing. Better than sitting back and watching harm done—watching the damage you're fairly sure is going to happen.'

Paula stayed on the sofa with an odd stillness, speaking with an unnerving fluency, while Anita paced and lurched around the room.

'This is so messed up,' Anita said. 'I can't—I can't believe . . . Can you hear the deluded shit you're spouting at me?'

Anita could hear herself sounding strident and unreasonable. Which was crazy, given that Paula was the one killing people. Which was, by most measures, a pretty unreasonable thing to do.

'How come you're allowed to set yourself up as judge and executioner?' Anita was almost yelling now. 'You do know that's wrong and egotistical, don't you?'

Paula nodded. 'Yes. But look, if Matt was standing in front of us now about to kill Stacey, you wouldn't hesitate to kill him to protect her, would you?'

'Well, of course not. But that's not what you did.'

'No one got here in time to protect Stacey and Cameron and Poppy. What if we'd had a chance to kill him before he had a chance to hurt them? If we'd seen Matt walk in here with the rifle, we could have a pretty good guess at what he was going to do. It was the same with Ian Ferguson—he was going to strangle Rochelle to death one day soon, to the extent you can ever be certain of anything. Same with John Santino. I killed those men because it was very, very likely they were going to kill those women. We were too late to save Stacey, but—'

'Stop saying "we". This is you. This is fucking *you*, Paula.'

'Sorry. You're right. It is me. And I'm not trying to convince you to approve of what I've done. I just want you to understand why I—'

'This is such self-justifying bullshit. On this basis—what—you draw up hit lists of dangerous people and kill them?'

'Of course not. But if a situation falls across my path, if a woman is in front of me and she's—'

'No. No. This is wrong. It's so wrong I don't even have enough words for the level of wrong.'

Anita's thought process was frying to a burnt mess. Paula had been thinking about this. She had her wording prepared. But Anita—she'd been caught off guard. She wasn't ready.

'Fucking hell, Paula, I know you don't believe in capital punishment, so how can you possibly—'

'This wasn't about punishment. Or revenge. I don't want revenge. If Santino had gone to jail, he couldn't have done Brooke any harm. Good. Leave him safe in jail—I don't care. I'm not interested in making him suffer. But he didn't go to jail. He was out and I felt I had to stop him doing any more damage.'

'I see,' said Anita sarcastically. 'You see yourself committing "preventative murders" for the good of the community.'

Paula didn't say anything. Anita then tried provoking her into some response other than the weirdly calm prepared-speech thing she was doing.

'Listen to yourself,' Anita snapped at her. 'You think you're so fucking wise. The wise doctor who knows what's best for everyone, better than they know themselves. You're so convinced your judgement is right, even if—'

'I'm not convinced,' Paula countered. 'What happened to Stacey and the kids—Jesus, that shattered any sense I ever had about being convinced of anything or being wise. But I believe that if the stakes are this high—if a woman is going to die—then me not being a hundred per cent sure is not a good enough excuse. It's not an excuse to do nothing.'

'Morally arrogant. Do you get how self-righteous this is?'

'I guess I can. It didn't feel self-righteous when I did it. It felt urgent and necessary.'

'You reckon killing people is the solution? There are other ways to—'

'Are there? They're not working, not fast enough.'

'So you're slaying monsters, are you? You're the good doctor, curing this disease. But what you're actually doing is violating every—I mean, aren't doctors supposed to uphold the sanctity of life?'

'Yes. Yes. And that's what this is about: the preciousness of life—the lives of women and children that anyone could see were at grave risk.'

'Why did you tell me?' Anita bellowed at her. 'Why the fuck did you tell me now?'

'I'm sorry. I shouldn't have. I feel the pressure of it inside me and you're the only person I could tell.'

'Great. Thanks. One of the cosy benefits of friendship. Are you planning to kill any more men?'

'No.'

'Well, I guess I should say "good on you". It'll just be the two murders then.'

Paula said nothing.

'Are you going to go to the police, confess?' Anita demanded.

'No. I'm not. I mean, in lots of ways that would be a relief. But I can't.'

'Because you're a special person, the wise doctor, and the world should simply trust your superior wisdom.'

'No. Not at all. But if I told the police how those men really died, that would be bad for Rochelle Ferguson and Brooke Lester. That would bring more pain into their lives because of something I did. That's not fair.'

'But it's okay to bring pain into my life by dumping this on me?'

'I'm sorry. I should never have told you.'

'Well, you have. So what am I supposed to do now? I'm an accessory after the fact now,' Anita snapped. 'And now I have to keep your murdering secret?'

'It's up to you. For Rochelle and Brooke's sakes, I hope you will.'

'And—fuck—it just hit me! You co-opted me into your preventative murder scheme. I told you so much stuff about Santino and you used that to kill him. You used me.'

'I'm sorry. I didn't set out to do that.'

'You've pulled me into it whether I like it or not. And now you're sitting there talking at me like some strange creature from another dimension. What you did was dangerous and wrong. Tell me you know that.'

Paula gave a slow oversized shrug of her shoulders. 'I know. But I can't regret doing it. Good things came out of those deaths. I'll have to live with the wrongness of what I did.'

'Listen to yourself. Kidding yourself. And you've betrayed our friendship. I don't know who the fuck you are, lady. I'm going to go now. Please do not call me. Stay away from me. I don't want anything to do with you.'

Anita walked out the front door of Paula's house and then sped up until she was almost running, around the corner and three hundred metres up the hill. The shock had burned away the last of the alcohol in her bloodstream and by the time she swung her body into the back seat of an Uber, she was brutally sober.

The next morning, Anita was sprawled in bed, semi-conscious. She rolled onto her belly to squash her forehead into the pillow, hoping to squeeze the thumping hangover headache out of her skull.

As she hovered in that little transition moment between sleep and waking, the conversation with Paula from the night before floated beyond any recall at first, then drifted into awareness as an implausible scene from a dream, then slammed into full consciousness as something that had actually happened, as the new reality Anita would have to handle.

She reached over to her bedside table to guzzle water and swill it around her parched mouth. When she picked up her phone to check the time, she noticed a missed call and several texts from Rohan.

Good morning, gorgeous woman. How are you? Having a sleep-in? Hope so. Rohan xx

Anita let the phone fall from her hand onto the sheets.

She imagined the scene of telling Rohan everything. Anita would calmly admit the truth of what Paula had done, remind him of the context and explain the reasoning behind her actions. She imagined Rohan listening in his respectful way.

Finally Anita would say, 'So in conclusion, Paula did unfortunately kill two people, but please understand she thought she was doing the right thing.'

She imagined Rohan nodding thoughtfully.

'Well, Anita, let's face it, they were horrible men. Having said that, do remind your friend that murdering is frowned upon and make sure she never does it again. Otherwise, it's all sweet,' Rohan would not reply.

Because that scene was impossible.

There was no way she could tell Rohan Mehta and expect him, as a cop and as an honourable person, not to report these crimes. Paula's argument for keeping quiet—that it would only cause distress for Rochelle Ferguson and Brooke Lester if this truth were to be told—that argument had merit. Maybe too, underneath the boiling surface of Anita's anger towards Paula, she wasn't ready to betray her friend.

She then tried to imagine her way through an evening at Rohan's place, the two of them having dinner and Anita not saying a word about the things she now knew. She imagined meeting Rohan's parents, and introducing him to her family, and still not telling him. She imagined him asking her why she didn't see Paula anymore and heard herself making up a lie. Those scenes were all impossible too.

Anita couldn't see a way to maintain a relationship with Rohan while this massive secret was sitting there, polluting the air they breathed together, rotting through the floorboards they stood on. She'd been the one to insist they must always keep their relationship candid and open. She could no longer offer that.

Later in the day, she composed a text.

Rohan, I know this seems like it's coming out of nowhere, but I'm afraid I have to end our relationship. I'm sorry. You're a wonderful man but I'm so messed up with everything that's happened, I need to be by myself and work some stuff out. I'm so sorry. Anita xxx

Immediately her phone buzzed as he tried to call her. She didn't pick up. The phone then dinged with a text.

??? I'm confused. Please can we meet and talk? R

Better not. Easier for me if we don't. Sorry. A x

I'm going to worry about you. Please. xx

This man was no idiot—he would need more of an explanation. And it was ridiculous and cruel to break up with him by text. So Anita agreed to meet at a cafe around the corner from the Downing Street court building at the end of the day.

Sitting at the cafe table, she looked for the shape of Rohan in the clumps of suited men crossing the street. She wondered if she would break, renege on her decision, blurt out the truth, betray Paula.

When she spotted him walking towards her, she felt how much she loved him like a pressure on her sternum, and at exactly the same time, she felt how impossible it would be to stay with him now.

Rohan signalled hello and then paused at the cafe counter to order a pot of tea. When he joined her at the table, she could feel him looking at her searchingly, wanting to understand. That made Anita fidgety, fiddling with the teaspoon, wriggling in the chair, as if by constantly moving, she could avoid being properly seen.

'Are you okay? Has something happened?' he asked, leaning forward, anxious for her.

'No. Well, only the stuff you already know.'

After that, he looked less worried and more wounded. He sat back in his chair, defensive.

'Then I'm confused,' he said. 'Have I missed something? Am I being thick about something that's going on?'

'No, no. I think it's just everything that's happened—I don't know—I thought I was ready to be in a relationship but I've realised I'm not.'

'Is this you wanting to even the score for that time I went to ground after the verdict?' he asked. 'I mean, I realise that was annoying, but I've explained and apologised and I thought we'd—'

'It's not that,' she said.

Rohan looked at her, waiting for more, so she blathered on, reminding him of her initial hesitation, the weird and painful way they had become connected in the first place. She poured blame onto herself: she had warned him she was an anxious, sometimes unstable person. The ending of her last relationship and then the trauma about Stacey had left her more of a mess than she'd acknowledged. Now she'd hit a wall and needed to be by herself to sort stuff out.

As she kept talking, not making eye contact, letting a string of unconvincing phrases tumble out of her mouth, Rohan listened silently, which only rattled Anita more.

She interrupted her own unimpressive ramble to ask, 'Can you please say something? You can say I'm a terrible, scatty, immature person who's toyed with your feelings and—I don't know what you think, but—oh . . .'

'I think you don't give yourself enough credit for being a strong person who can get through this stuff. And yes, okay, the way we got to know each other is connected to very painful things, but I don't . . . Look, I think you could give me more credit as someone who can handle whatever we need to—I mean, I love you, Anita. I think you should trust that more than you seem to.'

Anita dropped her gaze to the table. It was almost unbearable.

'Well, thank you,' she mumbled. 'I think it's a horrible shame that we met at the wrong time in my life. I'm sorry for messing you around like this, Rohan. I'm sorry if I've hurt you.'

She tried to give her tone an edge of finality, to make it clear no further discussion was welcome. She heard him sigh. The sigh sounded confused—understandably, because she was making no sense, given the reality of the relationship he'd experienced. And he sounded offended—also understandably.

'Am I supposed to make you feel okay about hurting me in this mystifying way?'

'No, no, it's not like that.'

'So were you just stringing me along all this time? I don't get it . . . Fuck.'

'I'm sorry.'

'Okay, you've said the requisite number of sorries.' There was a hard clip to his voice—something Anita had never heard before. 'Well, I don't understand it but I have to respect your decision. I might head off now.'

'Sure. Thanks for meeting me.'

Rohan got up from the table, gathered his work files, folding into himself, self-protective, and turned to go. But then he twisted around to gaze at her, suddenly defenceless again.

'Just tell me, Anita, are you really alright?' he asked. 'Is there anything I can do for you?'

The tenderness in his voice almost undid her.

'No. I mean, yes, I'll be okay. I'll find some professional help or whatever. You don't need to worry about me.'

'I will worry about you anyway,' he said. 'Do you mind if I message you occasionally so I know you're okay?'

'Of course.'

He nodded and walked out of the cafe. She could tell by the way he held his shoulders that he was fighting the urge to cry. Which made Anita want to rush out into the street after him and wrap her arms around him, soothe him, beg forgiveness, explain everything, declare her love. But she couldn't do that.

Travelling home alone, Anita pressed her cheek against the window of the bus, glad to let the vibration of the diesel engine rattle through her body.

It was just as well she and Rohan hadn't yet got around to doing the mutual family introductions. That made things easier now. Anita would not have to untell her parents and her brothers about the gorgeous police detective with whom she'd formed her most mature, healthy and joyful relationship ever.

She stumbled in the door of her flat and flaked out on the bed, sobbing like a teenage girl. In the last twenty-four hours she'd lost her best friend and the man she loved. That was bad enough. What made it worse was that they were the only two people who could've helped Anita get her head around what had happened, and now she couldn't talk to either of them.

NINETEEN

THE MOMENT AFTER ANITA WALKED OUT OF THE EARLWOOD house, it hit Paula with glaring clarity: she couldn't stay there anymore. Any good memories of Remy, Stacey or the kids that might be embedded in the house had been pushed out by ugly ones. And because of her own actions, and now what she'd done to Anita, Paula no longer belonged there.

She threw a change of clothes in an overnight bag and drove without any direction or plan, letting the stream of traffic take her, allowing the flow of traffic lights and turning lanes to make the decisions, until she ended up on the highway west out of the city.

As she drove, she found herself saying words aloud—'selfish', 'stupid'—like verbal slaps to her own face. She had vowed never to tell anyone what she'd done, but pressure had built up inside, a feverish need to share her secret with someone, and Paula had given in to that. But dumping it on Anita hadn't lessened the burden. All she'd managed to do was load this toxic information onto her friend, who didn't deserve it. She should never have told her. There was no excuse. It was unforgivable.

On the dark highway, Paula became aware that she was losing her sense of proprioception, unable to feel her body in the car seat, unable to orientate herself or the car in space. There was a risk she would run off the road or, worse, career into the lane of oncoming traffic and hurt someone. She pulled over to the verge and anchored herself by concentrating on the smoothness of the steering wheel under her palms and the tautness of the seatbelt against her collarbone.

After a few minutes, she steered back out onto the highway, fearing that if she stayed still, she would have to face up to what she'd done and it would be unbearable. She knew that wasn't logical.

Further on, somewhere past Lithgow, her eyes felt so gritty it was unsafe to keep driving. She parked in a truck lay-by, tipped the seat back and tried to sleep. Maybe if she got a few hours of rest, she could think her way through this, make some proper decisions.

But sleep was impossible. There were too many thoughts scratching around inside her skull.

She could possibly persuade herself that the first time—killing Ian Ferguson—had been a spur-of-the-moment act: she had seized an opportunity that fell across her path, without premeditation or even full self-awareness. But she couldn't delude herself about John Santino. With him, her criminal actions were planned with complete awareness and undeniable homicidal intent. After the second murder, Paula understood that she had crossed over into some other dimension, irrevocably, permanently.

She must've hoped—probably unconsciously, certainly childishly—that if she told Anita, then she could share the burden of this with someone. But she couldn't share it. That was impossible as well as being unfair and cruel to her friend.

Paula was alone with this. She had to accept that she was alone now.

Reclining in the driver's seat, sleepless, powerless to scrape unwelcome thoughts out her head, she stared through the window as the headlights of passing cars washed over the dark trees. Paula wondered if this was what it felt like to go mad. She thought about patients she'd dealt with when they were in the process of slipping into a psychotic episode. But she didn't think she was experiencing the onset of a psychotic break, because this mental disorientation made its own painful sense, given what had happened and what she'd done. This was appropriate anguish.

She must've dozed off for a while, probably a couple of hours, because when she jerked awake, the sky was starting to lighten. She returned the seat to upright and realised there were two semitrailers parked in the lay-by.

She clambered stiffly out of the car to stretch her limbs and then saw one of the truck drivers was pissing into the scrub, steam rising from the stream of urine in the chill of the early morning air. When the truckie saw her there, he turned his body away modestly and then, as he returned to his semitrailer, he nodded in greeting. The guy was unthreatening but it made Paula uncomfortable to have anyone look at her.

It was now thumpingly clear that she couldn't go back to work at Marrickville Family Practice. She couldn't handle seeing her own patients, couldn't bear to have their eyes on her, especially the patients who'd known her for years.

She walked in agitated loops on the gravel near her car, holding her phone, trying to think of the wording. She waited until seven forty-five, when Li-Kim would have arrived to open up the practice for the day.

Li-Kim picked up the call straight away. 'Paula. Hi.'

'Hi. Listen . . . um . . . I'm not in great shape.'

'Oh no. Are you ill?' Li-Kim asked.

'Not ill, but I think everything . . . it's kind of caught up with me.'

'Oh, Paula, I can hear in your voice, you sound rattled.'

'Can't really talk about it right now.'

'No, no, totally understandable,' Li-Kim responded.

Paula knew that everyone at the practice had been half expecting her to fall apart after Stacey and the children were killed.

'What can I do? How can I help?' Li-Kim asked. She was a deeply kind woman. Paula had been lucky to have her as a friend.

'I think I need to take a break,' Paula said. 'I'm sorry. I know it's a hassle.'

'Of course. Don't worry. Take the time you need, Paula. We'll cover your sessions.'

'Thanks, Li-Kim.'

'You need a break. Don't worry about anything here.'

'Thank you.'

Ending that phone call felt decisive, sharp—one more tie to normal life severed.

Paula pulled back out onto the highway, trying to make her crumbly brain work, unsure what to do next. In the rear-view mirror, she caught a glimpse of the ridiculous blonde hair on her head and she was sure she wanted to be rid of it.

She continued on into Bathurst, then drove around until she found a hair salon that was open early and could fit her in on the spot.

The hairdresser was reluctant to cut her hair super short. 'Are you sure? Sure you want to lose all your lovely long hair?'

Paula was sure.

The young female apprentice washed her hair and installed Paula in the chair with a cape around her. When the hairdresser came over, ready to cut, Paula smiled at him in the mirror, then quickly dropped her gaze.

The hairdresser sussed that this customer wasn't up for a chat and he began cutting her hair in blessed silence. Paula saw him exchange the occasional look with the apprentice, curious about who this strange woman was.

As chunks of blonde hair began tumbling to the floor, Paula met her own eyes in the mirror. She wasn't used to the confronting business of sitting in front of a salon mirror in strong lighting, facing herself. She closed her eyes and focused on listening to the swishing sounds of the guy combing her wet hair into sections and then the satisfyingly crisp snip of the scissors slicing through hunks of it.

So much had been subtracted from Paula's life—her parents, then Remy, then Stacey, Cameron, Poppy. Her sense of herself as an ethical person had gone. And now Anita had been subtracted too.

That was the moment Paula started to cry.

She felt the hairdresser rest his hand softly on her shoulder. 'Are you okay?' he asked. 'Too short? I can stop cutting it so short and we could give you some kind of layered bob.'

'Sorry, no. The hair is good. Keep going. Me crying is not about the hair.'

'Okay. If you're sure.'

'I'm sure.'

The guy resumed cutting but when Paula continued to cry, he stopped again.

'I'm okay,' she assured him. 'Please keep cutting. Sorry about the crying.'

'Well, usually when someone wants the big radical change to their hair, it's because of a relationship break-up or something along those lines.'

Paula shrugged. 'Something like that.'

'Look, if it's any consolation,' he said, 'I think the short cut will suit you.'

Paula nodded her thanks to him in the mirror. The apprentice passed her a few tissues with a shy smile.

The crying made Paula feel a little better. So did seeing the blonde hair being swept up from the floor and deposited into the bin.

Her head cleared enough that she could grab hold of one anchoring thought: as a doctor, she had useful skills. It must be possible to work usefully. It would need to be somewhere no one knew her, where she could keep her head down, somewhere she would not be constantly reminded of unbearable things.

After Paula walked out of the salon with what looked like a wavy pale yellow swimming cap on her head, she sat in the food court of a nearby shopping centre and started scrolling through websites for GP locum jobs.

In that same shopping centre, she bought underwear, shoes, a pair of jeans, a few shirts, two cheap but serviceable dresses, plus a suitcase to put it all in. She couldn't face going back to the Earlwood house—even for the few minutes it would take to fetch some of her clothes. Anyway, this seemed right. She could never be the person she used to be, so wearing new, unfamiliar garments felt appropriate.

Because Paula was prepared to go anywhere, on short notice, it only took a couple of days to nab a GP locum position. She signed on for a two-week fill-in stint in a town on the south coast. After that, there would be a locum job for a week out west, followed by two weeks on the far north coast.

Her theory was that it would be possible to keep working as a doctor as long as she moved around in temporary roles. That way she wouldn't become invested in patients' lives and wouldn't feel too responsible for what happened to them. She had no clue how long she could do this. Her capacity to think about the future had atrophied, her imaginative range only extending a day or two ahead.

The first gig down south required Paula to work Tuesday to Saturday in the general practice surgery and to be on call for the tiny local hospital on Sundays.

The town had absurdly beautiful beaches and a golf course draped between two dramatic headlands, but Paula's accommodation was on the low-lying, river side, facing the massive dark escarpment at the back of the town.

The one-bedroom serviced apartment came with job-lot chipboard furniture, a two-seater sofa covered in prickly grey fabric, angled towards the small TV sitting on a wood-grain laminate unit, and on the walls a couple of framed prints of lovely coastal views you couldn't see from the apartment. The place was good enough.

She needed to buy food—she hadn't eaten on the drive down south and it was now seven thirty in the evening.

By the time she drove to the main street, the IGA supermarket was twenty minutes from closing, so she hurried down the aisles with a basket in hand, grabbing tea, milk, eggs, bread, chocolate and the best she could find in the limp selection of fruit and vegetables. Because it was so late, there were only a few other customers in the place, which was a relief.

Unpacking her groceries onto the checkout counter, Paula exchanged a smile with the young woman on the till. Since the night she killed John Santino, she'd developed a way of smiling at strangers, conducting the unavoidable conversations with people, speaking to patients, all without truly connecting. It was a trick: she would aim her gaze at an object slightly to one side so the person's face remained out of focus. That way she never felt she made direct eye contact with anyone. She couldn't bear the idea that people would properly look at her, see who she was, see what she'd done.

Paula looked like a regular human to the young woman on the checkout, presumably, but she could no longer be a regular person. She imagined herself as one of those plastinated cadavers sometimes used to teach anatomy—once-living bodies with muscles, ligaments, circulatory systems, internal organs from which all the fluids had been extracted and replaced with silicone and polymers. They looked astonishingly normal and alive even though they were dehydrated, preserved in plastic.

While the checkout woman rang up the groceries, Paula half closed her eyes against the caustic glare of the fluorescent lights, but then a flash of colour, something red, caught her attention.

A small boy in a red T-shirt was darting back and forth between the drinks fridge and the confectionery display. He was five years old or thereabouts, grinning and cavorting like a naughty elf while a teenage girl tried to scoop him in with her free hand. In her other hand, she was holding a basket with a loaf of white bread and two cartons of UHT milk.

'No way you're getting fizzy drink, mister,' the girl said to him. 'We talked about that.'

The little boy dropped his head back and let out a groan of despair so tragic it made Paula smile to herself. But then, undaunted, he spun away from the fridge back to the rack of chocolate bars near the till, so fast that Paula had to duck sideways.

The girl turned to Paula. 'My brother's being a pain-in-the-arse little worm. Sorry.'

There was something defiant about the way this girl said 'sorry'. Not that she wasn't sorry, but she certainly didn't want anyone to mistake that limited 'sorry' for her being generally sorry about who she was and her right to exist in the world.

'You can pick one, Jye. A *small* one,' the girl instructed.

'Are you Ruby?' the checkout woman asked.

'What? Yeah. Why?' the girl shot back. There was that defiance again, a prideful and combative edge, always expecting a fight, always ready to fight.

'My little sister's in year eight with you.'

'Oh right.'

So Ruby must be about fourteen. Paula often found it hard to tell with teenage girls—some still looked like kids, while others seemed to have jumped straight to their mid-twenties. This girl was hard to pick because, even though she appeared small and young, she had the self-reliant edge of a much older person. With a wiry body, a pointy face and huge brown eyes, she looked like a pretty whippet.

By now, the boy was bouncing from foot to foot in front of the chocolate bars, moaning about the difficulty of choosing. Paula half expected his big sister to be irritated by this, but she just laughed indulgently at her brother and rested her hand on his shoulder, unobtrusively easing him from his bouncing into stillness. She made a little performance of joining him in the decision-making process, frowning, gasping and groaning along with him.

'Yeah, I know. Hard to pick one. If it was up to me, I'd—nuh, shouldn't say. It's your choice, mate.'

'Say! Say!'

'I'd go a Curly Wurly.'

Jye plucked a Curly Wurly bar from the display as if he'd won some glorious prize. Paula snuck her head around to exchange a smile with the boy, but then she realised that Ruby was glaring at her, suspicious, verging on hostile. *Why are you gawking at my brother, lady?*

Paula turned away, kept her head down. She didn't want any trouble. She didn't want to pry into anyone's life or have them scrutinise hers. Anyway, this was about as much human contact as she could handle in one go in her current state. She paid quickly and headed outside to her car.

Sliding into the driver's seat, Paula looked through the windscreen—the interior of the supermarket was bright against the dark street. Paula saw Jye come dancing out the door, with half the Curly Wurly already in his mouth and the rest of it making a chocolatey mess of his hand. Ruby hustled him forward while she put the bread and milk into a backpack.

As Paula drove out of the car park, she noticed Ruby and Jye climb onto a dirt bike parked around the corner from the supermarket. The boy hopped on the front, tucked in front of his sister, who reached her arms around him to grasp the handlebars. They puttered off on the little motorbike down an unlit side street, heading towards the escarpment.

Back in the serviced apartment, Paula unpacked her food supplies into the bar fridge and cooked eggs on toast. Once she'd hoisted the suitcase onto the bed and unpacked her small pile of new clothing, she felt profoundly tired—today had been a long drive—but she knew sleep was far out of reach without chemical aid. She took a temazepam, washing it down with a not-inconsiderable slug of vodka.

~

Anita and Paula had survived minor fallings-out in the past. Usually it would be because Anita had overreacted to something, with Paula being slightly condescending and infuriatingly reasonable in a way that only provoked Anita to behave more unreasonably. But very quickly, the two of them would make up and their friendship would be as strong as ever. They could both trust in that pattern.

In any past conflicts, Anita had been quick to admit she was an idiot and offer apologies. She was always quick to go to guilt.

And she was remorseful now, no question—guilty of a monumental failure of imagination not to have understood what was happening to Paula. Anita had been distracted by her own suffering and keen to recruit Paula into their exclusive club of Stacey's Grieving Best Friends. She hadn't stopped to think about the fact that it was different—much worse—for Paula.

Paula was already dealing with the death of her beautiful husband. Paula was the one who had been living with those kids for months. She was the one who'd walked into the house and found their bodies. She'd seen Matt shoot himself in the head. Anita berated herself for not fully weighing the trauma of that on any human being.

She'd been too quick to assume Dr Kaczmarek could handle everything as she always did. Arguably—and she could see this now—it had been harder on Paula than on a regular person. Paula had always accepted the obligation and responsibility to take care of other people, so the tragedy in that house would have been even more crushing.

Anita felt foolish for ever indulging in ridiculous hyperbolic talk about killing dangerous men. She'd only been venting, but still, it was a dangerous way to talk, given the raw emotional state Paula had been in.

She felt guilty for insisting that Paula follow the John Santino trial as a chance to see justice done, a chance for them to barrack together for the female victim. All Anita had managed to do was rub Paula's face in the terrible facts of Kendra Bartlett's death and then tear her apart with that verdict. Anita was culpable for relaying information about John Santino's life and what was happening to Brooke Lester. And now she was morally implicated in how Paula had used that information.

But those buckets of remorse didn't stop Anita from being horrified by what her friend had done. Not that she was sorry Ian Ferguson and John Santino were dead. Their deaths made the world better, no question, but that couldn't justify murder. It was as if the malevolence from those men had oozed out of them, infecting the air, spreading until it turned a truly good person like Paula into a murderer.

Then again, Paula had *let* that happen. She had allowed her certainty that she knew what was best for people to lead her down the track to a criminal act. Even if Anita had voiced some wild ideas about killing men, she would never condone it in practice. If Paula had ever hinted at what she was contemplating, Anita would've talked her out of it. But she'd never had that chance because Paula always thought she knew better.

Anita was left with surges of anger towards her friend, feeling used by her, lied to, and now lumbered with this information she couldn't offload, like a lump of radioactive material in her belly, contaminating everything. At the same time, she couldn't switch off her concern, the worry that Paula might harm herself. If it weren't for the risk of the crimes being discovered, Anita would've called the doctors in her practice, called in psychiatric help, something.

The day after Paula's confession, Anita had sent a text.

Are you okay? A x

I'm okay. And very sorry for what I've done to you. P x

Two days later, Anita messaged again.

People keep asking me how you are. A x

I'm okay.

After that, Paula no longer replied to Anita's messages. Well, if she didn't want to be contacted, fuck her then.

Meanwhile, Rohan was sending Anita a text every two or three days. Nothing pushy. It was like a cop doing a welfare check on an individual he was concerned about.

I hope you're alright. Call me anytime. Rohan

I'm fine. Thank you. Hope you're in good form. Anita

Over the coming weeks, Anita would be covering a big defamation trial and a coronial inquest into deaths caused when a stage collapsed at a music festival, so there was little possibility that she would run into Rohan in court. Just as well. If she saw him, she couldn't trust herself not to rush to him and blurt out everything.

In the past—before Paula started murdering people—Anita would have dissected the Rohan break-up with her friend, listened to her advice, soaked up her comfort, but that was no longer a possibility.

Anita begged off a couple of family events and avoided seeing any other friends. She didn't know how to be with people while she was carrying this knowledge in her guts. So the days sank into more and more solitude.

When two weeks had gone by with no word from Paula, Anita's anxiety began ratcheting up. She scrolled through the green column of texts on her phone: all the messages she'd sent to Paula with no response. She couldn't stand it—the not knowing—so on impulse, she drove towards Marrickville Family Practice, ringing ahead from her car.

'Hi. Could I make an appointment with Dr Kaczmarek, please?' she asked.

'I'm sorry. Dr Kaczmarek is on indefinite leave at the moment,' Jemma replied. 'Would you like to see one of the other doctors?'

'Uh . . . no. Thanks. Bye.'

Anita took the next turn to the left and drove on to the Earlwood house. She wanted to reassure herself that Paula was alive.

She parked a few houses down and walked along the footpath towards Paula's place. There was no sign of her car and the low metal gates across the empty driveway were closed. The curtains were drawn across the front windows.

Most likely Paula had chosen to go away. That was the most likely thing. She was a profoundly sensible woman who would take herself away to some tranquil place to recuperate. Then again, Paula had now revealed herself as a woman capable of killing two people, so who the fuck knew? Anita was queasy with apprehension as she approached the front door, imagining terrible scenes inside that house, imagining Paula killing herself.

She rang the doorbell. No answer. She thumped on the door, but there was no sound from inside. They'd always had keys to each other's homes and Anita was about to unlock the door herself when a voice behind her shouted, 'Hey! Who's that?'

Anita jerked with fright and spun around to see Mr Petrakis peering over the hedge from his front yard. The Petrakis family had lived in the house next door for forty years, having brought up their kids there, minded their grandkids there and grown grapes across the trellis in the backyard to make wine so putrid you could feel it corroding your stomach lining within seconds of ingestion. Paula had always had a great relationship with the family, scooting next door whenever one of the grandkids was sick or injured and graciously accepting homegrown vegetables and bottles of the corrosive wine over the fence. When Remy was sick, and in the weeks after Stacey and the kids were murdered, trays of food from the Petrakis kitchen would frequently appear on Paula's front porch.

'Hi, Theo,' Anita said.

Theo Petrakis hollered towards his wife, 'It's okay. It's just Anita.' Then he turned back to her. 'I didn't see your car, so I didn't know who it was.'

'Sorry if I gave you a scare.'

Theo made a no-worries gesture. 'She isn't here.'

'Do you know where she is?' Anita asked.

He shook his head and Anita felt a little stab of being judged by Mr Petrakis for not knowing where her friend was, for not taking better care of her. Or maybe she only imagined he was judging her.

'Dr K has been through a lot,' said Theo.

'Yes. That's why I want to make sure she's okay. Do you know when she's coming back?'

'No. She rang me, asked me to get my son-in-law to look after her yard once a fortnight. She sends the money to his bank account.'

'So it sounds like she's going to be away for a while,' Anita said.

Theo shrugged and nodded. 'We just want Dr K to be well and happy.'

Anita gave up any plan to check inside the house, figuring that would be too distressing, and she barely made it back to her car before the weeping overtook her. She wanted to ring Stacey and talk to her about what they should do for Paula. She wanted Stacey to be alive and Paula to be well and happy.

She thought about the day Stacey and the kids moved in to Paula's house, unloading Stacey's old red Subaru, carting their bags inside, the few belongings they'd brought with them when they fled the Maryvale property.

Mr and Mrs Petrakis had worked together to lift Poppy over the fence so she could feed their backyard chickens, while Cameron insisted on helping his mother unpack the bags.

Anita recalled the way Stacey looked at her kids—with such relief, amusement, pride, a staggering amount of love. When Stacey realised Anita was observing her, she had laughed, sending herself up for being such a pathetically besotted mother. She turned to Anita with that smile which could radiate joy through an entire room.

Anita suddenly felt the loss of Stacey so acutely, so freshly, it was like waves of pain through her body. And it struck her she'd never properly mourned her friend. Not the way you would normally miss someone and think about their splendid qualities and the amusing things they used to say and feel their absence in your life and all that. The shock of the way Stacey died had drowned out regular grief, robbing her of being properly missed, robbing them all.

Anita picked through the papers, tubes of sunblock, pens, loose Minties and other rubbish in her glovebox to find a packet of tissues. She allowed herself to sit in the car and howl for a good long time.

TWENTY

A RIGID SCHEDULE WAS THE ADHESIVE HOLDING PAULA together, the structure that stopped her crumbling into useless scraps or spinning beyond all social norms into a psychotic break.

She woke every day at six a.m., drank tea, went for a long half run/half walk, took a shower, ate yoghurt with fruit, then went to work in the medical centre. At the end of the work day, she pushed herself through another long walk, listening to an audiobook (non-fiction on subjects unlikely to churn up emotion), then returned to the serviced apartment.

Paula would plonk herself down on one of the two dining chairs in the place and sometimes an hour would have passed and the room had grown dark around her. She had been sitting all that time not moving, as good as paralysed.

These episodes of profound inertia had been happening to her quite often, a state of physical and mental torpor in which her breathing slowed, her limbs became immobile, her brain numbed. She guessed it was a self-protective mechanism, a temporary system shutdown to give her mind a reprieve from the endless churn of questions and shame. Paula would eventually rouse herself to switch on one of the overhead lights and cook dinner. She would drink one glass of wine in front of the TV, then take one temazepam and go to sleep at eleven p.m.

She regarded the life she was leading as a psychological breakdown in slow motion. A breakdown but under controlled conditions.

Paula had been in this south coast town for almost two weeks now and she'd discovered beautiful options for her morning run—through forest that swept right up to the edge of a headland where the huge trees met the cliff edge and the ground fell away sharply to the ocean.

She would finish by running along the beach, welcoming the burn up her ankles and calves from the strain of jogging on loose sand. This was probably some pathetic and futile act of self-punishment.

The medical centre was down the road from the town's tiny eight-bed hospital which mostly functioned as a respite place for elderly people and a first aid/transfer point to city hospitals for people injured in car crashes on the highway. Because it was winter now, there were few tourists around to swell the patient numbers.

The general practice was run by an old-fashioned but competent bloke, close to retirement, and a young guy in his first GP placement. Paula was employed to fill in for the other regular senior GP, Tanya, who was on an Alaskan cruise. Paula had quickly got the impression Tanya was a trusted and beloved doctor in the district.

Saturday was Paula's last day in the place. The doctoring required of her during the afternoon session was pretty straightforward stuff—three vaccinations, two medical certificates for days off work and one small laceration to be sutured.

Patients with anything complicated or delicate were unlikely to confide in the locum. They would hang on to their problem until Tanya returned to work and that suited Paula just fine. The last thing she wanted right now was to be drawn into the personal dramas of people in crisis.

There had been days when Paula couldn't avoid seeing the bruises on a woman's body or wondering how a woman's arm had been broken or noticing that a woman flinched at a sudden noise. Paula would feel the rage flare inside her, as if the pilot light was always on and any small sign would spark it up. When that happened, she worked hard to stay calm, regulate her breathing, to run through the standard guidelines in her mind and ask the patient the appropriate questions. Some of those women were most likely being abused at home but they were unlikely to trust a temporary doctor. And Paula wasn't going to push. She didn't trust herself.

She couldn't rely on her own perception anymore. When one woman sat up on the examination table and took off her shirt, Paula saw bruising on her ribcage. Bruises shaped like handprints from a large man. It turned out to be the blotchy shadows cast by the tree outside the window. When a woman made a few cracks about her husband being 'a difficult customer', Paula couldn't stop herself wondering if the jokes were covering real fear of the man. But maybe it was only a joke. Another female patient had a rasping voice, and Paula immediately pictured a man's hands around this woman's neck, crushing her vocal cords. But in this case, it was just laryngitis.

If there were enough worrying signs, enough red flags, Paula would speak to one of the permanent doctors in the practice about following up with the woman, making sure the mandatory reporting was done. Dr Kaczmarek was only temporary so it wasn't up to her. She couldn't be responsible. She tried not to let her mind follow those patients any further than the door.

This Saturday ended with another straightforward run: sinus infection, sprained ankle and a blood test for a gent at risk of developing type 2 diabetes. Paula put on a reassuring performance as a thorough and caring doctor, even though, in truth, she was keeping real human feelings in frozen suspension. It helped that this was her last day at the practice. On Monday, she would move on to some other anonymous locum job and she would have no idea what happened to anyone in this town.

After work, Paula planned to go for a last walk, filling her head with an audiobook rather than think about bruises or broken bones or strangulation injuries. She was untangling her earbuds as she passed the front office. Fiona, the receptionist, was on the phone, so Paula mouthed 'I'm off now' as she headed for the door. But Fiona signalled *wait* and beckoned Paula over.

'Hang on a sec, sweetie,' Fiona said into the phone and then turned to Paula. 'This kid says her little brother's got a temperature and a sore ear.'

'Well, I'll stick around if she wants to bring him in.'

'They live ten k's out of town and got no transport at the moment. I mean, if it was something more serious, we could send an ambulance, but not for this.'

'No. I understand. Okay. What would Tanya normally do in a situation like this?'

'She'd drive out there, take a bunch of antibiotics and whatever. But doesn't mean you have to.'

'Of course, yeah. A sick kid with no transport. Can I speak to her?' Paula asked.

Fiona handed the receiver across the desk.

'Hi, this is Paula. I'm one of the doctors here. What's your name?'

'Ruby. Jye's my brother. He's five.'

Paula immediately pictured the spiky whippety teenage girl and the little boy she'd seen in the supermarket on her first night in town.

'And Jye's got a sore ear, has he?' Paula asked.

'Yep. He had an ear infection last year and it's same as then. Forehead's really hot and he reckons the inside of his ear really hurts. He loses his balance if he stands up and that. He's just, like, quiet and doesn't want to eat, which for Jye is a big deal.'

Paula could hear the sturdiness in Ruby's voice—this girl was used to handling whatever shit was thrown at her—but there was a tiny quiver in the voice too. She was only a kid herself, anxious about her brother and scared to be handling this on her own.

'Okay, Ruby—that's a really good description you've given me. And there's no one at your house who can drive him in to see a doctor?'

'Nuh. His dad, my stepdad, he took the car. I mean, should I bring Jye in on my dirt bike?'

'No, don't do that if he's feeling wobbly. I'll come out to your house and see him. Hang tight, Ruby.'

While Paula chucked a few antibiotics and other supplies into her medical bag, Fiona took back the phone to write down directions to the house.

Paula looked at the names and address on the slip of paper Fiona handed her. 'Do you know this family?'

'Nope. Don't think they come to this practice.'

According to the GPS map in Paula's car, Lower Pinch Road branched off the highway, then ran almost parallel to it behind a wall of trees before winding back to join the highway again. Upper Pinch Road looped off Lower Pinch, travelling up a heavily wooded slope, passing a small number of houses. The dirt surface was rough but Paula was able to zigzag to avoid the big potholes if she took it slowly.

Finding herself back near the highway, she realised she'd overshot the house and had to do a precarious U-turn on the crumbly edges of the road. Approaching from this direction, she could see it—the roadside mailbox for 8 Upper Pinch Road.

She had to rev her car to coax it up the rutted driveway, until the forest opened into a clearing where the house sat. A small clapboard house perched on the hillside, with a front verandah built on tall wooden posts and ramshackle lattice covering the dark mouth of the underfloor area. The house was in poor shape, with paintwork flaking off so the exposed timber was rotting away in places.

The dirt bike Paula had seen Ruby riding away from the town supermarket was now tucked in the space under the steps. Next to it was a kid's tricycle. The carcass of an old truck was sprouting weeds beside the concrete water tank and other bits of rusty debris were strewn over the cleared ground. A corrugated-iron awning had been built against one side of the house to form a kind of open shed which housed a stack of engine parts and sections of car bodies.

There was no farmland nearby so this wasn't a farmhouse; Paula guessed it must have been a timber worker's cottage back when the logging industry still existed here. Now it was home for Ruby and her family.

The setting, nestled in the forest, was pretty, and with imagination and a bit of squinting to keep details out of focus, you could picture it as idyllic for kids. There was a blow-up swimming pool, deflated since the summer months, now with plastic toys floating among a few dead leaves. There was a tyre swing hanging off one of the big gum trees.

Paula remembered Cameron, when he was still little, hanging upside down on the tyre swing in the home paddock of the Maryvale property, grinning like a happy monkey. It was the first time she and Remy had driven up there to visit Stacey in the new place. With that move to Maryvale, Stacey had given up a teaching job she loved so she could support Matt in his new scheme to become a cattle farmer. They'd thrown a modest inheritance and all their savings into buying the small farm. Stacey had been fizzy like a little kid to have their first proper visitors, and she swept Paula and Remy through a tour of the weatherboard house they had started to renovate. 'This is what Matt needs,' she said, as if talking about treatment for a difficult patient. 'We're away from all the stresses in the city. It's just the four of us, loving each other.' Paula and Remy had smiled and made supportive noises. In private, they whispered about the precarious finances, Matt's changeable moods, the foolishness of the whole enterprise. Then again, the kids seemed happy and Stacey's chatter about their new adventure had functioned as a bright wall designed to deflect questions or concerns.

'You the doctor?' Ruby called out. The fourteen-year-old girl peered down at Paula from the verandah.

'Yes. Hello, Ruby.'

Paula fetched her medical bag from the passenger seat and picked her way up the wooden steps, avoiding the splintered boards, while Ruby held the front door open for her. Paula smiled but Ruby just squinted back, watchful and defensive, trying to read Paula's face, anticipating judgement.

The interior of the house was in better shape than you might expect from the outside. The furniture was shabby and mismatched but the place was clean and organised.

Jye was wearing clean pyjamas and lying on the nubbly mustard-coloured couch, rugged up in a mauve cotton blanket, watching *Bluey*, an animated series with dog characters, on a chunky old laptop. On the coffee table next to the laptop was a glass of water, a plate of half-eaten Vegemite toast, a bowl of green jelly and a bottle of children's paracetamol with a measuring glass sitting on top of the lid. It was obvious Ruby had constructed this little Sick Boy nest for him. Paula had an urge to spin around and grab the girl in a tight hug for being such a gorgeous big sister, but she assumed that wouldn't be welcomed.

'Hello, Jye. My name's Paula. I'm a doctor.'

'Hi,' replied the boy, an enfeebled version of the kid Paula had seen in the supermarket. It never ceased to amaze her how normally sparky children could so suddenly become wan and limp and knocked around by sickness and then so quickly bounce back.

While Paula examined the boy and took his temperature, Ruby dashed over to pause the Bluey video, then hovered close by like an anxious parent.

'I gave him some of that,' she said, indicating the paracetamol. 'That was the stuff they gave us last time he had the ear thing. I gave him the amount it says for five years old. Two hours ago.'

Ruby was earnest, as if she were doing a hospital handover, so Paula responded with a serious, respectful nod. 'That was exactly the right thing to do, Ruby.'

As Paula looked in Jye's ears with the otoscope, she asked, 'Are you guys home on your own?'

'No. Well, Jye's dad is out. He took the ute. But our mum's here. She's having a lie-down.'

Paula followed Ruby's gaze towards the closed bedroom door. The girl then took a step to plant her body between Paula and the view of the door. A protective impulse. She didn't want this stranger even to think about her mother, let alone go snooping. She didn't want some stickybeak middle-class doctor lady judging her family.

'You know what, Jye?' Paula said. 'I reckon your sister would be a very good doctor. She's exactly right about what's wrong. You've got an ear infection. The good news is I have some medicine here that's going to fix you up.'

Paula turned to Ruby. 'I see your bottle of paracetamol is almost finished. How about I give you this little one to last you until your mum can get to the chemist?'

'Oh. Yeah. Ta. I mean, if that's okay.'

'Definitely okay. And here's the antibiotic I want Jye to take.' Paula handed Ruby a bottle of liquid amoxicillin. 'If I write things down for you, you can measure out the right amount to give him, can't you?'

'Yeah. Yeah. No problem. I mean, I think so.'

'I'm sure so. You're doing a good job looking after your brother.'

Just as Paula was writing a list of instructions for Ruby, the bedroom door swung open.

A woman padded out of the dark bedroom in bare feet, wearing loose drawstring pants and an oversized man's shirt. She was probably in her mid-thirties but it was difficult to be sure. The physical resemblance to Ruby was clear—this woman had the same slight, lean build, the same sharp but attractive features, the same big brown eyes—but if she'd ever had the same fierce spirit and self-possession as her daughter, that was long gone. This woman was worn down, a defeated human being.

The mother was startled to see a stranger in the living room and she hugged her arms defensively across her chest.

Ruby jumped in. 'This is the doctor, Mum. Because of Jye's earache.'

'Oh right. Sorry . . . I didn't realise—uh, hi. I'm Nicole. Jye and Ruby's mum.'

'Hi, Nicole. Paula Kaczmarek. Good to meet you.'

'Thanks for coming. Sorry I wasn't up when you got here. I'm feeling a bit crook.'

'No worries,' Paula assured her.

'Do you want a cup of tea, Mum?' Ruby asked.

'No, honey, thank you. Oh, unless the doctor wants one?'

'I'm fine, thanks.'

Nicole went over to kiss Jye on the top of the head, asking him how he was feeling, making a fuss of him. Then she raised her arms to smooth down her bed-matted hair and the sleeves of the shirt fell back.

Paula could see bruises on the pale skin of Nicole's arms. Nicole quickly tugged the sleeves back down, realising the bruises had been seen. Paula froze for a moment—not wanting to jump to conclusions, not wanting to interfere and cause problems for these people, not wanting to overstep the new boundaries she'd established for herself.

'Nicole, would it be possible for you to bring Jye into the medical practice in town on Monday?' Paula asked.

'Oh, um, yeah. I'm sure I can get the car or, y'know, I could get my—'

'He's back,' Ruby interrupted, going to the front window. 'Earlier than he said.'

The girl had heard the sound of the gears grinding down on her stepfather's ute as it laboured up the driveway towards the house. Paula saw Nicole instantly shrink into herself, folding her arms around her torso again, as she listened to her husband slam the door of his ute and stomp up the steps.

Before he even reached the door, he demanded, 'Whose car is that?'

Seeing Paula standing in the living room, he flicked his chin up, belligerent. 'Hello?'

The guy was in his mid-forties, short but powerful-looking, with a solid chest like a keg of beer, shaved head, a tattoo of a fist emerging from flames that spread across his chunky neck.

His clothes were smeared with black grease, which made the fresh gash on his forehead stand out, bright red and glistening.

'That's my car,' Paula said, stepping forward with an instinct to place herself between this man and Nicole and her kids. 'I'm Paula Kaczmarek. Doctor from town. I'm here to see Jye, Mr . . . ?'

'Curtis Wigney.' Then he aimed his bullety head at Nicole. 'Rang for a doctor to come up here, did ya?'

'No,' responded Nicole, barely audible.

Ruby jumped in quickly. 'Me. I did. For Jye's ear. All good now.'

'Yeah? You all good now, little mate?'

Jye didn't answer.

'Beg yours? I asked you a question, Jye.'

Seeing the irritated way Curtis was glaring at his son, Ruby jumped in again. 'He'll be okay now he's got the medicine and that.'

'Just an ear infection,' Paula added. 'But Ruby did the right thing to call. With the antibiotic, he should be fine in a couple of days.'

'Doctor fixed you up, has she?'

Jye nodded, which seemed to be enough to appease his father. Curtis then scanned the other faces in the room—Paula, Nicole and Ruby—and he must've decided that no one was out to get him right at the moment.

'Quite a bad gash on your forehead, Mr Wigney,' Paula ventured.

'Oh yeah . . . fucking thing.' He poked his grease-black finger around the edges of the wound. 'The dropkick at the wrecker's yard doesn't know how to store shit properly. Huge fucking piece of junk fell on my head.'

'It'd be better with a few stitches,' said Paula. 'I mean, I'm here and I've got everything I need in the bag. I could stitch it for you.'

Curtis looked at Paula for several seconds, assessing if she was causing him grief or taking the piss or pulling some other scam he didn't quite understand. Eventually he said, 'Why the fuck not? Where do you want me?'

Paula swung one of the straight-backed dining chairs into a clear space and indicated he should sit there.

Curtis guffawed. 'How about this, Nicole? A doctor doing house calls! Pretty good, eh?'

'Yeah,' said Nicole with a weak smile.

'What about you, Ruby?' Curtis asked. 'Is there something wrong with you the doc can fix while she's here?'

'Nuh. I'm okay.'

Curtis's tone suddenly turned ugly. 'Sure about that? Maybe the doctor can give you a fucking pill to wipe that nasty bitch look off your face.'

Paula felt the air in the room tighten up like a held breath. She feared she'd made a mistake by offering to stay and treat his wound.

'Where can I wash my hands, Ruby?' Paula asked. 'Oh, and could you find me a clean towel, please?'

'No worries,' said the girl, leading the way to the kitchen.

While Paula rinsed her hands at the kitchen sink, Ruby brought soap and a small towel. Paula gestured for Ruby to stay a moment.

'Does your stepfather ever hurt you?' she asked in a low voice.

Ruby shook her head. Paula held her gaze—*Are you sure?*—and the girl shook her head again, emphatically. 'I won't take any shit from him,' she said firmly.

'I believe you.'

'If he gets riled up, I can go and stay with my grandparents.'

'But you want to stay here to keep an eye on your little brother?' Paula guessed.

Ruby shrugged. Yes.

'You know, there are people who can help you and your mum and your brother if—'

'Ruby! Get us a beer!' Curtis yelled from the living room.

'Okay!' Ruby called back, then she whispered to Paula, 'Mum worries the welfare people will take Jye off her. We'll be right. She's working herself up to leave soon.'

Ruby grabbed a beer from the fridge and walked out of the kitchen.

By the time Paula returned to the living room, Nicole had retreated to sit next to Jye, Ruby was perched on the arm of the couch and Curtis sat in the chair drinking the beer.

Paula set up her medical bag on the table and pulled out the supplies she needed. As she would with any patient, she talked Wigney through what she was going to do at each step of the process.

'There'll be a bit of a sting when I put in the local anaesthetic.'

'Yeah, whatever. Dad's tough, isn't he, Jye?'

Jye nodded.

Paula used the saline from her medical bag to irrigate the wound, flushing out the debris. 'How long since you had a tetanus shot, Mr Wigney?'

'Oh . . . shit. Dunno.'

'Well, all that rusty stuff in a wrecker's yard—good idea to update your tetanus. I've got some in my bag.'

'Yeah, whatever.' Then he turned his head to have a decent look at Paula, not sure if he should be suspicious. 'So how long you been living down here, doc?'

'I'm not living here. I'm only temporary. Leaving on Monday,' she explained.

That idea seemed to relax him, and while Paula stitched his head laceration, Curtis Wigney blathered on about his business plan to fix up cars and sell them. That was why he'd driven to the wrecker's yard, looking for automotive parts.

'I'm trying to get some cash together but it's always hard,' he said. 'Even if some people don't understand how fucking hard it is.' Wigney glared at Nicole and pointed to his head laceration with a hand gesture as if pointing a gun. 'See this, Nicole? This is what I go through trying to get cash for this family.'

'I know,' she replied.

'Do you? I don't reckon you do fucking know.'

Curtis shot Nicole a look so vicious it seemed to make the woman shrivel deeper inside her oversized clothes.

Wigney then aimed his hand, still shaped like a gun, at Paula's bag.

'Bet you got lots of goodies in there, doc.'

'Ah. Well, some,' she said. 'Keep still, please.'

As Paula continued stitching, she considered what goodies she might have in her bag that she could inject into Curtis Wigney in place of a tetanus vaccine. But then she blocked that line of thought. She mustn't let her imagination wander that way, even as a silly fantasy. Instead, she tried to focus on the task, the feel of the suture needle piercing the skin of the man's forehead, the thread pulling the jagged fleshy edges of the wound together into as neat a pink line as she could manage.

She didn't even have the facts of this situation. She couldn't be totally sure why Nicole was so nervous or where the bruises had come from. Curtis Wigney might be a bully, a man who enjoyed controlling people through fear, but Paula had no way of knowing how dangerous he was. And whatever was going on here, she must never cross that boundary again and act outside the law. Anita was right. She was totally right when she railed against the arrogance of Paula's actions, the danger of it. Choosing to kill a person meant shredding every thread of the fabric holding the world in civilised place.

She applied antiseptic ointment to the stitched wound and covered it with a sterile bandage. Glancing up, she saw Ruby was watching her. Paula smiled and hoped—absurdly, impossibly—that her smile could convey *I hope you're all okay. Call me if you're scared. Don't let this man hurt you or your family.* Who knows how Ruby interpreted Paula's intense look, but at least the girl didn't scowl or turn away.

Paula then realised that Wigney had twisted his head and caught the doctor and his stepdaughter exchanging looks. His expression darkened in a second and his voice came out hard and sinewy. 'Yeah, I reckon it's time you pissed off, doc. Don't reckon I need a tetanus injection.'

'Oh. Okay. Up to you.'

For a brief moment, Paula indulged the fantasy of this man dying of tetanus—first hit by stomach cramps, then his body contorted by muscle spasms so intense they could break bones during the agonising hours before his death. In her mind, Paula could hear the crack of his femur.

She turned away so the sight of him wouldn't make her do something foolish, then she said, 'Let me write a prescription for another course of antibiotics for Jye, just in case.'

She scribbled on a prescription pad and on the bottom, in clear block letters, she wrote her name and mobile number. She walked over to the couch to touch Jye's cheek gently.

'Hope you feel better soon, Jye.'

She handed the prescription to Nicole and, out of Wigney's eye line, she pointed out the phone number. 'Call if you're worried.'

Meanwhile Curtis Wigney stood up, huffing breaths through his nostrils, pugnacious, making it clear he wanted Paula out the door quick smart.

At the last minute, he bunged on a polite tone to say, 'Anyway, thanks for coming out here, doc. Thanks for sorting out the boy and stitching me up.'

'No problem. Please make sure Jye comes in for a check-up in the next couple of days.'

'I'll do that.'

Driving back down to Lower Pinch Road and along the highway to town, Paula made herself run through the guidelines any doctor should follow, going through them like a repetitive chant to control her breathing. Anything she did must be via proper channels.

The town's police station was small, with only one officer working limited hours, and by the time Paula drove there late on Saturday afternoon, it was closed for the rest of the weekend.

Paula sat on the steps of the locked police station and dialled the after-hours number posted on the glass. When she got on to the sergeant from a larger town further down the coast, she rushed through an explanation of who she was and the family she was concerned about.

The sergeant was patient, taking notes, asking the appropriate questions. Was there immediate grave concern for the safety of the children? Paula probably had to say no to that. Did the children appear well cared for? Yes. Did the woman ask for help or express fear for her life? No. Did the husband make threats in Paula's presence? Not as such, no.

The cop was very experienced and not a naive guy. He understood the subtle realities of these situations. But it was difficult. And what else could Paula have said to him? 'I feel in my bones that this man is dangerous'? She had to be honest with herself and acknowledge that her judgement could easily be skewed by the events of the last six months.

The phone call ended with the sergeant assuring Paula an officer would drive out to Upper Pinch Road and do a welfare check during the coming week.

That night, the temazepam and glass of wine were nowhere near enough to tip Paula into sleep. She lay awake most of the night on the lumpy mattress.

First, she tried to control the churn of thoughts in her head by making a list of the calls she would make in the morning to the police and the welfare authorities, to bolster the safety of Nicole and the kids. But afterwards, she would have to rule a line under this.

Lying there in the dark, Paula made another resolution: she would pull out of the other locum positions she'd signed up for. It was clear she couldn't go on working as a doctor, seeing what she would inevitably see and feeling so powerless to protect people. She'd been kidding herself to think she could function in a detached way. If she could no longer contain things in bearable compartments, it was too painful for her and not useful to patients. There was no choice but to quit being a doctor.

Next, she tried to summon happy memories—times with Remy, or with Anita and Stacey. She conjured up the day at Whale Beach when she'd taken that photo of Poppy doing the fake cartwheel, while Cameron looked back anxiously from the water.

As Stacey and Paula sat together on the beach that day, Stacey had said, 'Cameron's a tender-hearted boy.' Then she laughed. 'Am I allowed to say that about my own kid?'

'Yes, you are,' Paula answered firmly. 'He's spectacular.'

'I mean, I know he has the anxiety problem,' Stacey continued, 'but he also has this lovely urge to look after people. I like to think maybe some good things have come out of what he's been through.' She then did a grimace of desperation. 'Please agree with me, Paula, so I don't keep tormenting myself that I've damaged my kids forever.'

Paula wrapped her sunblock-greasy arms around her friend. 'You're a fantastic mother, Stace. And Cam's a beautiful, caring, empathetic kid. You'll all be okay.'

The memory of Cameron dragged Paula's mind back to Ruby—the girl's worried face, the steadfast way she looked after her brother. Paula couldn't bear to think she'd left Ruby at risk in that house. She needed to know how dangerous the father was, how worried she should be. The need to know for sure grew more and more desperate—however illogical the impulse was—until it consumed her.

Finally, at seven a.m. Paula appealed to the one person she could think of to help.

She sent a text. *Hi. Paula Kaczmarek here. Okay if I call you now?*

Rohan Mehta phoned her immediately.

'Hi, Paula. How are you?'

'I'm okay. Thanks for calling back, Rohan. I was hoping—please say if this is inappropriate. I'm hoping you could find out . . . If I give you a name and address, can you look up police records and check if a person is dangerous? If a guy has a record of violence?'

'Oh. Uh . . . I can certainly look someone up on the system but it's not okay for me to give out information like that.'

'No, no, you don't have to tell me stuff if you're not allowed. If you could check and make sure this guy's family aren't at risk or . . . just check if he's likely to hurt them. Look, I'll give you the name and address and you do whatever you think is right.'

TWENTY-ONE

ANITA WAS STEPPING OUT OF THE SHOWER WHEN SHE SAW her phone light up with a text from Rohan. She figured it would be one of his now-regular messages checking she was okay. She wrapped a towel around herself and reached for the phone.

The text read: *Just had a strange call from Paula. Ring me.*

Fear whooshed through Anita's body as if she'd been sluiced with a bucket of icy water. Had Paula phoned to tell Detective Mehta she murdered two men?

She quickly dressed and steadied herself before she rang back.

He picked up immediately. 'Hi. How are you?'

It was the first time she'd heard Rohan's voice since the break-up in the cafe. It was a beautiful voice.

'I'm okay,' she said. 'You?'

'Fine.'

He sounded more or less normal. He didn't sound as if Paula had just confessed to murder.

There was a long pause, as if they both harboured a faint hope that this was an awkwardly polite opening to a conversation in which they would suddenly launch into declarations of love and get back together. But it wasn't that kind of conversation.

Eventually Anita broke the silence. 'Paula rang you?'

'Couple of hours ago. Is she working down the south coast at the moment?'

'Uh . . . well, she sometimes . . . um . . .' she mumbled, reluctant to let on she had no clue where Paula was.

'Look, Anita, I've gotta say, she sounded weird.'

'What kind of weird?'

'I don't know her well enough to say. She seemed wired up, pretty agitated. I wondered if, lately, she's seemed—'

'Me and Paula haven't seen each other for a while. We sort of . . . we had a falling out.'

'Oh. Really? Oh.'

'Uh, yeah. I suppose the stress of everything took its toll on our friendship,' Anita offered, hearing how lame and phoney that sounded.

'Oh, Anita, I'm really sorry to hear that,' he said.

His tone was unbearably tender and lovely. Why did he have to be so fucking caring and adorable and perfect for her?

'Yeah . . .' she mumbled.

'And I'm surprised. You and Paula always seemed so close, like people who would stay friends for—anyway, look, none of my business.'

Anita could tell he was desperate to know the details but he was too damned considerate to pry. He left a pause, maybe hoping Anita would fill the silence with more explanation. When she didn't say anything, he added, 'I really hope you two can find a way through this together.'

'Thanks. So, um, why did Paula ring you?'

'She asked me to look up police records on a guy living down the south coast. Near where she's been working.'

Panic sparked Anita to blurt out questions too loudly, too urgently. 'Did she say why? Is the man violent? Is it a domestic abuse situation?'

There was a silence on the other end of the phone. Rohan was obviously trying to make sense of her explosive reaction.

'Do you want to tell me what's going on?' he asked.

'I can't.'

'Okay. But if you're worried Paula's in some kind of trouble . . .'

'I don't know what's going on. I haven't talked to her so I don't know.'

'Please tell me if there's something—I mean, the guy Paula asked me to check on, he's bad news. String of weapons charges, drug charges, assault convictions. He recently did time for a very nasty assault. Been dodging his parole officer since.'

'Did you tell Paula all that?'

'No. And I'm not going to. I've made sure the local cops are on to it, so she doesn't have to worry.'

'But on the phone, you got the impression Paula believes this guy is dangerous?'

'Well, yeah. Yes.'

'Did she mention his family being in danger?'

'She did. Fucking hell, Anita—are you going to tell me what's going on?'

'I told you: I don't know.'

There was another long pause. Rohan obviously knew there was something.

Finally, he said, 'Okay. Well, I think it'd be good if you call her. She sounds in a bad way.'

'I will. Thanks. Thanks for letting me know. Bye.'

Anita was shaking when she ended the call. Should she have told Rohan she was afraid her friend was planning to kill that man? Was that what a good friend would have done? What any responsible decent person would have done?

She circled her tiny living room. Chances were Paula wouldn't do anything. The fact she'd contacted Rohan was surely a sign she'd decided to operate through official channels rather than inject lethal substances into bad guys as part of her own unofficial protection service. This would be okay. Rohan would send the local coppers in to nab the bad guy and it would all be okay. There was no need to offer up Paula's secrets to the police.

She spun around to pick up her phone and tap Paula's number. When it went to voicemail, Anita breathed a bit after the beep but then hung up without speaking.

What message could she have left? '*Hi, Paula. It's me. Hey, are you about to murder another man? Maybe better if you don't. Call me. Bye.*'

She put the phone on the table next to her laptop. On that laptop were all the files collected for the feature article she'd put off writing. Case after case of women murdered by their partners. Men who had strangled, shot, bludgeoned, incinerated, stabbed, terrorised and destroyed those women.

Anita felt a spike of satisfaction to think Paula might be about to rid the world of one of those fucking monsters. Let Dr Kaczmarek make a hit list and kill some monsters and get away with it. The fantasy was thrilling, but only for a brief intoxicating moment, before it burned up in its own angry blaze like high-octane fuel. That kind of wrong-headed impulse had drawn Paula into this mess.

Anita's next thought was that it was up to her to find Paula and stop her from doing something foolish or dangerous. Whatever state her friend was in, whatever she'd done, Anita must try to help her.

~

Paula must have finally dozed off for several hours after the call to Rohan.

The blinds were drawn, so the apartment was too dim for morning light to disturb her. What did wake her was the sound of her phone vibrating and jerking across the laminate surface of the kitchen bench where she had left it charging.

She saw a missed call from Anita, then immediately the phone started vibrating again, this time with the caller ID *Hospital*, and Paula picked up.

She was still only half awake, but she could hear that the woman ringing from the hospital front office was flustered, not used to handling emergencies.

A truck driver had called 000 from the highway. He'd found a badly injured person, hit by a vehicle, and he was now bringing them to the hospital. A rescue helicopter was on its way down but Paula was needed to stabilise the patient before transfer.

Paula yanked on clothes and jumped in her car. She hadn't done trauma stuff for years, not since her residency days, and she wasn't sure she was up to it, especially on almost no sleep.

She turned into the hospital's drop-off zone at the same time as the semitrailer pulled over on the street outside, the brakes hissing. When the driver jumped down from behind the wheel, calling for help, Paula ran across the car park towards the truck. She saw Jye peering out of the small window in the rear section of the cabin, then she realised it was Nicole Wigney lying along the front seat.

The nurse on weekend duty hurried out into the car park with a backboard and a gurney.

'You're Dr Kaczmarek?' she asked.

'Yes. Paula.'

'Carol,' she said, tapping the name tag on her chest. She was in her forties, experienced, sturdy, unruffled.

Together, Paula, Carol and the truck driver eased Nicole out of the truck and onto the board. Her face was battered and raw, one eye swollen shut. She looked so limp that for a moment Paula thought she might be dead, but as they moved her, very gently, she moaned with pain and her eyes fluttered open.

'Reckon she might have a broken pelvis but I dunno,' the truckie said. The guy sounded distressed but determined to hold it together. 'The little kid flagged me down on the highway, took me up to his mum. I found her outside the house, lying next to the water tank.'

'Was she conscious when you got there?' Paula asked.

He nodded. 'She said her husband drove the car into her.'

'Was there a teenage girl at the house? Did you see a girl there?'

'No.'

As they lifted Nicole onto a gurney to wheel her into the hospital, she asked, 'Where's Jye? Is he okay? Where's Jye?'

'He's right here,' the truck driver assured her. 'Don't worry. He's a brave kid. He's a hero, this one. He's right here.'

Jye clambered forward into the front seat and the driver reached up his arms to lift the boy down from the high cabin of the truck.

'Down you hop, sunshine,' he said. 'I rang your nana and pa. They're coming here to pick you up.'

The gentleness of the man, the fatherly way he carried the boy—that little moment of kindness almost undid Paula. But then the urgency of what needed to be done took over and she managed to collect herself.

While Paula and Carol rushed Nicole towards the glass doors, the truck driver handed Jye over to the woman from the front office.

'Grandparents are on their way to pick him up,' he explained to her, then turned to call out to Paula. 'Do you need me? Can I do anything?'

'No, we're right. Grateful for your help,' Paula called back.

Nicole could only manage a small voice. 'Can you thank that guy for me?'

Paula raised her hand to get the attention of the truck driver. 'Nicole says thank you.'

The guy nodded. 'I hope she's okay. I'm heading to the police station now. Gotta make sure they find this mongrel.'

In the treatment area, Paula scrambled to recall all the emergency stuff she hadn't needed to remember for a long time. Examining Nicole, even without X-rays, it looked pretty certain the truck driver was right about the broken pelvis. Fractured ankle and ribs too.

'I know it hurts, Nicole, but you're going to be okay,' Paula said. 'We need to move you to a bigger hospital. A helicopter will be here very soon.'

'Where's Jye? My parents here yet?' Nicole asked. 'My mum and dad said they'd take him.'

'Don't worry. They're on their way. We'll look after Jye until they get here.'

Paula was confident—as confident as she could be with her limited trauma experience—that Nicole was not about to crash. The woman was in pain and in shock, but she was conscious, breathing well, and when Paula checked her over, felt her belly, there were no signs of major internal bleeding. The task now was to stabilise her and give her some pain relief for the helicopter journey.

While the nurse hooked up oxygen by nasal prongs, Paula set up a saline drip and put in a urinary catheter. There was a risk of bladder rupture, given the broken pelvis and the impact of a vehicle on a body.

'I'm going to give you some painkillers now, Nicole,' Paula explained. 'Might make you a bit woozy but you'll be much more comfortable, okay?'

Once Nicole was less panicky, in less pain, Paula asked her, 'Do you know where Ruby is? Is she safe?'

'Me and Curtis were arguing. Then he caught Ruby trying to use my phone to dial that number you wrote on the prescription. He took the phone off her, smashed it with a wrench. The two of them got into a big row about the phone. Ruby took off on her bike after that.'

'Where would she go?'

'Ruby's got her hidey holes for when Curtis gets aggro. She'll be okay.'

'And after Ruby left . . . ?'

'Oh, he got really wild then. I made a run for the ute with Jye but Curtis got there first. Drove it straight at me.'

'And he pinned you against the tank?'

Nicole nodded, then her face contorted into tears. 'At least he didn't hurt Jye.'

She let her head flop away sideways, drowsy from the pain medication or simply not wanting to talk anymore.

When they heard the *thoomp-thoomp* of the helicopter blades outside, Nicole panicked, terrified about going in a helicopter. Paula held her hand, reassuring her, as they wheeled her out to the landing area on the grass behind the hospital building.

Paula did the handover to the helicopter paramedics. Swamped by the noise of the rotors, she mouthed, 'You'll be okay,' to Nicole.

The chopper lifted off the grass pad and swooped away towards the Sydney hospital that would stitch Nicole Wigney together.

Walking back inside the hospital building, Paula could see Carol was now down at the reception area talking to a man and woman in their sixties—Nicole's parents. Jye was leaning into his grandmother's hip, as she rubbed her hand along his neck and shoulders with a regular soothing rhythm. The boy obviously loved his nana, felt safe with her.

Carol was filling the parents in on Nicole's condition, using calm gestures and the occasional reassuring touch on the arm.

As the doctor, Paula should also discuss things with the family members, so she quickly turned to the sink in the treatment area and splashed her face with water, hoping to settle herself enough to speak coherently to Nicole's parents. But by the time she straightened up and shook the water out of her eyes, Jye and his grandparents had gone.

'Well, that's something at least,' said Carol, as she headed back towards Paula. 'The grandparents are nice. At least the kid's got that going for him. Poor little bugger. Imagine seeing your dad ram a car into your mum and leave her there on the ground, smashed up. Far out.'

As Paula helped Carol tidy up the treatment area, her hands were shaking. Clumsy, she kept dropping gear on the floor, and when she stooped to pick things up, she stumbled, feeling faint. Carol looked at her, smiling but frowning at the same time—*Are you okay?*

Paula was already strung so taut that when the main door opened with a loud thwack, she jerked around anxiously.

It was Ruby, out of breath, looking for someone in the reception area.

Paula hurried towards her. 'Ruby! Are you alright?'

'People down the road reckon they saw some guy carry my mum to a truck. Where is she?'

'Your mum's okay. She was hurt, but she'll be okay.'

As Paula told Ruby what had happened, the girl shook her head, as if trying to shake what she was hearing out of her ears.

'It's my fault. I should've stayed at the house,' she said.

'It's not your fault, Ruby.'

Ruby shook her head even more vehemently. 'It's my fault. I pissed off. Should never've left. Is my brother alright? Where's my brother?'

'Your grandparents just picked him up.'

Ruby exhaled a shuddery breath with relief. Then she spun around and headed out the doors to the patch of concrete where she'd left her dirt bike.

Paula ran outside after her. 'Ruby, hold on.'

'Going to find my brother.'

'What can I do?'

'Nothing,' Ruby shouted over her shoulder at Paula, then revved up the dirt bike and swerved out onto the road.

Paula stayed in the car park, moving from foot to foot. She'd failed that girl. She'd failed Nicole. Maybe the whole world had failed them, but that didn't lift any of the responsibility off Paula.

Standing there, she realised her hands were shaking, sweat trickling down her back and chest, heart still racing from the surges of adrenaline that had been hitting her from the moment the phone woke her. Her legs suddenly felt boneless, as if they might give way under her.

She couldn't go back inside. Probably there was official stuff still to do, paperwork she needed to fill out, but she couldn't face it. Her bag and her phone were inside the hospital but her car keys were still in her jeans pocket, so she walked away from the hospital building straight to her car.

The adrenaline in her body was now converting into a pure, undiluted rage—a fierce metabolic process that tore away any threads holding her within normal bounds.

She headed south on the highway, driving too fast, towards the Upper Pinch Road house. She had no idea where Curtis Wigney was, had no viable hope of finding him. All she had was the certainty that if she saw that man, she would steer her car straight at him, ramming his body against a wall or a tree, so he could never hurt Nicole again and never have a chance to hurt those children.

She took a corner so fast on the loose gravel of Lower Pinch Road that the back wheels spun out, taking her into the ditch. She righted the car, took a breath and steered back onto the road. The compulsion to speed made no sense—the police would most likely find Curtis Wigney before she did anyway. But Paula needed to use this ferocious energy before it burned itself out and left her with nothing but her own useless fucking failure.

She roared up the driveway to the Wigney house. No sign of his vehicle. No sign of him.

She saw the welt of churned-up dirt that ran from the driveway to the base of the concrete water tank. That was where Wigney had accelerated to slam the bull bar of his ute into a woman, smashing her pelvis. It was really only by chance that Nicole hadn't been killed. It was only the difference of a few centimetres that the initial impact and the pressure of being pinned there hadn't pounded her internal organs to a pulpy mess.

Nicole's sandals were lying on the grass by the tank and Paula thought about the child seeing his mother lying there before he ran through the bush to the highway to flag down a passing truck.

Paula swung herself back behind the wheel of her car with the conviction that it was her responsibility to stop that man ever hurting anyone again and with the absurd belief that the intensity of her purpose would be enough to find him.

When she reached the highway, she turned south towards the town with the wrecker's yard Wigney had talked about. It was the only other place she could think of to look.

At the speed she was driving, she chewed up the kilometres rapidly, reaching the outskirts of the next town, passing a roadside pub. A second after she sped past, her brain processed what she'd just seen: Curtis Wigney's ute in the hotel car park. Paula swung her car into a U-turn.

Pulling into the car park, she was sure. The dusty green ute, a brawny steroidal thing—it was Wigney's. That dickhead was in the pub enjoying a cold beer.

As she walked from her car to the entrance, Paula regretted not having her medical bag or a weapon or any means of neutralising the man. The only 'weapon' she had was her vehicle, and she pictured ramming him with her car, pinning his body against the side of his own ute. That would require luring him outside and she had no plan for achieving that. She had no coherent plan at all.

Inside, the front bar was unexpectedly dim—one of those places with dark panelling and windows shuttered against the day outside. Coming straight in from the bright sunlight, Paula took a moment to adjust her eyes to the gloomy interior. The pub was almost empty, with a woman serving behind the bar and two patrons, one standing at the counter, the other on his phone in the corner.

She took a few steps further into the room and saw that the man at the bar was mid-forties, short, solid, with a shaved, bullety head. Another step closer and she saw the neck tattoo. It was Curtis Wigney.

Paula's heart rate hadn't slowed to normal since the hospital call, and the blood pounding in her head didn't allow for doubt or hesitation. She lifted one of the pub chairs. The chair—metal frame with a chunky wooden back and seat—was heavier than it looked, but she knew she had enough power in her arms. Whatever metabolic process had happened in her body, it was giving her the strength she needed.

'Wigney!' she shouted and hoisted the chair up to shoulder height.

Just as she swung it at him, he half turned towards her, so it collected him on the side of his face. Paula felt the jarring through the metal frame and felt the crunch of his jaw breaking.

As Wigney crumpled to the floor, the guy in the corner dropped his phone and dashed across the room.

'What are you doing? What the fuck are you doing?' he yelled.

Paula went to swing at Wigney again. The other guy reached out his arm to stop her and the chair smashed into his hand. Paula felt the juddering sensations of bones breaking, in the guy's wrist or hand or both.

She dropped the chair, heaving for breath. She scrunched her eyes shut for a moment to squeeze out the sweat and when she opened them again, she saw the face of the man on the floor. It wasn't Curtis Wigney. This guy's neck tattoo was an eagle, with no flames, no fist. She'd got it wrong.

Paula took a step back. 'I'm sorry.'

By now the bartender had run around to help the injured man. Paula could hear all three of them firing questions at her but she couldn't decipher anything they said. She couldn't trust her eyes or her ears or her judgement about anything.

She backed out of the pub. 'I got it wrong. I'm sorry. I'm sorry.'

Paula had almost no awareness of the drive back to town and to the medical practice. The whole journey happened in one of her blank fogs, a dissociative state that made it possible for her to function, but by the time she pulled up in the side parking area, her mind was sharply clear about what she had to do.

The place was deserted. She unlocked the door into the surgery but couldn't find the key to the drugs cabinet. She wedged the sturdy steel arm of a desk lamp into the cabinet handle, then picked up a heavy resin paperweight emblazoned with a drug company logo. After slamming the paperweight onto the metal rod a couple of times, she managed to lever the lock open. There was a sizeable supply of Schedule 8 drugs inside—plenty for her needs.

TWENTY-TWO

IN THAT PHONE CALL, ROHAN HADN'T MENTIONED EXACTLY where on the coast Paula was working. Anita contemplated calling back to ask, but she didn't want to compromise him.

Instead, she tried the old-fashioned plodding method she'd learned as a cadet journalist: hit the phone book. She made a list of medical practices in every town along the coast south of Sydney. Given it was Sunday, many of them were closed, with recorded messages. If she reached a practice with a person on the end of the line, she would claim to be a colleague of Dr Kaczmarek, urgently needing to make contact about a patient, but she had no luck. She tried looking up medical practice websites with smiling photos of their GPs but found no sign of Paula. If she were new on the staff, she probably wouldn't be on an 'Our Team' page yet.

Finally, in desperation, Anita looked up a website with doctor reviews and ratings and typed in *Paula Kaczmarek*. Thank God for the odd surname and thank God for Paula being such a fucking good doctor. There was one posting from two days ago:

Dr Kaczmarek is lovely, so it's a shame she'll be leaving us next week! Any chance we can persuade her to stay?

Under the post was a link to the medical centre, with the address.

Anita hurried downstairs to her car. Heading to that medical centre was the only move she could think of for now.

As she drove, she yanked her mobile out of her pocket and slid it into the holder mounted on the dashboard. Every time the phone dinged with a message, she was hopeful then disappointed. Paula obviously wasn't picking up or returning calls.

The next time the phone rang, it was Rohan.

'Where are you?' he asked.

'In my car. Going south. See if I can find Paula.'

'Listen, I'm not sure that's the best idea.' Rohan was using his serious police officer voice. 'That bloke Paula asked me about—the local cops are out searching for him right now.'

'Because of Paula?'

'Because he drove his vehicle into his wife, smashed her up badly. Attempted murder.'

Anita saw her own hands clenched so tightly on the steering wheel, it felt like she could snap it into pieces.

'Does Paula know about the attempted murder?'

'Uh, yeah. She treated the woman, got her into the medical chopper.'

'So do you know where Paula is now?' Anita asked, trying to keep her voice steady.

'No. The local guys haven't managed to make contact with her.' Rohan shifted his tone, sounding really anxious now. 'Look,

Anita, the cops down there will find this man. And Paula will show up eventually.'

'I hope so. But I still need to—'

Rohan cut in, 'Please. Hold on. This guy is dangerous. Wait until I get more information and I can—'

'Sorry. I understand what you're saying but I can't wait. Call me if you know anything.'

~

A patient had once described the calm he'd felt in the moment immediately after he made the decision to kill himself. Paula never thought she would find herself in that same kind of moment—not even after Remy died, not even after Stacey and the kids were killed.

As she drew up a lethal quantity of morphine into the syringe, she didn't feel calm so much as resigned and very, very tired. All that angry fuel in her body had burned away, leaving only the shame.

She'd exploited her privilege as a doctor to kill two human beings. Even if some good had come from those deaths, her actions were unforgivable. She had now assaulted two blameless people and then fled without helping them. She'd let down Ruby and Nicole. She'd failed to keep Stacey and Cameron and Poppy safe. Of course, it was self-important and ludicrous to think she had the power to protect any of them from danger. And there were so many other women, so many other children out there at risk, and there was nothing she could do for them either. The despair of knowing that was stirred in with the shame, all of it dragging her further down.

She reached for the tourniquet but then left it in her lap for a moment. Paula had cared for patients after someone close to them had killed themselves. She'd witnessed how cruel suicide could be to the loved ones left confused and guilty. That should have made her back off—knowing this action would hurt people—but the humans she cared about most were gone and she felt pretty much disconnected from everyone else. Except Anita. She hated the idea that this would hurt her beautiful friend, on top of everything else, on top of all of it. Worrying about Anita was what caused Paula to sit on the exam bed with the syringe loaded and the tourniquet lying in her lap for a long time.

But in the end, she could see no bearable way to go on. The numbed, structured life she had tried did not work. The shame would always be there. And she missed Remy so much, it was a constant dragging pain through her chest and belly.

She tugged the tourniquet into position on her arm and imagined who would find her body in the morning. It was a matter that should be considered. Paula wouldn't want to burden another person with a distressing sight. But she figured that by administering the overdose on the examination bed in the consulting room, it would most likely be a medical professional who would find her, someone who'd dealt with similar things before and could handle it.

Before injecting the morphine, she thought about Anita again, wishing she'd spoken to her, said a proper apology, expressed her love. She considered calling her now but decided that would only end up upsetting her friend even more.

During those few moments of hesitation, Paula heard knocking on the door that opened into the car park of the medical practice. She stayed very quiet. Whoever it was would give up and go away if the place seemed deserted. But the knocking continued, louder and more insistent.

Paula took off the tourniquet and put the syringe up on a high shelf before she opened the consulting room door a small wedge. On the other side of the narrow corridor, the knocking on the external door kept going.

Then someone yelled out. 'Hello? Are you in there? I can see your car.'

Paula recognised the voice—Ruby—and rushed to open the outer door. The girl stood there, blood smeared across her shirt, with the dirt bike lying on the paving behind her.

'What happened?' asked Paula, ushering the girl inside. 'You're hurt.'

'Not me,' Ruby said, and she took a step sideways so Paula could see Jye sitting on the planter box, with blood crusted on one side of his face, gluing his hair into sticky clumps.

Paula reached to pick the boy up, but Ruby said, 'Careful! He's got bits of glass in his head. I got most of it out but might be bits still in there.'

Paula took the kids into the consulting room and sat Jye on the exam bed. He was quiet and compliant as Paula checked his face and used tweezers to remove the last few slivers of glass embedded in his skin—luckily none too close to his eye. She started to clean up the lacerations, speaking softly to him, trying to be as gentle as possible. Even so, it must have stung quite sharply, but the boy barely flinched, silent and shut down.

Ruby was breathless but she was focused and clear. When she'd reached her nana and pa's place on the dirt bike, Jye was gone. According to the grandparents, Wigney had turned up, demanding to take his son, so the terrified boy locked himself in the bathroom. When Wigney forced the door open, he discovered that Jye had smashed the window, climbed out and disappeared into the bushland. The father could see traces of blood on the jagged edges of the window pane, so he knew the kid was injured.

By the time Ruby got to the house, her stepfather had already driven off and her grandparents had called the police for help. But Ruby wasn't going to wait around for the cops. She took off again on her bike, guessing that her brother had gone to one of their hidey holes. She found him near the Upper Pinch Road house, in a cave the two kids used as a cubby, a retreat where they kept supplies of lollies and bedding and toys.

Ruby didn't trust the police and she didn't think her nana and pa's house was safe. But she knew Jye needed medical attention, so she brought him here on her bike, hoping to find Paula.

'That's good, Ruby,' said Paula. 'But we really must tell the police and your grandparents that you're both okay. I don't have my phone with me, so can you use the one on the desk?'

It took Ruby a moment to remember her grandparents' landline number before she dialled. Then she held the receiver out so Paula could hear it ringing and would be able to speak to them. The phone rang a few times before Paula heard an almighty thumping noise coming from the door to the car park—someone kicking at the timber, then forcing the outer door open.

'Jye! You in there? Jye!'

At the sound of Curtis Wigney's voice, the boy froze and Ruby dropped the phone receiver onto the desk.

'You got him in there, Ruby? I saw you on the bike. You got him, you little bitch?'

Paula lunged across to shut the consulting room door, but Wigney slammed his weight against it before she could close it.

The man was making wet growling noises in his throat and snarling the same words over and over—he wanted his son, he hated that little bitch Ruby. His pupils were dilated and Paula could feel the heat radiating from his body even a metre away. Wired up on amphetamines, she figured. Then she saw the rifle he was holding down by his side, gripped tight.

She only managed to say, 'Please don't—' before he swung his arm out, thumping the butt of the rifle into her cheekbone and propelling her hard into the desk.

By the time Paula squeezed the pain out of her eyes and stood up, Wigney was reaching for Jye. Ruby launched her small wiry body at her stepfather, yanking at his neck and screeching at him with a piercing animal sound.

He was much bigger and stronger, but the girl was so fierce that Wigney had to put effort into prising her off his neck, dropping the rifle on the floor in the process.

While Ruby struggled with him, Paula thought about the syringe of morphine on the high shelf, but even if she could manage to stab the needle into him, it wouldn't work fast enough to help them now. And there was no way she could reach the gun.

Instead, she shuffled backwards to unsnib the back door that led to the toilets and the rear courtyard. Then she grabbed the weighing scales from the floor and slammed the corner as hard as she could into the back of Wigney's head. She felt the blow connect, felt the sharp metal edge penetrate the skin, squelch through flesh and hit the bone of the skull. She hoped it might be enough to knock him out.

Wigney just grunted in pain and spun around to glare at her, blood seeping down his forehead. But he staggered sideways a few steps—enough to open up a pathway for the children to slip past him.

Paula flung open the back door and yelled to the kids, 'Run! Now! Run!' Then she rushed at Wigney and jammed her fingernails into the injury site she had stitched on his forehead. She prised the stitches apart, felt the moist flesh as the wound split open, and blood began to ooze out.

Wigney hissed with pain and grabbed her arm. Even if she couldn't pull her arm free of his grip, he was still forced to fend her off, distracting him long enough for the two kids to escape through the door. Once Ruby had managed to hustle Jye out of the room, Paula kicked the door shut and slammed her body against it.

There was no way she would let this man past her, not until the kids had time to run far enough away, find help and be safe.

Wigney cursed and slammed his boot into Paula's belly until she crumpled to the floor. She landed across the doorway, which meant his access to that exit was still blocked. Pain sliced through Paula's face and abdomen like a knife, but there was still space to have the terrified thought: Wigney could easily pick up the rifle and go out the way he came in, through the car park door, then run around the building and catch up with the kids. Paula would not have the strength to stop him.

But Wigney was too wired up to think clearly, consumed by his anger at this bitch of a woman blocking his way. She felt the heat of his breath as he wheezed above her, the weight of his legs astride her and then his hands around her neck. He squeezed her throat, pumping his forearms to tighten his grip, crushing her larynx. Her head exploded with pain but she still managed to thrash her arms and legs, trying to fight him off. Air hunger meant the body would fight to survive and get the air it needed.

Then, with the sustained pressure from Wigney's hands, Paula felt herself shift down into a different gear, light-headed, her limbs tingling, hypoxic. She scrambled to calculate time—how much time had passed, how far the kids could have run—but she couldn't think anymore. Not enough oxygen in her brain to think. This was it.

~

The sat nav in the car showed she was virtually there. Over the last few kilometres Anita had seen half a dozen police cars on the highway, lights and sirens going—hunting the bad guy presumably.

She spotted the sign for the medical practice and pulled off the road, but the place looked very much shut on a Sunday—blinds drawn, *Closed* sign on the front door. She was about to drive away—try ringing again, maybe ask around at the pub—but then she saw Paula's car in the car park round the side.

Anita found herself smiling at the thought she was about to see Paula. She wanted to see her friend so desperately.

Then she realised the side door of the practice was open, hanging askew, splintered wood around the hinges. Anita stepped through the door and took a breath to call out to Paula. But when she heard strange guttural noises, it made her cautious, triggering the instinct to keep quiet as she moved further inside.

She saw a man crouched over Paula, hands around her throat, growling over and over that she was a 'fucking bitch', loud enough that he didn't hear Anita come in. Paula was limp, her face blue, dead-looking.

Anita rushed forward with the impulse to kick at this man to force him off her friend. Her foot hit something on the floor and she realised it was the butt of a rifle. The man heard that and when he looked up, his eyes black, monstrous, the muscles in his thick neck tight and shiny with sweat, Anita knew she didn't have the strength to haul him off before he killed Paula.

The decision felt simple and clear. She picked up the rifle. She'd had a go with one once, on her first visit to the Maryvale property. Matt had showed Anita how to fire his rifle at cans on a fence.

She aimed it at the man's head and pulled the trigger.

TWENTY-THREE

IN THE MINUTES IMMEDIATELY AFTER SHE SHOT CURTIS Wigney, Anita had limited awareness of the flurry of police activity around her. She was told the details sometime afterwards.

In those first minutes, she was so deafened by the gunshot, ears ringing, dizzy, she had to lean against the wall to maintain balance. She almost slipped over in a slick of blood on the floor, so she dropped to her hands and knees to crawl across the room to reach her friend. She was careful to avoid looking at Wigney's dead eyes. His body had slumped to one side, which meant his weight wasn't pressing on Paula's ribcage, thank Christ.

'Paula.'

Anita called her name over and over. Paula was unresponsive, her skin blue-grey, eyes closed, her mouth slightly open and slack, but when Anita grabbed her wrist, she was sure she detected a pulse. When she reached out to touch Paula's chest, she was convinced she felt the rise and fall of air going into her lungs.

She had no idea if Paula was conscious enough to hear anything, but still she leaned in close and said, 'I'm here. It's Anita. I've got you. I've got you.'

The next thing Anita was aware of was a police officer tapping her shoulder, asking if she was okay. She was still too deafened to hear any of the emergency vehicles outside.

The police sergeant took her elbow to help her off the floor and steer her out of the room. He did this gently but firmly so the paramedics could move past quickly to check on Paula and Wigney.

The grandparents had picked up Ruby's call from the consulting room and, even though the girl had dropped the receiver, they heard enough down the phone line to call 000. At the same time, Ruby and Jye had climbed over the medical centre's back fence and sprinted to a nearby house to bang on the door for help.

In the car park outside, Anita couldn't properly hear or process anything the cops were saying to her, so she said straight out, 'He was strangling her. He was killing her. So I shot him.'

When she saw the paramedics loading Paula on a gurney into the back of an ambulance, Anita called out to them, 'How is she? How is she? Is she alright?'

But with the overlapping sirens from approaching police cars and the clutter of vehicles and people and swirling lights, the paramedics didn't hear her. They whacked on their own siren and lights and accelerated out onto the highway.

The chunk of time after that felt unreal, impossible to measure or digest, even though there were familiar objects in front of Anita's eyeballs and people were saying words she understood, following procedures she would have expected. She was still pretty deaf from the noise of the gun, and presumably in shock too, which must have contributed to her disembodied sensation in the police station.

She wouldn't have described herself as being afraid during that time, except afraid for Paula. She recalled asking the officers several times if there was any word on her friend's condition and being told there was no information yet. The cops did confirm that Curtis Wigney had been declared dead at the scene.

Then at some point, maybe after two hours had passed, the sergeant came in to tell her, 'Thought you'd want to know—your friend, Paula Kaczmarek, she's in hospital in Sydney, conscious and stable.'

Knowing that, Anita felt her stomach muscles finally unknot and she knew she could handle whatever was going on around her.

The police were methodical, unhurried, polite. Later, when her head was clearer, she would recall that the cops were really very kind to her. And for her part, Anita was being as cooperative as she could manage, answering their questions, sitting compliantly in a room as officers came and went.

When she outlined the events of the day, she listened to her voice coming out of her body in coherent sentences, but she felt oddly disconnected from the lucid words. One moment managed to cut through the blur and lodge in Anita's mind with defined edges. When she followed one of the officers to the main desk to fill out another form, she saw a family group on a bench in the waiting area. A man and woman in their early sixties, both worn out, anxious lines gouged into their faces, sat side by side, whispering to each other. A little boy was asleep on the bench beside the woman, his head on her lap, the side of his face pocked with a dozen small scabs and stained yellow with antiseptic. At the other end of the boy, a teenage girl sat with her hand resting protectively on his ankles. A skinny, spiky tough-nut of a girl.

Later, Anita would understand that these people were Ruby, her half-brother Jye and their maternal grandparents. And later, she would realise that she had killed that little boy's father.

As she waited by the counter, Anita saw the grandfather lace his fingers through his wife's hand, giving her strength or maybe drawing strength from her. Either way, the two of them appeared to be sharing the load of this trauma together.

Then Ruby looked up and caught Anita staring. At first the girl gave her a filthy look—*What are you gawking at, lady?* But as she and Anita maintained eye contact, the look shifted into something closer to recognition. Maybe Ruby had sussed out who Anita was and what she'd just done. The girl fixed her with those intense brown eyes and nodded very slightly. A moment of connection before Anita was ushered back into the side room.

At some point—Anita had little concept of how much time had passed—she heard a familiar voice talking to the officers on the other side of the frosted glass door.

'Yeah, hi. Rohan Mehta. We spoke on the phone. But I'm here as Ms Delgado's friend.'

Hearing Rohan's voice, Anita suddenly found herself shaking and the tears came. She hadn't cried at all until that moment. And when he walked into the room, she didn't fall into his arms so much as let her whole weight drop against him. He stood there, holding her up as she sobbed.

'Oh, Anita. It's okay. I've been so worried about you. But this'll be sorted out. Might not feel like it now, but it'll be okay,' he said. 'I'm here. We'll get through this.'

Rohan brought her a box of tissues and a glass of water, and they had a few minutes to sit together in the small bare room. He explained that the moment he knew Anita was driving south, he'd jumped in his car, hoping he could prevent something bad from happening.

Anita nodded. 'Do you think what I did was—'

'Look, I'm—main thing for me is that you're okay. Better if we don't talk about the details now. We'll find you a lawyer and then . . .'

'Please tell me what you think,' she persisted.

Rohan sighed. 'Oh . . . obviously I wish none of it had happened.' Then he clasped her hands securely. 'But I reckon you made the best choice you could in that situation. You saved Paula. You did the right thing.'

Anita closed her eyes for a moment to absorb that. It wasn't that she required Rohan's sanction—she was sure she'd done what she had to do—but still, it was a blessed fucking relief to know he was on her side.

Rohan wanted to stay independent of the police handling of the case, so he left the room whenever there was any official questioning going on. But in the meantime, he was busy doing whatever he could to make things easier for Anita.

The sergeant's wife ran a small clothing boutique in town and, as a favour to Rohan, she opened up the shop late that Sunday afternoon. Rohan purchased several new items of clothing for

Anita—he did pretty well with the sizes—and brought them back to the police station so she could change into fresh clothes, putting her bloodied garments into evidence bags. She wouldn't have to wear a prison jumpsuit.

It was really only then that it hit Anita she would be staying the night in police custody. She was facing serious charges and there was no way she could appear before a judge to be bailed on a Sunday. She would have to spend a night in the station lock-up.

Rohan negotiated with the officer on duty to let him bring dinner back for Anita and allow the two of them to eat together in the lock-up. They balanced plates on their laps, with food containers on two stools like a small table set between them.

'Thanks for dinner. This is like a weirdly austere version of a private dining room,' Anita said, attempting to be light-hearted.

Rohan poked at his food and frowned. 'I'm sorry you have to spend the night here. Fuck . . .'

Anita realised he was annoyed with himself for not being able to fix everything.

'I'll survive,' she assured him. 'Thank you for looking after me. It pays to have a friend with connections on the inside.'

They both made an effort to smile at each other.

It struck Anita with absolute clarity that making a life with this man was something she desperately wanted to do. But that left the question of whether he would have any interest in pursuing a committed relationship with an anxious and impulsive woman who kept secrets from him and had now killed a man.

Anita slept surprisingly well in the lock-up that night. Rohan had talked about booking himself into a motel in town, but in the morning Anita discovered he'd chosen to stay close during the night, in case she needed him. The young constable described seeing Detective Mehta sleeping in one of the back rooms of the station, lying on a short vinyl sofa with his feet propped on a chair.

On the afternoon of the Monday, Anita appeared before the magistrate in the courthouse an hour up the highway. She was charged with murder—as she had expected—but the police didn't oppose bail and she was released on her own recognisance.

Everyone—the lawyer she'd called for advice, other mates in the judicial system, as well as Rohan—everyone was telling her that the DPP wouldn't proceed with the murder charge in the end. She concentrated on keeping hold of those assurances so anxiety wouldn't incapacitate her.

Anita walked into the Sydney hospital room still wearing the clothes she'd worn to the court appearance, because she'd driven straight here, wanting to see Paula before she did anything else.

She hung back from the hospital bed when she realised Paula was asleep. She looked awful. One side of her face, around the cheekbone and eye socket, was purple and swollen like an eggplant. Her neck was swathed in lurid bruises. But underneath all that wreckage, Anita could see Paula's skin was pink and alive, not the dead grey when she'd been lying on the consulting room floor.

Because of the severity of the attack, the doctors were keeping Paula in hospital to monitor her for blood clots, pulmonary oedema and whatever other damage could be done by a near-fatal strangulation.

By now, Anita had learned about the assaults in the pub. A woman had barged in, inexplicably struck two strangers with a chair and then rushed out. Rohan reckoned it was very clear from the CCTV footage that the woman was Paula and that she'd mistaken one of the male victims for Curtis Wigney.

When Paula finally opened her one good eye, Anita could see it was flecked with red from broken blood vessels. Her voice came out shredded and hoarse, 'Hello, friend.'

Anita leaned over to kiss her on the less-battered side of her face and said, 'I love the short hair. Not sure about the rest of this look you've got going.'

'Was that an insult?' Paula asked. 'You'll have to speak up if you're going to critique my look. My hearing's dodgy at the moment—ringing in the ears.'

'Yeah, well, I'm a bit deaf too, on account of the gunshot noise when I saved your life.'

'Oh good lord, am I going to have to grovel and say thank you constantly for the rest of our lives?' asked Paula.

Anita waggled her head. 'Well, you know, a generous amount of grateful grovelling would be appreciated. We can work out a voucher system.'

Paula smiled, but when she spoke again she sounded more serious. 'I'm sorry I lured you into becoming a violent criminal.'

'No, no, it's great. Liberating in a way. We should rock up to the next Parramatta High School reunion. Paula Kaczmarek and Anita Delgado: Most Likely to Commit Major Crimes.'

'Don't make me laugh,' Paula wailed. 'It hurts my throat.'

'Listen, doctor, because you assaulted those guys in the pub, you're going to need legal representation.'

'I know.'

'I can find you a good lawyer, have someone standing by.'

'Thanks,' said Paula. 'Do you know how Nicole Wigney is doing? And the kids?'

'Nicole's in hospital, St Vincent's, going pretty well. The kids are in good shape, I'm told. With their grandparents.'

Paula nodded, drew in a breath to ask more questions, but her breath was shuddery and she was too upset to speak.

'Paula. It's all good. Well, I mean, not *all* good obviously, given you're lying there half dead and we're both facing heavy-duty charges—but don't forget you saved those kids. You saved those kids.'

Paula flapped her hand in the air. 'Don't make me cry. Don't set me off. Crying hurts my throat too.'

Anita reached out her arms to hug her. It was tricky—with drips and catheters and battered body parts to be avoided—but the two women managed to fold each other in close.

TWENTY-FOUR

THE SEATBELT CHAFED ACROSS ANITA'S BELLY, WHICH WAS sticking out quite a bit now she'd hit the six-month mark in her pregnancy.

The prospect of the baby had gone some way to improving relations between her and Rohan's parents. The Mehta sisters had been lovely to Anita from the start, but the parents were, understandably, unnerved by the idea of their son shacking up with a woman who'd shot a man. Rohan promised her their last stiff layer of caution would melt away once the baby was born.

Anita always expected her parents, brothers and extended family would love Rohan, but under the circumstances in which they met him—as the lovely supportive boyfriend of a woman charged with murder—their positive assessment of him had spun up to the level of nauseating adoration. Rohan was considered so saintly, as well as being handsome with beautiful manners, the Delgado family felt the need to constantly remind Anita how very lucky she was to have him. Rohan claimed not to notice his perfect-man-beyond-anything-Anita-deserves status and that only irritated her more.

During the period the Department of Public Prosecutions was considering her case, Anita took leave without pay from the newspaper. She was now the subject of media stories, facing criminal charges, so it would be untenable and ridiculous to work as a journalist in the courts.

She used the time off to revisit the research she'd done into domestic violence and develop it into a book. Whether she liked it or not, Anita's personal story would always be connected to this material, now that she was notorious in a small way, so she gave in to that new reality and wrote about Stacey and about her own experience of shooting a man, including selected details about Paula.

All along, everyone kept assuring Anita the DPP would eventually drop the murder charges against her once they'd shuffled sufficient paperwork around for sufficient time. Even so, when that decision came through three months after the Wigney shooting, her relief was so overwhelming she began to hyperventilate and had to rush to the ladies and breathe into a paper bag to recover.

That night, she and Rohan celebrated with a ritual destruction of all contraception and they fell pregnant that same week. Anita liked to imagine her egg and his sperm hovering there, waiting for the DPP to make a decision—and then, the minute the no-bill came through, the gametes rushed towards each other to make a baby.

*

Anita knew her way around the car park at Silverwater Women's Correctional Centre now. She'd visited every week, sometimes twice a week, for the nine months Paula had been an inmate.

Paula had been arrested the day she was discharged from hospital, as expected, then taken to Central Local Court and charged with assaulting the two men in the pub. Rohan was confident she would be granted bail, but Paula had declined to apply. Everyone, except Anita, was bewildered by her decision.

From the very beginning, Paula offered guilty pleas to the assaults and, after four months on remand, the sentencing hearing was set down for a court in Wollongong. Anita wanted to be there for the hearing and Rohan took the day off to go with her. It was a strange kind of outing for the two of them.

Many friends, colleagues and patients had offered Paula financial help for legal costs and suggested themselves as character witnesses, but she declined all of that, insisting that nothing be done and no evidence presented to mitigate her sentence.

In the Wollongong courtroom, Paula's lawyer looked uncomfortable to be following her rigid instructions, anxious he wasn't doing a proper job for his client, but Paula appeared composed, resigned, relieved that this process was being finalised.

The judge, a thoughtful, compassionate woman in her fifties, seemed as uncomfortable as the lawyer about the lack of material being presented on Paula's behalf.

'This is a curious matter,' the judge said, baffled, scanning the papers in front of her as if they might suddenly offer up some clarification she hadn't noticed before. 'The accused is clearly a woman of prior excellent character and the court can take the early guilty plea as an indication of remorse. However, the accused has offered no explanation for her actions and the injuries she inflicted are serious.'

The judge sentenced Paula to eighteen months, with twelve months' non-parole.

On the drive home from Wollongong, Rohan didn't say anything at first and Anita didn't want to misjudge the moment by chatting about something trivial, so they travelled in silence for a long time.

Eventually he said, 'You know, Paula could have avoided a custodial sentence, most likely.'

'I know.'

'I mean, I would happily have testified on her behalf—about the trauma with Stacey and the children. We could've organised psych assessments, character witnesses. There was no need for her to cop a sentence that tough.'

Anita nodded. 'Paula knows that. But she wants to be punished. Because she feels guilty about the things she's done.'

The silence after that went on for several uncomfortable beats too long, long enough for Anita to realise Rohan understood that the bad things Paula had done must include more than the assaults in the pub.

He kept his gaze locked on the road ahead as he said, 'I'm not going to ask you what that means.'

'Okay,' Anita replied.

It was just as well this exchange happened when they were in the car, both facing forward. If they'd made eye contact in that moment, Anita wasn't confident she would have been able to conceal anything from him. Of course, Rohan had no reason to suspect Paula had killed Ian Ferguson, but it was likely he guessed Paula had something to do with John Santino's death and that Anita knew about it.

After that conversation in the car, there was a kind of tacit agreement: he would never ask her and she would never tell him.

Anita would always have to live with her guilt about concealing the two murders. It was like carrying a chunk of darkness around inside. For the sake of Rochelle and Brooke and their kids, she would keep Paula's secret, but she could never feel completely at ease with that.

In the months after she killed Curtis Wigney, Anita waited for something like crippling remorse to hit her, but it never really did. That man was going to kill Paula. She hated that it had happened, but she never doubted she'd done the right thing. It was surprising—she was someone generally simmering with self-doubt, but not when it came to the most extreme thing she'd ever done.

When Anita passed through security at Silverwater and entered the visiting area, she nodded hello to the prison officers she'd come to know. To begin with, the staff had assumed Anita was Paula's romantic partner, but when Rohan joined her on a few visits, it shook their theory. Then one of the staff twigged that Anita was the woman who'd shot the deadshit guy down the south coast and the officers were even more confused by her. She quite enjoyed giving off an air of mystery.

Paula walked out in her dull green prison tracksuit. 'Hello, lovely. Thanks for coming.'

'We've discussed this,' Anita reminded her. 'You don't have to thank me every time I visit.'

Paula shrugged and smiled. Even after all these months, Anita was struck by how different her friend looked. The blonde dye had grown out but Paula still kept her hair cropped very short. Her face was gaunt, with a scar around her eye socket where the butt of Curtis Wigney's rifle had connected. Her body was way more muscular from the tenacious fitness and martial arts regime she was following in jail. Her voice was different too, with a permanent husky tone from the strangulation injury to her throat.

Once the two women started talking, Anita would look into Paula's eyes and listen to her speak with such concern for fellow inmates, her plans to fix problems for everyone in her orbit. Anita would feel reassured that under the layer of prison uniform and toughened body, the old tender Paula was still there. But underneath that was another even deeper layer—the part of this woman that would always be altered because of what had happened, in ways that only Anita fully understood.

'Anyway, enough of me blathering about stuff in here,' said Paula. 'Tell me how the pregnancy's going. Is your heartburn still bad? When's the next scan? Have you and Rohan found a new place to live? Now I wish I hadn't sold my house so fast—you guys could've lived there.'

Paula had put the Earlwood house on the market when she first went to jail, then arranged, via a lawyer, to give a generous chunk of the proceeds to the two men she'd assaulted. Anita understood and respected that impulse, but she was trying to persuade Paula to keep enough money from the house sale so she could buy a small flat after her release. It was unclear how Paula would make a living once she was out, having been deregistered as a doctor.

Within the jail, she'd very quickly become known as The Doc, like something out of a cheesy prison movie. Some inmates needed convincing that Paula wasn't going to act snobby because she was a doctor, but once word spread about The Doc's story—she'd been almost killed defending two kids from a violent man—it earned her a degree of respect from her fellow prisoners.

Paula could talk endlessly to Anita about the vulnerable people she'd met in there, women trapped in abusive relationships, likely to be sucked back into those risky situations once they were released. She would launch into her slightly bossy benign doctor mode with some of the women, especially the younger ones, making sure they knew their legal rights and the resources they could use, urging them to learn self-defence techniques, encouraging them to believe they were worth more than being bashed and terrorised. Maybe the women were prepared to accept her helpful bossiness because they sussed out that Dr Kaczmarek truly didn't think she was morally superior to anyone.

For many of the inmates, Paula had become a mentor, a coach, a mother figure. A warrior-mother. A she-wolf.

Lately, Paula had spoken a lot about Leila, a young woman due for release in a couple of weeks, desperate to be with her kids, who had been living with her sister. But she was terrified of her violent ex-boyfriend—he'd threatened to follow the sister to the jail on the day Leila got out and track her down. So Paula had recruited Anita to help, coordinating with the sister to set up a safe escape route. Anita would whisk Leila away from the

Silverwater gates on the day of her release and take her to a place where she could be reunited with the sister and the kids.

Anita knew Paula had started developing ideas for a kind of underground railroad for women who needed support to escape dangerous men, help beyond the services official refuges could offer. In Paula's mind, it was something she could coordinate from inside the jail, with Anita's help on the outside, and then she could build on it after her release. The plan was probably crazy. Almost certainly dangerous and unwise. But there was never any doubt in Anita's mind that she would be Paula's ally in this campaign, in whatever way she was able.

Sometimes Paula would ask Anita for news of Ruby, Jye and Nicole. Nicole had written to thank Paula for helping her kids and Anita had stayed in contact with the grandparents. The latest report was that Jye was boisterously happy at big school and Ruby was doing well in year nine, only going off at the mouth and landing in trouble every now and then. Nicole's physical recovery was solid, and she'd started working at the council swimming pool.

The warning buzzer sounded for the end of visiting time.

'Oh, it's always too soon,' Anita groaned.

'Wait one sec,' said Paula. 'Give me a proper look at the belly.'

Anita stood up and posed flamboyantly with her gigantic belly.

'You're so beautiful,' Paula murmured.

Anita huffed a laugh. 'The security guy always gives me the greasy eyeball like he suspects it's a fake belly I'm using to smuggle drugs and weapons in here.'

'Forget that stuff,' said Paula. 'Sneak in some decent food.'

'Next you'll want me to smuggle in protein powder and anabolic steroids, now that you're in training to be a competitive bodybuilder.'

Paula gave her a sly smile. 'What can I say? My body is my weapon.'

~

The trickiest part of the day for Paula was trying to fall asleep on the unyielding narrow bed in her cell.

Prison hadn't proved as bad as her friends had feared. The many small deprivations and humiliations she faced as an inmate felt appropriate, even welcome, in what she realised was a deep-seated desire to be punished. But, really, none of that stuff mattered to her much. The burdens she was carrying in her head were far more important than the physical restrictions.

She'd met a number of extraordinary individuals in here: funny, damaged, spiky, strong women. She accepted she would never work as a doctor again, but there was satisfaction in offering medical advice and reassurance to her fellow inmates, though she was always careful not to encroach on the territory of the prison doctor.

There were nights when sleep seemed impossible. Worries churned in her skull about women she knew who would be facing perilous situations and violent men once they were released from jail. To control the traffic in her mind, Paula would compile lists of strategies to keep those women safe. Once she had a plan of useful things that could be done and solutions to suggest, she could usually settle herself.

If difficult thoughts still intruded as she lay there, Paula would resort to summoning up joyful scenes in her imagination. Scenes with Rochelle and Brody, Brooke and her baby, Nicole and Ruby and Jye. As she drifted into a drowsy state, the figures merged with each other, sometimes merging with Stacey and Cameron and Poppy too, but it was in a glorious way, all of them humming with life, and the hum would lull her into the sleep she would need to do the jobs she'd set herself for the next day.

ACKNOWLEDGEMENTS

I OWE ENORMOUS THANKS TO HELEN BARRY, MICHAEL O'BRIEN and Ben Hoffman for help with legal stuff and for generously answering my many questions. I'm very grateful to my sister, Dr Karen Oswald, for help with medical matters and insight into her career as a dedicated family GP. Thanks to Kerrie Laurence, Dr Michele Franks and Fiona Brown for help with various corners of the story. Thanks to Michael Wynne, Dale Druhan, Shelley Eves, Michael Lucas and Annabelle Sheehan for listening and/or reading as the story developed. I feel hugely fortunate to have my wonderful agent, Anthony Blair.

I'm so grateful to Jane Palfreyman for her enthusiasm for the book right from the start and for her passionate and astute guidance through the process. Thanks to Ali Lavau for thoughtful, generous, valuable notes, and to Christa Munns and everyone at Allen & Unwin for helping put this book into the world with such care.

As always, biggest thanks to my partner Richard Glover for his advice, draft-reading, support and for . . . well, everything.